The Whispering River

SUZANNE WINTERLY

Alizester Books

ALIZESTER BOOKS

First published in 2023

www.suzannewinterly.com

A CIP catalogue record for this title is available from the British Library.

ISBN 978-1-9993168-2-2

Cover Design: Books Covered Ltd.

Alizester Books
Monasterevin
Co. Kildare
Ireland

"Do nothing secretly; for Time sees and hears all things, and discloses all." - Sophocles

Novels by Suzanne Winterly:

The Neglected Garden
The Family Shadow
The Whispering River

Chapter One

The past - London, January 1896

Polly Brady's throat tightened as perspiration beaded on her brow. She lay still for several moments whilst slivers of winter light crept in the attic window. Voices of London street traders called out below, mingling with the smell of roast chestnuts and shellfish. Shrill cries of women selling eel pies rose above the clop of carriage horses' hooves.

She'd been back in Colgrannagh. She sat up in bed, trying to banish the image of the old house by the river with a ruined sixteenth-century tower looming over the wood.

How could she forget the huddle of figures on the lawn, shrouded in darkness? The mistress with her face hidden behind her hands. A man on his knees leaning towards that other... the body on the dry grass with its ghastly expression.

It wasn't a dream, no, not a dream. She was a long way from the Wicklow mountains. It was only a flicker of memory taunting her and dragging her back to that terrible night in August five months before.

Polly watched dawn sliding over the city rooftops as Colgrannagh faded away. A glass of water sat on the table beside her and, taking a sip, she lowered her feet to the floor. A lot of work to finish. She would dress and get on with it. Work obliterated her memories, dispersing shadows that lingered in the early morning. It helped keep at bay the guilt that sometimes threatened to overwhelm her; that tempted her to crawl into bed and draw up the covers.

A cheerful sparrow chattered on the sill outside as she pulled a shawl around her shoulders. She walked across the floorboards to the window, leaning her forehead against the icy pane, and the chill brought her back to the present.

Five months ago, she'd left Ireland but still the guilt remained; the fear of having done nothing, of having said nothing. She could imagine condemnation on the faces of others.

A little girl selling flowers looked up at the window, with round eyes and dark curls like… no, Polly wouldn't name any of the children. They had vanished from her life forever, disappearing with the mist along the path to the tower.

At least she'd left them a gift, those dear children. A gift with a secret to ease her conscience, and she hoped one day they or someone else might unpick the truth.

She smiled, raising a hand to wave at the girl on the pavement below. The truth was there at Colgrannagh, waiting to be discovered. Perhaps not this year, but maybe the next. Or in the future, decades later, a century even. Somebody, somewhere, would decipher the secret and reveal what had happened.

Chapter Two

The past – the previous year – March 1895

A sea mist wrapped around the railway carriage as it rumbled along the coast, droplets of moisture running down the glass. Polly glanced at her little brass pocket watch. The train had been late and, with only a few hours of sleep the night before on a lumpy mattress in the Dublin boarding house, exhaustion overwhelmed her.

She closed her eyes, searching with her fingertips for the letter in the pocket of her wool coat. The address of the house was clearly written in her new mistress's hand. She knew it by heart and had no need to unfold the pale ivory notepaper. Colgrannagh, County Wicklow. An old house, Mrs Manning had explained at her interview, built at the close of the last century, and she wasn't to expect comfort; far from it. Polly gripped the smooth paper between forefinger and thumb, summoning courage for what lay ahead.

Her aunt would have muttered a prayer, of course, although she'd bestowed no kind farewell blessings as she watched her niece's departure from the doorway of the Mayo cottage, her expression hard as flint.

"A chilly night ahead of us," a middle-aged man in a bowler hat murmured. "Are you going far, young lady?"

Polly switched her gaze to his ruddy face. A faded ginger moustache and beard under a hook nose; thinning red hair. "Yes, sir, it is cold. I'll be getting out at the next station."

An old woman beside her shifted her bulk and agreed. "'Tis cold indeed, child. There'll be frost on high ground tonight, of that I'm certain."

Child. A long time since she'd been called that but reassuring somehow. The woman's voice was soft, a Wicklow accent perhaps, and conversation about weather was always comfortingly familiar.

An inquisitive expression gleamed in the man's light blue eyes. Aunt Maureen had always told her never to divulge information unless asked a direct question. Keep her thoughts to herself. Don't go asking for trouble and mind her own business.

Polly smiled, clasping her fingers together in her lap.

"Perhaps you're going up into the hills to stay with a relative, eh?" the man enquired.

Was he interested or just passing the time? "Yes, but not with a relative," she replied. "I'm a governess and I'm taking up a new position." Her aunt would have clicked her tongue, irritated with her for disclosing that.

The woman on her left shot her a curious look.

"A governess, eh?" the man repeated. "You must be an educated young lady." His gaze slid over her black gown with its cream lace collar. "Pretty too, with your auburn hair."

A flush burned her cheeks as she pulled the front of her coat together and fumbled with the hooks.

"English, French, music… and all that," he said. "I had it drummed into me once long ago. Can't remember a word of French now and I can't say it made any difference to me." He laughed, a loud guffaw that filled the compartment. "Ah well, good luck to you, young lady. Up in the hills, you say? You must be going to Mrs Manning's household of urchins."

Polly made no comment.

He continued, "Would they be your charges? They're a wild lot."

"A wild bunch of hooligans, I've heard." The woman tilted back her head and yawned, reaching up a wrinkled hand to pat her mouth. "It's time Mrs Manning made an effort to civilize them… but her soft-hearted father kept taking in other folks' problems."

Polly picked at the hem of her coat, twisting the fabric in her fingers while the other two carried on talking. She noticed a threadbare patch that would need darning.

They appeared to forget about her, absorbed in their discussion of her mistress's lack of discipline and unorthodox ways, as they continued to debate about the eccentric but beautiful widow in her late thirties.

"Perfectly pleasant… quite charming, in fact," the man said, "a lovely lady, truth be told, but with some unusual ideas. As strange at times as her father was, may God rest his soul."

"Ah yes, that's the truth," the woman agreed.

Claudia Manning had explained to Polly at the interview in a small Dublin hotel that not all the children were hers. She and her husband had only been blessed with one son but her father had taken in a few orphans, in an attempt to give them a decent life, an education and a more privileged upbringing than they could ever have expected. She'd flashed a bright smile at Polly, patting her shining dark hair and adding that her father had been a physician and keen on philanthropy, but he'd also considered it an interesting experiment. Claudia's brown eyes sparkled with enthusiasm.

Polly had warmed to her. But an experiment? What did that mean? A servant girl in the hotel arrived with tea and sandwiches, cutting short Claudia's explanations and, when they were on their own again, her employer switched the subject to the house and the surrounding countryside.

The Wicklow mountains would be a big change from the west of Ireland, a world away from the Mayo coastline dotted with islands where the salt wind from the Atlantic stunted the trees and bent hedgerows into grotesque shapes; where great squalls of rain lashed the headland. March had arrived like a savage beast, the locals said, with its roaring wind and violent hailstones.

Wicklow would be calmer than her home county, no doubt about that. It would be an oasis of gorse and heather, rocky granite outcrops and sweeping forests of oak and Scots pine. And sheep, of course, always lots of sheep in the mountains.

"Glendalough is nearby," the man said. "The round tower of Glendalough is a fascinating sight." He cleared his throat as if to attract her attention. "You'll have to pay a visit to that. You're not from Dublin… I can tell by your accent. Not from Ireland, are you?"

Heat flared on Polly's cheeks and she glanced out of the window. Lamplight in the distance, a golden glow in the murky mist, which meant the station lay ahead. She longed to escape from the railway carriage and these questions. "I'm from Ireland. I was born in Mayo." She swallowed, her mouth dry. No need to mention her London schooling. Those years were gone and she would say nothing more.

The woman gave her a nudge with a surprisingly sharp elbow. "So… you must be gentry then, with an accent like yours. Imagine you coming all this way to teach books and French and the piano to Mrs Manning's wild creatures… and you only a child yourself."

"I'm twenty-two years old."

"Twenty-two years old but with little experience of the world," the man replied. "Still, we all have to make a beginning somewhere. Learn to stand on our own two feet… and you'll soon learn, my girl, you'll soon learn… where you're going. A baptism of fire, mark my words."

The train was slowing, wheels jolting and brakes screeching.

The shriek of its whistle pierced the air and a cloud of smoke wafted past the window, laced with an acrid smell of coal.

The man stood and reached for his leather Gladstone bag on the rack above his head. He lifted it down and placed it on the seat beside him. "Give my regards to Mrs Manning, my dear."

"Your name, sir? She will wish to know your name."

He stroked his whiskers. "Tell her… tell her Henry Fitzpatrick was asking after her. She'll remember me, don't worry."

The woman gave Polly another poke with her elbow and cackled with amusement. "Indeed, she will." She leaned nearer, a whiff of whiskey on her breath. "Oh, indeed she will for Dr Fitzpatrick is on the board of the local workhouse and also the orphanage. He knows all about badly behaved children, don't you, sir? And their wanton mothers. He'll have met your little charges, to be sure."

Chapter Three

The present – August 2022

"Aha, you must be Fiona Foley?" A man with thick white hair pulled open the cottage door. "You're early. That's a good sign… welcome to Colgrannagh. Come in, come in."

I followed Daniel Manning into the tiny hall, his head almost brushing the ceiling, a tall man for his advanced years, with only a slight stoop.

He bent under a low doorway into another room and beckoned to me. "Come along… this way. You've made good time. No trouble finding me?"

"No trouble. Do you mind the dog? I can leave him in my car." I looked down at Archie, my Jack Russell, who scampered into the sitting room ahead of me and was about to leap onto the sofa. I clicked my tongue and he shot me a reproachful look before flopping to the floor.

"Not at all," Daniel replied, "a fine fellow… grand little chap. I used to have one similar, a little brown and white terrier. She was a great character and kept me on my toes. Take a seat while I put on the kettle and we'll have tea in the garden while I explain everything. Lovely weather, isn't it? A good August, for once, with plenty of sunshine here in Wicklow." He had a deep voice, full of expression as it rose and fell and I could imagine him on the stage in a theatre delivering a monologue from Hamlet or Othello. Perhaps he'd been keen on amateur dramatics in his youth.

"Thank you. Tea would be great. Have you lived here for long?" I asked, sitting on an armchair beside the fireplace and holding up a forefinger to warn the dog to stay on the rug.

I remembered my mother's text.

> *Old Daniel is a widower with a stash of money and no kids. He'd be the ideal client for you.*

There was warmth in his eyes. "About six months now, since I came back from… used to live in the south of France… near Aix in Provence. I moved there when I retired. You know the area?"

I didn't and admitted this. Antique furniture surrounded me and I spotted a wedding photo on top of the piano, displaying a much younger Daniel with a pretty brunette.

"Yes, in Provence… a beautiful place. A wrench to leave it but there you are… life changes, doesn't it? We have to go with the flow, as young people say nowadays. Go with the flow even if we long to resist."

"Yes, we do." I glanced down at Archie, lying beside my feet with his tongue lolling, the picture of innocence.

"Now, I'll make tea. Follow me." Daniel stepped towards an open door into a kitchen and I noticed he had a limp.

I said, "You knew my mother quite well, I believe, when she was a nurse."

He poured boiling water into the pot and stirred, obviously not the sort of man to just toss a tea bag into a mug. "Your mother and I worked in the same hospital for some years. We were in the cardiac unit of the Mater in Dublin. I worked in

England too, but the Mater was where I ended up. She still sends me a Christmas card every year, bless her."

I stepped towards him and laughed. "It's more than she sends me. No, no, I'm joking. She contacts me quite often." Too much since the demise of my ill-fated marriage to Dominic. My mother took an avid interest in the progress of my separation.

The spoon hovered in mid-air and he grinned. "You're like her, you know. You have the same dark blonde wavy hair and blue eyes. Oh, I remember your mother vividly. I think many of the doctors did."

I forced a smile. My mother had succeeded in charming Professor Daniel Manning.

He chuckled, giving the contents of the teapot another stir. "Your expression says it all, my dear. Your mother and I were good friends but that was it… I know what she's… ah, I see you frown but she was a vivacious woman and fun. We all thought that in cardiology. A good nurse too but perhaps not suitable for the intensive care unit." He raised bushy eyebrows. "A little lacking in discipline but the patients took to her."

"I like to think I'm a bit more responsible than my mother." I hoped that didn't sound too sharp. Bossy, my mother called me.

"She told me she's living in Lisbon now." Daniel raised one shoulder in a shrug. "Another man, I take it."

I nodded but didn't elaborate. My mother never allowed an inconvenience like responsibility to get in her way. She'd cast us off years before, my brother and me. Cast off my father too, poor man. Dad never stopped missing her. Never stopped waiting for her to return; the rest of his life until his death three years before. She'd come back for his funeral. At least she'd managed that.

Daniel opened a tin and took out shortbread biscuits, placing them on a china plate beside the teapot on a wooden tray with the mugs and a small jug of milk. "Sugar? No, I guessed you wouldn't take it. Not many do these days. Bad for the health. I have to be careful… diabetes, unfortunately." He nodded towards the patio doors leading to a paved terrace outside. "Would you mind opening them, please? There's a table on the right. Yes, over there."

We settled ourselves on cane chairs and I admired the garden. A small herbaceous border ran along the high granite wall separating the big house from the cottage. The old house towering above the wall caught my eye, built of granite, dark and rather formidable. I hadn't seen the pitched roof and finials from the entrance to Daniel's cottage, with carved stone figures above the arched windows.

If anyone were standing inside watching us, they would be impossible to see. Did Daniel mind the lack of privacy in his little garden? The house looked secretive, brooding. My imagination was already running away with me.

"It's an interesting place," I said, waving a hand at it. "How old is it?"

"Georgian period, late eighteenth century but, as you can see, it fell victim to that dramatic Victorian trend, the Gothic Revival." He chuckled. "I've done a little research. A banker rented it to my great-aunt Claudia and her father. Her son ended up buying it years later."

"I saw a ruined castle when I drove up the avenue," I replied. "Does that belong to your property too?"

He lifted his mug, pushing the plate of biscuits towards me. "It used to. It's a tower house, owned by the state now, like many historic ruins, and they oversee its upkeep. A sixteenth century listed building."

I sipped my tea as he lapsed into silence. He seemed to be composing his thoughts, tapping a forefinger on the top of the table and smiling at Archie, who lay on the lawn, snoring softly.

Daniel cleared his throat. "Your mother recommended you to me, as I mentioned on the phone. She said you're the one to do research. Thorough and diligent, those were her words." When I didn't reply, he added, "You're a history teacher, I understand."

I would have to tell him, admit the truth. "I was a history teacher… until the end of last term. I'm not sure about being good at research but I enjoy doing it."

His eyes held mine. Wise understanding eyes. An urge to confide in him surfaced; to explain about the difficult new principal who'd upset so many of us and who'd picked on me in particular. At the beginning of the summer, she'd lost one third of her staff and it served her right. I said nothing. I didn't want Daniel to realize how desperate I was to get the project.

"Your mother told me you're at a bit of a loose end right now." He stretched his arms above his head, his gaze moving away. "I'm sorry about your marriage."

Oh God, thank you, Mum! Why did she have to tell the entire world about Dominic running off with a journalist?

"I'm sorry if I've embarrassed you, Fiona, but from what your mother said it sounds like you're better off without this man."

A flush burned my cheeks. I was thirty-three years old, not a gauche teenager, but I worried what else my tactless parent had divulged.

"So, you were a heart surgeon? That's a great achievement," I said, a hurried attempt to change the subject. "Think of all the lives you saved over the decades. There must be many thankful families…"

"There were some, yes, but it's all in the past now. I'm ninety, can you believe it? Don't be so surprised. People tell me I only look eighty but I'm ninety years old… and I'd like to feel I've achieved something else apart from being a medical man."

"Tell me more about the research, please. Claudia Manning was your great-aunt?"

He leaned towards me. "Yes. My great-aunt was a doctor too.

Well ahead of her time in the late nineteenth century... in an era when ladies weren't encouraged to work... kept down, you understand, in spite of their intelligence."

"Wealthy Victorian women were. The unfortunate poor ones had a tough life... hard work and many children."

"Indeed. Tough times, no doubt about that. My great-aunt must have cared about the less well-off and their health. I admit I don't know much about her but she tried to help women in her day and she must have been one of the first female doctors in Ireland." He came to the point. "I want to write a book about her, you understand, my great-aunt Dr Claudia Manning. It would be a shame to die and allow her life to fade away... her achievements... I'd like our family to remember her, to be proud of her. That's where you come in."

"You want me to compile information about her for your book?"

"Yes, exactly. We have a room full of her papers in the main house. My nephew Kenny... he's my great-nephew, actually. He and his fiancée moved in last year and the place was a terrible mess, I'm afraid. Claudia's son Solomon left me the property when he died but I rented it out for decades. I already had a house in Dublin and then the villa in France."

I nodded to show I understood.

He continued, "So much work is needed to get it in order because the tenant died ten years ago and it was left empty. There's a room full of boxes of diaries, letters and photographs. The details of Claudia's work are in that old schoolroom, I'm sure of it, and if you could collect it all together for me, catalogue it or whatever, so that I can access the information with ease... well, that would be wonderful."

It sounded intriguing. A female doctor in the late Victorian era might make my research project look good on my CV. I'd suspected Daniel Manning had called me here to compile his family tree but work for a book that actually might get published sent a thrill coursing through me. My name in the credits, hopefully helping me to build up a reputation.

And money, because I badly needed money. I couldn't go on living with my friend Jessica's aunt in Wexford for the rest of my life, kind though she was. I'd kept her company during the long months of lockdown during the Covid-19 pandemic but I needed to find a home of my own.

I'd stayed with Jessica in Dublin during the school term but she was planning to move in with her partner and sell her apartment.

He interrupted my thoughts. "What do you think? Does it sound interesting?"

I realized I hadn't replied and my words tumbled out. "Sounds fascinating… a doctor, a female doctor back then. I'd love to… I'm sure it would be really interesting."

"Quite a strong character and allowed no one to stand in her way." His tone rose with enthusiasm and Archie woke up to cock an ear. "We'll discuss payment in a minute but are you sure you want to take this on?"

"Oh yes, definitely. I've done some family research for a relation of a good friend and I've also been hired to research two other family trees, one for an American in Chicago and another for a man in Edinburgh with Irish grandparents. Family history is popular nowadays but a book… research for a book would be exciting."

"I can offer you accommodation here while you work on it. Plenty of room in the big house if you don't mind… um… if you don't mind roughing it a bit. Not exactly luxurious."

I said I wasn't used to luxury.

"Splendid!" Daniel clapped his hands and the dog leaped to his feet, wagging his little tail and probably imagining that we were going for a walk. "Thank you so much, Fiona. Now, let's get a notebook and make a plan…" His words trailed away as a woman, with long dark hair and large sunglasses covering a thin tanned face, appeared from the door in the wall leading towards the main house.

She advanced across the lawn with a purposeful step. "Daniel, a word, please."

He frowned. "Not now, Millicent. Can't you see I'm…"

"A word, Daniel." Her voice was sharp to match her features. A cigarette glowed between red-painted nails on the fingers of her right hand and she took a quick drag. "Who's this?" She nodded towards me.

"My dear, where are your manners? This is Fiona Foley, my researcher."

I liked the way he called me his researcher. It made me feel needed, more useful somehow. I was growing fond of Daniel and his old-world charm.

"You're both about the same age," he continued. "You'll be company for each other." He turned to me. "Millicent North, my nephew's fiancée."

She held out a hand with silver bangles jingling on a slender wrist. "Fiona, pleased to meet you. Now, Daniel, I…"

He groaned and held a palm to his brow in a mock theatrical manner. "Can't this wait?"

"Listen to me," Millicent insisted. "A leak, a burst pipe! The overflow tank or something in the attic and water is dripping through the ceiling into the room below."

He sat up, alert. "Which room?"

Was that a gleam of triumph in Millicent's dark eyes? She took another drag from her cigarette, inhaled and breathed out smoke. "The schoolroom with the boxes of junk… those papers you're always going on about. Great-Aunt Claudia's clutter is becoming waterlogged as we speak." She glanced at me with a brief twist of her lips. "He loves to dream about the past but

I wish he'd focus on the present and our crumbling house. It's much more important than faded letters and dead people no one remembers."

Chapter Four

The house towered above us as Millicent set off at a brisk pace along a gravel path to the front entrance, a grey hulk with a solid door at the top of granite steps. I noticed that some of the lower windows had been replaced but, when I looked up, the glass in several on the third storey was cracked. Finials adorned the pitched roof and little grotesque faces carved from stone peeped down on us from under the guttering.

Millicent pushed open the door, beckoning when I hesitated at the bottom of the steps. A deep paved area dropped down from a grassy bank, running around the base of the house and reminding me of a small moat. A Georgian basement lay behind barred windows.

"Where's Daniel?" I turned and saw him at the corner near a large oak tree, stopping to lean on his walking stick. "He seems out of breath. Will he be able to manage these steps on his own?"

She waved a dismissive hand. "He's fine... better off walking at his own speed."

Archie bounded towards her and she frowned. "This your dog?"

"Yes. Do you mind if he comes inside?"

"I do mind. You'll have to tie him up out there. The decorators have just painted the hall and I don't want…"

"All right," I interrupted, turning away to slip the lead from the pocket of my jeans. At least the delay would give poor Daniel a chance to catch up with us.

I waved at him and looked for something to tie Archie to.

"The garden seat there." Millicent pointed at it. "That will do. Do hurry up. I haven't got all day. Kenny will be back soon with the interior designer and we have to make decisions about the bridal suite. Professionals are expensive… can't keep her waiting with the price she charges."

I secured the dog, who slumped on the grass and would have rolled his eyes if he were able.

Daniel shouted, "You go on, Fiona. I won't climb all those stairs up to the third floor. I'll go to the kitchen and phone the plumber."

"Kenny is my fiancé," Millicent continued. "Did Daniel mention him? We're going to turn this semi-ruin into an upmarket wedding venue." She gave me her frozen smile when I joined her in the hall. "Though you wouldn't think it suitable for guests when you see some of the bedrooms upstairs. Plaster flaking, damp patches and mildew on the walls… what a dump!"

A fanlight arced over the door and threw a shaft of sunlight on the wooden floorboards in the hallway. The room smelled of fresh paint and a tall vase of floribunda roses stood on a round mahogany table.

I stopped to admire them. "A beautiful shade of dark pink." I reached out to touch the layers of petals. "Such a lovely scent and so old-fashioned!"

"Yeah, the landscaper guy found them hidden among weeds at the bottom of the garden… He told Daniel that there were probably rose beds once, like years and years ago, before the property was abandoned."

"Are you restoring the garden as well as the house?"

"Obviously we'll have to unless we expect the bride and groom to have their photographs taken in long grass and briars." She uttered a short sarcastic snort. "Daniel hired a landscaper from France. One of his friends over there recommended him but… well, he may know what he's doing with plants and stuff but he hardly speaks a word of English. In this day and age, can you believe it? I thought everyone learned English now."

"That must make communication difficult."

"It does, yeah, a serious pain. Daniel can talk to him in French because he's fluent, having lived over there, but it means I can't give him instructions."

I pulled a face, hoping I looked sympathetic and not amused.

Millicent pointed a glossy fingernail. "So far, we've renovated this hall, the dining room over there and the drawing room opposite. Do you like the paint? I chose pale apricot because it's warm."

"Very nice," I replied.

She nodded in agreement. "This way, up these stairs and then on to the end of the corridor."

I followed her, admiring how elegant she appeared in black linen trousers and a silk shirt, compared to my T-shirt and faded jeans.

A row of photographs, faded to sepia, with heavy wooden frames lined one wall of the passageway above. I lingered in front of a woman with dark hair, fashioned into curls at each side of her face, sitting on an ornate chair at the top of the front steps. "Is this Dr Claudia Manning, Daniel's great-aunt?"

Millicent didn't bother to look as her gold sandals clattered along the wooden floor. Clack, clack, clack. "Probably. Daniel said there's one of her here."

"And who's this beside her?" A man with lighter brown hair almost to his shoulders, quite long for the late-Victorian era, with piercing eyes that seemed to follow me as I stepped away.

"Might be her husband, I forget his name, but Daniel said he was some sort of botanist and plant hunter and died out in South America. I'm going to get rid of all those depressing portraits. The local charity shop can have them."

We climbed another set of stairs to the third floor and Millicent opened a door at the end of the gloomy corridor. "In here. This is where it gets really uncivilized, I'm afraid… the part of the house we've left till last. Watch where you put your feet because some of the boards might be rotten. This was once the schoolroom."

Heavy cobwebs laden with dust clung to the corners of the ceiling. I bent to examine a glass container on the ground and saw a stuffed ferret, its fur faded to pale yellow, and a dead rabbit lying in front of it.

"Gross!" Millicent shuddered. "The hall was full of dead animals and birds and stags' heads. Kenny hid them away up here. I don't think even the charity shop would accept them."

"Very Victorian," I replied.

"Can you imagine how they'd go down with my wedding guests? The animal rights brigade would close us down. The letters and diaries are over there."

Piles of cardboard boxes sat on the faded rug among other discarded objects: the ends of a brass bed and a gigantic wrought-iron baby's pram overflowing with books. An ancient trunk stood in a corner, dark green and covered in stickers from sea voyages decades before, and a cluster of flies buzzed against the glass of the window.

"Wow, so many belongings crammed into this room," I said. "How many generations left their possessions behind?"

"Too many. Why couldn't they get rid of their rubbish before they moved out?" Millicent stepped over and heaved up the bottom sash of the window, flapping her hands at a peacock butterfly. "Shoo, shoo, out you go."

I summoned patience. "If people threw everything out, there'd be no trace of the past. No footsteps left behind for us to follow."

"I'm in the minority here, I guess. I think we should live in the present. The past is gone. Why bring it back?"

It was a good question and one that had often been thrown at me in the classroom. Who cares about history, miss? All those people are dead anyway.

"We need a sense of belonging," I replied. "To learn from mistakes… to help create a better future for the rest of us." I thought that might appeal to thoroughly modern Millicent.

It didn't. She shrugged and pointed up at the corner nearest the window. "See the leak over there? You'd better move whatever papers you want to keep."

A crack in the ceiling was dripping water into a red plastic bucket and I could see one box already sodden and a damp trail across the floor where Millicent had pulled it out of the way.

"How did you spot the leak if no one comes in here?" I asked.

"I saw a mark on the ceiling in the corridor. Luckily, I checked this room or the whole ceiling could have fallen down if left for days and that would have been expensive to fix. I hope the plumber comes today. You can work in this room out of the builders' way. You can dwell in the past here to your heart's content." She lit another cigarette.

"Thank you." My love of the past was more than a longing to dwell in it, much more. In a house that age, more than two centuries old, layers of time hung in the rooms; rooms once filled with laughter and the patter of feet where families had lived and loved and cried.

I picked up a leather-bound notebook and opened the first page. Dr Joshua Burroughs 1883 scrawled in faded ink. I turned the page and saw lists of names with details of illnesses and treatments. An interesting casebook. I didn't know much about Victorian era medical practice but the notes might help. Perhaps there was a medical dictionary somewhere among these overflowing boxes.

Millicent watched me from the window, mobile phone in hand. "Are you going to accept this project?"

"Of course. I like the idea of researching the life of a Victorian doctor. It's great Daniel wants to write a book about her."

"It's just another of his crazy ideas. He has at least five a week. If I'd known… if Kenny and I had known what he was like before we accepted his offer, we wouldn't have come."

"But you must have been told that the house had been unoccupied for years?"

"Yeah, we were but we didn't realize it would be like this… so run-down and in need of a ton of money to get it sorted… and we don't have the cash, that's the problem. If we did, it wouldn't matter so much." She drew on the cigarette. "Daniel can do what he likes but we're… we're relying on him to pay for a lot of it… until we get our business up and running."

I ran my eyes down the page in front of me and spotted an illness I recognized. A twelve-year-old boy named Peter had scarlet fever in 1883, often a death sentence for children back then. Even those fortunate enough to survive were left weakened but today the illness was rare because modern antibiotics cured it. Peter had a rash on his chest and abdomen, a flushed face and pale area around his lips but Dr Joshua Burroughs didn't record the outcome. Probably just as well. I picked up another notebook from the box.

"I worked as a wedding planner in London," Millicent was saying. "Kenny is a professional photographer so that's how we met. One day we hope to buy the property from Daniel but he can keep the cottage."

I smiled at her to show I was paying attention. "It's going to take patience and money. Couldn't you rent somewhere nearer the city, put up one of those semi-permanent marquees… wouldn't that be easier?"

"Everyone does that," she replied with scorn. "We want to be different, more special, a boutique wedding venue with a beautiful view of the Wicklow mountains."

"Ah, okay, I get you." I spotted the name Claudia Manning written on the first page of the second notebook. The year was 1895. Pages crammed with an untidy scrawl that was hard to read. "A special unique venue, you mean?"

"Yeah, exactly. Wouldn't you prefer that for your wedding?"

"I had the marquee and the city wedding."

"Oh, I didn't realize you were married."

"I'm not… not any more. My husband left me three years ago."

"Oh," she said again and looked at her golden sandals and red-painted toes. "Sorry, I'm sorry to hear that. Here's me rambling on about weddings and you're… you probably don't want to hear."

I managed to laugh. "I don't mind, but I've had enough of marriage." Would I confide in Millicent? Tell her how Dominic had expected me to mother him since our college days and pay for everything while he gambled away his salary at the end of each month? No, she didn't seem the sympathetic type and I'd managed to push Dominic out of my mind. He didn't deserve to creep back in.

I held up the two notebooks. "I'd like to borrow these… show them to Daniel. One looks like a diary written by his great-aunt and the other belonged to a Dr Burroughs."

"He was Claudia's father, I think." She moved away. "Take whatever you want. I've got to go."

Chapter Five

The past – March 1895

"Here we are… my darling Papa's grave." Claudia waved a gloved hand. "He was a wonderful doctor, so enlightened. I really do believe him to have been a man born ahead of his time. So far ahead of his time that others sometimes struggled to comprehend his ideas."

Polly followed Claudia Manning through the long grass towards a granite headstone. Her mistress was taller, with a longer stride, and Polly quickened her pace to keep abreast.

Flurries of wind snatched up wizened leaves and bowled them along the gravel path, forming heaps against the larger tombstones. An early morning frost still glittered in shady corners.

Polly read the epitaph:

Here lies the body of Dr Joshua Burroughs
departed this life November 16th 1885
Beloved husband and father

"You must miss him," she said, raising her eyes to the bell tower of the church, with its backdrop of pine and oak trees. On her right, Colgrannagh House lay hidden in the shadows, still slumbering in the early morning mist. Her mistress was an early riser.

"I miss him every day," Claudia replied. "This burial ground is part of the estate. Our landlord is a wealthy man and he leased us the house after his wife died."

"Colgrannagh doesn't belong to you?"

"My father didn't believe in owning a house. Too much expense and palaver with maintenance. People were his real interest." She stooped to pluck a dandelion from the blanket of grass covering her father's grave. A clump of daffodils, their trumpets facing the sun, huddled beside the path. Overhead, a flock of starlings landed on top of the tower and burst into a chorus of twittering.

"He sounds like an inspiring man."

Claudia held her gaze. "He was, indeed he was. The children loved him. They all loved him." She pulled her pocket watch from her coat and peered at it. "Look at the time! I visit my first patient in half an hour and must return to the house. I imagined you would enjoy seeing the garden, the river and the church. At least you know where to take the children on a walk. I like them to have exercise and fresh air every day, weather permitting."

"Yes, Mrs Manning, I will do my best. I'm certain country air is good for us all."

Claudia's hair shone in the sunlight under a stylish green hat, adorned with a small feather. She laid a hand on her father's gravestone, as if touching it would bring him back for a moment. She closed her eyes. A silent prayer? "I miss my dear Papa and come often to his grave. He lived to ninety-one years."

Polly smiled. "An example to us all. No doubt he was extremely healthy in old age." How odd that she didn't mention her late husband and his grave. Was he buried elsewhere?

"Indeed, he was very robust. He never once asked us to call Dr Fitzpatrick… just fell asleep one night and never woke up… a lovely way to go. Come along, my dear, I don't wish to delay. I abhor being late."

Polly remembered the condescension in Dr Fitzpatrick's voice on the train when he discussed Claudia Manning and her father with the woman. He'd been scathing about the children. A baptism of fire for a new governess. What had he meant by that? Polly had met the children before bed the previous night and they'd seemed mannerly, each extending a hand when introduced. Perhaps the physician had been a rival of Dr Burroughs in the locality.

Claudia stepped towards the wood, calling over her shoulder, "I must tell you more about your pupils, Polly. As I mentioned when we first met, only one of them is my child… my son Solomon. He's eight years old, the youngest, and loves his older sisters as if they were his own flesh and blood."

"What age are the girls?"

"Annie is sixteen and Hannah is twelve."

They walked into the wood, the sun slipping behind the highest branches, a chill on the breeze. Their footsteps crunched on the dry leaves strewn along the path beside the river. Not a wide river but peaty and meandering, making its way around large boulders covered in moss.

"They were only infants when they came to us, poor lambs," Claudia continued. "Papa took pity on them. Hannah's mother was abandoned by her husband and died in the workhouse, so the baby was sent to the orphanage. Such a beautiful child with her green eyes and raven hair." She glanced at Polly, as if to ensure she was paying attention. "And then Annie, little serious Annie, was found at the gateway of the rectory, bundled up in a fine wool blanket and an envelope of money tucked into the basket, so she must have belonged to a family wealthier than most around here. Perhaps a desperate young woman discovered she was in trouble and saw no other way out." Her earnest gaze lingered on Polly. "We never found out who she was. Heart-breaking."

Polly murmured agreement. What would her aunt say? She'd

been critical of Polly accepting the position, so far away from Mayo and with no idea of the sort of family to which she was going. The children would most likely be monsters, she'd pointed out, spoilt and badly behaved. Polly would regret her rash decision and return home with her tail between her legs. Aunt Maureen would have preferred her to remain in Mulranny to work with her as a seamstress for the rest of her life.

"Poor girls… but they were fortunate that your father found them."

"Yes, indeed." Her mistress added with a laugh, "I confess that I didn't tell you too much about the children. I feared I might put you off."

The trees thinned into a clearing and, on the other side of the river, a ruined castle stood on a slight hill amongst gorse bushes. A tall tower with ivy clinging to its granite walls and arrow slits for windows. One turret had fallen away and a heavy iron door barred the entrance below. Jackdaws circled overhead.

"What's that?" Polly asked, stopping to gaze at it.

"It's an old tower house. It hasn't been lived in for centuries. You can see it from Colgrannagh," she replied. "Locals think it's haunted. They see lights sometimes at night and hear a banshee wailing. All sorts of nonsense." She shook her head and continued along the path that led onto a wooden footbridge across the river.

She grasped the handrail and stared at the deep pool of water below. "I was afraid you wouldn't come if I told you too much about my charges. People can be so… so prejudiced against those born into poor homes. There are many in Wicklow… the offspring of parents who struggle with poverty every day. We are privileged, you and I, to have so much."

Polly nodded, watching the glistening water swirling in little eddies. A huge rock sat in the middle of the pool with a narrow path carved out of stone winding to its summit. The breeze sighed in the branches overhead, creating a swishing sound like waves on the beaches in Mayo.

Claudia squeezed her arm. "Yes, my dear, education is so important and exactly what my father believed in. His dream was to educate children from less well-off backgrounds and see how they developed… both boys and girls. He wished to see if they progressed in a similar way to the sons and daughters of better-off parents. Indeed, why wouldn't they, if given the same privileges?"

The good doctor sounded like a kind philanthropist but Polly's pulse quickened. The adoption of the children was too similar to an experiment.

"I imagine you've heard of Sir Francis Galton?" her mistress asked, fixing her with a direct gaze. "My father was a staunch admirer. He read his book Hereditary Genius many times."

"I'm sorry, no, I confess I haven't read his work."

"No matter. Sir Francis was a pioneer of eugenics and also coined the phrase nature versus nurture… a half-cousin of Charles Darwin, as far as I remember. It was his work on psychometrics that impressed my father whilst Gilbert and I admired his travel writing, particularly his adventures in South-West Africa… well known for his cartography. I could lend you his Art of Travel, if you're interested."

"Thank you, ma'am, I love to read." Eugenics? Did that mean breeding with select attributions in mind? She didn't dare to ask.

Claudia took out her pocket watch again. "Ten minutes. Yes, dear Papa adopted these children and I wish to continue his work and ensure they receive a good education. Unfortunately, the two previous governesses… they didn't stay long. One left to marry, between ourselves a rather frivolous and wayward creature, and the other… she said she found the house too lonely. We keep to ourselves and don't mingle much in society. Life here must have been too tedious for her." She looked into Polly's eyes. "I feel you have strength of character, determination. You will not desert us so readily."

"I hope not, indeed."

"I'm sure you won't." Claudia replaced the watch, leaning over the wooden railing of the bridge and pulling out a coin. She handed it to Polly. "I'd like to show you a local custom. Throw the coin into the river and make a wish. There's a tale this pool was blessed by a druid centuries ago. I often meet people here, wishing for a better life no doubt, poor souls. They tell me that when we make a wish... before the coin hits the water and sinks to the depths, the trees along the riverbank whisper our yearnings to each other." She laughed. "They call it The Whispering River. It's a fanciful belief but a rather beautiful name. Perhaps belief helps wishes come true. Come along, Polly, toss in the coin and make a wish for I must hurry back to visit my patient and her ongoing struggle with insomnia."

Polly clutched the coin. What would she wish for? The answer was simple. She tossed the penny into the dark water, listening to the plop as it hit the surface, watching it whisked away by the current.

"What did you wish for?" her mistress asked, but held up her hand. "No, don't tell me... it might not be granted."

No, Polly wouldn't tell her. She longed to succeed in her position, determined to escape from her aunt and create an independent life. She wished for the children to like her. Dr Fitzpatrick's words in the train carriage had caused ripples of unease.

"Mrs Manning, was your husband... I was told he was an explorer too, like Sir Francis." Polly recalled Lizzie the housemaid's chatter as she'd laid the fire in her bedroom that morning.

"Not an explorer as such... a plant hunter." The smile on Claudia's face faded. "Gilbert was a brave man who collected plants and endured many hardships for his employer, the owner of a horticultural nursery in England. He died last year."

"Oh, I'm sorry. I shouldn't have asked… "

"No, please, don't worry. He will always be spoken of at Colgrannagh with love and respect. It was a tragic accident. He slipped when attempting to reach an exotic flower on the edge of a ravine in Brazil."

"Oh, Mrs Manning, I'm truly sorry."

"I thank you, but we won't dwell on such thoughts. Pray, let us go back to the house. My mother is longing to meet you. She's been confined to her bedroom with a cold in the head all week. I'm sure you'll think her kind-hearted and amusing." Claudia turned away and walked off with Polly hastening to keep up.

Chapter Six

The past – March 1895

Three pairs of eyes stared at Polly, curious and assessing.

"Have you learned French?" Polly asked the children sitting at the long table and pressed her fingertips together. She would have to appear confident from the outset if she were to gain their trust and obedience. Children had an uncanny way of sensing unease and some took advantage. Perhaps she should have begun with an easier subject, such as English spelling or some simple addition.

"We learned a bit of French, miss," the girl with dark curly hair replied. Hannah's unusual eyes lingered on Polly's face. "Miss O'Brien... she was our last governess... she taught us a few words before she left."

Annie frowned, light brown hair framing a thin pale face. "Miss O'Brien didn't speak French. She merely wrote words on the blackboard."

The boy, Solomon, yawned and looked towards the window. He resembled his mother with his straight dark hair. A wise child, Claudia Manning had told Polly, but shy, requiring encouragement to participate.

"Have you been to France, Miss Brady?" Annie asked.

"I was fortunate to spend a year at a French school where I

learned the language," Polly replied, turning to the blackboard and writing the word *cheval* on it with a piece of chalk. "Now, what does this mean?" She read the word aloud. "Anyone know the answer?"

Silence fell as sunlight flittered on the wall of the schoolroom, throwing shadow on the tall bookcases. The creases on Annie's brow deepened and Solomon continued to gaze out of the window.

"A knight," Hannah ventured.

"Close, that's quite close. What does a knight ride upon?"

"A horse!" The boy turned his head, interested.

Polly wrote the English word beside the French one. "Very good, Solomon. Now, all of you repeat it after me."

A chorus of young voices rang out, copying her accent.

"Did you go to Paris?" Hannah asked. "I'd love to go to Paris and see all the ladies in beautiful clothes and… what age are you, miss?"

Annie nudged her. "That's impolite… you shouldn't ask a lady that."

A lady, how grand to be called a lady! Polly allowed herself a smile. "Older than you."

"You're much younger than Miss O'Brien," Hannah muttered. "She was silly."

"Hannah!" Annie said and apologized on her behalf. "I beg your pardon, miss. She shouldn't say such things."

Solomon crumpled a sheet of paper into a ball and threw it at Hannah. "You're horrid," he shouted. "You shouldn't ask a lady her age. Rude, rude, rude…"

Hannah stuck out her tongue at him.

Polly was losing control already and would have to be firm. "That's enough. Quiet… please. Annie, what do you think this means?" Polly wrote the word *fleur* and stood back to scrutinize their faces. "Anyone? Please raise your hand… don't shout it out."

Nobody replied. Hannah sighed and Annie looked blank. Solomon's gaze drifted back to the window.

Polly cleared her throat. "It's flower. Now Hannah, will you come up here and write the word beside the French? Perhaps you could draw a flower for us as well."

Hannah got to her feet, pulling her pinafore down over her knees and brushing out a crease. "I like drawing. Annie is better but I like painting. Mrs Manning likes flowers and makes them into medicine to cure people who are sick."

"Yes, indeed," Polly said. "Come over here, please."

Annie added, "Mr Manning used to search for flowers. He hunted for them in South America."

"My papa," the boy added. "He went on an exped… an expedi…"

"Expedition." Hannah tossed her thick hair over her right shoulder and took the chalk. "A plant-hunting expedition to South America… and he never came back."

"My papa died." Solomon looked at Polly. "He fell into a ravine."

The three children regarded her with interest, perhaps attempting to gauge her reaction. It was fortunate that her mistress had already told her about the tragedy so that she wasn't caught unawares.

"I'm very sorry," she replied. "Mrs Manning told me yesterday."

Hannah leaned towards the board with the chalk in her fingers and drew a round circle with petals protruding from it. "It was last year. Solomon's papa died last year and we were very sad because he was a kind man and used to read us stories at bedtime about adventures in foreign lands. Will you read us stories, miss?"

"I'll have to ask Mrs Manning. Perhaps she likes to read to you now?"

"Sometimes," Hannah said, drawing another shape, "but she's

always so busy with her work and the books she chooses aren't very exciting. I prefer to hear about dragons and wild animals and horses and…"

"Adventures at sea," Solomon added. "Especially books about pirates. I'd like to be a pirate."

Hannah scoffed, wrinkling her nose. "I don't think you would. You'd probably be seasick." She stepped back from the board and waved a hand. "There's a wild creature, miss. Can you guess what it is?"

How quickly the children had distracted Polly's attention from the French class. The wooden clock over the bookshelves revealed that half an hour had passed and they'd only learned two words. She looked at Hannah's drawing. Two pointed ears, a long nose and sharp teeth. What was it? A dog of some sort, a wolf perhaps.

Solomon giggled and even serious Annie's pale blue eyes lit up with amusement.

"Go on, miss, guess what it is," Hannah insisted. "Guess what it is, go on." She peeped at the others under her long eyelashes and put a hand over her mouth to smother a laugh.

"It's a… a dog."

"No, it's not a dog. Have another guess."

Polly would have to regain control because exuberant Hannah was assuming the position of schoolmistress and pointing at the drawing with her forefinger.

The girl adopted a high-pitched, wheedling country accent. "Does that look like a dog, children?"

"Oh Hannah, you sound just like Miss O'Brien." Solomon laughed. "Doesn't she, Annie? Miss O'Brien had a shrill voice, so she did."

"Hannah, please sit down." Polly stepped forward and removed the chalk from the girl's fingers. "Sit down and we'll learn more French words. Three more words for today."

Hannah dragged her feet back to her desk, scraping the toes of her boots across the wooden floorboards, and flopped onto the bench with an exaggerated sigh. "It's not a dog, though, miss."

Annie's gaze flicked from the drawing to Polly's face.

"What is it then?" Polly asked. "Tell me and perhaps we could learn the name in French."

Hannah wiped chalky hands on the front of her pinafore and whooped. "I knew you wouldn't guess. It's a fox, of course. A fox that comes out at night and trots through the wood and up to the house. A cunning fox who knows everything that happens here because he watches everyone."

Solomon tittered again and Annie's lips twitched.

Really, Hannah was too boisterous but Polly knew she would have to proceed with caution as it would not do to alienate the girl during the first lesson, and she was obviously the leader of the three. "The French for fox is *renard.* Can you say that? Roll the R at the back of your throat. *Rrrr-en-arrrr. Le renard.*"

At least the children attempted it, Hannah pronouncing the word perfectly. She was an intelligent girl and would need to be challenged to keep her interested in lessons. Her drawing was competent too and she'd managed to capture the shine on the creature's fur. Why hadn't Polly realized it was a fox? It seemed obvious but why would a fox create such amusement amongst the children?

"As cunning as a fox," Hannah murmured. "If you were an animal, miss, what would you like to be?"

Polly shook her head, refusing to allow the girl to distract them further. "Now, let's repeat all three French words you've learned this morning and write them in your copybooks. Then we will learn three more before its time for luncheon. Two words each. Annie will write hers on the blackboard in a few minutes."

Hannah opened her mouth as if to object but closed it again. She cast a look at the other girl but opened her book and picked up her pencil.

The children settled down and Polly managed to persuade both Annie and Solomon to write the French words on the board and recite them aloud. When the clock displayed half-past twelve, she announced the end of the class.

Solomon let out a shout of joy and ran from the room, leaving Annie to tidy up his paper and pencils.

"Now, wash your hands, please, before luncheon," Polly called. She would have to change her dress before the meal because it was dusted with chalk. As she walked towards the door, a hand tugged at her sleeve.

It was Hannah. "Miss Brady…"

"Yes?"

The girl whispered, stepping closer, "Did Mrs Manning tell you what happened to her husband?"

Polly smiled. "You mustn't dwell on such unpleasantness, Hannah. She told me he slipped when trying to reach a plant."

A light gleamed in the girl's eyes, secretive, almost furtive as she replied, "No, no he didn't."

"But Mrs Manning… surely she knows?"

Hannah moved closer; her breath warm on Polly's ear. "Somebody pushed him."

Chapter Seven

The past – March 1895

The old house was like a labyrinth after dark. Polly placed her candlestick on the top of a large chest of drawers in the hall and struck a match. Oil lamps glowed in the downstairs rooms but long dark corridors lay above. Darkness had arrived early, with cloud descending on the hill on which Colgrannagh stood, and a rising wind carrying rain.

The match flared and she held it to the wick of the candle. She would have to concentrate on her bearings because the previous night she'd turned left instead of right after opening the door at the end of the corridor and found herself outside the schoolroom. Lifting the brass candlestick, she moved across the hall.

The storm was gathering strength, groaning in the trees. From the window at the foot of the heavy oak staircase, Polly saw dark silhouettes of pines shuddering in the wood by the river. Claudia had warned her that wind was always more blustery up in the mountains, but Polly was used to gales sweeping in from the Atlantic Ocean and battering her aunt's tiny cottage. She'd loved to stand in the doorway on wild nights and hear the crash of waves on the beach.

She held the candlestick higher as she climbed the stairs.

Gloomy paintings glowered from the walls; one of a dog with a chain around his neck serving as a collar, a long snout and sharp teeth bared in a snarl with a limp hare lying in front of its huge paws. It reminded her of Hannah's drawing of the fox and she shivered, averting her eyes as she passed by. What had the girl meant by that creature? The other children knew and seemed amused. A joke at her expense obviously, and now, too late, she wished she'd asked Hannah to explain the significance.

A sound creaked above, similar to footsteps on floorboards, and Polly froze, holding her breath and straining her ears to listen. Claudia had been called out to visit a patient expecting a baby and the children were in bed. Mrs Delaney, the cook, left after dinner had been served and Lizzie would have retired to her room near the kitchen, for it was almost ten o'clock, and both servants had to rise early in the morning.

A draught breathed from the window at the top of the stairs and the candle shivered and almost went out. No, please, not here in the darkest part of the house. She turned away to shield the flame with her hand. It flared again and threw dancing light across the landing. She could see no one and the only sound came from the gusts outside, whistling through a crack in a pane behind. Her imagination was running amok and she silently scolded herself. She wasn't used to such a big house. On stormy nights, the rooms of the cottage in Mayo had seemed warm and safe.

Was someone watching her? The hair on the back of her neck prickled. One of the children playing a trick, perhaps? But all three had gone to bed two hours before. She'd consented to read them a story before they settled down to sleep.

There'd been a minor argument about the choice of book, Solomon requesting *The Coral Island* by R.M. Ballantyne and Hannah insisting on *Alice's Adventures in Wonderland.* Annie, receiving a pleading look from the younger girl, had sided with her and Polly, suppressing a stab of guilt, picked up the Lewis

Carroll novel. She'd assured the boy that he could have his book read aloud the following week.

Solomon had crept from his bed in the adjoining room and climbed onto Polly's lap, snuggling under a blanket until his eyelids closed and his head drooped. He felt warm and sturdy on her knee and she couldn't resist stroking his shining dark hair before waking him and helping him to bed. The girls had seemed drowsy and happy to bid her goodnight.

Further down the corridor, the floorboards creaked again.

Polly held the candle aloft and called into the darkness, "Hannah, is that you?"

No sound or reassuring answer. Perhaps the girl was hiding behind the large wardrobe on the left and would jump out any minute to frighten her. That was just the sort of trick she might play on her new governess. Had antics like that driven away Miss O'Brien?

Polly stepped across the oriental rug, her eyes growing more accustomed to the dim light. No figure crouched beside the cupboard or behind the military chest belonging to an ancestor of her mistress who'd fought in the Battle of Waterloo. Solomon had pointed that out to her with pride.

If there were no one up here, she must be imagining the sounds. How foolish to allow her fears to get the better of her!

Polly continued along the corridor on the right, her pace quickening as she resisted the temptation to glance over her shoulder. Perhaps it was natural to feel unease in a strange house, with unfamiliar nooks and crannies where the children might be lurking, waiting to screech with laughter at her timidity. She wasn't usually a nervous type but being alone here on the side of the mountain with only sleeping children and Lizzie was disquieting. A desolate spot, no doubt about it, with its sweeping view of the valley below and, further off, the rearing peak of Tonelagee.

A thump against her legs and a sudden yowl sent her heart

racing but it was only Claudia's black cat scurrying past. She'd given him more of a fright because he shot into the sanctuary of an open doorway.

Polly glimpsed her face in the round gilt-framed mirror, white with anxiety, but she was nearly at her bedroom. She swung to the left and reached out to turn the door knob.

A shape loomed beside her and she screamed, dropping the candle, which instantly went out. She sank to her knees in the darkness and groped for it with shaking fingers; blood drumming in her ears.

"Don't worry, child." A whisper came from the gloom behind her, a female voice laced with mirth. "Hold still there while I light your candle again. I'm afraid I gave you a dreadful fright, my dear."

The woman moved closer and lit a match. Polly saw a gleam of white untidy hair, wisps straying from the pins that held it up and a soft face with a small nose and bright birdlike eyes.

There was mischief lurking around her lips. "I alarmed you, to be sure. You never saw me in the darkness."

"I… I'm sorry but you frightened me… I thought I heard footsteps."

"No one hears me. I am like an owl and can move in silence, in spite of my advanced years." There was satisfaction in her strange girlish tone.

Polly stood upright and held out the candle.

The woman lit the wick. In the flickering light, she appeared elderly, wrinkles on her brow and soft folds of skin beside her mouth. "I'm Dora Burroughs, Claudia's mother… your mistress's mother."

She pushed open the door into Polly's bedroom and followed her in, the candlelight guttering and sending shadows creeping up the walls.

Polly sank down on the bed. "I must apologize. Mrs Manning

mentioned you to me, indeed she did, but she said you were poorly… confined to your room."

"Please don't distress yourself. I shouldn't have been standing in the dark but I know this house like the back of my hand." The older woman walked towards the window and pulled the curtain back, exposing the garden and a slim silver moon unveiled for a few moments by scurrying cloud. "A wild night… a very wild night. The house comes alive at such times. It shakes off its habitual lethargy and springs to life like a restless creature."

Polly hesitated, finding the analogy unnerving.

Dora added, "I've been keeping to my room but I'm feeling better now. Tell me, Miss Brady, what do you think of us all so far? The children… are they easy to manage?"

Her heart rate returning to normal, Polly smiled. "They are lively but… they are cheerful happy children."

"They've been allowed to run a little wild, I fear. My husband was… he wanted them to grow up with confidence, without too much discipline so that their personalities would develop, but my late father always said we should not spare the rod and spoil the child. My husband was a man with different views… alternative views, you might call them. Who am I to question his judgement?" A gust of wind hit the windowpane and Dora stepped back, turning to face Polly. "Dr Fitzpatrick didn't agree with my husband's actions, of that I'm certain. I heard you met the doctor on the train. What did you think of him?"

"Oh, I… I don't know. He seemed… pleasant enough."

Dora put her head to one side again, her bright eyes fixed on Polly's face. "Pleasant enough, ha! He doesn't approve of my daughter… of women meddling with medicine. He didn't exactly see eye to eye with my husband either, but at least he was a man."

Polly remembered the comments that had passed between the doctor and the old woman on the train.

Dora muttered, "He thinks Claudia should have become a

nurse or a midwife. That was her place, according to him. She shouldn't administer herbal treatments or yearn to study medicine. Is that not unreasonable?"

Polly shifted her feet on the floor, clutching the counterpane with both hands. "I don't know. I'm not… I don't know anything about medicine, but… but I'm certain Mrs Manning is good at what she does. She appears very knowledgeable about many things. Why shouldn't she study medicine if she wishes? She may well be better than some men."

The other woman took in Polly's discomfort nodded. "Of course she is. She is intelligent, which is more than can be said for our local doctor, who is an ignorant and arrogant man."

Polly didn't dare agree but bent to unfasten the hooks on her boots. If she looked like she were preparing for bed, perhaps Dora would depart.

Dora turned back to the window as a fresh burst of rain rattled against the glass, displaying no sign of wishing to leave. "Claudia took you to the graveyard today. I saw you from my window."

"Yes, she did."

"It's a pretty little church with its grassy banks of primroses and violets at this time of year. Sheltered from the south-west wind by the wood. You thought it a charming place?"

"Oh yes, indeed I did," Polly replied.

"A picturesque spot for my husband to rest and at least he is near us."

"That must be a comfort for you."

The woman nodded and asked, "Do you believe in ghosts, my dear? Do you think the dead walk?"

"Oh no, I don't, I…"

"Not even on a night like this?" Dora whispered the words, as if talking to herself.

"No, definitely not," Polly said with a firmness she didn't feel.

What a strange woman Mrs Burroughs was! Not at all like her practical daughter and seeming to delight in making Polly feel uncomfortable with her direct questions.

"You can see the old castle from this room. You must have passed it on your way back from the graveyard."

"We did. I asked Mrs Manning about it."

Dora raised a thin finger to point at the darkness outside. "So, ghosts don't exist, eh? And yet sometimes, yes sometimes, there are lights in that tower house and no one is there. What do you make of that?"

"What sort of lights?"

"A kind of shimmering glow on the walls, like a lantern. We never see them up close because they vanish. By the time we reach the tower, the lights have gone." The old lady laughed, a shrill titter. "The locals believe they are a bad omen. Our Lizzie saw them before poor Gilbert... my daughter's husband, died in Brazil. Mind you, Lizzie is fond of the sherry so her word might not be reliable."

Polly twisted the counterpane in her fingers. "Perhaps that's all the lights are... figments of people's imagination."

Dora shook her head. "No, they're more than that, I'm certain. When they appear in the tower house, something bad happens, or so people say. But what say you, Miss Brady?"

"Boys." Polly tried to sound convincing. "Boys meeting for a bit of sport, daring each other to be brave in an old building at night. I imagine that is all it is."

"You imagine that, do you?"

"I do."

She laughed again. "Confidently spoken. Well then, my dear, we shall see, shall we? When next these strange lights appear, I will come and fetch you and you might like to creep out into the garden and over the bridge and spy upon those daring boys. In the meantime, I will leave you to rest. Goodnight."

Before Polly could reply or politely turn down the unusual proposition, Dora slipped out of the door and pulled it shut behind her.

Chapter Eight

The present – August 2022

The schoolroom had been tidied before my arrival and I liked it on bright mornings when the sun flooded both windows, shadows capering across the floorboards. The rusty hands on the old oval clock above the bookshelves remained forever at ten to five. Blotches of damp disfigured its faded face but it possessed a certain dignity, witnessing so much over the years.

How long had that clock hung there? Children would have watched eagerly, hearing the loud ticking and covering their yawns with ink-stained palms; longing for the hour their governess would release them into the garden to play. The clock had stopped decades before, with no one or no need to wind it up, but in that silent schoolroom the past came creeping back.

I stood at the window and watched Daniel on the lawn exchanging a few words with Millicent. She was gesticulating and shaking her head while he donned his usual placid smile. A second man joined them and pointed towards a clump of briars beside the gate into the wood on the far side of the lawn. The French landscaper, Tobie Desjardins?

He stood at an angle that made it difficult for me to see his face but he had thick sandy hair and wore well-cut red dungarees.

Yes, he probably was speaking French because he addressed Daniel and ignored Millicent. She wouldn't like that. I'd only known Millicent for a week but I could recognize a control freak when I met one.

After a few minutes, the landscaper threw his arms in the air, hunching his shoulders in a shrug, and strode off. Millicent scowled, rolling her eyes at Daniel, before marching towards the house. As she neared the door, she looked up at the window and I stepped back, anxious not to be caught spying.

Bookshelves lined two sides of the schoolroom and I suspected that it had been used as a library over the more recent decades when governesses were no longer required. Paint peeled on the ceiling and a spider's web of damp circled one corner where the leak had occurred.

"You'll have to do your research in the schoolroom," Millicent had reminded me when I'd arrived with my luggage and she'd shown me to my bedroom on the third floor. "I need the rooms below for guests. I'm sure it will suit you well and all the junk that you have to search through is there anyway."

I agreed that it was an ideal place to work, away from the hammering and clattering of the builders who were attacking the kitchen below.

"And that dog, too." Millicent frowned at Archie. "Keep him up here under control. I don't want him annoying the others."

I'd managed to sort through some of the boxes of papers, placing the more interesting-looking ones beside the old pine table running down the middle of the room. I sat on an office chair provided by Millicent, with a broken armrest, and ran my fingertips along the uneven surface, marked by children many years before. Someone had dug a hole with a penknife at the top of a leg and carved initials. H M. Who was H M? A bored child, no doubt.

Daniel had been interested when I showed him the 1895

journal belonging to his great-aunt because it was before she'd studied medicine, mainly containing information about patients she'd visited and her herbal treatments, a common practice in Victorian times. Many old cookery books, such as Mrs Beeton's, outlined everyday remedies for use in families. I'd come across such cures before and they usually featured plants that could be grown at home, not like the more toxic concoctions supplied by druggists' shops such as arsenic, opium and similar poisons. Another fact I'd discovered was that Claudia had studied at the Chelsea Physic Garden in London. Further research told me that women were limited to a course on botany because only men were allowed to become apothecaries. Claudia's university training obviously came later.

I reached into the cardboard box nearest to me and untied a red ribbon around a bunch of letters; yellowed envelopes and faded ink. Perhaps I would learn more about Claudia in her personal correspondence. This was the era before the telephone when letter writing was an important way to keep in touch with family and friends.

The first envelope was addressed to Mrs Gilbert Manning and postmarked London 1889. I read the page of neat handwriting. It contained news of a female cousin's family in England and suggested a visit to Wicklow later in the year. Nothing significant jumped out at me, the cousin writing about minor ailments and an excursion to Brighton.

The rest of the bundle was much the same: news from relations about holidays and how children's schooling was coming along. I relegated all these to a shoebox.

Underneath another diary owned by Claudia, again listing her visits to patients, was a bundle of letters tied with a black ribbon. Black might mean something solemn in the Victorian era. The letter at the top looked formal, dated 1894 but shorter and with the address of a horticultural establishment at the top:

Withersham's Seed and Plant Nursery. I began to read:

> *"Dear Mrs Manning,*
> *It is with great regret that we inform you of the disappearance of your husband, Gilbert Manning, missing from our plant-hunting expedition in South America. Mr Manning became separated from the party during a tropical storm.*
> *We received the worrying news by telegram from our contact in Brazil this morning and we can only pray for more hopeful tidings in the coming days."*

Poor woman! What a shock she must have got when she opened that letter. I read the lines again. Millicent mentioned her husband was a botanist and plant hunter who'd never come home. It was a daring but dangerous profession in those days. I wrote down his name and the date.

A few taps on the keyboard of my laptop told me that there were around two hundred seed and nursery firms in Britain by the year 1800. Many of them were family owned and some of the larger ones had premises on the King's Road in Chelsea during the middle of the century. I found an alphabetical list and there was Withersham's near the bottom, a large business based in Devon.

Another lengthy search on the internet revealed that one of the important plant hunters of the nineteenth century was David Douglas, sent by the Royal Horticultural Society to North America in the 1820s. He brought back plant material to grow trees that transformed the landscape and timber industries: the Douglas fir, Sitka spruce and the giant Monterey pine that grew up to thirty metres in Britain and Ireland and over double that height in New Zealand.

New plants from foreign countries were all the rage in Victorian Britain; status symbols for owners of large gardens, and nurseries paid their plant hunters big money to track down unusual exotics.

Anthony and I had visited some of the more famous gardens in Ireland with Dad when we were in our teens and my brother had begun to show an interest in botany. I remembered Kilmacurragh in Wicklow, owned by the Botanic Gardens, where huge rhododendrons from China dropped deep pink blossom like confetti on the paths of its historic landscape.

I clicked on another famous plant hunter's name: William Lobb from Cornwall was dispatched by the Veitch nursery business to South America. Had Gilbert Manning accompanied someone like him?

Lobb was renowned for introducing the prickly-boughed Chile pine, better known as the monkey puzzle tree, to Britain. He'd also sent home branches and cones from a gigantic sequoia tree of the Californian forests. It was named Wellingtonia after the Duke of Wellington.

Some of the plant-hunting adventurers came to unpleasant ends. David Douglas was gored by a bull when he fell into a pit and William Lobb picked up debilitating diseases on his travels, including yellow fever and dysentery. He died in San Francisco in 1864 so his voyages seemed unlikely to have crossed with those of Gilbert Manning.

I tapped my biro on the table and frowned. Was that what happened to Claudia's husband? Some horrible disease carried him off and he was never seen again? Or perhaps he'd met with an accident during the tropical storm. Daniel hadn't known anything more, except that he'd died in Brazil.

I keyed the words Gilbert Manning plant hunter 1894 into the search bar of the archives of an Irish newspaper. The internet signal was slow and unpredictable in the schoolroom and, while the page was loading, I got to my feet and walked to the window.

The landscaper had built a bonfire and was forking great

heaps of branches and briars onto the flames. Was that allowed in these days of more rigid environmental regulations? He obviously didn't care.

I thought it would be interesting to discover more about the old garden at Colgrannagh and maybe I might find plans somewhere. If Gilbert had been a plant hunter, he might have brought home some rare specimens, which could be still lurking in the undergrowth all these years later. I would ask the landscaper about that but my French was rudimentary. More than a decade since I'd worked as an au pair for the summer in Brittany. I'd spotted what I guessed was a Wellingtonia tree at the edge of the wood, taller than the tower house, but no monkey puzzles.

A page opened on the screen on my laptop: Death in South America. That looked promising. I tapped on the title and glanced at my phone while new columns of text loaded.

No messages. Not even from Dominic who'd taken to sending regular threats about what his solicitor was advising him to do. My husband was convinced that he deserved half of the proceeds from the sale of my late father's house. I was equally determined that he had no right to any of the money.

I leaned towards the screen and saw that the date of the death notice was also 1894:

> *"The death has occurred of Mr Gilbert Manning of Colgrannagh, County Wicklow, whilst taking part in a plant-collecting expedition in Brazil. Sadly missed by his grieving widow and family."*

No mention of why he died. I took a screenshot of the notice and my eyes slipped to the boxes of papers at my feet as I tapped my biro against my cheek. The details might be in those somewhere.

Most of the correspondence in the bundle tied with black

ribbon turned out to be letters of condolence after the death of Claudia's husband and of no use as far as my research was concerned.

"Time for lunch," I said aloud to Archie, who was asleep on the moth-eaten rug under the table. He raised his head and thumped his tail.

Volumes of poetry and natural history sat on the book shelves on this side of the room. Rather beautiful leather-bound books by William Wordsworth, Lord Byron and Coleridge. I stepped over and took down the Wordsworth and noticed the name Polly Brady written inside. Who was she? Perhaps a friend or relation of Claudia.

Archie stood up, whining and stretching, as I replaced the poetry volume and stared around the room. So much old junk, Millicent had moaned. She longed to dump the lot. I moved over to a wooden box of toys, painted bright blue with a golden star motif on the lid.

"Let's see what's in here," I said to the terrier, who wagged his tail and yawned.

The box was large and quite heavy. A cursory look revealed toys from the Victorian era onwards: a skipping rope, lead soldiers with their red coats chipped, a doll with only one arm and a dreadful haircut (attacked by a child with a pair of scissors, no doubt), a collection of marbles and a striped spinning top.

There was also a stack of hardback exercise books filled with looped writing; lines of French and Latin. *Annie Manning* was the name inside one of the covers.

I lifted out a green notebook, smaller than the rest, with different children's handwriting across the pages. *The Game* was the title on the first page. What was this? The names of children descended in a list below. What was this game they played? Each child had been given an animal's name.

'Luke Manning – Age: 22 – The fox
Annie Manning – Age 16 – The deer
Hannah Manning – Age 12 – The cat
Solomon Manning – Age 8 – The mouse"

All these Manning children! Daniel had only mentioned one, the boy Solomon. I recognized him for he was Claudia's son; the man who'd lived in Colgrannagh before it was left empty for so long and allowed to fall into a ruin, according to Millicent. Who were these others? Cousins, perhaps, come to visit. I turned over the page to find a single paragraph set out under the heading *Rules* on the following page:

'The Game is our secret. The oath of loyalty must be sworn. No one must speak of this to adults. Our duty is to watch, listen and report back.'

The children had scratched their signatures in formal agreement under these rules. Who exactly were these children and who were they watching and reporting on?

At first, this seemed similar to a childish type of secret society, common enough in those days when there were no video games or mobile phones to keep young people occupied. I remembered my friend Jessica and I had joined a secret club in school. We used invisible ink to pass hidden messages in the classroom. Often the teacher would confiscate them and turn over the paper to find nothing written there while we smothered smirks and giggles. We met in the garden shed belonging to the parents of an older girl and had to whisper a password before we were allowed in the door. Usually all we did was draw pictures and eat biscuits pilfered from our parents. All harmless fun that we soon outgrew when boys became much more interesting.

Archie watched me, bored with my research.

"All right," I said. "Why don't you and I drop in on Daniel for lunch and see if he has any idea who these children might have been?"

Chapter Nine

The present – August 2022

"Do you like our new marquee?" Millicent pushed open the double doors and ushered me inside. "It's the company's latest model. Kenny discovered it when he was a photographer at a wedding last month."

Tempted to point out that I'd suggested this to her before and she'd scoffed at my suburban taste, I decided that might plummet me even further in her estimation.

A meringue confection was probably the perfect description for the marquee, a billowing mass of cream and pale pink with one end opening onto the courtyard at the back of the house.

"Very stylish," I muttered. "I'm sure your bride and groom will be delighted with it. Looks as if they'll be able to fit at least two hundred people inside."

Millicent smiled, gratified. "Yeah, it's huge. Thankfully, the bride chose the white dance floor, just as I hoped she would." She frowned at Archie. "Mind that dog of yours doesn't lift his leg in here… the last thing I need is the stink of pee. All the tableware is included in the price, with serviettes, glasses… It's perfect for this courtyard because it's sheltered in here and the paving stones underneath are quite level. The Frenchman did a good job, I have to admit, even though it took him several weeks.

Such a slow worker."

"I'll take Archie outside… just in case." I called the terrier. Millicent had just given me the perfect excuse to escape.

"I'm sorry, Fiona, perhaps it's upsetting for you to see this… another wedding venue. I forget that you're… did you tell me you're divorced?"

I laughed with what I hoped was a carefree manner as I moved to the door. "Not yet but hopefully soon. Don't worry, it's not upsetting for me. I hope the bride made the right choice." I watched her eyes narrow and added, "I was just out of university when I married Dominic. Far too young, so I didn't know what I was doing."

"I sympathize. I'm divorced. My ex-husband was a serial adulterer. Kenny and I are hoping to tie the knot next year. We're saving up for a big wedding… a day to remember."

"Ah, okay. Hopefully you'll be much happier this time around," I replied. Dominic and I had a wedding day to remember. Not easy to forget the rain lashing down and the power cut halfway through the church ceremony that caused both lights and organ to fail. My mother, always late for important events, had crashed the car on the way and my father cut his head on the broken windscreen. He'd arrived at the church door to ferry me up the aisle clutching a bloodstained handkerchief to his brow, while Mum blamed a sharp bend in the road that somehow hadn't been there on her way to the rehearsal.

Dominic's best man made a speech salted with rude puns and peppered with his own guffaws of laughter that shocked my genteel grandmother into an uncharacteristic silence for the remainder of the afternoon.

The grand finale came when my brother Anthony and his school friends drank fifteen pints of lager each for a bet and were sick all over the dance floor. After that, I decided my marriage could only improve. How wrong I was.

Archie obligingly lifted his leg outside against the pedestal of a large urn overflowing with flowers, receiving a dark look from Millicent. Her mobile phone rang and she tapped the screen. "Yes… oh, Siobhan, hello. Yes, everything's nearly organized now for you to pop over and check it out. The dance floor has been fitted… just waiting for the indoor floral arrangements now."

I whistled at Archie and we hurried out under the stone arch that led from the courtyard to the front garden, around the clump of silver birch until we were safely out of sight.

"You shouldn't pee in front of her," I reprimanded him. "Millicent thinks dogs are uncivilized and you let us down."

Archie tipped his head to the side, his tail wagging slowly, as if uncertain what to make of my tone.

"Come on," I said, pointing towards the lawn, "let's go and explore."

In the distance, the tower house rose above the trees, what was left of its stone turrets reaching towards the cloudless sky. Sixteenth century, Daniel had mentioned, and now considered a national heritage site and maintained by the state. I liked tower houses, which were fortified dwellings similar to the keeps built by the Anglo-Normans after they'd invaded a number of centuries before. Normans were great builders and many of their magnificent stone constructions were still standing over a thousand years later, including the historic castles of Dublin, Kilkenny and Trim.

Strange that Daniel hadn't known anything about the other children when we'd looked at the book about their game over lunch. It appeared to be a collection of notes by the girls, Solomon and another young man called Luke; secret observations about the goings-on of the family, servants and visitors at Colgrannagh.

Daniel handed it back to me and said it was probably just a bit of amusement for the children, but perhaps I would read through it in more detail when I had time.

A bonfire smoked on the far side of the mown grass, the scent of wood ash on the breeze. I headed towards it, glancing over my shoulder to ensure Millicent was still preoccupied with her bride and not hot on our trail.

Archie bounded ahead of me, his nose to the ground tracking some wild creature. He darted into the shrubbery on the right, yelping with excitement.

"Hey, come back here!" I shouted. "Come back here now."

No sign of the dog returning, just a series of hysterical barks from under the tangle of branches of an overgrown laurel.

A man pushing an empty wheelbarrow appeared and came to a standstill when he saw me; the landscaper Tobie Desjardins, whose surname amused Daniel because it translated as 'Tobie of the Gardens'.

"Sorry about the noise," I said, "my dog... he's gone into the bushes and I'm trying to get him back."

The man made no reply. Still wearing his dungarees and a pair of leather work boots, his gaze shifted from my face to the laurels. Now that I was close to him, his eyes looked hazel or that in-between shade between green and brown.

Millicent had told me that the landscaper didn't speak much English so I considered addressing him in my rusty French but Archie's yaps were growing more frantic. What had happened to the dog? He sounded further away, as if underground. Down a damn rabbit hole. It had happened before in a friend's country garden and her husband ended up having to dig him out. Why, oh why, did the Jack Russell breed have to chase every creature they met? When Archie belonged to my father, he never left the enclosed back garden of the house in Dublin without his lead clipped to his collar. It hadn't taken me long to discover why.

What was the French word for rabbit? *Lapin*?

"He loves to chase things." I abandoned the effort to speak French. The landscaper probably wouldn't understand my terrible accent anyway. "Excuse me, I must crawl in here and try to find the dog." I pushed aside the branches, sending a swarm of flies buzzing into the air.

Tobie folded sun-tanned arms across his chest and watched. Was that a smile playing around his mouth? Surely not.

"Archie, here Archie, come here, boy."

"*Ce chien est vraiment obéissant*," he said and broke into a sudden laugh.

A flush crept from my neck up to my cheeks. His last word sounded like it meant obedient and was obviously an attempt at sarcasm. Which I could do without. "Yes, well… he's… he's not usually this bad. Archie! Come back here."

The yelping ceased and there was silence for a few moments, except for the twittering of a robin partly hidden in a wild cherry tree to our left.

"*Et maintenant il n'est pas là*."

"He is here, somewhere. He might be down a rabbit burrow."

"*Ah oui*."

I ignored this last comment because I was now on my hands and knees under the laurels and spotted a large hole in the ground. Bigger than a rabbit burrow. More like a badger's sett with a pile of soil lying nearby. Didn't badgers clean out their underground homes at regular intervals? I pushed my head into the earthy darkness and called, "Archie, Archie, are you there?"

No answer, not even a whimper from the little wretch. I groaned, imagining the terrier galloping along endless passageways that spread for miles like a maze under the ground. Would he ever come out again? What if he came face to face with the badger? It might be in a territorial mood and attack him; tear him to shreds. I'd never had any dealings with badgers but I knew they were considerably bigger than Jack Russells. My mouth went dry. Why hadn't I kept the dog on his lead?

I listened again, my head still down the yawning hole. No

sound from him. It was no use; I would have to ask for help. I twisted my head round to look up at the man who had stepped closer and was peering into the shrubbery, his thick eyebrows drawn together and a curious expression on his broad features.

"The dog might be in danger," I said. "Have you got a spade I could borrow?" I scrambled to my feet and imitated a person digging, throwing invisible soil over my left shoulder and hoping he would understand the urgency. Archie might be suffocating down there in the dark, his little throat gripped in the jaws of a furious badger.

The landscaper considered me, his mouth twisting to one side.

What was the French for spade? Surely he could understand what I meant by the way I was miming the action.

"*S'il vous plaît*," I added, wondering if a display of courtesy would encourage him to help. A pity Daniel wasn't at home to translate but I'd seen him drive off to the local supermarket after our lunch together.

Tobie scratched his head and frowned again.

"Surely you possess a spade!" Impatience seized me. "You're a gardener, for goodness sake. You must be able to lend me one."

His mouth stretched into a grin. "And you are going to dig out the little dog all by yourself, eh?"

"I have to try. He might be in danger." I brushed soil from my jeans. How could he find it amusing? Archie's life was at risk. I realized only then with a stab of indignation what the man had said. "You speak English!" I cried. There I was, making a fool of myself, acting like an idiot with an imaginary spade and all the time he could understand me perfectly.

"Of course."

"*Of course*… what do you mean *of course*? Millicent told me… she said you don't speak English."

"I only speak French to *Madame*… for obvious reasons."

I stared at him. "Oh, I see. I see what you mean. So that she leaves you alone?"

"Yes. She can only speak to me through an interpreter… Daniel." He spread his hands and shrugged. "And so… I am left in peace."

"What if I tell her?"

"I think maybe you won't."

"How do you know?"

"Because I am going to help you dig out your little dog… your naughty little dog. Would you like me to do that?"

Relief flooded through me. "Yes, I would be really grateful. Thank you, thank you so much."

"Besides, I've seen you speaking to *Madame* and you might also wish you could speak French." He grinned again and turned away. "Wait here. Perhaps you'll hear him bark again. I'm going to get my spade."

I crawled back under the branches and thrust my head into the entrance of the badger's sett, calling again. Was that a whimper? A soft yelp?

"Archie, Archie, is that you? Are you there?"

Yes, definitely a muffled bark coming from deep down under the ground. The dog was still alive. "Stay there, Archie, good boy. Stay there. We're coming to rescue you."

Tobie reappeared, a long wooden handle over his shoulder. He beckoned for me to get out of his way and pushed the branches aside, driving the blade of the spade into the earth. Clods of soil landed beside my shoes.

"I heard the dog bark while you were away," I said. "He's still alive."

"Of course he's still alive. He is exploring. I expect he would come out on his own later but, just in case, I'll help you. I'm fond of dogs."

"Even disobedient Jack Russells?"

He thrust the spade into the ground again. "Especially disobedient Jack Russells. My grandfather owned one."

"Where did you learn to speak such good English?" I sat on the grass and watched him dig, beads of sweat gathering on his brow, his hair growing damp where it curled around his ears.

"My mother is English. She comes from Derbyshire."

"I see. So, you pretend you speak only French and all the time you are half-English. Isn't that a bit deceptive?"

"Definitely deceptive, yes, but I believe it is necessary." He added, "You don't know Millicent as well as Daniel does… and he was the one who suggested I should only speak French."

I laughed. "Daniel was trying to protect you. Millicent can be rather overbearing."

Archie barked again, as if growing impatient with our conversation and wondering why we weren't making more of an effort to hasten his rescue.

Tobie dug faster, earth and stones gathering in a heap. He slashed at the laurels with his spade before stepping forward and bending to peer at the ground. "Hey, look at this."

"What is it?" I moved closer.

"The bottom of an old wooden door… see here to the left of the badgers' sett. Looks rotten where that hole is. I bet your dog squeezed through there. There must be something behind it… a shed maybe."

"Yes, but what is it? An icehouse? See the step there. Is it an underground potting shed? The house and garden were owned by a nineteenth-century plant hunter. Perhaps this was where they stored plants or kept implements."

"A plant hunter? Interesting. Daniel never mentioned that." He rattled the handle. "What you suggest makes sense… some sort of old garden structure where they might have kept pots and tools."

Tobie dug more soil out of the way before leaning on the door with his shoulder and giving it a push. It groaned and creaked open, rusty hinges complaining. More steps led downwards, damp and slippery with moss. He pulled his phone from the back pocket of his dungarees and switched on the flashlight. "Yes, look at this… you're right, it's an underground storage area. I can see a wooden workbench and… ah, there's your dog gazing up at us and wagging his tail."

Chapter Ten

A pungent earthy smell rose from below when I followed Tobie into the dark shed. I placed my hand on the wall to keep my balance as I descended the steps; cold trickles of water running down the rough brickwork.

The beam from his phone swept over a paved floor, where puddles gleamed in the dim light. A wooden workbench ran along one side and sagging shelves clung to rusty iron bars at the far end.

"A long time since anyone's been down here," I said, my breath turning to fog in the chill. "Looks like it was abandoned."

"I suspect it's very old," he replied. "Perhaps it was forgotten about when the garden was left to turn into a wilderness."

"Yes, after the First World War, when everything changed. And after Irish independence… the civil war, many of these old properties fell into ruins. And no staff, or no money to pay the staff. I don't know if Solomon was keen on gardening."

"The last owner? Was he the man who left it to Daniel?"

"Yes, Daniel inherited Colgrannagh and told me that the place was left empty for years when his tenant died."

Archie was jumping at my legs, overjoyed to see me after his ordeal.

Tobie bent to caress the terrier. "You're a clever dog. You led us here, didn't you?"

I laughed. "A coincidence, I think."

"You believe in serendipity and not fate?" His voice had a faint trace of a French accent.

"I'm not a fatalist. If I were, I would still be living in Dublin and married to my ex-husband." As soon as the words slipped out, I regretted them. This man had only just met me; he wouldn't be interested in my failed marriage. I blamed Millicent because, with her incessant talk about weddings, she'd dragged Dominic back from the depths of my memory where I'd buried him.

Tobie continued to stroke Archie, pulling his soft ears through his fingers, but didn't reply.

"Perhaps they sprouted plants or bulbs down here years ago?" I muttered, changing the subject. "As I said earlier, they were keen gardeners… the people who lived here in the nineteenth century. The husband of Daniel's great-aunt went on expeditions to South America in search of unusual species to bring home."

Tobie seemed interested. "But is this true? It was a dangerous profession back in those days."

"I read about a few of them… many died from illnesses like dysentery or malaria."

"I learned about the plant hunters in horticultural college," Tobie said. "The French missionaries in China brought back many botanical treasures in the nineteenth century… priests like Armand David, Jean Marie Delaney and others."

"You went to horticultural college in England?"

"No, in Rennes… in Brittany." He leaned against the bench and swung his flashlight along the walls, as if examining the brickwork.

I decided I liked Tobie Desjardins. I liked his down-to-earth manner. "Your name is very apt," I said, "for a horticulturist… Tobie of the gardens."

He laughed and flicked the light onto my face and off again. "I suppose in English it would be Gardiner. Tell me about this plant hunter who lived here."

"He died while collecting plants on an expedition in Brazil. I found a report this morning about him in a newspaper in 1894 and a letter from the nursery he worked for. They'd didn't know exactly what happened to him because he disappeared during a tropical storm."

"That doesn't surprise me. There were many deaths. Courageous men, but all explorers are brave, aren't they? They enjoy pushing the boundaries. They have to, or they wouldn't do it. They'd stay at home with their wives and children by the fireside. It takes a certain type of person to want to leave home and go off to risk their life for something like that. Are you writing a book for Daniel?"

"No, he is paying me to carry out research on his great-aunt Claudia Manning. He's the one who's going to write a book about her."

Tobie gave a low whistle. "At his age, he's amazing, isn't he? A nineteenth-century lady doctor, that's interesting. How are you getting on with the research?"

I picked Archie up and held him in my arms while he wriggled and licked my face. "I haven't discovered much about her medical career yet. She was a herbalist before she went to university. I suspect she was knowledgeable though... knew more than many women of her time because her father was a doctor."

Tobie shrugged and waved a hand. "Women in those days... they weren't allowed to study for serious professions."

He crouched down to shine the beam of light under the bench. "Many people don't value plants in spite of all the famous medicines produced from them. Digitalis, the foxglove, for heart treatment and lots more. My father didn't want me to study horticulture... thought I should become an engineer like him. I take after my mother."

"She likes gardening?"

"More than that. She opens her garden to the public in Brittany."

"Impressive. My brother is a botanist." I remembered Anthony with his vague smile, so different to Tobie, and how impossible it was to get him to answer emails. Where was he now? I would have to track him down.

"We have interests in common, your brother and I. A noble profession!" He swung the flashlight under the bench again. "See here… old terracotta flower pots, mostly broken. I think this could have been a potting shed decades ago." He stood and continued his investigation of the underground space, fixing the beam on the back wall. "Look at that. Those bricks seem different, don't they? A different shade, as if from a later period."

"I've seen red brick walled gardens from the eighteenth century," I replied. "Maybe they patched it up."

He stepped over to the wall and examined it. "No, it's more like a doorway… that arch there… it's like a doorway that was bricked up for some reason. I wonder what's on the other side."

"You could check later. I expect it's underneath another clump of laurel, whatever it is."

He walked away and ran a hand along the bench, pointing at a tin box on one of the sagging shelves. "What's that?"

I put Archie down and he scampered after Tobie, spinning in circles of excitement. He'd taken to the landscaper.

Tobie reached for the tin and placed it on the table. It was quite large, the size of a small trunk with a rusted clasp and padlock.

"Locked," Tobie said.

"Bang the padlock with your spade," I suggested, keen to see what was inside.

"Okay, hold my phone and stand well back in case I hit you

by mistake." He handed me his mobile and grasped the handle of the implement, raising it in the air and bringing the blade down on the padlock with a crack.

The metal catch snapped open as the lock fell to the floor and rolled into the darkness.

I peered over Tobie's shoulder and shone the flashlight into the chest. Books, white with mildew, and rows of small bottles with faded labels. "What are they?"

He lifted a bottle to the light, squinting to read the faded label. "Tinctures… this one held gum myrrh. Some of the words are difficult to read." He picked up another. "This other one is called *Tincture of Lobelia*."

I clutched at his arm. "These must be Claudia's… her herbal preparations she used on patients." Heat bloomed on my cheeks in the dark and I released my grip with an apology.

He passed me the small book. "Check what is in it."

I laid it on the table and turned to the first page. The writing was long and looped and in ink so faded it was almost impossible to read, even with the aid of Tobie's phone. I recognized the handwriting, the same as in the journal and definitely Claudia's.

The paper felt soft, almost spongy under my fingertips, as if it might fall apart before I had a chance to decipher the words. I read the sentence at the top of the page aloud: "*The human body and herbs used in the botanic practice. 1886.*"

"Wow, look at this," I said, gently peeling open another page. "*Marsh Mallow… excellent to cure coughs, stomach ulcers, dysentery and stones in the urinary tubes.*"

"You'll have to dry this book out carefully, or the pages will stick together. Search on the internet… to see how to do it, I mean."

"Good idea, thanks."

He bent forward, shining the flashlight into the tin box. "There's something else there at the bottom."

"Looks like a folded sheet of paper. What is it?"

Tobie picked it up. "A map of some sort. Move along the table, please, let's see what this is."

I stepped sideways and gave him room to open it out. "It is a map, you're right."

He nodded, leaning closer. "So difficult to read the words. A plan… yes, definitely a plan. I think it's a design for a herb garden. See this word *physic* beneath?" He grinned into my face. "A physic garden… medicinal herbs grown for the tinctures in those bottles. This is fascinating, isn't it? The physic garden must have been here at Colgrannagh. I'll have to show this to Daniel."

"Hello, hello! Fiona!" A call rang out, distant and muffled, but instantly recognizable.

"It's Millicent," I said.

Tobie held a finger to his lips and I nodded.

"Fiona! I need to talk to you. Where are you?" Millicent shouted.

"I'll wait until she moves away and then I'd better go." I placed the precious notebook back in the tin and closed the lid. "I don't want to share this with Millicent. She has no appreciation of the past. She'd only wrinkle her nose and tell me to chuck the whole lot in the rubbish bin."

Tobie lifted the metal chest back to its resting place on the crooked shelf. "We'll leave it here for now, where it belongs. When Millicent isn't around, perhaps you could take it back to the house and keep it somewhere safe or give it to Daniel. I'll be interested to learn what other plants your Claudia used."

My Claudia! His words gave me a thrill, a sudden dart of possession. As did our shared sense of conspiracy.

"Our secret for now." Tobie pointed up towards the shaft of light creeping in at the top of the steep steps, while Millicent's unheeded calls grew fainter. "I'll say nothing, I promise. And in return you must promise that you won't give me away. When

Millicent sees you talking to me, she must believe that you're speaking French."

Chapter Eleven

The past – March, 1895

"What is the name of this plant?" Polly stooped to pick three leaves of sage and placed them on her outstretched palm in front of the three children. "Take a leaf each, squeeze it between your fingers and hold it to your nose."

Annie reached for one and sniffed. "Oh, it smells like mint. Is it mint?"

"That's a good guess," Polly replied, smiling. "It's from the same family as mint. Solomon, do you have any idea?"

The boy stood motionless on the gravel circle around the sundial, where clumps of herbs brushed against its stone pedestal. He ignored her and stared at the door in the brick wall from the kitchen garden. He was more easily distracted than the two girls, which was understandable because of his age, but Polly would have to encourage him to concentrate. Claudia would question the children later to test how their lesson in the physic garden had progressed, keen for them to learn botany.

Polly had spent several hours with her mistress earlier in the morning, learning how to identify herbal plants. Claudia suggested beginning with names the children might recognize from everyday cooking: sage, bay, rosemary, lavender and thyme.

Polly wondered if she should have mentioned Hannah's comment about Gilbert Manning's death but a suitable opportunity had never arisen. The girl might consider it a betrayal but the mistress would surely want to be informed about such a serious allegation.

Hannah crushed her sage leaf and inhaled its scent. "Oh, it's strong, isn't it? I don't think it's mint. It has a much heavier scent… Solomon, what are you doing?"

The boy threw an arm into the air and pointed. "There's Mama with Mr Kingson. Mama!"

Two figures were making their way along one of the six paths that radiated out from the sundial in the centre of the garden. Each path was lined with beds of medicinal plants, a profusion of different aromas when Polly's skirt brushed against them. It was too early in the year for their flowers to bloom but she admired the geometrical design of the borders and the neatly clipped shapes. There was a pleasing orderliness to it.

"It's sage," she told the children. "The Latin name is *Salvia officinalis* and it's used in herbal medicine for coughs and digestive disorders and in cooking for… Solomon, please come back."

He gave no reply and ran towards his mother, his arms outstretched, whooping with excitement. Hannah tossed her sage leaf away and followed, snatching up her cotton dress as she ran, her hair streaming behind her in the spring sunshine.

Annie remained at Polly's side and gave her a timid smile. "*Salvia officinalis*. Would you like us to learn the common name as well, Miss Brady?" A conscientious girl and by far the easiest to teach. If only the other two were more like her.

"Yes, thank you, Annie. I'm sure Mrs Delaney uses sage in her cooking, especially mixed with onion and breadcrumbs when stuffing a goose."

Her employer came closer, with Solomon and Hannah trotting beside her, sleek dark hair pinned in a coil on the top of her head and her arm looped through that of a tall fair-haired gentleman in a well-cut navy coat.

Annie raised her hand in greeting. "That's Mr Kingson and he's Mama's new friend. He's kind and brings us gifts when he comes to visit."

"Generous of him, to be sure," Polly replied. She saw him bend to listen as Hannah whispered to him and he laughed, turning to glance in Polly's direction. What had the girl said?

"Hush, Hannah, please mind your manners," Claudia reprimanded. She raised her voice, "Miss Brady, I would like to introduce you to Mr Robert Kingson. Miss Brady is our new governess. And Mr Kingson is a member of the Pharmaceutical Society of Great Britain. Isn't that how you would describe yourself, Robert?"

"That sounds far too grand. I sell medicines to physicians around the country… although I acquired a qualification at the School of Pharmacy in Bloomsbury Square."

"An enlightened group," Claudia added. "They admitted two women as members over fifteen years ago."

Polly inclined her head. "Pleased to meet you, sir."

"Miss Brady." Robert gave a slight bow and his eyes rested on Polly's for several seconds before he turned to Solomon. "What has Miss Brady been teaching you today?"

The boy shrugged. "About plants… medicine plants." He turned his back on Kingson and grabbed his mother's hand. "Mama, will you come with me now and see the tree house I'm building in the wood? Eamon has been helping me with it and it's almost finished."

"Solomon, please… don't pull at me like that. You'll knock me over. I'd love to see it but later… I am taking a stroll with Mr Kingson and you are well aware that Miss Brady is in the middle of a lesson."

"Yes, Solomon, you must do as your mama tells you." Kingson

reached his hand towards the boy's shoulder but Solomon spun away. "You must stay with Miss Brady and finish your lesson. I'll be here all day and will come with you later. I'm looking forward to seeing your tree house." He beckoned to Polly. "Pray forgive our intrusion and continue with your instruction. We'll observe your teaching methods and appraise them."

Polly flushed again as she summoned the children, a scowl on the boy's face.

Claudia tapped his sleeve. "Oh no, Robert, Miss Brady wouldn't appreciate that… too much of an imposition. Let us continue with our walk to the graveyard. Miss Brady will follow with the children after another ten minutes… when she's finished her instruction." She took his arm again and they continued on towards the gate into the wood.

"Isn't Mr Kingson a handsome man?" Annie sighed. "He wears such elegant clothes and he always smells divine."

Hannah nudged Solomon. "Divine, if you please! The poor girl is in love with Mr Kingson. How unfortunate that your mama met him first!"

Annie dropped her gaze to the sage plant and poked at the soil with the toe of her little boot. "You think him handsome too, don't you? You said so only last week."

"No, I don't. I don't think of him at all. I never do."

"Neither do I," Solomon shouted. "I don't want to think of him." His big eyes filled with tears. "He will never take the place of my papa."

Polly put her arm round his shoulders. "Of course not, my dear, but he seems a nice friendly man and he's interested in your tree house."

The boy slowly shook his head from side to side.

"Come, Solomon." She clasped his hand. "Allow me to show you a plant and you must try to guess what it's called." She led him back to the sundial where she attempted to distract him with the history of thyme. "It was once used by the Ancient Egyptians to embalm their dead. The Romans threw it on their floors to prevent snakes from entering their homes."

He made a hissing noise through his front teeth. "Ooh… I've never seen a snake. Would Mr Kingson be a snake if he were an animal?"

Hannah giggled, lifting a hand to cover her mouth.

"A snake isn't an animal. It's a reptile." Annie frowned. "Mr Kingson would be a lion, with his fair mane and…"

"He could be a giraffe," Hannah interrupted with another snort of laughter. "He's as tall as a giraffe."

"He is not!" Annie cried.

Polly silently cursed Mr Kingson and Claudia for their interruption of her lesson. "Please, children, let us forget Mr Kingson for ten minutes."

"If you could be an animal, Miss Brady, what would you choose?" Hannah grinned at the other children. "Let's play our game."

They all looked at Polly.

"What game is this?" Polly asked.

"Our other governess Miss O'Brien was an owl." Annie ignored her question. "She wore round spectacles and Hannah said she was always twittering. She didn't know we called her an owl because she would have given away our secret."

"The game is our secret. I'm the cat," Hannah added. "I have black hair and I'm good at climbing trees."

Solomon laughed. "And I'm the mouse because I'm the smallest. I'm good at hiding."

"Miss Brady would be a cat too if she were an animal," Annie said.

"Why a cat?" Polly noticed her pale serious face. She recalled how her aunt had never been able to abide cats and once threatened to drown a tiny kitten found in the scullery. Polly had carried it away to the farmer's barn down the road, where she fed it on scraps until it was old enough to fend for itself.

"Yes, indeed," Annie replied. "I think you would be a cat because you are clever and you don't fawn all over us like a dog would. You notice things but you are quiet and reserved."

Hannah said, "Do you have secrets, Miss Brady? I suspect you're good at keeping secrets, not like Miss O'Brien. Miss O'Brien told Mrs Manning everything we said."

"We couldn't trust her," Annie added.

Hannah giggled again. "That's why she had to go." She reached out a hand and laid it on Polly's arm. "We don't want you to go, Miss Brady. We like you."

That's why she had to go. Why had the girl said that? But perhaps it was just her usual abrupt manner of speaking and Miss O'Brien had left because she hadn't been able to maintain discipline; or because she found Colgrannagh too isolated.

She thanked Hannah, bending down to pluck a sprig of rosemary from the herb border running along the wall. "Now, back to our lesson. What plant is this?"

"Can we go to the graveyard soon?" Solomon asked. "I like the graveyard and my tree house is only…"

"In ten minutes. You heard what Mrs Manning said," Polly replied, her voice rising a fraction.

Annie reached for the rosemary and twirled it in her hand. "I know this herb. It's rosemary, like the girl's name. I've seen Mrs Delaney use it when she roasts lamb."

"Correct, well done." Polly clapped her hands. "And now…" She noticed Hannah glancing towards the rows of oak and pine trees that ran behind the railings along the north side of the physic garden.

The girl murmured, "The fox. It's the fox."

The others turned to look. Polly peered into the cool dappled shade but could see no fox, nor any other animal. She pointed at the lavender and said, "What about this one? A beautiful pale purple when it's in flower and used as a scent by ladies."

The children paid no attention to her and continued to stare towards the wood. Polly opened her mouth to reprimand them but a shape moved in front. A face looked back, a freckled face amongst the tree trunks. A young man about the same age as her, with a mop of golden hair, crouched half-hidden in the shade, regarding her with an enigmatic smile on his lips.

Chapter Twelve

The past – March 1895

"I've invited you to accompany me today to help you understand my work," Claudia said, placing her medical bag in the trap. She sat on the driver's bench and picked up the reins.

"Thank you, ma'am. I'm grateful for the opportunity to learn." Polly gripped the wooden side of the carriage as she climbed up.

Her mistress encouraged the white pony to move off. "Walk on, Misty. I apologize for always being so busy. I don't seem to have much time to talk to you… so tell me how you are getting on with the children. How are they progressing with their lessons?"

Polly hesitated, wondering how much Claudia learned about what went on in the schoolroom. How had her charges answered when questioned about their new governess? "Oh, I… we appear to be getting used to each other and I'm pleased Solomon's spelling has improved."

Claudia kept her eyes on the road ahead as the pony trotted out of the gateway under the sweeping branches of a chestnut tree. The sticky buds had burst into life and waved huge pawlike leaves in the breeze. A mild day for late March, primroses and tiny clumps of violets dotting the banks of the hedgerows as the pony's hooves rang out a metallic rhythm on the stones.

"That's encouraging," Claudia said. "Most encouraging, because I often despaired of Solomon and his studies. He showed so little interest with Miss O'Brien. Nothing she could do would persuade him to listen… but he tells me you have been reading stories about pirates at bedtime."

"Yes, I had to insist that he should be allowed to choose a book," Polly replied. Hannah had begun to object but had given way with grace.

Polly remembered the young man peering from behind the trees the day before; the way he'd raised his finger to his lips as if to silence her. The children made no reply to her queries after he'd slipped away into the shadows. They refused to speak of him and, when Polly pressed them, Hannah said it was their special game and they were sworn to secrecy.

Was Claudia aware of this game? Perhaps she would have recognized the man. Polly wouldn't betray the children's trust unless necessary but this young man, this fellow they called a fox, unnerved her. If the children seemed in any danger, she would have to expose their secret.

They drove on in silence, Claudia's brow drawn into lines of concentration as she negotiated several sharp bends and a steep slope down the hill towards a stone bridge over the river. Trees behind them shielded Colgrannagh, standing silent in the sunshine. No whispering from them today.

"Did you know, Polly, that women are not permitted to study medicine in Trinity College Dublin?"

"I imagine that is the case. Medicine, like many serious professions, is considered a man's prerogative."

Her employer shot her a look. "A man's prerogative… yes, that's true. Far too many intelligent women are denied education because of what men deem correct. They feel our delicate natures to be unsuitable for the strain of higher learning. Fortunately, my father thought it nonsense and often took me with him as his assistant. Thanks to my dear papa, my greatest desire is to study to be a physician." She added, "I shall apply to the Royal College of Surgeons in Dublin because they are more enlightened. They admitted their first female student ten years ago."

"I'm pleased to hear that."

"Since then, another woman called Miss Hannan was the first to receive a licence in 1890 and now she works at a hospital in India. An outstanding achievement."

Polly agreed. "I hope you will soon be able to do likewise."

"Ah but it's not that easy, I'm afraid. The medical course and lodgings in the city cost money… money which I don't have at present. However, I'm resourceful. Women need to be resourceful, don't you think, if we are to outwit the men?"

"Yes, Mrs Manning, and I imagine you are most resourceful."

"You've heard of the first female doctor in England? Elizabeth Garrett Anderson. She succeeded in slipping through a loophole and qualified with the Society of Apothecaries. The Society changed its rules as soon as they were forced to give her the certification. They made certain no other woman would take advantage in the future. Such petty small-mindedness and jealousy!"

"She must have been a determined woman."

Claudia laughed. "Indeed, she was. She was refused admission to medical courses in the English universities so do you know what she did? She learned French and attended the University of Sorbonne in Paris, from which she qualified in 1870. It can't have been easy, studying medicine in French. An admirable woman and a shining example to us all."

Polly agreed and they drove on in an amicable silence. When they reached the river, Claudia reined in the pony and waved her whip towards a purple mountain peak on their left. "Tonelagee, the third highest peak in the Wicklow range. Perhaps we should take a picnic there with the children. Have you heard of the heart-shaped lake that lies near it?"

"No, I haven't."

"A beautiful spot… we must go when the weather is more reliable. It's a challenging walk and might be too much for Solomon. It can be wet and muddy after rain but the view… oh, you'll love the view of Lough Ouler and perhaps, if it is warm, we could swim. The water is cold and dark… cobalt blue, you might say." Claudia added, "Can you swim?"

"Yes indeed, ma'am. I was brought up near the sea in Mayo. I was fortunate to have lessons from… from a local man when I was a child." Splashing in the waves while her aunt looked on with disapproval; her thin figure on the beach, hands on her hips. But those were the good days; days when he paid attention to her.

The pony tossed her head, pawing the ground.

"Oh dear, Misty is growing impatient with us. Steady, steady! How beautiful the coast of Mayo must be! I've never visited although there's now the new railway line, isn't there?" Claudia clutched at her hat as the wind rose. "Gilbert and I used to walk to Lough Ouler when we were courting. The lake is like a glittering jewel… a sapphire. Then we'd return to Glenmacnass Waterfall. I remember the thunder of the cascade after heavy rain… it was so invigorating. It brought one… brought one alive." She continued with a sigh, "I mentioned my husband to you before. A brave man. I miss him."

"I'm sure you do."

Claudia changed the subject. "I know you've been spending time with my mother. She tells me she keeps an eye on you."

Dora had certainly been keeping watch over Polly. She would pop up in the most unexpected places, with her untidy mop of fluffy hair. When Polly was reading a book on the bench under the dappled shade of the fig tree, Dora would sit beside her and ask her about her family in Mayo. The old lady was inquisitive and persistent with her questions.

"Well, you're a quiet one," Dora would say and utter her high-pitched titter. "An oyster. A veritable oyster. Do you not reveal your secrets to anyone?" Polly would deny this, protesting she had no secrets to reveal. A lie, a deliberate lie.

Claudia's words brought her back to the present. "Did my mother mention my husband?"

"Yes, she enjoys talking about him."

Her mistress clicked her tongue and Misty trotted on with a swish of her tail, happy to be on her way. "He collected plants for a nursery in England. Indulging his wandering spirit, I called it. He loved the adventure of it, the excitement… but it was dangerous, you understand. Many plant collectors become ill and die. So many diseases. He came home delirious with a fever once and I nursed him back to health."

"Very worrying for you."

"Oh, Polly, I pleaded with him not to go out there again, pleaded for days on end but there was a plant he'd been told about. A plant growing in the rainforest used to alleviate pain in the indigenous people and he was determined to bring it back. Nothing would stop him. He believed it would provide a medical breakthrough." Claudia said, while the ears of the pony moved back and forth as if listening to the emotion in her voice.

The scent of pine, cool and fresh, wafted from the woodland on either side.

"Gilbert thought he was invincible," Claudia continued. "That's why he kept going back to Brazil. Some would call it an obsession, but I don't think he yearned for fame or money. It was the dream of bringing home new plants that drove him. The lure of a discovery that might ease the sufferings of many…"

"And did he? Did he find this plant?"

Claudia made no answer at first. Her gaze swept over Polly's face with an uncertain expression. "He mentioned it to his employers, certainly, and they were as excited as he was but… the following week he… he died."

"How dreadful for you… and for the children."

"Solomon and the girls doted on Gilbert, although they rarely saw him. We were all distraught… bereft. The manner of his death… so strange and…" She blinked and pressed her lips together, before adding, "What upsets me most is we parted on bad terms. Our last words to each other weren't kind. I regret he left Colgrannagh without me bidding him goodbye."

"I'm sorry." Polly peered up at the sky through leaves of beech branches as the carriage passed underneath. What else could she say? A thrush burst into song, clear notes repeated several times before it skipped on to its next verse. Her father had always loved birds and had many ornithological volumes in his library. He had ones about plants too, although it was difficult to grow more delicate ones in the bracing coastal wind. Hannah's words came into her mind, the tug on her sleeve and the girl's whisper about the plant hunter's death.

Claudia glanced again at her. What had she said?

"I beg your pardon?" Polly asked.

"I said there is jealousy in the plant-hunting world… envy of anything that can make money, that might have a high commercial value. Treasures like that are sought after, and the nurseries and botanists keep expeditions secret."

"I imagine the expeditions are expensive… all the travel costs and the wages for men required to look after the collections."

"Indeed, you're correct. Nowadays, plant hunters are searching for ornamental specimens for nurseries to propagate... to sell to wealthy clients in America and Europe. Occasionally they come across an unknown plant with medicinal value. Gilbert… well, Gilbert was a good man but he couldn't resist a drink every now and then. When he drank, he became expansive. It was part of his charm." Her tone softened. "Part of his charm… but he'd tell stories and sometimes let slip what he shouldn't."

Polly felt a stab of worry. "You think another plant hunter might also have been looking for that plant and… that person might have wished him harm? I should tell you, ma'am, for it is on my conscience, that Hannah told me…"

"What did Hannah tell you?" Claudia asked.

"She said… she told me your husband's fall into the ravine was not… was not an accident."

"Did she indeed? Hannah has a vivid imagination." She clicked at the pony, urging her on.

"But why would she say such a thing?" Polly picked at a splinter in the woodwork of the carriage. Would her employer think she was being gullible, believing the far-fetched story of a child?

"Hannah has been listening to my eccentric mother and Lizzie… how they love to speculate. But I fear there might be some truth in Hannah's words."

The pony shied at a branch blowing in the hedge and the carriage lurched. Polly grabbed the seat with both hands. Was her employer implying her husband had been murdered? Sent to his death because of a plant someone else coveted?

"I see the doubt in your eyes," Claudia said. "Why am I telling you this? You have a calm disposition, Polly. I feel you are wise beyond your years and you appear… discreet. I've told you about my longing to study medicine and now…"

"But surely you don't think your husband… someone deliberately plotted to… take the life of your husband?"

"You'll think me hysterical, my dear."

"No, ma'am, of course not but… perhaps you should go to the constabulary."

"What can they do? Brazil is so far away."

"If you had evidence… some sort of evidence."

"Indeed, and that I do not possess."

Polly paused before asking, "Did he mention anything in his letters?"

"He mentioned this plant... how it cured crippling pain and fever in the locals. One of the tribesmen was friends with a local priest, an Irish priest who worked out in Brazil. That's how Gilbert heard about the plant. The priest told him of a miracle cure."

"You don't think the priest had anything to do with your husband's death?" Polly's aunt would be horrified. A priest! A man of the cloth. A man of God. The parish priest held a position of power in her Mayo village. When he came to visit, her aunt baked scones and laid out her best tea set. Polly had never warmed to the priest because he looked at her with a cold calculating gaze. He knew her background and he didn't approve, calling her *Miss Polly* and loading the name with sarcasm, while her aunt summoned her mirthless smile.

"Not the priest, no, but Gilbert mentioned another Englishman." Claudia pulled on the reins and lifted one shoulder in a half-shrug. "I don't know. I really don't know what happened. Perhaps it was an accident."

They were nearing a village, passing a thatched cabin with a half-door on their right where a cluster of barefoot children gathered to watch the carriage pass by. The little ones waved, while older siblings stared.

Claudia dropped the subject of her late husband, but added, "The girl who is ill comes from a wealthy family and lives in a house at the other end of the village, just beyond the church. Dr Fitzpatrick says she has pulmonary consumption... a terrifying diagnosis for the family, if he is correct."

Polly's thoughts swept her far away from her Claudia's concerns. Far from the dusty village, its road pitted with holes, and the gaggle of urchins who ran beside the trap as they shouted greetings to the lady herbalist.

The lush damp vegetation of a Brazilian jungle reared in her imagination, huge exotic plants towering overhead. In the sweltering sticky heat, Gilbert Manning hacked his way through the undergrowth with a sharp blade, while another man tracked him, waiting for his opportunity.

Chapter Thirteen

The carriage turned down a long avenue lined with beech trees and, as it rounded the last bend, Polly noticed the mansion towering above them with tall chimney stacks and a hipped roof. An imposing building.

A brougham stood outside the front door, with a bay horse in the traces resting a hind leg, its head hanging as if half-asleep. The elderly man on the coachman's seat was smoking a cigarette and raised his cap when Claudia's trap drew up beside him. "Mrs Manning, ma'am, good day to you," he said and turned to Polly, giving her a nod. "And to you too, miss."

Claudia called, "Good afternoon, Johnnie. Doctor inside?"

"Aye, that he is. Must be going on half an hour now." The coachman blew out a cloud of smoke and surveyed it gloomily. "Won't make much difference, doctor says. Consumption… may the good Lord have mercy on the poor young lady."

"A concerning time for any family." She swung round on her seat to face Polly. "Perhaps you would stay here and hold the pony for me?"

"Of course."

Claudia climbed down from the carriage and waited on the

gravel as three figures emerged from the darkness inside the open front door. Polly recognized the burly outline of Dr Fitzpatrick as he put on his top hat. A man and a woman followed him to the steps under the portico, the woman dabbing at her eyes with a handkerchief.

"Doesn't look good," the coachman said and shook his head.

What fear and dread the illness brought! An outbreak of tuberculosis had struck the local village in Mayo eleven years before. One family had died within a week and several others had been seriously ill. So tragic, young people dying in their prime. Life wasn't fair, life was never fair.

"Ah, Mrs Manning." The doctor's greeting boomed across the gravel. "You're here to enquire about my patient, I imagine. I know the family are acquaintances of yours. The parents sent for me but there's not a lot I can do. Miss Lydia's fate is in the hands of the Almighty now."

A heart-rending sob burst from the stricken mother and she ran back into the house. Her husband cast an irritated look at the doctor before hurrying after his wife.

Claudia said nothing but her mouth formed a firm line.

"Not a lot you can do, either," Dr Fitzpatrick continued, walking towards her. "A wasted journey, I'm afraid. The poor girl is not long for this world."

She gazed towards the house. "Nevertheless… where there's life there's hope. My father always said that."

"Your father… forgive me, my dear," Dr Fitzpatrick replied, scratching his thick beard with a forefinger. He cleared his throat. "As far as I'm aware, your father had no cure for consumption either, but at least he was qualified to administer to the sick."

The coachman shifted on the wooden seat and released another slow breath of smoke, as if knowing what was coming next.

"Unlike me, you mean?" Claudia replied, her tone chilly.

Dr Fitzpatrick issued a snort, before attempting to disguise it as a cough. "You do your best, my dear, I'll give you that, but herbal potions are no match for more serious diseases. You comprehend that as clearly as I do."

"I beg to differ, sir. We have used herbal medicines for centuries."

"Pah! Even modern medicines cannot retrieve a victim of consumption from the jaws of death. No hope unless caught early and the patient sent to a sanatorium for the correct medical treatment and fresh air. I suggested the sanatorium last week but the parents wouldn't listen." He squinted at her in the sunlight. "They told me you didn't believe it was consumption."

"I don't believe it's consumption."

"You know better than the medical profession, do you?" He grunted and stepped towards his carriage, his fingers tightening their grip on his Gladstone bag.

A brave woman to tackle the doctor, Polly decided when he gave her a cursory nod before pulling open the door of his brougham.

He placed one boot on the step and looked in her mistress's direction. "I don't suppose there's much harm you can do now, anyway. The poor girl is beyond help. A few floral remedies won't make any difference." He climbed into the carriage and rapped the roof with his cane. "Drive on, Johnnie, I've another three calls to make this afternoon to patients who, thank the Lord, are too sensible to encourage meddling women."

The coachman raised his cap in a salute to Claudia. He nodded a farewell to Polly, pulling on the right rein to turn the bay horse towards the avenue.

Polly watched the brougham rattle under the trees and stroked the pony's forehead. An impolite and arrogant man, Dr Fitzpatrick, and one who resented his diagnosis being challenged, especially by a mere woman. A prickle of anger stirred in her chest. Men could do what they liked. Utter whatever hurtful words they pleased and walk away feeling justified, self-satisfied in the knowledge others would agree with them.

"We'll pay no heed to him," Claudia said. "The man's a dinosaur. Like many of his kind, he's reluctant to examine his female patients physically. The older doctors believe it improper and come to a diagnosis by asking questions. What a nonsense! How can he state Lydia has tuberculosis without listening to her lungs? She has only lost a little weight and there's no coughing up of blood."

Polly surmised she was asking a rhetorical question, expressing her irritation, and she decided to remain silent.

"Ah, there's Lydia's father back on the steps. I'll go indoors now. I'll try not to be too long. If the pony frets, just lead her around in a circle or take her for a walk down the avenue. I'll be back as soon as possible." She hurried away, swinging her bag.

The pony rested her head against Polly's arm and rubbed the side of her nose on her coat, leaving a trail of white hairs.

"No, Misty, stop that." Polly brushed her sleeve with her glove. The pony stamped a hoof with impatience. Should she lead the animal around the gravel sweep? Curtains billowed from an open sash above the portico. Was that the bedroom where the patient was lying? She could imagine Claudia leaning over her, resting her cool hand on her brow and murmuring reassuring words in her confident way.

"I'd much prefer your mistress tend to me than that old physician, even if she doesn't hold a medical qualification," Polly addressed the pony.

Misty nodded her head as a fly landed on her ear, as if in agreement.

Footsteps crunched behind and Polly spun round. A young man stood watching her; a lean figure with an amused expression.

With a jolt, she recognized his unruly golden hair. The man

she'd seen hiding in the garden; the one the children called the fox! She stepped nearer to the pony, her cheeks flaming. Had he been listening to her words?

"Don't be so embarrassed. I agree with you." He stepped over to the pony's head and stroked her nose, leaning close to Misty's ear and whispering inaudible but soothing words. She stopped fidgeting and raised her nostrils to his face.

After a long silence, Polly said, "I was talking to the pony."

"No harm in that, is there?" He had a slight Dublin accent. "Sure, don't I often talk to you myself, Misty?"

"You recognize the pony?"

"I do."

"Mrs Manning has gone into the house."

He grinned. He must have known where Claudia was, so why did she have to utter such an obvious statement? She decided to try again. "Lovely day, isn't it?"

He raised his eyes to the sky, as if just noticing it, a feigned note of surprise in his tone. "Indeed, it is." He continued stroking the pony's nose.

"I'm certain Mrs Manning would make an excellent doctor," Polly added. "She is called out to visit so many people who are poorly and many say she has helped them."

"She uses medicines that are very old," the young man replied. "No mercury, blood-letting, opium or arsenic. She doesn't believe in most of these modern patented preparations that are little more than poisons." He shrugged. "It's my belief the likes of Dr Fitzpatrick could learn from Mrs Manning. But many people hold the doctor in high esteem so…" His words trailed away and he hunched his shoulders again.

Another silence fell between them. Should she mention seeing him amongst the trees that day in the garden? What was he doing there and why was he watching them? Perhaps she should begin with an introduction.

"My name is Polly Brady."

"I know that."

His confident tone was irritating. What else did he know about her? A blush crept up from the neckline of her indigo walking dress.

He laughed, a soft chuckle. "I know what goes on at Colgrannagh. I have… I have friends there."

"The children?"

"The children and others."

"Does Mrs Manning know you are friends with the children? I must ask you why you were spying on us last week."

Her curiosity seemed to amuse him all the more. He leaned towards Misty's ear again and whispered, "The governess is worried. She doesn't trust me."

She said, "You might at least tell me your name."

He stepped away from the pony and gave Polly a deep, rather mocking bow. "Please accept my apologies, miss. I'm Luke Manning, at your service."

"Luke Manning? Oh, now I understand…" She acknowledged his bow with a slight inclination of her head but she would not smile. He was playing games with her. "Mr Manning, if I was of a nervous disposition, I would suspect you were following me."

"Oh, no, not at all. I'm following Mrs Manning."

"But in the woods that day... you must understand the children are my charges. I'm responsible for them and need to know they are safe."

Luke ignored this and looked towards Claudia, who appeared in the doorway.

She strolled across the gravel towards them, placing a hand on his shoulder, a brief touch. "Ah, Luke, how nice to see you. Are you well?"

He replied, "I'm very well, thank you."

"And enjoying your work? I hear you're a treasure when it

comes to keeping accounts. Your ability to add up columns of figures doesn't go unappreciated because your employer has been singing your praises to me just now."

"That's kind of him. I enjoy the work."

Claudia turned to Polly. "My father adopted Luke at the age of thirteen."

"Oh, I see," she replied. Why hadn't he said so instead of teasing her?

"How is Miss Lydia?" Luke asked.

Claudia deposited her bag in the trap and summoned the governess. "We must be off. Miss Lydia has a cough and I've listened to the tightness in her chest. It's nothing that regular wineglasses of a combination of horehound, hyssop, vervain and coltsfoot won't cure. Your employer… Miss Lydia's father is relieved Dr Fitzpatrick's dire conclusions are unlikely to come to pass."

Luke grinned. "The doctor won't enjoy being proved wrong."

"I don't suppose he will." She climbed into the carriage, reaching for the reins.

"I expect we'll meet again before long," Luke said to Polly. "A pleasure to meet you, Miss Brady."

She lowered her voice, casting a quick look at Claudia engaged in untangling a knot in the long leather reins. "You didn't answer my question… about the garden and why you were there."

He leaned forward to whisper, his mouth close to her ear. "I'm Mrs Manning's guardian angel. I watch over her. The children will explain when they trust you."

Chapter Fourteen

The present – August 2022

"What have you discovered about the children?" Daniel rubbed his right hip and grimaced. "Ah, this damn pain… my arthritis is playing up today."

I expressed sympathy while the afternoon light danced on the wrought-iron table, and shadows from leaves of the tree above us created moving patterns across our faces and bare arms.

"I've read through their notebook about the game, as they called it." I bent to scoop up and throw a tennis ball for Archie, who bounded after it across the grass. "They spied on other members of the family and certain visitors too, and wrote short reports in this book. There's a man called Luke… twenty-two years old, who was also involved. I saw in a subsequent letter that Dr Burroughs adopted him and he got a job working as a bookkeeper for a friend of the family."

"How curious," he said. "I'd no idea there were any adopted children." Daniel gazed across the expanse of freshly mown lawn to where the mechanical arm of a mini-digger clanked and clattered; its bucket biting into a mound of overgrown shrubbery behind the potting shed. Tobie was clearing undergrowth from a piece of ground Millicent wished to use for wedding photographs.

"It's strange you never heard of them," I replied. "They took it in turns to write about what the family did. They mention their governess Polly Brady, a young woman from Mayo with a mysterious past. There's also a man called Robert Kingson who appears to have sold medicines for a pharmaceutical business at that time. The young people didn't like him much… apart from sixteen-year-old Annie. He worked for a subsidiary of an American company, selling patented pills and potions to doctors… some quite dubious by the sound of them, or certainly by our standards today. I looked a few up and they contained some alarming ingredients."

Daniel laughed. "Let me guess. Arsenic, chloroform and opium? They were regulars found in drugs in Victorian times. Even babies were dosed with concoctions that could turn them into little addicts. The herbal remedies in household management books back then were probably a lot safer, to be honest."

"Yes, that's what I think too."

"Find out anything more about Claudia?"

"I read in a letter received from a cousin in England that Claudia told her she'd studied botany in the famous Physic Garden in London… in Chelsea. You've heard of Nicholas Culpeper, the English herbalist who compiled a famous herbal book in the early seventeenth century? He trained under the Apothecaries' system in the Physic garden."

"I once visited the garden. An interesting place on the edge of the Thames."

"I discovered in the late nineteenth century women were allowed to study there, as long as the course was botany and not pharmacy. Apparently, it proved a popular course and women outnumbered men on it. They were even allowed to sit exams."

"Women couldn't be trusted with important men's work," Daniel replied drily, as he watched the rise and fall of the digger's arm while it wrenched away the debris of decades. "But that's the stuffy Victorians for you."

I saw the top of Tobie's head in the cab, sunlight on his hair. I hadn't spoken much to him since the day he helped rescue Archie, only a few words as I passed by.

"Thankfully your great-aunt ignored the stuffy Victorian men," I replied. "What did you make of the old plan of the physic garden we found in the underground shed? Wouldn't it be interesting to replicate it? I bet Tobie would love a project about herbs."

Daniel sighed and rubbed his hip again. "I'm thinking of getting the plan framed… an important part of the history of this place. Millicent, I'm afraid, wouldn't be interested in renovating a herb garden… at least not on that scale. I wouldn't dare suggest it."

The terrier dropped the ball at my feet and looked up, tail wagging. Millicent appeared from the direction of the house, carrying a tray. The dog abandoned the ball and bounded over to greet her. I hoped he wouldn't trip her up. Millicent viewed Archie as a constant nuisance but, with his usual exuberance, he seemed oblivious to this fact and determined to win her heart.

"Here's a welcome cup of tea," I said, smiling at Daniel. "So, I've now discovered your great-aunt didn't study medicine until nearer the end of the 1890s, when she enrolled at the Royal College of Surgeons in Dublin. Even then, she had to complete a two-year course on Arts subjects before she could move into medicine."

Millicent's frown deepened as she approached. "Fiona, please call your dog! I can't see where he is with this tray in the way."

"Archie! Come here."

He ran back and flopped down beside me.

"Kenny has gone to the hardware store in Wicklow," Millicent said. "One of the hanging baskets is missing a hook. So many details to sort out at the last minute before our first wedding reception tomorrow."

A big day for them both, I thought as I stood to take the tray from her while she unfolded a pale blue cloth and smoothed it over the table in front of Daniel.

"How exciting! Your first big event," I said to appease her. She placed mugs and plates on the cloth; a sponge cake with glistening icing, butter filling and a delicious aroma of coffee. Millicent's Polish assistant was a skilled cook.

Archie raised his head and sniffed the air but I gave him a reprimanding nudge with my foot.

"It's exciting, certainly it is, but I'm terrified… just dreading everything will go wrong." Millicent pushed her sunglasses back on her head. "Kenny tells me I worry too much."

Daniel let out his sudden booming laugh. "Kenny is right. Relax, my dear, all will be well and I'm sure the day will be a resounding success. I have every confidence in you because you're always so organized." He raised his bushy eyebrows. "Don't you agree, Fiona?"

"I've never met anyone as… as organized as Millicent." I suppressed a smile.

Seeming mollified, she poured tea into a mug and handed it to Daniel. "Add your own milk. No sugar, remember your diabetes. I'm not sure you should have the cake… okay, don't complain, but just a small slice."

"How cruel to expect Fiona to eat it all!" Daniel winked at me.

Millicent ignored this. "The flower arrangements arrived this morning and are stunning. All white roses and lilies with green foliage. Very tasteful, and I assured the bride… she's turned into a nervous wreck, that everything…" She broke off as the engine of the digger cut out and Tobie appeared from behind the pile of uprooted laurels, waving at us with unusual agitation. "Now what's wrong with him? I really want that job finished by this evening but there's no hurrying that Frenchman… a law unto himself."

I'd never seen Tobie run before and his normal pace at Colgrannagh was careful and methodical.

"Perhaps the digger has broken down," I suggested. "That would be unfortunate if he's under pressure to get the work finished."

"A bloody disaster…" Millicent began.

"*Daniel… Daniel! Nous avons un sérieux problème*!" The landscaper came to a halt in front of us, slightly breathless.

"Did he mention a problem?" Millicent's features tightened. "What now, for God's sake?"

Tobie addressed Daniel who joined him in a rapid exchange in French, indecipherable to Millicent.

Daniel listened and scratched the side of his face, never one to panic. He'd had years of training as a heart surgeon and doctors never displayed emotion.

"What is it?" Millicent demanded. "What has happened?"

I'd understood the occasional word. Tobie had found a hole under the ground.

"Daniel, what the hell is wrong?" Millicent's question ended in a screech.

The older man cleared his throat and rubbed his cheek a little harder. "Ah, yes, that sounds like a problem. He's found a … something unusual so we should all take a look."

"Something unusual?" Millicent repeated, a scowl gathering on her features similar to a dark cloud.

"Under the laurels." Daniel kept his face expressionless as he reached for his walking stick and slowly got to his feet. "Tobie has uncovered a cavity with the digger and it appears there is something in the bottom of it."

Millicent threw her arms in the air, her face flushing. "How long will this take? I don't want children falling down a cavity at the reception. What would Health and Safety say? It's just what would happen and then we'd end up being sued."

"Millicent, please," Daniel muttered.

Tobie's eyes darted to my face and away again. Did they hold a glimmer of amusement?

"I'll come with you," I said. "I want to see what it is."

I followed behind Tobie, Archie dancing around his ankles.

"Kenny's not going to like this," Millicent said. "Another delay. This area needs to be tidy before tomorrow."

I knew her well enough at that stage to notice she always invoked her fiancé's name when she was determined to get things done.

"My French isn't great," I replied. "I wonder what Tobie told Daniel."

"My French is non-existent," Millicent panted, clutching at my arm to regain her balance when her high heels sank into the lawn. "I was hopeless at languages in school. Communication is so difficult when the guy doesn't speak English."

The pile of debris lay on the opposite side of the lawn, nearer to the gate into the wood. Tobie led the way round the side of the mound where the digger lurked like a silent metal monster.

He pointed at an open hole in the ground among the splintered broken branches, a gaping mouth edged with red bricks. Gesturing at us to come closer, he pulled out his mobile phone, directing the flashlight into the black cavity below.

A smell rose from the depths; dank, cloying, like rotting fungi. The bricked-up wall in the potting shed? Was the cavity behind that?

Daniel rested his hands on a large granite block, leaning forward.

Tobie shouted, "*Regardez! Voilà.*"

His words hung in the dry August air. No need for a translation from Daniel when the powerful beam picked out what was at the bottom of the pit. My heart gave a lurch. Among the dry leaves and sticks lay a human skull and bones.

Millicent's piercing scream made Archie yelp and run off barking. Tobie raised his eyebrows and gave me another glance, as if attempting to gauge my reaction.

Only Daniel appeared unperturbed. He stood upright and let out a long whistle. "Well, that *is* a surprise. We'll have to notify the police… the Gardaí."

Millicent grabbed at his arm, her voice pleading. "No, no… you can't. The wedding… what about the wedding tomorrow?"

"But, my dear, we can see the remains of a body down there. We can't just ignore it… all sorts of procedures attach to this kind of discovery."

"But the bride… think of the bride. It will ruin her day. We can't have the place swarming with cops."

He frowned at her. "What do you suggest we do?"

"Cover it up again." Millicent close to panic. "Hide it. We can't have the forensics and detectives here tomorrow with all their crime scene tape… how would it look?" She added, "Oh… no, please, no… Daniel, I've worked so hard… and the bride… she'll be distraught. Her mother will be furious. A skeleton at the reception! You can't inflict that on them."

Daniel looked at Tobie and then at me. "What should we do? We'll have to report it."

I gazed into the gloom at the hollowed-out eyes and ghastly clenched teeth; the cream bones mottled with green on the damp earthen floor. "I suppose the skeleton has been under the ground for a long time… goodness knows how long… we'll have to wait for a pathologist to work that out. Would one more day make any difference?"

"Thank you, Fiona." Millicent still clutched Daniel's arm. "Listen to her, please. One day won't make any difference. Cover it up and no one will be any the wiser."

"All right… just one more day." Daniel waved his hand at the hole and issued instructions in French to Tobie. He turned to me. "How interesting, a body hidden away all these years. Must have been a long time because there was so much vegetation on top. Who is it, Fiona? How did it get there?"

His excitement was infectious and I sounded slightly breathless when I replied, "I don't know. Do you think it could be one of your ancestors?"

"I hope not, but who knows?" He clapped me on the back with such force that I almost toppled into the shaft. "Let's write this damn book! Let's find out what happened here at Colgrannagh all those years ago."

Chapter Fifteen

The present – August 2022

The granite rock reared above the pool, its crevices softened by ferns and moss, reminding me of a damp green beard on an ancient face. Winding its way between boulders, the river slipped under the bridge. A kingfisher darted past, a bright flash of turquoise and orange, while I rested my hands on the wooden railing, its smooth surface warmed by the afternoon sun.

It was peaceful in the wood, away from the activity in the garden. Birdsong drifted from the branches above my head as I watched the shapes move across the lawn; plastic tape flapping around the opening into the underground cavern. Navy uniforms of the Gardaí and white suits of the forensic team huddled together in groups. A division of the local crime unit was taking photographs of the scene and collecting evidence.

I heard their voices, low and urgent, above the trickling of water and the whisper of a breeze in the treetops.

The local detective sergeant had interviewed Daniel before lunch and outlined what would happen. He said one of the state pathologists was on her way. After her inspection, the skeletal remains would be removed in an undertaker's hearse. The Gardaí would enlist the services of forensic anthropologists, given the length of time the body had been concealed underground. In the meantime, the detective stressed, no one was to go near that area of the garden.

Another figure came into view, appearing through the gap in the trees and strolling onto the path below the pool. He stooped to drop a hand into the water and sent ripples spreading across the dark surface. Tobie Desjardins.

He hadn't seen me on the bridge and I waited in silence. Had he been ordered away from his work and told not to return until the police presence had finished its investigations?

He looked up, caught my eye and waved a hand in recognition.

"Hello," I called.

He came towards me, his gaze on his feet as he stepped across the broken slippery planks of the bridge. "This seems dangerous. Someone should mend it."

"Yes," I replied. "I'm surprised Millicent hasn't ordered you to fix it. Imagine if one of her guests fell through into the pool below."

"It would be a catastrophe. How did *Madame*'s wedding reception go?"

"Very well, according to Kenny… told me at breakfast this morning that even the bride's mother was satisfied with the day. A great relief for Millicent. I haven't seen her today. I'm sure she's lying in bed with an ice-pack on her forehead, recovering from a migraine brought on by all the stress."

"Are you being serious?"

"No."

He laughed. "I thought not. I've been told to clear off by the police. A pity because I wanted to get a closer look at the skeleton."

"The detective sergeant told me to keep away too. I left Archie with Daniel in the cottage just in case he got up to mischief. You know what he's capable of doing. He'd probably run off with the skull or one of the bones in his mouth."

Tobie laughed again and lines beside his eyes crinkled. "You need to train your dog. He's totally heedless."

"Jack Russells usually are. They have minds of their own. Do you think you discovered part of the other shed… the bricked-up wall we saw? The other side of that?"

He shrugged. "It might be. The police will probably knock a hole through the bricks to check."

I was enjoying talking to Tobie. "I searched the National Archives website and the census records for 1901 and 1911. There were only women in the house back then apart from the son… Claudia Manning and her mother, Dora Burroughs, a young maid and the two girls, Annie and Hannah."

Tobie leaned closer and held up his mobile phone. "That's interesting because I took photos… before the police arrived. I got as close as possible and took some shots of the bones. Would you like to see? It's really hard to tell whether the bits of clothing belonged to a male or a female. Look…" He tapped the screen before he handed me his phone.

I shielded the mobile screen from the sun and examined the image; the staring skull with its vacant eye holes and the tangle of bones with tatters of dark fabric. "The clothing must have deteriorated over the years. The body wasn't laid out in a formal way and looks as if it was just thrown there."

Tobie's shoulder brushed mine as he bent over the photo. "Yes. It's hard to tell anything from this dark image and I'm sure the forensic guys will let Daniel know, but that could take a while. Weeks or months... who knows?"

A knot of excitement twisted inside me. "Nineteenth century! Suppose this body was connected with Claudia in some way?"

"Was it someone in her family?"

"Perhaps. It couldn't be her husband because he died out in Brazil, but I'll check the headstones in the graveyard for Gilbert Manning's name, just in case his body was shipped home. I'm on my way there now… beside the ruined church. Just up here." I pointed to the path along the river bank. "Are you busy or will you come with me?"

"Okay, I'd like to come with you. It's not often I have time to relax with Millicent around."

I led the way across the bridge, gripping what remained of the handrail and relaxing only when my feet touched the ground on the other side.

His words floated over my shoulder, above the rustle of our feet among dead leaves on the pathway. "The richer Victorians collected plants from overseas as trophies and status symbols. I've been to look at one of the original Wellingtonias in Devon. A vast giant of a tree."

"There's one in the garden here, isn't there? Over there, near the top of the avenue."

He nodded. "They were tourist attractions back in nineteenth-century America. People came from everywhere to see them. I read about one that was cut down, either a redwood or Wellingtonia, I can't remember which, but it was over three thousand years old and they hollowed it out to fit a piano and forty visitors inside."

"Wow! I suppose it would attract the same excitement as an enormous skeleton of a dinosaur today."

"I'd prefer to see the tree."

We laughed and continued on along the river. A jay screeched somewhere in the branches overhead, alarmed by our intrusion. No sign of the bird but they were shy, elusive and often difficult to spot.

"The church was built later than the eighteenth-century house," I said. "Around the beginning of the following century. Daniel said it belonged to an estate here but the big house is no longer standing… abandoned like so many during the decades of high taxes. I suppose the family, what was left of them, moved back to England. I was told in the supermarket in the village that the granite from the old house was sold off years ago." I looked back at Tobie over my shoulder and noticed a tall ruin on our right. "Oh, the tower! I didn't realize we were so close to it."

He followed my gaze. "Daniel showed it to me... so many ruins in Ireland. Castles, towers, huge houses. I find them fascinating."

"Yes, it gives a... a sense of history, I suppose. The past still lurking in the present, no matter how dilapidated they are."

Tobie joined me as the path opened into a clearing in front of the ruin. "Would you like to take a look inside? There's still a stone spiral staircase leading to the parapet. A bit dangerous, I guess, but it's possible to climb up it. Good view from the top."

"All right," I said. "Show me."

He unclasped a chain on the rusty iron gate into the enclosure. "I can tell you love historical buildings. As I said, they interest me too but I prefer plants and their history. Plants are living things." He looked into my eyes for a few seconds before waving at me to go ahead.

An attractive man, I decided. If there hadn't been Dominic and his persistent aggressive lawyer, I might have allowed myself to think more often about Tobie, but the last thing I needed right now was to stumble into another relationship.

"You find history everywhere," he said. "But you're a teacher."

I nodded.

"Daniel said so."

"I was... for years."

"My wife is a teacher too."

"Ah." I should have known he would have a wife; a good-looking man like him in his early thirties. Though he didn't wear a wedding ring, not that it mattered to me, of course. It didn't matter one bit because I was determined not to show too much interest in Tobie Desjardins, in spite of his interesting name and sudden smile. I had no wish to blunder into a relationship with a married man.

"You say *ah*. Why is that?"

Why did he have to question everything? "What I mean is… I mean we have something in common, your wife and I." That sounded worse, as if I wished I were married to him. I hurried on, "We're both teachers." I turned my face towards the ruined tower to hide my embarrassed blush.

My mother would have loved this awkward situation. She'd have batted her eyelashes and sidled up to him, asking him to tell her everything about his wife and how well they got on. She'd once informed me, in front of my father and brother, that the reason I put up with a gambler like Dominic was because I'd married too young and had no experience of other men. Dear Mum. She'd never have made the diplomatic service. Anthony had guffawed with laughter and said she needn't worry about him because he wasn't the marrying type.

"Who lived in this building?" I asked.

"There's a sign beside it outlining the history. See that doorway over there? That's where we go in."

I followed him under the low stone arch into a dark interior. A huge open fireplace stood in front of us and, to the right, steps leading upwards where a beam of light shone through a hole in the roof. A bird shot out of an arrow slit window, making me jump.

"The place is full of them," Tobie said. "They must have nests here."

I ran my fingertips along the wall as we climbed, anxious not to lose my balance on the narrow stairs.

Tobie stepped over a fallen rock at the top and turned to hold out his hand to me. He gripped mine and pulled me up into the glare of sunshine. The ground fell away from a low wall in front and my legs shook. I drew in my breath and took a step back.

"Careful," he said. "Watch where you put your feet. Don't go too near the edge."

"I don't intend to, don't worry. I'm nervous of heights."

We stood side by side, gazing across the trees towards Colgrannagh, where figures still moved around in the garden, and I willed myself not to look down.

"Is your wife French?"

"Yes, Isabelle is from Paris. She doesn't enjoy living in Provence, especially where we live as it's… it's a bit too rural for her."

"But isn't the south of France supposed to be glamorous and sophisticated? Cannes, Saint Tropez, Juan-les-Pins… and all those other lovely places on the French Riviera where the beautiful and wealthy hang out."

"Glamorous and sophisticated is not exactly my style. Not for me… but Isabelle adores parties and dressing up. Maybe she likes my clients more than me. I have some rich and sophisticated clients in Provence."

My mother would ask Tobie if he had a happy marriage and if there were any children. I didn't have the nerve to enquire. Not my business.

As if he'd read my mind, he said, "We have one son, Victor, who's seven. We had to find a name that my English mother's family could pronounce." That secretive smile lingered around his mouth, as if an amusing thought had popped into his mind that he didn't want to share with me. "Did you tell me you are no longer married, Fiona?"

I hesitated. "Yes… my husband left me."

"You're divorced?"

"Not quite. I suppose I soon will be. It's a long sad story but, to cut it short, I was just out of college when I married Dominic." I sighed. "It's not a subject I enjoy talking about."

He dropped his gaze to the rough stones at our feet. "I

understand. I was young too… but let's talk about something else." He turned to face the river. "There's a man over there… can you see him on the path? I wonder what he's up to."

I shaded my eyes with a hand as I looked into the sun. "Oh, yes, I see him." An older man, possibly in his late sixties or early seventies, with thick white hair. He was wearing a short jacket and jeans but that was all I could make out from that distance.

"I've work to do," Tobie said, checking the time on his phone. "I'm going back to the garden. *Madame* will have surfaced from her boudoir and be wondering where I am. I'll help you down the spiral staircase if you feel it would be easier for you. It's often more difficult to go down than up."

"I'm fine, don't worry. You go first. If I fall, I'll land on you."

He laughed. "Are you still going to the graveyard?"

"I think I will. I want to check the headstones for the Manning family. I want to make sure that Gilbert isn't buried there and see if there's any sign of the adopted children. I've seen Solomon's gravestone already."

When we reached the path beside the river, Tobie murmured, "Thanks for asking me to come with you. Perhaps we could do some more exploring another day."

"Yes, why not? Think of somewhere we can go." I moved quickly away. Why had I said that? So much for keeping him at a distance.

He strode away and I continued along the track. I'd reached the next bend in the river when the white-haired man appeared. "Hello there." He stepped towards me and held out his hand. "I'm Stephen. Pleased to meet you. I'm guessing you're Fiona Foley."

"Yes, I am. How did you know?"

"Local gossip in the village. I live there and I've heard all about the young researcher Daniel has hired to find out about his great-aunt."

"Nice to be called young. What did they say about me?"

"Don't worry… all good things." He chuckled and added, "This latest mystery is intriguing."

"What mystery?"

"The mystery of the body in the Colgrannagh garden. I've seen the Garda vans and the detectives swarming around the Mannings' place. I came here hoping for a better view." He pointed a finger in the direction of the house. "Can't see much from here, either, because of all the trees in the way but perhaps you know something?"

I didn't reply, waiting for him to continue.

"I know Daniel well," Stephen added. "What do you make of the house? A bit too much Victorian gothic for my taste."

"It was probably nicer when it was a plainer Georgian house."

"Yes indeed. Unlucky house, so they say. Two sudden deaths there."

"Two deaths?"

"Two, if you count the latest body."

"What was the first one?" I asked.

Stephen shrugged slightly. "A servant died in the house in mysterious circumstances back in the mid 1890s. It's one of the stories about the place that you'll hear in the village, along with the more fantastical one about people seeing ghosts on the lawn."

"Ghosts on the lawn? Daniel hasn't mentioned them."

"The path to the village runs along the boundary here and ends up at the back of the post office. Naturally some more imaginative types see ghostly figures when they look into the grounds of what was an old empty house for years."

I laughed. "I'll keep an eye out for them."

"So, tell me, what's the verdict about this latest corpse?" He regarded me, as if trying to read my mind.

"I don't know much about it."

"You can tell me. I'm a historian, an amateur but I have a

particular interest in the Manning family."

"That's interesting." I wondered if he had accumulated useful information that might help my research.

Stephen ran a hand through his unruly hair. He had soft, rather pink skin, similar to that of a child. "I'm related to someone who lived there. Distantly, but I'm related to a woman who once lived in that house."

I detected a hint of drama in his statement when he paused, hoping I would question him. Was he related to the Mannings? To Daniel and Claudia? "What's her name?"

"Polly Brady. She worked as a governess at Colgrannagh when she was young. Polly was my great-grandmother's sister."

Chapter Sixteen

"Polly Brady," I repeated. "I saw her name recently in some papers in the house. I'd be very interested in reading anything you have about her." I told him the children had mentioned their governess and seemed to like her.

"I was on my way to visit Daniel. He might know more about the human remains in the bushes."

"In the shed," I replied.

He looked at me. "Ah, so you know about the crime scene, eh? A body in a shed. A local said it was in the bushes but that's gossip for you… not always accurate. Any idea who it might be? Recently deceased?"

How much should I tell him? I didn't know anything beyond the fact that the skeleton had lain there for many decades and it was possible that part of the shed had been bricked up. If Stephen was a relation of the young woman who'd lived in the house in the 1890s, perhaps he would be keen to tell me more if I helped him.

I folded my arms and leaned against an elderly oak tree, watching the sun flicker on the west end of the house beyond the trees; the old place guarding its secrets. Holding them close. What would those walls whisper if they could talk?

The man followed my gaze. "It's a strange old house, isn't it? Dark and austere with those long corridors."

I agreed with him. "I'm staying in the house with Daniel's nephew Kenny and his fiancée."

Stephen stepped closer. "Interesting, very interesting. I'm hoping you might be able to assist me. I could tell you a few things about my great-aunt and, in return, you could keep me informed about the Gardaí and their murder enquiry."

"What makes you think it was a murder?"

"Don't you think so? It would be a strange accident."

And the shed had also been bricked up. Definitely not an accident. "It seems unlikely he or she wouldn't have been missed and discovered..."

He pursed his lips and sucked in his breath. "What date? Any idea of a date?"

"Not yet. The sergeant told Daniel that a forensic anthropologist would need to work that out."

"Ah yes, indeed. They use radiocarbon dating and DNA... those sorts of tests. I watched a television series about it once... fascinating. All living things absorb carbon from the atmosphere and food... forgive me, I'm going off on a tangent. I tend to do that and it drives my poor wife crazy. No wonder she spends so much time with her sister. What were we talking about?"

I'd met enthusiasts like Stephen before; ardent, talkative and obsessive. I told him I'd taught history in a school of uninterested teenagers in Dublin and he uttered his sympathy.

"History is wasted on the young," he said. "We don't appreciate it until we're middle-aged, especially family history. We don't care what happened to our ancestors until we've grown older and, even then, many people..."

"Many people never appreciate it. Only a few of us can see any relevance, I suppose."

He raised his arm and pointed towards the ruins of the tower house. "See here, the past around us… imagine all the people who must have died in battles over the centuries. Do they deserve to be forgotten?"

A cloud of jackdaws circled over the crumbling turret. "Perhaps some do. Or perhaps there is no one left to remember them, but I agree with you. I can feel the presence of the past breathe in a place like this." I remembered the plant hunter. "Have you read all the headstones in the graveyard, Stephen?"

"Yes, I certainly have. I've recorded a list of them and where they are placed."

"Do you know if Gilbert Manning's grave is there?"

He shook his head. "But… no, it wouldn't be because he died out in South America."

"Does he have a grave out there?"

"I would imagine so. He slipped… fell off the edge of a cliff of some sort. That's what the family always said and I found the report in newspaper archives… tragic accident when searching for a rare plant. I wrote an article about it for a historical magazine years ago so I did quite a lot of research."

"Would you tell me a bit about Polly Brady, please?"

He pushed back the cuff of his jacket to uncover his watch. "What's the time? I'm supposed to be meeting someone at four o'clock. Maybe we could meet up again soon? Hopefully you'll have learned more about the skeleton by then." He noticed my hesitation and added, "I can certainly give you a few quick details now about Polly. She was my great-aunt from Mayo who came to educate the son and daughters."

"Annie, Hannah and Solomon."

"Yes, and the two eldest were adopted. Mrs Manning's father, Dr Burroughs, was a sort of philanthropist. He rescued youngsters from institutions and tried to help them. Victorians were well meaning sometimes but you wouldn't think that from reading Charles Dickens, would you?"

"Dickens saw a different world to the one at Colgrannagh. How did Dr Burroughs help them?" I asked.

"Gave them a decent education… sent them out into the world to earn a respectable living. That sort of help."

"I'm sure they were traumatized when they first arrived. Anyone in that era had a tough time in institutions."

Stephen's eyes lingered on his watch. "That's true. Polly came to Colgrannagh to help improve those children, the two older girls, and to educate the son, Solomon, before he went off to boarding school at the age of nine. I've discovered letters written by her, when she was in her early twenties, sent to my great-grandmother, and a journal. Polly's aunt… well, it's complicated, because she wasn't her real aunt… she lived near a seaside village in County Mayo, a place called Mulranny. The aunt was a seamstress and used to take in sewing and darning work. Polly was keen on sewing too."

"Was Polly adopted?"

He frowned, his bushy eyebrows joining above his nose, but made no reply.

I took out my little notebook and pulled the pencil from its sleeve. "Polly came here in the 1890s. When did she leave?"

Stephen cleared his throat. "Sorry, Fiona, I have to go. I'll meet you again and show you Polly's letters and journal then. Perhaps you'd like to have lunch next week? Here's my phone number." He read it out.

I scribbled it down. "Thank you. Lunch would be nice."

He held out his hand and shook mine. "I look forward to that. It's nice to meet a fellow historian." He walked off towards the graveyard, making me wonder if he'd come along the path by the river to talk to me or to get a better view into the garden.

I picked at moss on the trunk of the oak. Polly might have written about her employer and her work with herbs. She would have known about the death of the plant hunter in Brazil. It would be fascinating to read what she thought of that.

I'd make sure that Stephen remembered about our lunch. He'd seemed reticent about handing over information so I would keep my cards close to my chest, as my grandmother would have said, and I wouldn't give Stephen information about the skeleton unless he helped me. Would Polly's papers reveal more about Claudia? Daniel would be delighted, if so. That was what I found exciting about research: the breakthrough that came out of the blue. A sudden lifting of the fog and a glimpse into the past took shape, but I wouldn't get too excited. I realized the fog could descend again in an instant.

The jay screeched and I spotted it over the treetops, a quick flash of pinkish brown with white and blue as it disappeared among the branches. An eerie sound, that bird call, quite mocking in its intensity, and I imagined the laugh of a maniac hiding in the vegetation.

Daylight was fading and shadows crept among the trees. They would have walked along the path, wouldn't they? Claudia and her family would have come that way to the graveyard or to attend services in the church. It wouldn't have been a ruin back then. Unfortunately, many small country churches became derelict from lack of use after Anglican congregations died out after the First World War or emigrated to England or America, and the dioceses were left with no option but to close the churches and deconsecrate them. I'd seen so many lying roofless and abandoned around Ireland, a refuge only for nesting birds like the tower house beside the river. Yet another swathe of history swept away.

When I rounded the bend before the rickety wooden footbridge, Tobie was on top of the large rock that loomed over the pool and waved at me.

"How did you get up there?" I called.

He pointed to the back of the stone. "Over that way… a

path, very overgrown now, and hasn't been used for a long time. I can see into the garden from here through a gap in the trees."

An outcrop of granite, barely visible among the ferns, formed the track to the summit. I stepped over briars, bending to disentangle their thorns from the legs of my jeans.

"Wow!" I said when I stood beside Tobie and glanced down. "It's quite a drop to the water."

"Yes, it is. It would make a good place to dive from. Do you think they used it for swimming? The pool appears big enough... and deep."

"Maybe. I'm not sure how much bathing they would have done in those days, though they believed it was good for their health. Have you spotted anything interesting in the garden?"

"I watched them remove the skeleton. They zipped it into a body bag and drove away. The forensic team looks like they're finishing up."

"Who was it?" My face glimmered in the water below, white and distorted, with Tobie's deathly pale beside it; a trick of the greenish light among the trees. The pines seemed to press in behind us, dark and oppressive, silently watching. "Who lay in that bricked-up tomb for all those years, alone and forgotten?"

Chapter Seventeen

The past – June 1895

Polly watched Annie and Hannah step down from the bathing hut to join Solomon on the river bank. Sunlight played on the striped paintwork and a robin landed on the apex of the roof, regarding the strangely clad group of humans with its head tilted to one side.

"I fear the water will be cold," Annie said, shivering.

"It's not." Solomon wriggled his toes in the river before kicking a spray of water over her. "See! It's not cold, is it?"

She shrieked and jumped back, snatching at Hannah's arm. "Stop that, Solomon. Stop! Miss Brady, please make him stop."

Polly called out, "Solomon, don't do that, please. It's not kind."

"It's quite shallow here." The boy laughed and slid into the water.

"That is because we've had no rain for three weeks," Polly said. "Eamon is worrying about the drought. He told me this morning that the weather station has recorded its highest temperature this year."

"June often has lovely weather," Annie replied. "No, Hannah, don't poke Solomon like that!"

Polly intervened and asked the boy to move further along the river bank. "I want you to show me how brave both of you girls are. Your mama is keen on fresh air and bathing."

Annie's serious voice asked, "Can you swim, Miss Brady?"

"I learnt to swim in the sea in Mayo and I assure you that the Atlantic Ocean is cold, icy cold. Why, it comes all the way from America and it also joins with the Arctic Ocean near Greenland and Iceland. Imagine the chill of that stretch of water!"

"Could a polar bear swim all the way to Mayo?" Solomon slapped the surface of the pool with his palm and sent the two girls scurrying back to the steps of the bathing hut.

"It would be too far for the polar bear," Polly replied. "I imagine he would find the Atlantic too warm in Mayo with his thick furry coat."

"Did your mama teach you to swim, miss?" Hannah stooped to pick up a handful of pebbles and tossed them at Solomon.

He shouted, sticking out his tongue and disappearing under the surface. Polly was relieved when he surfaced again, gasping for breath. He seemed happy, a smile stretching across his face. His skin was sallow beside petite Annie, her white arms reflected in the water as she advanced once more towards the pool. Overhead, the sun had risen above the tallest of the pines and a golden warmth drenched the hollow in the river.

"Miss Brady, did your mama…"

"Yes, Hannah, I heard you the first time. I was taught to swim by my… by my father." Polly kept her eyes on the robin as it hopped from the roof to a carved post over the double doors. She'd loved those summer days, with long picnics on the sand while his big dog capered in circles of joy, the breath-snatching chill of the ocean and a light breeze fingering her long hair. Those were the most precious days, when her aunt was away measuring for curtains or gowns, and she could slip out of the cottage to meet him.

Hannah took two strides towards the river and, with a shout

of glee, leaped into the air. She landed with an explosion of water, catapulting waves over the far bank where the beech leaves hung limp in the heat. She resurfaced, arms flailing, legs thrashing, and shrieked that the water wasn't cold at all.

Startled, the robin took flight into the pines. Polly remembered the first day Claudia had taken her onto the wooden footbridge. She'd told her to throw a coin into the river and explained about the local superstition about whispering trees that carried people's wishes along the bank.

The pines stood silent in the heat. No whispering of secret longings.

Annie sat on the bank near the bathing hut and carefully lowered her body into the water, shivering in anticipation, each limb inching in. First her toes, followed by one slender leg hidden by her bathing bloomers, until she stood beside Hannah and Solomon, water lapping around her waist.

The children watched Polly who drew in her breath as the chill hit her. She warned Solomon to remain still until she was under the water.

He chuckled but obeyed.

They stood in a circle, waist-deep in the pool, with the sparkling sun warming their hair. Her wish had come true, no doubt about that. She'd wanted to be accepted by the children and be happy at Colgrannagh. Past experience had taught her that happiness was often fleeting, but she pushed that thought away.

"Let's sing *Frère Jacques*," Hannah shouted. "We'll sing about the sleepy monk and the bells. Come on, let's sing!"

They clasped hands and swung in a circle, singing in French before letting go and falling backwards into the water.

"Faster!" Hannah shouted as she struggled to her feet. "Let's go faster."

Their singing echoed through the woodland:

"Frère Jacques, Frère Jacques,
Dormez-vous? Dormez-vous?
Sonnez les matines! Sonnez les matines!
Ding, dang, dong. Ding, dang, dong."

Arms were flung into the air as they sank under the water. Polly glimpsed the base of the great lump of granite beside them, green weed streaming from its wrinkled surface like strands of hair. Perhaps she would tell the children that she'd found the entrance to a hidden cavern where river mermaids lurked, or some such story. When she could hold her breath no longer, she burst to the surface, gulping in air. Hannah was laughing, her head thrown back; her wet hair clinging to her shoulders and her unbridled joy infectious.

The sound of footsteps came from the far bank and a man's voice called out, "Hello, hello," followed by the tap of his boots on the wooden bridge.

Polly looked up.

"A collection of water nymphs. How delightful!" It was Robert Kingson, with an amused expression as he said, "Ah, do please continue your dancing and singing. I have no wish to disrupt such merriment."

A flush burned on Polly's cheeks. What would he think of her throwing herself around like a boisterous child?

"Mr Kingson, we were just…"

"I enjoyed watching what you were doing, Miss Brady. You and the children… cavorting in the water. If I had a bathing suit, I would join you in an instant but, alas, I have not." He smiled down at them.

She turned away to call, "Children, time to get out. We don't want to get cold. Hurry now, come along, Solomon, your lips are purple." She pushed through the water towards the bathing hut.

"You could swim in your clothes, Mr Kingson," Hannah shouted. "Or in your shirt and drawers."

"Please, Hannah!" Annie whispered, mortified.

Hannah gave her a push and followed Polly to the bank. She clambered onto the grass and twisted her hair between her hands to wring out the water.

Annie held out her hand for Polly to grasp while Kingson continued to talk, seeming oblivious to any embarrassment.

"I've been to the church with Mrs Manning," he explained. "She's arranging flowers for Sunday's service and I helped her carry them from the garden. Regal lilies and white roses and a large bunch of greenery. I watched for half an hour and then left her to her task. May I join you?"

"The children must get changed now."

He made a half-bow. "Of course. I will wait here while you go into the bathing hut. I promise not to come down and peep in through the window."

Annie blushed scarlet and Hannah said, "There's a blind so you wouldn't see anything."

"You go first, Solomon," Polly said. "If you have trouble dressing, please call out and I will come and assist."

The boy got to his feet and walked up the steps of the hut, directing a scowl at Kingson before closing the door behind him.

Hannah tossed her hair over her shoulder, throwing a small stone into the water and watching the ripples spread. "Do you like bathing, Mr Kingson?"

"I do, to be sure."

"Can you swim?"

"After a fashion."

She considered his words. "What does that mean?"

"It means I'm able to swim but not well."

"At least you are honest," Polly replied. She liked his easy manner and the way he made an effort to talk to the children.

He often visited the house when he was in the area and always brought a treat for them. Earlier that week, his gift was buns with soft icing and sugared almonds. So many adults ignored young people and believed that they should be seen and not heard; produced in the early evening to be admired by their parents and visitors for ten minutes or so before being sent back upstairs.

Claudia Manning didn't hold with that because she was different from other women in her social circle. Claudia wished the children to experience life. Polly had witnessed the looks of disapproval when Claudia brought the children with her in the carriage to the village and sometimes into the shops. She'd even let them peer inside the public house once and they'd encountered Dr Fitzpatrick eating his luncheon. The physician had risen politely to his feet to address Claudia but his eyes narrowed when he caught sight of the three children and Polly.

"Will you sing a song for us please, Mr Kingson?" Hannah asked.

Annie's blush spread upwards into the roots of her damp hair. "Oh no, Hannah… don't embarrass Mr Kingson."

Kingson strode across the bridge and jumped down beside them on the bank. "Mr Kingson is not embarrassed, not in the slightest, my dear girl. But…" He beamed at Polly. "Mr Kingson is not a good singer. Perhaps you would like to sing, Miss Brady?"

"Certainly not."

"You sang earlier. Quite beautifully, in truth. You all sang well."

"Did you hear Annie?" Hannah nudged the other girl and grinned. "Miss Brady says Annie is the most musical. I sing like an old crow."

Polly laughed. "You certainly chatter like a magpie, my dear." She was aware of Kingson sitting beside her and admired the cut of his jacket. A fine wool cloth similar to the one worn by her father when he'd come unexpectedly to the house that day. The last day of her childhood. He'd called her out into the garden to explain why she had to leave and she'd kept her gaze on his shoulders, on the tailored coat, in an attempt to hide her disappointment.

Kingson appeared in no hurry to depart and waited for them to finish dressing, conversing with Hannah in front of the bathing hut about butterflies and moths. He possessed a large collection of them, he told her. Red admirals, peacocks, painted ladies. Perhaps she would like to see them. He explained that the Ancient Greeks gave the name *psyche* to the soul and also to butterflies.

"Did you know," he said, "that they imagined the souls of the departed in the shape of a butterfly? Isn't that a lovely image?"

"The souls wouldn't last long as a butterfly," Hannah replied in her clear, matter-of-fact tone. "Miss Brady says butterflies only live for a few days. You could hardly call them immortal."

"A couple of weeks, perhaps. A short but glorious life." He stared into the river; his expression suddenly serious. What thought had crossed his mind? He turned to look at Polly. "I would like to walk back with you, Miss Brady, if I may?"

Hannah raised her eyebrows at Annie and giggled.

"Of course," Polly replied, inclining her head.

He rose to his feet. "Is everyone dressed? Good, good, let us go. Now run along, girls, and take young Solomon with you. I wish to ask Miss Brady a few questions about botany. Perhaps she knows the answer to a particular query."

Annie and Hannah ushered the boy along the gravel path and they skipped out onto the lawn where Eamon was cutting the lawn with the new rotary mower, purchased from England the previous month. He raised his cap as they passed and wiped a handkerchief across his sweating brow, muttering about the heat under his breath.

The girls waved at him and swung their bathing garments in

circles over their heads, singing another verse of *Frère Jacques*.

"How can I assist you?" Polly asked as they followed behind the children.

"Your mistress is a keen plantswoman," he said, "like her husband was."

She waited for him to continue and, when no words came, asked, "Did you meet Mr Manning, sir?"

"Oh no, indeed. I never met him. I would have liked to… very much. He sounded so knowledgeable about plants and other subjects."

She would like to discover more about Claudia's late husband. He sounded an obsessive man, with his constant voyages overseas. Was it for fame or money? Perhaps he had a restless spirit and couldn't remain in one place for long. Not easy to be married to, she decided, and it was hard on poor Solomon, who'd obviously adored his father.

"Mrs Manning is a skilled botanist, especially with herbs." Kingson opened the door into the physic garden, standing aside for her to go through. "Shall we make our way over to the bench there? It's in the shade."

Polly followed him along the path past the sundial as the scent of lavender rose from the borders when the skirt of her dress caressed the leaves. Drowsy bees droned on the flower heads and a small butterfly landed on a purple spray, its wings outstretched.

"You understand, no doubt, how she upset our venerable doctor when she cured the girl with consumption," Kingson said. "She was like Lazarus, rising from her bed and walking."

"That was no miracle, indeed, for Mrs Manning never believed she had consumption, merely an inflammation of the lungs."

He laughed softly. "It didn't go down well with Dr Fitzpatrick. He mentioned something to me about witchcraft."

Polly swung around to face him but he was smiling. "Oh, you jest."

"I jest. Not witchcraft... but the physician doesn't like being put in his place by a woman. Now, take a seat, my dear Miss Brady, and I will begin."

She sat on the bench and he moved closer to her, reaching out to take her hand for a few seconds. She blushed and edged away.

Her embarrassment appeared to amuse him because his lips twitched. "Claudia assured me that you have learnt a lot about plants over the last couple of months... a studious pupil, she said. Have you ever heard your mistress speak of a tree bark similar to Slippery Elm?"

"*Ulmus rubra*? I believe it was used by some of the tribal people native to America for fevers and coughs. The red slimy bark inside was stripped and mixed with water. Forgive me, I'm not certain that's correct for I am but a novice. Mrs Manning has been a patient teacher."

"I'm impressed by your knowledge. Claudia mentioned another tree... bark from a similar tree in Brazil that her husband... that Gilbert Manning sent home. I'm wondering if you've seen it."

A peacock butterfly flittered closer. Polly fixed her gaze on it, on the false eye on its wing, and said, "I'm sorry, no, I know nothing about such a tree. Was it another Slippery Elm?"

"It was like *Chinchona* and smaller than an elm. You know the *Chinchona officinalis* tree? The bark helps many ailments and there are several species. Quinine for malaria comes from *Chinchona*, a plant named by the famous botanist Carl Linnaeus in 1742. One story says that it was called after a Spanish countess who fell ill of a fever in Peru and was cured by the bark of this plant. It used to be ground up and added to liquid or wine as a drink."

"Is the tree you enquire about native to South America?"

"Yes." He smiled at her, a gleam of excitement in his eyes. "My dear Miss Brady, you have no idea how important it may prove to be. What I need to know is… is if you ever observed packages here at Colgrannagh, which would have been sent back by Mr Manning and his team of botanists. A similar bark to that of *Chinchona* before… before his tragic accident. Or if you recall Mrs Manning ever mentioning this to you?"

He slid nearer on the bench and Polly resisted the temptation to stand up. A handsome man, she couldn't deny that, and so close that she could smell his pomade, its strong and intoxicating aroma.

"Your mistress mentioned that I am a member of the Pharmaceutical Society." He glanced through the open door at Eamon pushing the lawnmower. "I distribute pills to doctors and surgeons around the country. The company for which I work has an excellent range of patent medicines. You've probably heard of our well-known remedy: Farrell and Thompson's Fever Powders? Dr Fitzpatrick finds them most useful. We have recommendations from the…"

Polly attempted to rise from the seat but he put out a hand and held her arm, giving it a slight squeeze. "Miss Brady, pray don't leave."

"I'm sorry, sir, but I haven't seen the bark you seek. I could ask Mrs Manning about it, if you wish, but surely it would be better coming from you. You and Mrs Manning share a medical background… an interest in medicine while I…" Her apology trailed away.

"I apologize," he said. "Forgive my enthusiasm. I didn't want to bother Claudia because I'm sure such reminders of her late husband would be upsetting. That's why I decided to ask you for I know she found his death devastating."

She should have thought of that. He would think her insensitive. She was more foolish than a child. Even poor besotted Annie would have handled the situation better than she had.

"I believe that Mrs Manning would make a wonderful doctor,"

Kingson continued. "There will come a time when all universities will open their doors to women. She is hoping to apply to the Royal College of Surgeons and may have told you this. There is already a lady who… The ladies might be more open to our patent cures than some of the older physicians with their leeches and blood-letting." He winked at Polly. "You wouldn't believe the opposition we encounter sometimes. Dr Fitzpatrick is more open-minded."

Dr Fitzpatrick seemed anything but open-minded but Polly resolved to keep her opinion to herself. "I hope I understand you correctly… you and others from the company that employs you… you're interested in bark from a South American tree possibly sent back to Ireland by Mr Manning. Would he not have sent it to his employers in England?"

"I made enquiries and it appears he did not. The nursery for which he worked is only interested in ornamental plants for propagation. This tree bark, if it exists, might prove a valuable addition to the fight against fever if it could be stabilized and produced in a palatable formula. Just imagine if we could stop epidemics in their tracks… in hospitals, in workhouses… even in the navy and army. Contagious fevers cause devastation where there are many people living together."

Polly could feel a damp patch of perspiration on her dress between her shoulder blades. The excessive heat or the anxiety caused by Kingson's request? "Would you like me to ask Mrs Manning?"

"How kind you are. I don't wish to upset her, as I mentioned before, and I'm certain you will be able to broach the subject with your more ladylike intuition." He made as if to pick up her hand again and she lifted it away, clasping her fingers together in her lap.

He shifted his weight on the bench. "If you get a chance to have a look in the potting shed… I know Claudia gives you lessons on how to take cuttings down there. If you see anything that might be the bark down there, perhaps you would be so kind as to inform me."

"Oh, sir, I couldn't. Not without asking Mrs Manning."

He frowned for a second but patted her arm. "Of course, of course. You must assure her that I don't wish to bring back painful memories but I believe this bark might be an important discovery. A valuable and important discovery that might be worth a lot of money."

Polly got to her feet. "I will, sir. I'll let you know what she says. Now, if you'll excuse me, I must check that Lizzie has lit the fire in the nursery so that the children may dry their hair." She gave him a quick nod and hurried away before he could make another attempt to detain her.

Chapter Eighteen

The past – June 1895

The heat of the day melted into a heavy humid night. Polly retired early to bed and, when Claudia expressed concern before departing for a dinner engagement, assured her mistress that she was only suffering from a mild headache. She didn't mention her conversation earlier with Robert Kingson, in spite of having thought of little else since.

She stood at her bedroom window, looking out on the lawn and woods towards the top of the tower house, a dark shadow looming behind the trees as dusk fell. Perhaps it would be better if she searched the potting shed for the bark and, if she found nothing, she could tell Kingson that she'd tried to help him. What would he do with the bark, if it existed? Persuade her mistress of its potential medicinal value? Perhaps he would send it off to be examined for healing purposes.

She'd heard of books of pharmacopoeia but surely her employer, the daughter of a physician and the widow of a plant hunter, would know if the tree bark were valuable? It was unlikely she would have been so overcome by her husband's death that she would dismiss a horticultural discovery he'd shipped back to Colgrannagh for safekeeping, presumably with his detailed instructions regarding its possible uses.

Polly resolved to discuss the matter with Claudia instead of conducting a clandestine search. She was about to close the shutters when a knock rapped on the door. Three urgent taps. That would be Dora Burroughs, who sometimes visited on the way to her own chamber. Lizzie was often requested to bring drinking chocolate to the bedroom where Dora and Polly would sit either side of the mantelpiece in the candlelight, discussing different topics but nearly always returning to the goings-on of family members. Her mistress's mother liked to be kept informed about the progress of the children's education.

Polly opened the door and smiled at her visitor.

"Ah, my dear," the old lady said. "I understand you're feeling poorly and I thought I'd ask if I can be of any assistance. I have an excellent preparation for headaches… even better, dare I say, than what my daughter would prescribe. My husband found it worked splendidly for his female patients."

"No, I thank you, but do please come in, Mrs Burroughs. I'm perfectly well. A headache, that's all it is, and most likely caused by the oppressive heat today. Come, have a seat and I'll ring for Lizzie to bring us chocolate."

Mingled scents of lavender water and peppermint rose from Dora's black bombazine gown as she rustled across the rug. Lowering herself onto the chair, she fingered a paper bag in her beaded reticule and offered up a hard-boiled sweet. Polly thanked her but shook her head.

"When Lizzie arrives, I'll request a little brandy," Dora said, her eyes twinkling. "You might need a beverage stronger than chocolate tonight. My husband, God bless him, believed it exacerbated headaches… chocolate and cheese. You'll join me, I hope?"

"Oh, I don't… I don't usually drink spirits."

"Try some, my dear. It will help you sleep."

Polly pulled the bell rope and Lizzie eventually appeared,

a little breathless and her cheeks flushed. Dora adjusted the needlework cushion behind her back and gave the maid a sharp look. "It appears that you've been sampling the brandy too."

Lizzie pushed a stray lock of hair away from her face and tittered. "Oh, Mrs B, you do have such a wicked sense of fun… I always tell Cook about your droll remarks, indeed I do. As if I would do such a thing! You know I prefer the sherry."

Polly raised a hand to her mouth to hide a smile. Lizzie and the older lady got on well because Dora turned a blind eye to the servant's frequent raids on the decanters in the drawing room, apart from uttering the occasional dry remark.

Two brandies were ordered and the maid trotted off along the dark corridor outside.

"Poor Lizzie, I don't like to be too critical because the woman works long hours and she's so useful… a mine of information about the locals." Dora turned to Polly, popping a sweet into her mouth. "I noticed you in deep conversation with Mr Kingson today. A clever young man, by all accounts, because he studied physiology in Oxford."

"I didn't realize." Hadn't he told her it was a pharmaceutical course in London? There'd been no mention of Oxford.

"Yes, indeed." Dora made loud sucking sounds, rolling the boiled sweet around in her mouth. "He held aspirations of becoming a physician, I believe… his father died, alas, and there were no longer the funds to support his education but he acquired his present employment with the drug company… I imagine he mentioned this occupation to you during your little tête-à-tête today…"

"That's interesting. He told me a little about his work. I suppose he is successful."

Dora nodded, the satin ribbons on her widow's cap swinging. "An ambitious fellow. The owner of his company worked in America and studied in Philadelphia. He employs well-educated gentlemanly types to sell his wares to the medical profession and hospitals. Indeed, he has chosen well in Mr Kingson for he's a clever young man. He knows how to charm the doctors." When Polly made no reply, Dora winked and added, "I understand he's paid a good wage in his position, over £300 a year and that's a lot more money than many country physicians would earn." She sighed. "I recall only too well how poorly paid my dear late husband was… if Joshua could actually persuade his patients to pay their bills in the first place."

Polly wondered, not for the first time, where Dora had acquired such information. She rarely left the house and appeared to spend most of her time wandering the corridors, peering out of windows, or sitting with a book in the drawing room. When she occasionally ventured into the garden, if the weather was cooler because she abhorred the sun, it was to sit on the iron bench in the physic garden in the shade of the fig tree.

With her bombazine dress, dark green reticule and wisps of hair under the cap of black lace, she reminded Polly of a character from the works of one of the more sensational novelists. A lurking presence who watched from the shadows, all-seeing and all-knowing, missing nothing.

It might be Lizzie who unearthed nuggets of tittle-tattle for the old lady. Hadn't Dora just told her that the maid was a mine of information? Yes, Lizzie was most likely her informant.

Dora appeared disappointed that Polly showed no interest in discussing Kingson. She cast a petulant glance in her direction. "You don't seem impressed, my dear. I decided he might suit you."

Polly flushed. "I beg your pardon? Suit me? Surely you are jesting, ma'am."

"Not at all, not at all. Wouldn't he be a fine catch for a young woman like you? A man with over £300 a year and likely to go further in life."

Polly recalled the way Kingson had edged closer to her on the seat in the garden and taken her hand. A heat prickled along the neckline of her dress. "I'm certain Mr Kingson wouldn't be interested in someone like me."

Dora rocked back and forth on her armchair, as if excited and amused by the discomfort she was causing. "He would consider himself most fortunate, my dear. An educated woman like you, who has been to Paris and can speak French, play the piano and paint… you do paint, don't you? I'm sure Claudia told me you can paint."

"You overestimate my accomplishments, ma'am."

"Oh fiddlesticks. Claudia was singing your praises and mentioned your needlework too. I was told you're making new dresses for both of the girls."

They chatted for a further ten minutes, with Dora teasing and the governess protesting until Lizzie's loud knock on the door propelled Polly out of her chair with a surge of relief. She no longer hesitated about trying the brandy and sipped gratefully from the crystal glass while Dora eyed her.

"My daughter told me that you've made friends with Luke," the older woman said, after Lizzie had closed the door behind her and departed. "He comes to see the children regularly on his days off. He's another potential suitor for you, my girl."

"Oh, really, Mrs Burroughs, I hardly know him."

"But the same age as you, I understand. That must be diverting for you… someone of your own age because Kingson is a little old perhaps… in his late thirties."

"The children are fond of Luke," Polly replied, hoping the change of subject would not appear too obvious. The man fascinated her in a strange way. When she'd first spoken to him, he'd said he was keeping an eye on her mistress. Why would he feel that was necessary?

Dora's wrinkled face cracked into a smile. "They are, indeed they are, bless them."

"You must know him well. He lived here, after all."

A tinkle of laughter in between sips of brandy. "He was brought up here at Colgrannagh, just as the others were. One of Joshua's best boys, in fact. An intelligent young man in spite of his past. Aha… I see you're interested in our Luke… I can tell by the sudden sparkle in your eye."

Polly protested, "No, no…"

"Miss Brady, do please indulge an old woman."

Polly smiled. "Well, perhaps I am interested, a little. Tell me more."

"His parents lived in Dublin. His mother died young from some horrible disease, I forget what and his father… well, I'm sorry to say that his father was a ne'er-do-well. Imprisoned many times for larceny and drunkenness. A ne'er-do-well of the very worst sort."

"Oh, I…"

"Not the boy's fault. He was handed over to his grandparents as a baby… lived here in County Wicklow and his grandfather worked in the mines over near Glendalough, the lead mines at Glendasan… past their best now, of course, but they employed a lot more people earlier this century. Young Luke returned to the city when he was older and his father decided he could put him to work, make use of the boy. He fell into bad company there, which was hardly surprising with a despicable father such as his."

"Into bad company?" Polly remembered how Luke often lifted Solomon onto his shoulders and cantered like a horse across the lawn, the little boy shouting with glee. He was trusted to work as an accounts clerk by his employer, wasn't he?

"Bad company, yes indeed, he became a thief… he was starving, poor child… so many were in that part of the city. No mother to care for him and… no wonder he ended up in St Kevin's."

"What is St Kevin's?"

"A reformatory school… an industrial school for boys aged ten to thirteen run by the Oblate Fathers, a missionary order from France originally." Dora sipped her brandy before tutting and shaking her head. "That's where the judge sent young Luke for stealing bread when he was ten years old. Perhaps it was for the best… probably saved his life for the Lord only knows where he would have ended up if left to wander on the streets of our capital city."

"Poor Luke," Polly replied. "It's shocking how some children have to…"

Dora waved a hand. "All in the past for Luke, gone now, thank goodness. Tell me more, my dear, about your life. You were sent to London at a young age, weren't you?"

"Yes, ma'am. I was ten years old."

"A mere child, indeed. And why were you sent there?"

Polly would have to be careful about her answer. "To boarding school. I was sent to a boarding school in London." She thought of the long cold dormitory with its rows of beds, the girls sitting in their pinafores in the dining hall, but a welcome change all the same from living with Aunt Maureen..

Dora seemed enthralled, clapping her hands and exclaiming, "How wonderful! Another little orphan rescued by education!"

"I was brought up by my aunt."

"A rich aunt, I'll be bound, if she could afford to pay for London schooling." Dora raised her glass. "And you're a credit to her generosity, no doubt about that. A well-educated young woman! My husband would have liked to meet you… would have been impressed by you." Her gaze lingered on Polly's face, almost mocking in its intensity, and bringing a glow to her cheeks.

Was she poking fun at her? Polly stood to light the candles on the mantelpiece because the room was growing dark.

"No, wait… don't strike a match just yet." Dora's eyes shot to the window and she rose from the armchair and bustled across the floorboards. "See there! Oh yes, come here, quickly. You see those lights in the trees… there, at the ruin. You see them?"

Polly hurried to join her and saw a distant glow; a sporadic flickering like that of a lantern inside the building.

"Someone is climbing the spiral steps," Dora said. "I wonder who it could be. The ghost of a sixteenth-century warrior?"

"I doubt that." She remembered the old lady's words two months back. Lizzie had seen lights in the tower before Mr Manning died in Brazil and some believed them to be a harbinger of doom.

"Then who?"

"I don't know, Mrs Burroughs. Local boys, perhaps, but certainly not ghosts."

Dora turned to face her, a note of excitement in her voice. "Bravely spoken, my dear. Now you must go out. You must go out and see who it is."

Chapter Nineteen

"I can't do this, ma'am, indeed I can't," Polly protested as she crossed the cobblestones of the yard with Dora leaning on her arm. "Suppose the men in the tower are dangerous."

"Hush, girl, Eamon will look after you. No need to be afraid with him there. Don't you want to find out who it is waving these mysterious lights around… terrifying half of the countryside and allowing them to believe they are ghosts or ghouls and warnings of death?'

Polly was curious, no denying that, but it was all very well for Mrs Burroughs to send her off on this mission while the old lady waited in the safety of the house. What would Claudia say about this escapade? Surely she wouldn't approve of her governess being dispatched into the dark woods if there was danger involved?

Dora rapped on the door of the coach house and called into the heavy night air, "Eamon, wake up, man! I know you're still up for you keep late hours smoking your pipe. I can smell the tobacco. Open up!"

The hinges whined as the door slowly opened. "Mrs Burroughs, what is it?" Eamon stood blinking in the light of an oil lamp clutched in one hand, still dressed in his working clothes. "Is there anything amiss?"

"Indeed there is. Make haste. Miss Brady and I have spotted goings-on in the tower. This courageous young woman is willing to hurry there to unearth the culprits and she needs an escort. Get your jacket… make haste!"

No point protesting further at this stage, Polly decided, as Eamon eyed her with a hint of admiration. Too late to back out now. Dora would have her own way as usual.

The governess followed Eamon across the lawn towards the wood, while Dora watched from the archway into the yard. Her boots were soaked through in minutes from the dew on the grass and she wished she'd brought her shawl. The humidity of the night was seeping away, leaving a chill in the air.

"There are stories about the old tower and the lights people sometimes glimpse there," she addressed Eamon, an effort to make conversation. "Mrs Burroughs wants me to find out who's behind them."

The man coughed and laughed. "Aye, Mrs Burroughs… she's the inquisitive one, no doubt about that. I didn't believe it was you who wished to venture out into the dark. I can tell by your face, young lady, for aren't you as pale as a ghost yourself?" He shook his head and held up the lantern to help her find her way along the path towards the river. "Isn't that typical of old Mrs Burroughs? Ah, she's a character, there's no doubt about it. You'd be wise to ignore her suggestions in the future, miss. Mind your step, if you please, there's a fallen branch across the way there."

If only she'd had the strength of mind to pay no heed to the old lady and her request but Polly felt a tingle of curiosity and, with Eamon beside her, she was no longer afraid. She imagined telling the children about the boys she would encounter in the tower house late at night, smoking cigarettes and laughing about frightening the locals.

Even Hannah might be impressed by her courage.

The river gurgled, dark and glittering in the light of the moon floating above the treetops. Eamon led the way along the path, his lantern swinging and casting shadows on the trunks of the pines. They fell silent as they walked. It would be a waste of time, no doubt, and the tower would have been abandoned when they arrived. She and Eamon would be easy to spot from such a height, in spite of the cover of trees. Polly's limbs trembled as they neared the ancient stone building, its ruined stone turrets jagged like broken teeth against the night sky.

"Ah, sure, the old lady was right," the manservant said, halting behind an oak tree and nodding towards the tower. "See that light inside?"

"Yes, yes, oh Eamon, what should we do?" She clasped her hands together. Suppose they weren't boys playing games but housebreakers, ruffians planning their next robbery or dividing the spoils of one recently carried out. She squeezed her eyes shut to block out her fears. Ridiculous. Her imagination running away with her.

"I think it's best if I go alone, miss," Eamon suggested. "I'll creep across to the door and have a look inside while you wait here with the lantern. Keep it behind the tree and make no sound."

She agreed and reached out to touch the sleeve of his jacket. "Take care, please. Don't let them see you." She watched him as he moved away across the damp grass, his cap pulled low over his forehead.

She had grown accustomed to the darkness and she noticed the iron door blocking the entrance had been pulled back.

Eamon reached the pile of fallen stones on the left of the arched doorway and slipped behind them. No light shone from the arrow slit windows. Had the intruders extinguished their lamps?

Or perhaps they'd already left by another exit on the opposite side of the building?

She heard a sudden soft screeching sound behind her, like the protest of a rusty gate hinge, and swung around. No, it was nothing to worry about. Just the cry of hungry long-eared owl chicks on the approach of a parent. She'd heard it in Mayo years before and her father had explained what it was. Unnerving though.

She turned back to watch Eamon approach the entrance, each step bringing him closer to possible danger. What if the intruders attacked him? Hit him on the head with a stone and then saw her hiding behind the oak? She should never have agreed to Dora's request.

The screech rose again and leaves on the ground rustled behind her. A twig snapped and she froze, gripping the trunk of the tree with her free hand. Her lantern shook, sending light shivering across the ground. She listened but there was only the gurgling of the river. Minutes slipped past as she waited, the thumping of her heart loud and painful in her chest.

Eamon stepped into the tower house and disappeared from view.

A movement on Polly's right made her cry out but it was only an animal, sniffing the earth and raising its head in surprise. A beautiful fox, deep red in the moonlight with a white tip at the end of its bushy tail, stood so close that she could reach out to touch it. A musty scent reached her nostrils. The fox stared at her, ears pricked and its almond eyes assessing this strange and unexpected sight in its territory.

The creatures were nocturnal, weren't they? She held her breath, not wishing to frighten the animal. Unusual that it hadn't run away.

Another snap of a light branch and footsteps rustled on the pathway. She crouched down, hiding the lantern behind her. One of the robbers from the tower must have crept over to the river path on his way home. He would find her for certain and she would be caught.

The fox turned away, moving into the undergrowth, the tip of its tail vanishing into the briars.

"Well, if it isn't Miss Brady," someone muttered. "May I ask what you are doing here on your own in the woods?"

Luke stood before her, wearing a dark wool jacket, a small sack in his hands.

Relief flooded through her and she stood up. "I might ask you the same question. Have you come from the tower?"

He didn't answer.

"Eamon is in there now so I'm not alone. I wouldn't be so foolish as to come here on my own."

Luke grinned. "Indeed, I hope not. You never know who you might meet in the woods at this time of night." He stepped closer, laying down the sack.

"What have you got there?" Had Luke been in the tower with others? She recalled her wild thought of robbers dividing stolen spoils.

"It's nothing."

"There must be something in the bag. What is it?"

"Just scraps of food. Stolen, I admit, from the kitchen. Lizzie gives me leftovers to feed the animals at night."

"Is that all?"

"I'll show you, then. Did you see Rufus?"

"I saw a handsome fox just before you came. Was that Rufus?"

He nodded and bent to open the sack, revealing pieces of bread and the fatty remains of a leg of mutton they'd eaten for dinner. The children had told her that Luke was fond of animals and had a special way with them. Solomon had mentioned a tame jackdaw.

"Yes, that's Rufus," Luke said. "He eats meat out of my hand but you must have frightened him off. You're nearly as bad as the poachers that hunt through this wood with their guns and lanterns after dark. But my fox is clever and can usually smell humans before they see him. He's wily, is my old friend Rufus." He moved closer to her. "You are here with Eamon. What are you doing?"

She shrugged, lifting one shoulder and turning her face away as her cheeks warmed. "Oh, it was foolish… a foolish adventure, no doubt, but I was with Mrs Burroughs in my bedroom and we saw lights shining in the tower. She asked me to investigate and sent Eamon with me."

His eyes, the unusual shade so similar to the fox's, gazed into hers. "What a brave woman you are! You could have met poachers, or republicans… there are plenty in the mountains of Wicklow."

"Would they have harmed me?"

"Perhaps not." He chuckled and added, "Perhaps they would have been more careful like Rufus and slipped away when you approached. I can see the lantern at the top of tower now. That must be Eamon carrying out his search."

Polly had forgotten about the manservant. She turned to follow Luke's gaze. "I hope he's on his own. Who do you think would have been in that lonely place at this hour?"

He yawned, covering his mouth with a hand. "Like I said… poachers or republicans… or young boys on a lark."

"I told Mrs Burroughs they were just young boys when she suggested ghosts of warriors. Such nonsense. And as for the stories about people dying after seeing the lights…"

"There'd be no one left in the countryside if somebody died whenever I saw a light in the tower," Luke replied with another grin.

"You see lights often?"

"At least once a fortnight. I ignore them. None of my business. Whoever it is, I go my own way and they go theirs. I have no wish to be dragged into political shenanigans or come across local children drinking and smoking when their papas think they're in bed. And, if they are poachers or hunters, I don't want them to see me feeding Rufus or the owls."

What a strange fellow he was! She felt at ease with him though, in spite of the darkness and the fact that Eamon hadn't returned.

"Old Dora is too curious for her own good," Luke said.

"Indeed, she is. She astounds me with her knowledge of this family."

Did he look a little wary at her words? "Does she mention me?"

Yes, he was concerned about what Dora might have told her. If he'd made mistakes in his youth, what did that matter now? Claudia and her mother obviously trusted him, as did his employer. He was no longer the boy thief sentenced to spend time in St Kevin's.

"Mrs Burroughs told me that you used to live here at Colgrannagh, when her husband was still alive." She kept her tone matter-of-fact. No need to mention the reformatory school or the conviction for stealing. She had no wish to embarrass him.

He hesitated for a few seconds before saying, "Yes, I did. Dr Burroughs was kind to me. He took me in when I was thirteen years old and educated me… or at least Mrs Manning did, for it was she who helped us with our reading and arithmetic back then before the first governess arrived. I thought she was an angel… an angel sent to change my life."

Polly could imagine why. Claudia with her earnest confidence, her belief in these young people, her lack of regard for the usual prejudices, must have seemed like a fairy godmother to a motherless boy. A boy whose father drank and probably beat him.

"I understand how you would believe that."

"You do? I believe that Mrs Burroughs must have told you

my history… my sad and reprehensible past. Indiscreet of her… but she isn't known for her discretion." He lowered his voice. "I spent nearly three years in a reformatory school."

"I'm sorry for you. Was it very difficult?"

He shrugged, leaning back against the oak. "Not so difficult." His smile came and went like a shadow. "Do you forgive me?"

"It is not my place to forgive you but we all have things of which we aren't proud."

He raised one eyebrow in mock surprise. "Really? Even you?"

"Even me." Out of the corner of her eye, she saw a man stepping out of the tower doorway. "There's Eamon coming back to us."

"But what could you, an upright young woman… a respectable governess… what could you have to regret in your past?"

Polly pointed at Eamon and moved away from Luke. He was unsettling, the way he stared at her and stood so close. The nickname of the Fox suited him for there seemed something almost wild about him. The tension, the intense focus of his gaze made her uncomfortable.

"We're not responsible for our parents' actions, only our own," he said. "Remember that."

"What do you mean?"

"Your father's actions. My father's actions. They are not ours. *The son shall not suffer for the iniquity of the father*. I know my bible, Miss Brady. Dr Burroughs used to quote that often for my benefit. I'm certain that is as apt for a daughter as it is for a son."

"What do you know about my father?"

"I've been told that he is a kind man, but reckless when young."

She turned her head away. How did he know anything about her father? Was it from Dora? Had she ferreted out information and passed it on to him?

Luke reached out and laid his hand on her arm, adding, "I

beg your pardon. I should have said nothing."

"I don't... I don't know what you mean."

His fingers tightened on her sleeve as he watched her expression.

"Eamon will be here in a minute," she said. "It's time I went back to the house."

He bowed his head, pushing at the dead dry leaves with the toe of his boot. "I understand your..."

When Polly said nothing, Luke changed the subject. "There's a lake near here, a heart-shaped lake in the mountains. Would you like to see it? I promised the girls I would take them. Perhaps Mrs Manning would like to come too."

"Mrs Manning mentioned it to me. I'd like that, thank you."

"Nobody there, Miss Brady," Eamon called as he drew nearer. "I saw no one at all. They must have spotted us and slipped away before I climbed the spiral stairs. Ah, it's young Luke! How are you, my lad?"

Luke released Polly's arm and took a step back. "I'm well, thank you."

She smiled at Eamon. "I'm grateful to you. I'll report back to Mrs Burroughs and no doubt she'll be disappointed but I confess I'm relieved that we can abandon this foolish adventure."

Chapter Twenty

The present – September 2022

"What do you think of my choice of restaurant?" Stephen waved a hand towards chairs with leather seats, embroidered tablecloths and an eclectic collection of antiques adorning the walls.

I decided it was exactly the sort of café an enthusiast like Stephen would choose, packed with memorabilia from the past. His cottage in the village was probably crammed with similar remnants from period house auctions, or handed down to him by relations eager to declutter.

A gilt-framed portrait of a Victorian matron glowered at me beside the stag, bristling in her widow's gown with its stiff lace collar, as if she too resented being put on display to satisfy the idle curiosity of villagers and tourists. Her expression of distaste appeared to emphasize her indignation.

"It's… it's interesting," I replied, turning to face Stephen who was running a hand over his thick hair in an effort to make it lie flat. A vast gilt-framed mirror hung on the wall opposite and he couldn't resist checking his reflection.

Removing his tweed jacket and hanging it on a hat stand beside us, he held out a chair for me. "I thought you'd appreciate the décor because you're a fellow disciple of the past. I'm sure we have so much in common. Please take a seat, Fiona."

"Thank you."

Stephen sat beside me at the head of the table and raised a hand to attract the attention of a teenage girl leaning against the counter with a bored expression on her face, her right hand resting on the rectangular shape of a mobile phone in the pocket of her short black skirt. She crossed long legs and yawned, staring at us.

He nodded a greeting to her and smiled at me. "I recommend the lamb. Straight off the mountain, it is. Delicious."

"Thank you but a sandwich will do me. I don't usually eat much in the middle of the day."

I'd left Archie with Daniel, who'd offered to keep him in his enclosed walled garden, away from Millicent who was entertaining a group of businesswomen to lunch to discuss a topic entitled *The Role of Social Media in the Modern Marketplace.* She'd invited me to attend and I'd feigned disappointment about having a prior engagement. Millicent assured me her own social media profiles were buzzing with excitement about the delegation's arrival. The women were part of an important entrepreneurial group.

If she succeeded in impressing them, put on a good spread and convinced them that her food and her venue were worth including on their website, then all sorts of opportunities might land in Millicent's lap. Kenny had been dispatched in the Volvo to the local wine merchant where he was to pick up carefully selected vintages. Millicent's other recently recruited assistant, a serious but competent young woman from Lithuania, had been cleaning the house for days.

It was vital that my Jack Russell didn't come across these business women and attempt to befriend them. I hoped Daniel would remember to keep his garden gate shut.

The girl slouched towards us and held out a menu. "D'yer want me to tell you about the specials?"

"Yes, indeed," Stephen said. "I've been explaining to my colleague here about the lamb."

So, I was his colleague already? I smiled. Perhaps that might encourage him to divulge more of his research.

"Lamb's off," the girl replied with another lengthy yawn. "It's fish pie or roast chicken and ham. Or the vegan option."

"What's that?" I asked to compensate for Stephen's disappointed sigh.

"Mushroom soup." She glanced at the menu and read aloud, "Local gourmet mushrooms, picked by our expert in the woods."

"How expert?" Stephen let out a sudden guffaw of laughter that reminded me of Daniel. "We don't want to be poisoned, do we?"

The girl scoffed. She'd heard that joke before.

"Ladies first." Stephen gestured at me.

"Do you have sandwiches?"

She eyed me coldly. "No."

"Then I'll risk the vegan mushroom soup."

"Aha, brave woman… indeed you are a brave woman." Stephen chuckled. "I admire your courage. I'll settle for the chicken and ham." He turned to the girl. "Got that down on your notepad? Thank you, my love."

She scowled at the endearment and slouched off towards a swing door into the kitchen.

"The owner's niece," Stephen said, as if that explained her lack of enthusiasm. He poured me a glass of water and sat back, linking his fingers together and resting them on the table. "So, here we are at last, Fiona. It must be two weeks since I met you in the graveyard. Do tell me if there have been any developments about the body… the skeleton in the shed?"

I pulled my notebook out of my handbag. "Nothing yet. Daniel was warned that it could take quite a while for the forensic laboratory to date the skeleton."

"Did you get a chance to talk to Daniel about the discovery? Does he have any idea who this unfortunate might have been?"

"None whatsoever. You probably know there were only women living in the house after Dr Burroughs and Gilbert Manning died, apart from Solomon."

He frowned, sudden deep furrows across his forehead. "Could it be one of the women?"

I stared at him, surprised, and replied, "I never considered them, to be honest. Not Claudia, obviously, or Solomon, but what about the servant you mentioned who died in the 1890s?"

"I had no reason to check her out until now. Might just be the gossip machine in the village… you understand how… how people love to talk, especially in rural areas like this."

I opened my notebook and pulled out a biro. "What are these people saying?"

"That a maid died unexpectedly in the house around that time but I don't know if that's even true. She wasn't a local, lived with the family, but this might just be people's imagination taking flight. Mention a body and… it was on the TV news. Did you see the report?"

"Yes, Daniel and I watched it together. He's had to send several journalists away since then. I'd like to find out the name of the maid and where she was buried… if she was buried."

He replied, "I suppose newspaper archives would be your best bet. If you find anything useful, perhaps you would email a copy my way at some stage? I would like to have it for the file."

I wondered what else he had in his file and decided to push the conversation in the direction of Polly Brady, his great-aunt, the governess hired by Claudia Manning. "I'll take a photo of any info and send it to you."

He pulled a business card out of the breast pocket of his jacket and laid it on the table. "There you go… my email. Did I mention my little venture?"

"No, I don't think you did."

The door of the kitchen swung open and a waft of steam issued forth, followed by the girl bearing a silver tray with cutlery. She placed this on our tablecloth and, as if an afterthought, tossed two linen napkins in front of us.

"I'm writing a book about Polly and women of her generation who found themselves in similar circumstances. The research is most interesting, I can tell you."

I sat upright. "Similar circumstances?"

"Young women who were obliged to go out and work for their living in the nineteenth century. There were a lot more than people realize. Not just governesses but journalists, nurses, seamstresses… Sometimes you'd think the twentieth century invented work for women but that's not true. Not true at all."

"Women were employed in factories during the industrial revolution," I replied. "When factories opened, that brought families flocking to the cities in search of work and wages. Poorer women had to work long exhausting hours."

"I've got an agent interested in my book." Stephen said in a whisper, as if worried the elderly couple at the next table might be listening. "One with good contacts in London. Early days yet, of course, and he's been avoiding me of late… not answering my calls, but I'm hopeful. If I could spice up the manuscript a bit… the skeleton, the identity of same… a large dollop of scandal hopefully. Then who knows what might happen with the agent? I'd imagine publishers might be keen to get their hands on my book then and might even offer a decent advance."

Should I try to discourage him? If Daniel wished to write his book about the same incident, the body in the underground shed… He'd stated as much, hadn't he, that day Tobie unearthed the bones with his digger? I couldn't allow Daniel's story to be snatched from under his nose.

Stephen seemed to sense my reluctance and switched his gaze

to the girl who reappeared with the silver tray carrying a bowl of mushroom soup and a large plate of chicken, sliced ham and mashed potatoes swimming in gravy. She placed them in front of us, wished us a curt "enjoy" and returned to her post beside the counter, this time unable to resist the temptation to whip out her mobile and scroll.

"Could the skeleton be Polly Brady? Do you know where she ended up after she left Colgrannagh?" I picked up a spoon and stirred the mixture in the porcelain bowl, a collection of beige stalks and black gills. What had I let myself in for? The rising steam smelled of garlic and an earthy aroma, suspiciously like rotting wood and similar to the stink of decaying leaves and debris that came out of the cavity uncovered by Tobie. Not an appetizing thought.

Suppose the expert mushroom collector had had a bad morning? He could have been suffering from a blinding hangover from too much whiskey in the pub the night before and, in his befuddled state, his shaking fingers might have plucked up lethal fungi that would soon send me to an agonizing and untimely death.

Stephen eyed the stalks with obvious distrust. "I've no details about what became of Polly. Her diary ends in the summer of 1895 and she wrote the letters soon after she first arrived. My grandmother didn't know what happened to her."

"You said you'd lend me the letters and the diary." Would there be anything significant in the governess's journal that Stephen might have missed?

"I've got those here. I can also give you some information about Polly Brady." Stephen stuck a fork into a morsel of chicken, lifting his eyebrows. "*Quid quo pro*… if you like. You scratch my back and I'll… though only metaphorically speaking, I hasten to add. Is that a deal?"

The first spoonful of soup tasted surprisingly good. I replied,

"A deal? Well, if we could help each other... yes, that would be good. I'm interested in Polly's accounts because she would have been close to Claudia, I imagine, being a governess. She might have written about subjects only someone working inside the house would know."

He chewed his chicken and nodded. After a brief silence, he reached into his jacket pocket and produced a small leather-bound book and a number of envelopes, saying, "Here's what I have. There's not a lot of relevant information in them but they might help you in some way, I hope. Her journal ends with an odd statement… quite odd, but you'll see what I mean when you read it." He stopped talking, looking around the room in an almost furtive manner, before dropping his voice and adding, "I feel obliged to tell you that Polly was a bit of a misfit in my family. She had a sister, who was my grandmother, but she wasn't a blood relation, you understand, because Polly was adopted. I only recently discovered that when I looked up the church records in Mulranny in Mayo. My grandmother's mother was a respectable seamstress in what was a remote village back then, a windswept place where the local landlord ruled the tenants… you know what I mean."

I flicked through the diary and saw neat handwriting in ink, but only a few lines on each page. Some sketches of flowers. Polly appeared to be an accomplished artist. "The landlords had so much power," I said. "Was that one difficult?" I dropped the book and envelopes into my handbag, yearning for a chance to look through them.

"On the contrary, he was a kind man by all accounts. His father before him had fed his tenants when the potato crops failed during the famine years and never tried to force them off the land. His son was the same. Affable, you might say, and did his best for the locals though…" He popped a piece of ham into his mouth.

I waited; biro poised over my open notebook. "What was his name?"

He swallowed and cleared his throat, helping himself to a slurp of water. "I can't remember offhand… got it written down somewhere. Anyway, it seems Polly's mama got herself in the family way."

"The respectable seamstress?" I asked, surprised.

"No, not her, not my great-grandmother. Polly's real mother. That's how she came to be adopted, you understand? Her birth mother… that's the right expression, isn't it? Her birth mother was a servant in the landlord's house. The usual story… pretty young housemaid catches the eye of the son in the big house and one thing leads to another and next there's a… a bun in the oven."

My lips twitched at the quaint expression. "It happened a lot in those days. The seamstress was kind enough to take in the unwanted child?"

"My grandmother always made out that her mother didn't really want the child but she was paid well, apparently, and her husband had died several years before so the money helped bring up her own daughter as well. Polly and the seamstress's daughter were educated at a boarding school in London, a decent education, and Polly subsequently went to Paris for a year to study the French language. I think the bribe of a good education for her own daughter sealed the deal, because my great-grandmother realized this would be an advantage for her daughter, as well as help to get Polly off her own hands. All paid for by the errant son of the landlord. Only fair he should pay when he was the one who…" He paused to shovel more chicken into his mouth and patted at his rather large lips with the linen napkin.

I made notes and sipped my soup. No ill effects from it so far. Perhaps I'd been unkind to question the mushroom expert's skill.

"No, indeed," Stephen added. "The family letters tell us they thought the son a gentleman like his father. He never shirked his duty to his child."

"And what about the housemaid?"

"You mean the mother of the baby girl? She ran off, apparently, so the story goes. She scarpered with her meagre belongings, leaving no clue as to where she ended up."

"Why didn't the generosity of the land owner's son extend to the poor maid?" I noticed the sharp edge to my words. Why would he lavish money on the child and ignore the woman he had wronged? It seemed unfair.

"She was a wild one, my grandma said. Ran off with a local lad, no doubt. We've no idea although my grandmother…"

The girl advanced from the counter. "Finished? D'yer want dessert? No? Fair enough. Coffee then?"

I ordered a cappuccino while Stephen asked for an espresso with a spoonful of sugar.

"Sugar comes with it. You can put that in yerself." She threw the words over her shoulder as she walked away.

"What a little ray of sunshine!" Stephen said. "I do apologize, Fiona. Normally the owner's wife is here and she's a charming woman."

I waved a dismissive hand. "No problem. I'm used to bored teenagers because I taught history. It doesn't bother me. So, what happened to the maid?"

"Did you enjoy teaching?" he asked, ignoring my question.

"I did… for years until… One profession that robots haven't managed to replace just yet."

"That's good." He chuckled. "Robots! My goodness, there's a thought."

"The housemaid," I prompted. I didn't want to have to explain why I'd given up teaching. I'd only recently met Stephen.

"Ah yes, her. We never found out where she went but my grandmother once let slip… she once told me something after a night out at a wedding, when she'd had one sherry too many and wasn't minding her words."

"What did she let slip?" I was beginning to feel sorry for Stephen's future editor. Difficult to get him to stick to the point.

"She said that a position was found for Polly as a governess. They sent her down to Claudia Burroughs… Claudia Manning, I mean. I suppose she was the ideal choice because her father had a reputation for being a philanthropist. He took in all sorts of waifs and strays from a variety of disreputable backgrounds, so Polly would have fitted in well. Claudia seems to have been the sort who wouldn't have cared if she were illegitimate."

"They sounded like kind people. I read about that in one of Claudia's letters from a cousin in England. Her father liked to give children from poorer backgrounds an education and help them find employment."

"Yes, that's what I was told too," he said. "There are a number of people in the village descended from some of Dr Burroughs's protégés."

"But you mentioned that your grandmother let something slip. What exactly?"

His frown lines returned. "It was about the housemaid who ran off. My grandmother said she was an ungrateful hussy. That's what they all thought of her. The landlord's son was soft on her, apparently, fancied himself in love with the woman and she was offered a cottage on the estate in County Mayo. She had the cheek to turn down his offer and vanished one night taking the other child with her."

I blinked. The other child? What other child? Had I missed an explanation about this among all the different strands of Stephen's story?

He smiled at my confusion as the coffee cups arrived with a clatter on the table, hot liquid slopping into the saucers.

"A boy," he added. "She kept the boy, my grandma said. The

ungrateful hussy left her daughter and took her boy."

"She had two children?"

"Yes. No doubt from a different liaison, brought up by her mother perhaps. She was lucky to get a job in the big house in the first place, especially with a reputation like that." Stephen was enjoying himself, imagining scandalous scenarios in a more conservative era.

While I digested this information, the girl at the counter looked in my direction. Had she been listening to us? She walked over.

"Have you heard anything about the body?" she asked me, ignoring Stephen. "Only… like, my uncle was asking when he rang me. He's keen on all this old history and stuff."

I shook my head. "Nothing yet."

"There's a needlework thing here," she said.

Stephen looked up from his espresso. "A needlework of what, my dear?"

She shrugged. "Like plants and herbs, I guess. It's on the back wall behind the bar and my uncle bought it in the house auction years ago when the old guy who owned Colgrannagh died."

"That's correct," Stephen said. "Solomon Manning sold off quite a lot of furniture and paintings over the years. Broke, poor man."

"I could show you the needlework," the girl offered with a knowing smile. She waited.

Stephen frowned. "You want a tip for showing us, I suppose. I could ask your uncle instead."

She shrugged. "Please yourself. He's away for two weeks with my auntie in Spain so you'll have to wait."

"I'd like to see it," I said, opening my purse and producing a five euro note. The poor girl probably didn't get paid much for working in the restaurant.

She whipped the money from my fingers and hurried off

before I could change my mind or Stephen stopped me.

"I hope she comes back, Fiona. She's a saucy one, that girl. Always in trouble in school, or so I hear."

I sipped my coffee. She would come back; I was confident of that.

After five minutes and much complaining from my companion about the lack of manners of the young in the contemporary world, the girl reappeared with a framed embroidery under her arm.

She held it up beside me. "You can borrow it for ten euros."

"Now, see here, missie…" Stephen protested. "Hand it over or I'll be sending a report to your uncle… and your teacher as well about your antics."

She pushed the frame towards me, turning on her heel with what sounded like a muffled curse.

I examined the needlework and its beautiful neat stitching in silk threads of different hues. It depicted a herb garden with circular beds, spirals edged with stone, and a tall sundial in the middle. Yes, an exact replica of the old design plan Tobie and I had found in the underground shed. Some of the herbs had been stitched along the outside border in more detail, including their names underneath. Blue flowering rosemary, tiny white elder blossom and a brighter one called borage, among several others.

"It's beautiful," I said. "So delicate. Whoever created this knew what they were doing." I peered at a tiny name stitched in the bottom right hand corner of the embroidered scene. Polly Brady! Claudia's governess had embroidered the exquisite work of art and what I held in my hands could only be the old physic garden at Colgrannagh.

I looked across at the girl and she was by my side in a flash, pocketing my ten euro note with a smirk.

Stephen tut-tutted at me and gave the needlework a cursory glance, obviously not interested in plants. On impulse, I placed my fingers over Polly's name to hide it and said, "It's lovely, really brings the herb garden to life. Daniel and the landscaper will be excited to see this."

Chapter Twenty-One

As I drove back up the hill towards the main gates of Colgrannagh, I wondered what had happened to Polly's brother and her birth mother. Stephen hadn't known the age of the boy and it sounded like he hadn't shared the same father. Where had the mother taken him? I wouldn't waste time finding out as it might be just a wild goose chase and irrelevant to my research. Interested as I was in the maid from Mayo, I had to focus on what Daniel needed. Polly, a witness to what went on in Claudia's family at the end of the nineteenth century, was more important.

The death of the other maid in the house was intriguing. Why had she died? If it had been newsworthy, I might find a coroner's report in the archives online. I made a mental note to check.

I reached the ornate gates, hanging on their granite pillars, and stepped out of the car to open the latch. Millicent's little sports car was heading towards me. She drew to a halt at the entrance and, to my horror, I saw Archie peering out of the back window, his nose pressed to the glass. He let out a howl of excitement, or perhaps relief, when he spotted me.

"Fiona!" Millicent leaped out of the driver's seat.

I remained where I was, clutching the gate.

"Fiona!"

"Oh hello, Millicent." I attempted a welcoming smile.

"We need to talk."

"Right... okay."

She reached into her car and gave a sharp yank on the dog's lead. Archie yelped and fixed me with beseeching eyes.

"Why have you got my..." I began.

"Don't start... just take the damn dog."

"Has Archie done something terrible?"

"I found him digging in the new flower bed beside the marquee. New plants, Fiona, only put in yesterday. You should have seen the devastation! He's completely out of control."

I groaned and apologized. How had he escaped from Daniel's walled-in garden? Perhaps one of the builders or Tobie had opened the door and the little wretch had slipped out. "But where were you taking him?"

"Daniel told me you'd gone to the café in the village to meet someone. I had to pop into the post office so I brought him with me. Now that I've found you, I've got something important to say."

I took the lead, my fingers brushing her cold ones, and frowned at Archie. "Did you have a nice afternoon?"

"It went quite well, thanks. The women are an ambitious bunch and they feel I can play a useful role in their business group."

I smiled. I wouldn't tell her I'd addressed my question to the dog. "That's good. Sounds encouraging."

She pulled out her cigarettes and lit one. "Yes, it was encouraging, especially after my name had been blackened by that witch who owns a guest house down on the coast." She waved a hand. "Forget I said that. She's not worth bothering about but she's jealous I have this place at my disposal and she's trying to turn others in the women's group against me."

I feigned sympathy. Millicent was always falling out with people.

Tobie's Land Rover appeared round the bend in the lane outside the gate and he stopped, squinting in the sunshine. I recognized bronze fennel plants on the passenger seat, feathery fronds shielding most of his face.

"Can you give us a moment alone?" Millicent snapped at him.

His eyebrows rose in surprise and he glanced first at me and then at the terrier. He didn't move.

"For God's sake, doesn't he understand anything?"

I explained in my basic French what Millicent wanted and translated his reply for Millicent. "He says he wanted to check a few things with you later on but he's going now."

"Good." She exhaled smoke. "Where did you learn to speak the language?"

"I spent six months in Paris when I left school... minding children for a friend of my mother's. My French isn't great though. I've forgotten most of it."

Tobie's lips curved, his secret smile. He saluted Millicent and drove off up the avenue.

She pointed and we moved across to a stone bench on the left side of the entrance gate.

"Sit down," Millicent ordered.

I joined her on the sun-warmed seat and reeled in my dog, urging him to lie by my feet and behave.

"I'll come straight to the point, Fiona."

"Please do."

"I'd like you to give up this research."

For a moment I thought I'd misheard her. "I'm sorry? Give it up?"

"Yes. Yes, that's what I said. It's not a good idea."

Archie's bright eyes looked up at me, as if checking my reaction.

"But why?"

"It will only cause trouble around here. Daniel has no intention of writing a book about his great-aunt. He's too old. It's just another of his whims."

I opened my mouth to object to this ageist remark but she hurried on. "Give up your research and he'll soon forget about the idea and move on to his next one."

I leaned back, my shoulders tensing, but said nothing. Thoughts raced each other around my mind. What about my bank overdraft? And the risk I'd taken. I'd given up my teaching job to concentrate on family research projects, to focus on making a new career for myself. And, worst of all, I still had nowhere to live.

"You must understand, Fiona," she said, her tone a little softer, "Kenny and I have worked so hard to get this place under control. We've put time and effort into the house and… the grounds…"

With Daniel's money, I thought. They couldn't have done it without Daniel's money.

"Daniel is…" I began.

She interrupted, "A whim, I tell you. He has a different idea every month. Forget it and go home."

Should I explain that I needed to save up to rent a home? That my soon to be ex-husband had gambled his way through all our savings and run up such massive debt that we'd had to sell our house. That I'd only that morning received another demand in an email from his lawyer, looking for nearly quarter of a million euros which deluded Dominic claimed was his fair share of the money from the sale of my late father's house. A house Dominic had never even lived in.

No, I wouldn't mention it because I didn't want her to realize how desperate I was to keep my job. I said, "Daniel seems pleased with my research. He's got notes… a big file of notes that I've given him."

"It passes the time for him, that's all. Can't you see how it's going to cause trouble for our business… our wedding business?"

"No, I don't see how it will cause trouble. It's got nothing to do with your wedding business."

She inhaled and frowned.

I sighed and said, "You'd better explain what's bothering you."

Smoke trailed from her nostrils. "It's obvious, isn't it? If you keep digging up family history… stuff that's been forgotten about for decades… more than a century, in fact… who knows where it will end?"

"Are you worried I will discover shocking deeds committed by Daniel's family?"

"I certainly am. The locals in the village are already gossiping about it… about the damn skeleton. That attracted all sorts of unwelcome questions from journalists. The phone rang for a week afterwards. Every time I went to the supermarket, I had to… That's hardly going to impress couples planning their dream weddings here. It's too much of a distraction."

"I doubt it would put people off. They might even think it was exciting."

She snorted. "They won't. They want a beautiful stress-free day full of sunshine, champagne and roses. A lovely country house and dreamy garden setting… not another forensic scene with detectives and tittle-tattle about murder."

"Do others think it was a murder?" I asked.

"Of course they do. What else could it be?"

"I think it's likely too. The body must have been hidden there. I heard today that a maid died in…"

Millicent snapped, "You're not paying attention, Fiona. I don't actually care who was hidden, or if a maid fell down the steps or if she was murdered. I want it all covered up and forgotten about. It happened long ago and it's none of our business… nothing to do with you. You're going to tell Daniel that you're leaving."

"What? You must be joking. I've no intention of leaving," I replied, and Archie glanced up at my curt words..

Her eyes widened, as if astonished I would even consider disobeying her orders.

"I've agreed to help Daniel and he's agreed to pay me," I said. "This research is important. It's my job, not some frivolous whim. I won't abandon it… or him."

"I hope that you change your mind. I'd like you to think very carefully about this."

Was she threatening me? I couldn't leave just as I was beginning to make progress. Millicent North with her grand ambitions of wedding functions and the women's business group wasn't going to stop me. What could she actually do anyway? Threaten Daniel? Maybe she'd denounce me to the business group. I swallowed a smile.

"I'll make sure Kenny hears about this," Millicent continued. "He's even more worried than I am about you exposing horrible stuff."

I doubted that. Kenny was easy-going with his friendly grin. He always stopped to chat to me whenever I met him on the staircase or in the garden. He also had the sense to realize that Daniel was the one who kept their wedding business afloat.

No, I wouldn't let Millicent bully me out of a project I desperately needed to complete. An important step for my future. I couldn't go to the principal of the school with my tail between my legs, begging for my teaching position back. Besides, she hadn't seemed at all sorry to see me go because we'd never seen eye to eye.

I stood, picking up the dog and placing him under my arm. "I'm sorry, Millicent. I can't agree to your… um, to your request. This project is really important to me. It's also important to

Daniel. If he wishes me to continue, then continue I will."

I hurried towards my car; jumped in and deposited a relieved Archie on the rear seat. I drove off before she could stop me.

Chapter Twenty-Two

The past – June 1895

Claudia came out of the front door and handed the picnic basket to Polly. "I wish I could accompany you to Lough Ouler, my dears. If only my patients had chosen a more suitable day to fall ill… six visits to the sick lie ahead of me, would you believe?"

"Inconvenient of them, to be sure," Dora muttered drily from her perch on the top of the granite steps. "I'm thankful I'm not going with you. Can you imagine me attempting the steep climb up Tonelagee Mountain? It would surely bring on apoplexy at my age." She turned to Solomon and patted his hand. "This young man and I will have a lovely afternoon playing chess. I'm determined to beat him today."

Solomon scowled, resentful at being left behind. He hung his head and made no reply.

Luke handed Hannah into the carriage, an old four-wheeler similar to a landau and borrowed from a nearby landowner; large enough to accommodate the four of them. Eamon had driven it round from the stable yard with Misty and the farmer's cob in the shafts. The pony was sweating and restless in the heat, tossing her head and pawing at the gravel with a front hoof, impatient to move off, while the solid bay cob dozed beside her.

"It will be cooler up the mountain," Luke assured Polly. She took a seat opposite him between Annie and Hannah, raising a hand to wave to the three on the steps. Mrs Delaney had packed enough food to feed twice as many, judging by the size of the basket strapped to the back of the carriage.

The girls chattered with Luke as Eamon drove the horses along the road towards the village, their iron-clad hooves ringing out a rhythm on the dusty stones.

"How long will the journey take?" Annie asked.

"Less than an hour," Luke replied. "Once we reach Laragh, we'll soon be on the Military Road and then you'll see the view of your life."

In the village, Robert Kingson was standing with Dr Fitzpatrick outside the public house and Hannah called out a greeting.

Annie reached across Polly's lap to snatch at the girl's arm. "Hannah, please! Pray don't make a spectacle of us." A flush of heat blazed on her pale cheeks. Poor Annie, always so worried about what others thought.

Hannah shook her off and shouted, "Good morning, Mr Kingson. We're off to Lough Ouler for a picnic."

Kingson raised his bowler hat. "Good morning, ladies. A beautiful day for it."

Dr Fitzpatrick leaned forward to whisper in his ear and Kingson's smile faded.

Luke glanced at Polly and shook his head. "Thick as thieves."

What did he mean? Dr Fitzpatrick's greeting had been lukewarm, a mere nod of his head before he turned away. Perhaps it was the sight of a carriage load of orphan children that repelled him. The doctor had lived a sheltered life compared to them, brought up within the security of society. He hadn't been reared with a drunken criminal for a father like Luke. He hadn't been sent as a baby to the local orphanage like Annie, when her unmarried mother died in the workhouse, or abandoned outside a church like Hannah. No matter what the parents had done, the sins they may have committed, the children were innocents but alas not in the opinion of snooty Dr Fitzpatrick.

As Eamon urged the horses up the hill from the village, Hannah giggled. "Mr Kingson likes Miss Brady." She shot a mischievous smile at Annie. "I see the way he looks at her."

"Nonsense," Polly said. "He rarely looks at me."

Luke's eyes were on her face and she turned away.

The girls exclaimed with delight when they reached the Military Road above Laragh. A wide expanse of heather bloomed, shimmering in the haze of heat and the air was filled with the coconut scent of bright yellow gorse flowers stretching away to the mountains.

"There's Brockagh on our left." Luke pointed. "And Tonelagee further along. That's where we're heading, ladies."

"It's beautiful up here and not so hot," Polly replied. "The wildness reminds me of home… of Mayo. Wicklow isn't quite as dramatic as our mountains of Nephin and Croagh Patrick but breathtaking all the same."

Luke smiled at her but Hannah and Annie weren't listening. They were arguing about the cut of Robert Kingson's navy coat and how he'd once mentioned that Luke keeping a fox as a pet was dangerous because the creatures carried unpleasant diseases. Poor Annie. She would do well to try to be more discreet about her admiration of the man because she was an easy target for Hannah's taunts.

"The military road was built at the beginning of the last century," Luke told Polly, "by the British army after the insurrection of 1798. They knew rebels were hiding out in the mountains and this was their attempt to keep them under control. They built four army barracks along the road. One was at Glencree."

Dora had mentioned that St Kevin's Reformatory was built

on the site of the Glencree army barracks.

Luke said no more until they reached a cabin near Glenmacnass Waterfall, where he jumped down and handed over a few coins to a lanky boy with a mass of freckles, a tattered shirt and bare feet under trousers that were too short.

"He'll keep an eye on the carriage and the cob until we return," Luke explained. He turned to Eamon, who was unbuckling the picnic basket. "You might as well stay here too. I know you are good friends with the boy's father. Take some beer and your sandwiches from the basket and rest yourself."

Eamon touched his cap and grinned. "If you're sure, Master Luke, and thank you."

"Certainly I am. You deserve a few hours off. I'll strap the basket onto Misty's back and we'll continue on foot. It will take about an hour and a half to walk from here, with a few stops to catch our breath, and perhaps another quarter of an hour to reach the ridge… where we get the best view of the lake. It's rough underfoot and often wet even in summer so we need to watch where we're going."

The girls exchanged smiles, Annie's irritation forgotten, as if blown away by the breeze that stirred her light curls. They set off in front towards a narrow river, following a path through grass burnt by the sun.

"Over there," Luke said, with a wave of his hand. "We must climb across the stepping stones. One at a time, please, and I will help you."

Hannah scrambled across the boulders with the agility of a mountain goat while cautious Annie clutched Luke's hand. Polly declined his assistance and was soon on the opposite bank.

"An independent woman!" Luke laughed. "No doubt you'll tell me you've had plenty of practice crossing rivers in Mayo. Wait, Hannah, while I go back for Misty. I'll have to ride her across further down where there aren't so many rocks."

The two girls ignored him, setting off up the hill in the direction of a track created by sheep that cut through the heather.

"Girls, wait for me," Polly called.

"Don't go too far ahead," Luke added, pulling on the pony's rein. He smiled at Polly. "See how they ignore their governess and me. Hannah is headstrong but Annie is sensible. A good balance, don't you agree?"

"Most of the time. Hannah can be too determined and I fear she will lead Annie into trouble. Make haste, we must follow… they are walking fast and Mrs Manning will not be pleased if I lose them."

"No fear of that. I'm certain quite soon, in several hundred yards or so, they will lose their initial enthusiasm." He shifted his gaze from Misty, ambling behind them on the end of her lead rope, to Polly's face. "Are you a keen walker, Miss Brady?"

"I enjoy it, yes."

They fell silent, concentrating on the climb. When Polly checked her pocket watch, half an hour had passed.

He kept pace with her stride, watching the girls ahead of them. "The hem of your dress is damp. It's wet underfoot and this climb is steep for a while. You must miss the freedom of Mayo now that you are a governess."

"I didn't have much freedom in Mayo, I assure you. My aunt is a taskmaster and I had to help her with her sewing. I came to Wicklow for freedom, such as it is."

His eyebrows knitted together.

She added, "As a child, I wasn't given the freedom that Mrs Manning's children are permitted."

"Nor was I. A punch on the ear if I gave cheek… three years in St Kevin's Reformatory for snatching a loaf of bread for my dinner." His tone wasn't bitter. Ironically it sounded almost triumphant. "I survived."

"A harsh sentence, indeed," Polly replied, "but our courts

are rarely kind to child offenders. The judges see the need to discipline… to correct."

"I knew a girl only a little older than I was… the judge handed down a sentence of three years in prison and five in a reformatory for stealing a side of bacon. Another boy received the same for stealing a bible. Wouldn't you imagine the judiciary would have been happy he stole the holy book? Life is never kind to children unless they are born with silver spoons in their mouths."

He could hardly accuse her of that, could he?

She wondered again how he knew about her father. Or did he? Perhaps he was bluffing; merely giving her an impression that he knew about her background in the hope she would reveal more of it. Like a gypsy's trick when telling fortunes to those foolish enough to hand over their coins. That trick wouldn't work with her. Aunt Maureen had trained her well.

Hannah and Annie slowed their pace in front, Annie doubled over and clutching her side.

"See," Luke said. "I told you, didn't I? Those girls won't be able to walk up this hill at that speed. Too much heather and too many loose stones."

Polly stopped for a moment to catch her breath. The slope fell away behind her. A bird hung in the air overhead, with wings outstretched. She pointed at it.

"A kestrel." Luke smiled. "The wind-hoverer. Unlike horses, it faces into the wind."

"You are keen on nature, Mr Manning."

He nodded and pushed a lock of hair back with his palm. "Call me Luke, if you please. Mr Manning sounds rather formal if we are to be friends."

"You are named after the most literary of the apostles."

"And a physician, don't forget. Mrs Burroughs always told me that St Luke was a physician." Misty stopped to eat the grass behind them. Luke asked, "May I call you Polly?"

"As you wish." She feared this sounded abrupt and added, "I would be happy if you… certainly you may."

"Are you tired, Polly? This is a tough climb. You can ride on Misty and have a rest, as long as you carry the basket on your lap. The girls will be dismayed if we abandon the picnic."

"I'm perfectly capable of continuing on foot."

He frowned. "I'm sure you are. I was just being polite… not meant as a slight, I assure you." He tugged at the lead rope, the pony plodding behind them.

They walked on, another half hour slipping past in silence, both girls back on their feet and forging ahead.

Polly silently cursed her aunt for teaching her to be suspicious of people she barely knew. And even of those she did know. It had become a habit and sometimes she feared she sounded too abrasive.

They reached a bank of heather where the path continued over stones set into the hillside like steps. Luke held out his hand. "Allow me to assist you up here."

She hesitated, regarding the stones, willing herself to decline. Patches of perspiration dampened her cotton dress between her shoulders and in the hollow of her back. He was looking at her in that mocking way. She held out her hand and he clasped it in his firm one.

"There, Polly Brady, that doesn't hurt, does it? Independence can be a hindrance at times."

"A hindrance to what?"

"To making friends… I meant only to be friendly." He leaned closer to her, his freckled face almost touching hers before he swung away to look further up the slope. "I see our young ladies are once again sitting in the heather awaiting us."

She clambered up over the heather bank as Misty stumbled behind her and Luke pulled on the rope. He squeezed Polly's hand, releasing it when she was once more on the worn grassy path.

"I have a tame jackdaw. Would you like to see him sometime?"

She smiled. "Solomon told me about him. That would be interesting. I've never seen a pet bird before apart from a canary in London." Luke Manning, with his golden hair and perceptive gaze, was an unusual young man. With eyes that could see into her soul, or certainly into her mind. Half-man, half-boy.

"What age are you?" she asked.

"Twenty-two."

"The same age as I am."

"I know that." He tilted closer to her and she wondered if he was going to raise a hand to touch her face, but he didn't. He whispered, "It seems like fate, doesn't it? The two of us…"

"I… I don't know what you mean." He peeled away her protection, all those layers so carefully laid down over the years, skin upon skin like an onion. His words challenged her, leaving her vulnerable and exposed.

He regarded her, his mouth stretching into a grin.

"I want to know how you know my age," Polly said. "Did Mrs Manning tell you?"

He laughed. "You don't trust me… you don't trust people. Perhaps you're wise not to do so. Wise not to trust me. Let me tell you. I've a friend in St Kevin's who has acquaintances all over the country. Oh, don't be so disapproving. Your lovely blue eyes have turned cold and as for that aloof expression… the network of priests is very respectable, I assure you. Your aunt would agree."

Her aunt! What had Aunt Maureen to do with this? Polly clasped her fingers together and twisted them. "What can you mean?"

"The parish priest in your village in Mayo… he knows one of my teachers in St Kevin's. It was easy. Brother Eugene corresponded with your parish priest and enquired after a certain young lady who recently came to work as a governess for Mrs

Manning. A perfectly normal enquiry, I feel, brought about by my concern for your employer and the children and so… that's all."

Anger stirred inside her, a burning flush on her cheeks. How dare he! How dare he pry into her background like that. She stepped away. "It's not your business and the parish priest may be friends with my aunt but he is not… he has never been a friend to me."

"I'm fortunate that Brother Eugene, who taught me mathematics, is a popular man with a wide circle of friends. He shares my enthusiasm for…"

"Spying?" Polly spat the word at him. "Is that how a priest… how a man of God should behave?"

His grin slid away.

"It's not your concern," Polly added more softly. "All you had to do was ask me, if you really wanted to know."

Luke shrugged, as if disappointed with her reaction to his cleverness.

A silence fell between them when they continued up the path, the sun beating down on them when the wind dropped, perspiration forming on Polly's brow. She tasted salt on her lips. Not tears, no. Never tears. Colgrannagh had seemed a refuge. An escape and yet even there the past had caught up with her. It was Luke's fault. He was to blame.

They reached Annie and Hannah, who lay prostrate on soft tufted grass, hot and tired, their faces glowing from the exertion of their climb.

"How much longer to the lake?" Hannah pulled at Luke's sleeve. "I'm hungry and thirsty and Annie is exhausted."

"I'm not," Annie replied, her voice rising. "Why do you always blame everything on me?"

"So much for our pleasant day out, eh Misty?" Luke pulled one of the pony's ears through his long fingers and bent to kiss her hairy forehead. "Looks like you and I are the only ones enjoying ourselves." She raised her nostrils and blew into his face.

"How much further?" Hannah demanded.

"See where the ground levels out over there?" Luke waved a hand. "There's a ridge and the land drops beyond it… a magnificent view of the lake. When we've admired it, we will sit down and enjoy the picnic."

After another five minutes' walk along the sheep track, Lough Ouler lay below them like a jewel, a sapphire pendant under the cloudless sky, its heart shape unique, clearly defined, reminding Polly of a locket given to her by her father before she left for London. She'd asked him for a lock of his hair and he'd cut off a dark curl with his pocket knife and placed it behind the glass.

Her irritation diminished as she stood beside the girls and gazed down on the dark water glittering in the sunshine. A breeze lifted her hair, sighing up the slope, welcome and refreshing. Perhaps it had been the heat and not Luke that had provoked her.

"It's wonderful," she said. "Just wonderful. Thank you for bringing us here."

The frown on his forehead vanished and he smiled, placing the basket beside them and shaking out a tartan rug. He stepped over to slacken Misty's girth, searching for a branch or a rock on which to tie her lead rope. There was nothing suitable so he gripped it in his fingers.

The girls joined them on the rug on the grass, uttering their approval of the lake but more interested in the picnic basket. Polly handed out sandwiches, Mrs Delaney's soft homemade bread oozing butter, filled with tomatoes, cucumber and thin slices of cheese. A bottle of lemonade for the girls to share, poured into metal cups and another bottle for her. Beer for Luke. His fingers brushed hers as she passed it to him.

Annie nudged Hannah and the two girls rose, taking their food and drink further away, huddled together in a more companionable way, their frustration spent, heads close together.

Their bickering rarely lasted long. Hannah looked at Polly and Luke, giggling.

Polly chewed in silence. She swallowed a mouthful and sipped her lemonade.

"You seemed annoyed with me. Do you dislike me now?" Luke asked.

She clicked her tongue. "Don't be foolish. I don't dislike you."

"You forgive me, then?"

"Forgive you for what? For prying behind my back?" Really, he was maddening. Persistent and almost childlike with that pleading tone.

"Yes. For meddling… for trying to discover your secrets."

"I have no secrets."

He took a couple of gulps of beer and wiped his mouth with the back of his hand. Polly passed him a sandwich and he bit into it. "You're quite frightening when you're angry."

"You're being ridiculous. I'll forgive you if you don't spy on me again."

"Thank you." His expression brightened. "Do you want to hear another secret?"

She stiffened. Not again. What else had that interfering priest told Brother Eugene about her?

"Oh, not about you, Polly. Not about you. I'll leave well alone there because I can see it offends you." He looked away and added, "No, this is a secret about someone else… I haven't even told Mrs Manning."

She stared at him. "Mrs Manning?"

"Yes, I haven't told her. I thought I would seek the advice of a sensible friend first. In case I am overreacting, you understand. A governess with strong discipline who will reprimand me if I'm overstepping my…"

"What is this secret?" Polly suppressed a smile. "Who are you talking about?"

Luke fumbled in his pocket, his fingers searching. "Another snippet of information from Brother Eugene who knows a missionary abroad."

"Abroad. Where?"

"South America." Luke pulled out a scrap of paper and unfolded it. A photograph. An old faded photograph. He held it out, pushing it into Polly's hesitant fingers.

"Does Brother Eugene know who these people are?" She looked at the figure of a priest; his neatly brushed hair; his collar and dark suit. He stood in the shade of a banana tree. The other man beside him, tall and fair, smiled at the camera, his hand resting on the shoulder of the priest in a confident manner. Her stomach quivered. Surely not? It couldn't be…

"One mile from the ravine where Gilbert Manning plunged into the water." Luke moved closer and she could feel the warmth of his breath on the back of her neck. "Do you recognize who it is?"

Her fingers shook and she had to grip the photograph with both hands. "I do… I think I do." She lifted her eyes to his. "Oh, Luke, it's him, isn't it? It's Robert Kingson."

Chapter Twenty-Three

"Who's that?" Hannah leaned over Luke's shoulder and reached for the photograph.

He snatched it away from her, pushing it deep into the pocket of his trousers. "Nothing of interest to you. I was just showing Miss Brady some of the priests at St Kevin's Reformatory."

"Luke was merely telling me about his time there with Brother Eugene," Polly said. The lie slipped off her tongue so easily but the last thing she wanted was Hannah's sharp eyes to spot Robert Kingson.

"The Missionary Oblates of Mary Immaculate." Luke smiled at the girl. "I've told you stories about my time in Glencree. It was difficult, especially when we had to dig our way through drifts of snow to get to the lavatories but I enjoyed playing in the school band. We had our own gas manufacturing plant to provide lighting. Are you ready to go home?" He gestured towards the heart-shaped lake below them, a bank of puffy cloud reflected in its depths and he added with a grin, "Or do you wish to bathe?"

Hannah's attention drifted from the photograph. "No, thank you. Indeed, I've no wish to swim there. It looks deep and cold in spite of the sunshine." She turned away and called to Annie who was still sitting on the rug, threading a long piece of heather through her fingers, a wistful expression on her pale features. Was she dreaming of Kingson? Poor Annie would no doubt learn that men could be fickle when she grew older and wiser.

The girl held up her hands. "I'm tired. Help me up, Hannah. Do we have to go down that mountainside again?"

"Yes, you lazy thing," Hannah replied.

Annie pointed. "Perhaps there's another way over there. See where those people are walking towards the woodland… wouldn't that be easier for us?"

Luke agreed and the two girls helped him and Polly fold the rug and pack the picnic boxes and bottles into the basket. Luke strapped it onto Misty's broad back, gave the pony a quick pat and pulled the reins to turn her head towards the stand of trees further down the hill.

"We'll try this way then, Annie, to save your legs. Are you feeling poorly? You've turned pale."

She shook her head. "Just tired, that's all. Could I ride on Misty in front of the picnic basket?"

Luke hoisted her up, instructing her to hold on to the pony's thick mane and they moved off down the slope, Hannah skipping in front and Polly bringing up the rear.

No further discussion about the photograph took place while Annie was with them. A crisis averted, Polly thought. The silence would give her time to consider what Luke had revealed. She stepped through the tufts of heather, the hem of her skirt caked with mud and her boots sodden as she followed behind Misty on the narrow trail etched into the slope by sheep.

What was Kingson doing in Brazil? He worked for a British pharmaceutical company so he could have been sent there to find the bark because there were bound to have been whisperings in the medical world of a new cure for fever; perhaps even typhoid fever.

Misty swished her long tail when flies landed on her solid rump. A cure for scarlet fever, Polly thought, which carried off many unfortunate infants and children, would be a medical breakthrough, would it not? A cure worth paying handsomely for. Worth killing for?

Either she or Luke would have to broach this subject with Mrs Manning. He was suspicious of the man, suspicious of anyone who got too close to his guardian. She'd felt he was overprotective at first but perhaps he had reason to be concerned. If word had got back to the pharmaceutical company about a miracle cure for fever, a cure in the possession of Gilbert Manning, Kingson might have been sent out there to persuade the plant hunter to hand over the bark.

The Brazilian bark might be worth a lot of money if it could be changed into a stable medicinal drug and patented for distribution. Enough money to make it worth doing away with Manning if he objected and refused to cooperate? The fine hairs on Polly's neck and arms rose. If Kingson had something to do with the plant hunter's death, that would make him dangerous if thwarted. She would have to approach her mistress and ask her advice.

Behind them, the sun slipped towards the mountain peak of Tonelagee. Mrs Manning had already hinted that her husband might have died an unnatural death.

How long had Luke known about the photograph? Another reason why he kept a close eye on his guardian.

They climbed down from the sheep track onto another path worn through the soft grass where patches of mud squelched underfoot. The pony stumbled, nearly tipping Annie over her head. The girl shrieked and asked to be helped down. She hurried away to join Hannah.

Luke led the pony down the track, clicking his tongue to encourage her and whispering endearments.

Why had he gone to such lengths to find out about Polly's home in Mayo? Suspicion? He must have been suspicious of her, a stranger coming to stay at Colgrannagh, and had attempted to find out all he could by enlisting Brother Eugene's help. At least he appeared to trust her more because he wouldn't have shown her the photograph otherwise. At that moment, Luke looked around and smiled.

"Are you managing to keep up with me?" he asked.

"I'm a country girl, don't forget. I was brought up near the mountains."

"I suspect if you were tired you would never admit to it."

She glanced away. Annie and Hannah were holding hands as they clambered over an outcrop of boulders, chattering together like contented sparrows, and for a moment Polly envied them. How she would have loved a sister when growing up! Not one like her aunt's daughter, with her scheming ways and mocking words, but a real companion with whom she could have shared experiences.

She became aware of Luke watching her and said, "I suppose I should tell you about the bark and Robert Kingson's questions."

His smile vanished. "What did he ask you?"

Polly moved closer to him, holding onto the pony's mane as she edged past on the narrow track, trying not to look down on the sheer drop to the lake below.

She explained how Kingson had come across them swimming in the river pool and had deliberately drawn her aside when they walked back to the house afterwards.

Luke's freckles joined across his forehead in a frown. "Tree bark for fevers... must be a tribal remedy. If it were worth money... if Kingson hoped he could make money from it... or the company that employs him..."

"Yes, and if Mrs Manning's husband refused to give it to him..."

"He must have been involved in his death. The priest in the photograph would remember a visitor from home. He was a missionary out there and he'd have known about cures used by the local people… he may also have had nuns working with him, nursing sisters who cared for the sick." Luke gripped Polly's arm. "We must warn her. We must warn Mrs Manning because Kingson is not to be trusted."

Hannah called out, "This fork in the track goes towards the woods. Would you like us to go that way?"

Luke released Polly's arm, peering into the distance. "The path through the woods might be a shorter way back to the Military Road. The other takes us further up the Glenmacnass River."

The shade was dark and cool when they walked under the trees, a welcome relief from the sunshine. Luke pointed out sessile oak and Scots pine, with a tangle of holly underneath.

Annie cried out with glee when a red squirrel leaped from the top of a pine and scrambled down the branches. "Look, look! How sweet!"

Polly watched its fluffy tail disappear into the pine needles above and Luke bent to examine a toadstool.

"What's that?" Hannah kneeled beside him and reached out.

He caught her fingers in his. "No! It's poisonous. Don't touch."

She scowled and snatched her hand away. Luke looked up at Polly and said, "The common inkcap, *Coprinus atramentarius*… see the shiny cap here and look at those in a group growing over there… the way they melt away and turn black."

"Poisonous?" Polly asked.

"When consumed with alcohol, yes, it is toxic. It used to be made into ink when boiled with water and cloves. There's also another inkcap, its outer flesh shaggier in appearance, which is edible and starts off looking like a long finger. They grow in grassland."

Annie twisted her mouth. "I don't think I'd like to eat it."

"Brother Eugene showed me an inkcap left on the kitchen table overnight," Luke said. "The next morning it was only a dark stain on the pine surface, having melted away overnight."

Hannah laughed. "I should like to see that. Mrs Manning showed me the border of poisonous plants in the garden. Foxgloves and monkshood. I thought they were exciting but she told me not to touch them."

Polly helped Hannah to her feet. "She told me the wild monkshood called *Aconitum napellus* was used around the world on tips of arrows for hunting. I don't think it's deadly poisonous but I'm not sure. It's better to be cautious. Come along, we still have a journey ahead of us and Misty is growing impatient."

The pony took a mouthful of grass in the clearing, pulling long strands of soft stems with her strong teeth, green saliva foaming in her mouth.

"The Brothers in St Kevin's knew what fungi to pick in the woods around Glencree." Luke nodded in the dappled light. "They were from France originally and they have great knowledge."

They continued on their way, the two girls skipping ahead playing a game of hide and seek, taking turns to slip behind tree trunks and leap out at each other, the silence of the wood pierced by their shrieks.

"May I make a suggestion," Luke asked, at last.

"Certainly," Polly replied.

"I believe it would be better if you mentioned Kingson's questions about the tree bark."

"To Mrs Manning?"

"Yes. Inform her that he's anxious to know the whereabouts of the bark."

"Perhaps he has already asked her."

"I don't believe so. If he had, he wouldn't have enlisted your assistance."

"Perhaps she doesn't have any bark." Her mistress might wonder why Polly suspected Kingson.

Luke swung Misty's reins over her head. "Come on, greedy pony, stop eating grass and move. Mrs Manning may not have the bark but he might believe she is hiding it from him and this is why he has approached you. He thinks he can charm you."

Polly frowned. "You think I find him charming?"

"I know that some women do. Annie seems to have fallen under his spell. He knows how to flatter… to cajole ladies in order to get what he wants."

"You're an expert, are you?" Polly replied, her tone sharper. Did Luke think she was a foolish young woman, like Annie, taken in by charming but insincere speeches?

Luke kept his eyes on the two girls in front, Hannah bounding ahead of Annie in her eagerness to find a safe hiding place, and he remained silent for a few minutes before taking one of Polly's hands in his. She pulled it away but not before he'd given it a quick squeeze.

He chuckled. "How nervous you are! I will not hurt you. Why are you afraid?"

She flushed. "I'm afraid of nothing."

"Well then…" He shook his head. "Don't be afraid. Summon your courage and inform your mistress about Kingson's questions."

"But she knows you better. Why can't you do this?"

"I don't have the same opportunity as you…besides, he didn't approach me. He asked you." He added, "I've an ominous feeling about him, I have. If Mrs Manning is in danger… if anything bad happens to her, wouldn't you feel remorse? Please, you must do this, Polly, you must… not for me but for her."

Chapter Twenty-Four

The past – June 1895

Butterflies floated into the air when Claudia's skirt brushed against lavender plants spilling onto the path, their purple flower spikes alive with the hum of bees. Polly followed behind and hoped she would be able to broach the subject of Kingson and the tree bark while they were alone. Two days had passed since the excursion to Lough Ouler and her mistress had been away from home for many hours, a number of children with whooping cough requiring her attention in the cabins further up the mountain.

Claudia turned to face her, dark hair shining in the warm light. "My dear, I meant to tell you before but I've been so busy, I'm impressed with how well the children understand their plants. Even Solomon was able to recite the many advantages of lavender. You're an inspiration to them."

Polly thanked her. "The girls are showing interest and Solomon is eager to please." She suspected that Annie wished to appear knowledgeable in front of Kingson, but even Hannah suggested they should learn to mix potions from herbs.

"Wonderful, how wonderful to hear that," Claudia said, reaching out a hand and resting it on Polly's arm. "You're a natural teacher and it's also your enthusiasm for botany, I'm certain of it. Our last governess showed little interest and the children became lost in a fog of apathy but," she added, pointing at the seat under the fig tree, "you've changed all that. I'm so grateful you've encouraged them to learn… to appreciate how important plants are."

They sat beside each other, Claudia's soft voice trailing away, as she bent to pluck a sprig of rosemary and hold it to her nose. "Rosemary is a useful herb. I use it to rinse my hair as well as in a salve to help painful muscles. Quite extraordinary how successful herbal treatments can be for minor ailments. When I'm permitted to study medicine, I won't abandon my most useful plants."

Polly took a breath, inhaling the mingling scents around them. "Mrs Manning, I wonder if I might ask you a question?" Luke would be waiting for her report, growing more impatient by the day.

"Certainly," Claudia replied. "What is it? Nothing troubling you, I hope?"

A bumblebee droned in front of Polly's face before it dropped on a bunch of chives bobbing at the edge of the gravel.

Polly turned to her. "Nothing troubling me, I assure you. Nothing at all…" Although that wasn't strictly true, but she needed to appear calm and logical.

"The trip to Lough Ouler went well, I gather." Claudia smoothed her skirt with a hand. "The girls were delighted with their day out, the sunshine, the picnic, the view… they've told me about it many times since. You enjoyed it too, I hope?"

"I did, thank you. Luke was an excellent guide and very careful of us all."

Her employer's dark eyes held hers. "Eamon mentioned that Luke left him behind with the cob at a cabin. I'm surprised, I must say. Was that a good idea, Polly?"

"I beg your pardon, ma'am, I didn't realize that Eamon was supposed to accompany us to the top of the mountain. He had an enjoyable few hours playing cards and drinking with his friend. Luke said he would have found our company tedious."

"Was it your idea or Luke's to leave Eamon behind?" Claudia asked in a more reproving tone.

Polly blushed. "Not mine, I assure you. I had nothing to do with it." She had no wish to get Luke into trouble and added, "I don't understand the harm."

Claudia looked away. "I see no harm but if others heard about you… the likes of Dr Fitzpatrick and his cronies… or some of the more matronly types in the village. They wouldn't approve of a young woman and a young man left alone with two children up a mountain. That would really set tongues wagging. I sent Eamon with you as a chaperon, truth be told."

So that was it. She was worried about a scandal. Unlike her, out of character, but Kingson might have brought back some ridiculous tale from narrow-minded gossips in an attempt to discredit Luke.

"I beg your pardon. I didn't think to…"

Her employer frowned. "I don't suppose Luke thought about it either. He can be… rash, a trifle foolhardy at times. An enthusiastic young man but sometimes he needs to keep his impulses in check."

Polly looked away. A red admiral butterfly fluttered its wings on a chive flower, basking in the sun. Was this a gentle warning? To be careful of Luke? She stammered another apology.

"Please don't be distressed," Claudia said. "I trust him but I don't wish to appear careless in your father's opinion."

Her father! Did she intend to tell him?

Claudia added, "Your father would not be impressed with me." She shot a look at Polly before snapping off another sprig of rosemary and plucking the leaves from the slender stem. "Luke is attractive, isn't he? He has such an ardent, winning nature that it might be difficult to resist…"

Polly stiffened, willing away the flush that scorched her cheeks. "Oh, but I… I mean, he is a nice young man, but I…" She added with vehemence, "My aunt brought me up to be careful of men, I assure you."

Claudia patted her arm. "That is sensible. I can't help but feel a responsibility for you. Luke can allow his imagination and his feelings to run away sometimes and you'll understand that caution is necessary. He wouldn't be a suitable match for you, I'm afraid. I know him well, and I'm fond of him… very fond of him, but he wouldn't suit you."

Mortified, Polly made no reply. Claudia had never attempted to put her on her guard before. Perhaps Luke had misbehaved in the past and another young woman had been swayed by his persuasive powers.

"Mrs Manning, have you been in touch with my father?" she asked. "I have written to him to tell him how I am progressing but have only received one letter in return."

"I've heard from him several times… a letter only last week." She frowned, turning her face away.

"Oh, did he say… was he well?"

"Perfectly well, but he mentioned… he gave me quite startling news," Claudia said, "but I'll let him explain about that. Now, perhaps you would like to ask me that question you mentioned earlier."

"Yes. I… well, it doesn't concern Luke. It's about Mr Kingson." She hesitated, taking a breath before blundering on. "I wanted to mention that… that he wanted me to find out…"

Her mistress smiled. "Please continue. What does Mr Kingson wish to know?"

"He mentioned a… and I'm afraid that I didn't understand about it so I decided I should ask you…"

Claudia's tone sounded gentle and encouraging. "Why, Polly, you understand that I will always try to answer your questions to the best of my ability, don't you? Why such hesitancy? I fear my reprimand about Luke has upset you. Please, don't be anxious… pray continue."

"Mr Kingson… he asked me about a… bark from a tree… bark that your husband brought back."

"Bark?"

"Yes, from a special tree, presumably."

"From Brazil?" Claudia asked, as the butterfly on the chives fluttered from one purple bauble to another.

"Yes… that's what he said. I didn't know anything about it but I remember you mentioned a rare medicinal plant your husband came across."

"Perhaps he's talking about a substance similar to that taken from the cinchona tree, which has been used to treat malaria since the 1600s. Is that the one you mean?"

Polly remained silent.

"If so, my husband certainly discovered a bark used by a tribe for controlling high temperatures and sweating. Yellow fever is rampant there, spread by the bite of an infected mosquito."

"I believe that must be the one."

"Quinine has been derived from the cinchona for centuries and used to alleviate the symptoms of malaria… the headaches and chills. If a new discovery could help with typhus…"

Polly wondered if she was deliberately distracting her; leading her away from Kingson. Luke appeared in her mind, urging her to seek an answer. "I've no idea but… would what Mr Manning found in Brazil help against typhus?"

Claudia frowned. "It might control the fever but typhus is a deadly disease and epidemics sweep through many countries. Any breakthrough in medical treatment for contagious fevers would be a blessing."

"And valuable too?" Polly held her breath. "You said before that..."

"Valuable for the medical profession, you mean? Yes, of course. If a cure for fever could be derived from the bark, it would surely be a worthwhile investment. I'm sure they would be grateful for such a breakthrough. Scientists are already making great strides with willow."

An opportunity dangled and Polly grasped it. "Mr Kingson's company… the company for which he works... would people there be interested in such a find?"

The other woman stroked the lace at the end of her sleeves. "Has he told you about his employer? A man who used to work for a large American veterinary business… and, more recently, human medicines. He is ambitious, very ambitious indeed."

"I understood that to be the case when Mr Kingson…"

A smile settled on Claudia's lips. "Poor Robert has to succeed in convincing the local physicians… to persuade them to try new patented remedies. Many are reluctant to change… those who are stubborn like Dr Fitzpatrick, an old-fashioned man who believed my father too ahead of his time. And as for me…" She laughed and leaned towards Polly to whisper, "I often suspect Dr Fitzpatrick imagines my work akin to that of a witch."

"Surely not?"

She nodded. "He does. He has a poor comprehension of medicinal plants and once threatened to take a legal case against me for poisoning my patients. Ah, you look doubtful but it happened. He's droll, very careful not to sound entirely serious when he speaks to me about it but I feel he's watching and waiting."

A knot of indignation twisted in Polly's chest. "Dr Fitzpatrick perceives you to be a threat. He fears you are better than him, I'm sure of it. You have more success than him! Why, only the other day, your mother told me…"

"Kind Mama will always take my side… and you too, Polly. How sweet of you to defend me."

"Yes, but Mr Kingson…"

"Robert, unlike Dr Fitzpatrick, understands how modern medicines can be formulated from plants. Take the willow bark I mentioned earlier, for instance, which has an interesting history."

"For headaches and fever?"

"Yes, indeed. It was used by the Ancient Greeks. A Scottish physician recently used a compound from it most successfully to treat rheumatic fever. I hope I'm not boring you, my dear, but it is really most exciting because now, only this decade, a pharmaceutical division of a well-known company is to run further trials on salicylic acid derived from willow," Claudia replied, leaning towards Polly. "There is talk of its great potential and, if its quality and properties can be stabilized, that will certainly be an important step forward."

If her employer were a man, Polly thought, she would be working in laboratories researching new medicines for she was as intelligent, if not more intelligent, than many men. Instead she had to endure derisive comments from boorish physicians like Dr Fitzpatrick.

"So," Polly summoned courage and continued, "did Mr Manning send back a similar bark to you for safekeeping? This is what Mr Kingson asked me to find out."

Claudia's fine eyebrows rose. "He asked you to enquire about that, did he? But I don't understand…"

If only Luke were there to help her explain. That photograph with the priest. The man was identical to Kingson. What had really happened to her husband? A wave of inadequacy overcame her when she saw doubt replacing interest in her employer's expression.

She hurried on. "Perhaps… perhaps Mr Kingson's employers will pay you well for the tree bark."

"Oh yes, I do hope so because Gilbert sent back a small quantity of it for analysis. We're calling this a joint venture."

"A joint venture?"

Claudia got to her feet, tossing away the bare stem of rosemary and reaching for her little gold pocket watch. "Is that the time? I have to visit Mrs O'Leary in the village, the postmistress. One of her earaches." She brushed the remaining leaves of herb from her skirt. "A joint venture between Robert and me. It's exciting, Polly, so exciting! He has promised to present me to his employers in London and assures me that they are impatient to examine Gilbert's discovery. You are quite correct about its possible worth for, if they decide it important enough to merit further testing, it might be extremely valuable in the future. I'm grateful to dear Robert for encouraging me."

Polly remembered the frown on Luke's face as he pressed the photograph into her hands and his suspicions. She couldn't leave the conversation like this… had to say something. "But, Mrs Manning, forgive me please if I offend… can you trust him? Can you trust Mr Kingson?" She wondered why the man had asked her to find the bark if he'd already discussed its value with her mistress. It didn't make sense.

Claudia drew in a sharp breath and swung round to face her. "Trust him? Why, Polly, what a strange thing to say. Of course I trust him. I trust him implicitly because he has my best interests at heart. Robert Kingson has asked me to marry him."

Chapter Twenty-Five

The present – September 2022

I found Daniel in the kitchen with a wooden spoon poised over a stainless-steel saucepan, peering through half-moon glasses at a tattered cookery book perched on top of the toaster.

He looked up and smiled. "Ah, Fiona, how did your meeting with Stephen go?"

"I think it went pretty well, to be honest. He gave me a diary written by the governess and some letters. He's wondering when I'll be able to repay him with information about the skeleton."

"Ha! That sounds like old Stephen. He's searching for nuggets of gossip about the forensic team's discoveries, no doubt."

"Have you received any information back from them?" I sat on a pine chair, Archie slumping at my feet as if exhausted from his terrifying ordeal with Millicent.

"I asked the local sergeant in the village yesterday. Their work is still ongoing and will take time. All sorts of tests. I'm sure they'll uncover everything eventually. Carbon dating and DNA tests are sophisticated now. Perhaps they'll use me to find a match."

"I'll have to offer some sort of research detail to Stephen. Perhaps there's information about Polly Brady in Claudia's journal… though what I've read so far is all to do with ailments and treatments."

Daniel kept his eyes on the saucepan. "Help yourself to coffee. I'm battling with a hollandaise sauce here." He liked cooking, had taken to it after his wife died and found solace in it, he explained. It was a challenge and a way to occupy his mind, an escape from the waves of grief and the pressures of being a heart surgeon.

"No coffee, thanks. I had several cups at the restaurant with Stephen." I reached down to stroke Archie's nose. He twitched in his sleep and whimpered. "I've borrowed an interesting embroidery of the herb garden, stitched by the governess. The proprietor bought it at Solomon's auction and his niece hired… er… lent it to me. I think both you and Tobie would like to see it."

He squinted at me. "Oh yes? I'd like to see that… Claudia was first and foremost a plantswoman."

"I'll show you later." I continued with a groan, "I've just been accosted by Millicent. She wants me to stop your research project and leave."

"She's been on about that all week to me. You didn't agree, I hope?"

"No, I didn't. I want to keep going with it. No intention of leaving now, just as we're beginning to get somewhere."

Another chuckle as he stirred the contents of the pan. "And stay you shall. Stay you shall. We won't let Madam Millicent have it all her way. Poor Kenny. Why doesn't he see what he's going to marry? A domineering wife, that's what she'll be and the unfortunate lad will be trampled underfoot. Oh well… so be it. Can't say I haven't warned him often enough but he won't listen. Too blinded by love, I suppose."

"Too frightened to back out now," I replied with a laugh. I'd been accused of being bossy by my ex-husband. A bossy teacher, Dominic used to call me and my mother agreed. They hadn't met Millicent though. What would have happened if Millicent had married Dominic? Perhaps she'd have sorted out his gambling problems and forced him into passive submission. She might have made more of a success of the marriage than I had.

"Oh dear, this hollandaise looks like it's going to curdle." He pulled the saucepan from the heat and stirred again. "That's it, that's it. I think I've just saved its life." He glanced at me. "Let's just ignore Millicent. The more stressed she gets, the more she interferes in the lives of others. She's convinced I would be better off in a care home… my diabetes, you see. She suspects I'm going to collapse and die one of these days. Forget her and tell me about Stephen's great-aunt."

Poor Daniel; one of the problems of growing old was unsympathetic relations. "Stephen says Polly was brought up in Mayo by a seamstress in a village near the coast. She was illegitimate, the daughter of the local landlord's son and a servant in his house."

I imagined the young girl leaving home with her baggage, taking the Royal Mail coach from Westport to Dublin. Or perhaps she'd gone by train.

Daniel's voice brought me back to the present. "If Polly lived here in the late nineteenth century with Claudia, she must have seen and heard a lot of family goings-on. Governesses always did, part-family part-servant as they were. They lived their lives between the two classes." He leaned over the hob and cracked two eggs into a pan of simmering water. "I'm making Eggs Benedict. You're going to eat with me."

"Thanks, but I'm not…"

He shook his head. "No excuses. I can't possibly eat on my own in front of you. How impolite that would be!"

"Okay, thank you."

"I've been reading through your file and notes," he said. "I have to admit, Fiona, the accident that happened to Claudia's husband Gilbert in Brazil… falling into a ravine there… was strange. I looked up the internet and plant hunters from Britain followed the expanding empire into far-flung corners of the globe but South America attracted more continental plantsmen… the Germans, the French. What was Gilbert Manning doing there?"

"Do you think he was searching for something in particular?"

"There's a reference in one of Manning's letters to a cure for fever. Did you notice that?"

I stared at him. "Fever? I thought he just collected the seeds and cuttings of decorative plants for gardens as most plant hunters did in Victorian times. Medicinal plants were much earlier. Are you talking about medicinal?"

"I am. I suppose I noticed that because of my background. He doesn't say much about it but I got the impression that he was searching for a specific plant." Daniel lifted the poached eggs with a spatula, placing them on slices of toast and pouring the hollandaise sauce over them. He sprinkled chopped-up parsley and pushed a plate towards me. Archie woke up, his nose twitching.

"Thanks, that looks delicious."

"We know where he was based because of the address in the letter," Daniel continued. "What exactly was he hoping to find?"

An idea popped into my mind. My brother Anthony was a plantsman; he'd worked in botanic gardens across Europe and had even done a two-years' stint in Jardim Botânico in Rio de Janeiro. He might be able to help me about the area where Gilbert had stayed, or might have contacts out there who would be able to find out more.

"You seem inspired," Daniel said. "Is that my hollandaise or have you had a brainwave?"

"A brainwave… actually both. The eggs taste amazing."

"Don't let my culinary skills distract you. Please, tell me your brainwave."

'My brother worked in the botanic gardens in Brazil. It's just occurred to me that he might know something useful or might be able to help me find out who to talk to."

"Excellent. Use my phone and give him a call."

"Probably best if I email. Anthony is hard to get hold of and hopeless at answering his mobile. I haven't spoken to him for several months."

"Your mother's son." Daniel gave me a smile and tossed a corner of toast to Archie, who swallowed it with a mixture of gratitude and guilt.

"You shouldn't feed him from the table."

"I'm sorry. He always looks at me with such an appealing expression. Your mother, yes, the adventurer. We never knew what she'd do next."

We ate the eggs, Daniel telling me a story about my mother. She was always the impulsive one in our family. Poor Dad, so placid and down-to-earth all his life; mystified by her leaving him until the day he died. Not his fault, I often told him. She always claimed she was a free spirit and I knew, once an idea was lodged in her head, she would move on. No wonder she'd always thought me too conservative. Jessica told me I compensated by having the sense of responsibility my feckless mother lacked.

A shadow fell across the floor and Archie growled. Millicent's face was at the window, her hand raised. "Hey, Daniel, I want a word."

I hurried to clip on the terrier's lead and muttered, "I'll leave you now and email my brother. See you later." I escaped by the back door as Millicent came in the garden one.

As I walked towards the door in the wall, Tobie appeared from the back of the cottage. "Hey," he called. "*Madame* the Dragon is breathing flames. Watch out!"

I laughed at the expression on his sun-tanned face. "She's about to harass poor Daniel now. I've already had a lecture today so I'm avoiding her."

He fell into step beside me and we strolled along the path towards the front entrance of the main house. The side windows were still shuttered, hiding the builders' debris. What had gone on there in the late-Victorian era? What secrets lay hidden behind its walls? I'd read through so many of the letters belonging to Claudia Manning in the schoolroom and nothing significant had jumped out of them. The governess had to hold the key to the past. She was there, a witness in the house. I would start her diary that evening.

"She was in bad form… Millicent?" Tobie asked.

"Yes. She tried to push me out of my job here."

He whistled air through his teeth. "That's bad… that's bad. I hope you didn't…"

"I didn't."

"Good. I would…"

I said, "You would what?"

He shrugged, raising both hands. "I would miss you. It's quiet here." He added with a laugh, "I would miss that badly behaved dog too. I would miss Archie." He turned his face away as he stroked the Jack Russell who, on hearing his name, had jumped up on Tobie's legs and was licking his hands with affection.

"Well, thanks." I decided to make light of his remarks. "Don't worry, I'm not going to allow Millicent to have her way. Besides, I need the money right now."

"Your divorce?"

I groaned. "I'm being bombarded with solicitor's letters from my husband… from Dominic. He thinks he's entitled to half of the money from the sale of my dad's house even though he never lived there. It's difficult at the moment."

"Where is he, this profligate husband of yours?"

I liked Tobie's use of language. The half-mocking tone, the dancing light in his eyes. In fact, I liked Tobie. I liked him a lot. Too much, perhaps, for my own good.

"Dominic is in Dublin," I replied. "He's staying with a friend of his but he wants an apartment of his own and that means he expects me to pay for it... or at least help him with the deposit."

"Doesn't he have a job?"

"Yes, but that's never enough for Dominic. He always spends all of his wages at the end of the month betting on slow horses and online poker. Leopards, as you probably know, never change their spots. I can't see how he will ever manage to support himself. My mother told me I spoiled him... looked after him too well. She might have been right, much as I hate to admit that."

Tobie placed a hand on my shoulder. A fleeting squeeze before he stepped away. "Poor Fiona. You must extricate yourself from this gambler and ignore his demands."

"Even if I end up in court? It's not easy, Tobie. Not easy at all because he's so determined. He's desperate, I suppose, and he realizes only too well that I'm his last hope."

"You're not his last hope. The man is an *imbécile*. Ignore him. He has to grow up some day."

I grinned at his indignation. It was kind of him to show an interest in me and my boring problems.

"Marriage is difficult. Divorce is even harder," I said.

He shrugged again. "Sometimes when people are young, they are too keen to get married and later there are difficulties."

Was he talking about my marriage or his? I glanced down at the dog, trotting at my heels, blissfully oblivious to the murky waters in which our human lives drifted.

When I made no comment, he continued, "I mentioned before... the incompatibility in my marriage. My wife who loves Paris, and me who prefers life in the country. And our son... caught between two adults... entangled in a mess he can't comprehend. But I must try... I must try to make things right. I can't give up."

"You can't give up," I agreed. "You have to try to make it

work for his sake unless…"

He shot a look at me. "Unless?"

"Unless you realize that your son is happier without conflict in his life. Parents arguing all the time is not good… not a good way to bring up a child. I have no children, so it's easy for me to preach…"

He raised his voice. "You think I don't know this? I think about it a lot."

"I'm sorry."

"No need to apologize. Not your problem, Fiona."

I decided to change the subject. "I'm going to email my brother about a tree in Brazil. Daniel and I are wondering if Claudia Manning's husband was sent out there to find it… bring it back for his employers in England. He mentions it briefly in a letter to his wife. I need to get my brother to find out all he can about plant hunters in that part of the world in the late 1800s. With luck, someone might have met Gilbert and might know the truth."

Interest glimmered on his face. "That will keep you out of Millicent's way for a while. Perhaps you should get amnesia and forget how to speak English… like me. It's the only way to avoid her, I tell you. Goodbye, my friend. I'll see you soon." He waved a hand and disappeared round the side of the house towards the back yard where he kept his gardening tools.

I watched him go. Definitely an attractive man but I would be a fool to venture down that path. No, I would continue up the staircase and along the dark passage to the old schoolroom, where I would open up my laptop and send a cheerful enquiring email to my long-lost brother, pleading for his assistance.

Chapter Twenty-Six

The present – September 2022

I enjoyed the peace in the schoolroom in the evening, the builders usually leaving at five o'clock, putting aside their hammers and persistent drills, so that the rooms below in the turmoil of renovation lay silent, the big house almost sighing with relief. Millicent often watched their departure with barely concealed irritation; if she'd had her way, they would work until midnight.

That night, it meant I could focus on Polly Brady without interruption. I yearned to read her diary but first I would send Anthony an email. I selected his name and clicked, sitting for a few minutes and wondering what to say. I typed a few lines, asking how he was and outlining Daniel's research project.

The most important information I required was whether Gilbert had discovered a new cure for fever. Surely that would be easy for my brother to find out? If so, there would be records in the Botanic Gardens and the tree might even still be growing there. I added that any details about the plant hunter would be appreciated.

I signed off with a few cheerful lines about our mother and her latest antics, and asked him to get back to me as soon as possible. Anthony had always needed a nudge to get things done and, with Millicent breathing down my neck, it was vital I made progress.

Box files of correspondence lay on the scarred wooden table. A child had gouged out a hole near where my left hand lay. Perhaps a boy with a penknife bored with mathematics and spelling. Could it have been Solomon? Or Luke perhaps, the boy from the reform school in Glencree, who'd been sent there by a heartless judge for stealing food. I picked up a letter I'd come across the day before from Claudia, addressed to a friend in Derbyshire, an unfinished account in her neat handwriting and never dispatched:

"Colgrannagh,
September 1886

My dear Lucinda,

I mentioned in my last letter to you that I would send an update on our new arrival, my father's latest protégé, a thirteen-year-old boy from St Kevin's Reformatory. Luke is older than the others when adopted by Papa but shows kindness towards Annie and Hannah.

Mama thinks he's a wild boy at heart, with his shock of golden hair, but he certainly has an affinity with the Wicklow landscape and its creatures. Luke delights in helping Eamon in the garden and even Misty, our strong-minded Connemara pony, will do anything for the boy.

Our latest governess reports him to be intelligent but lacking concentration but I suspect her method of instruction is to blame. The children haven't warmed to her; a woman with airs and graces from Dublin. I don't think she'll stay long. She tells me that Luke's eyes flit to the windows, watching the birds fly from tree to tree as he fidgets on the bench. He can name every garden bird, thanks to a book Gilbert gave him for Christmas. Such a thoughtful gift and one that…"

At least Gilbert had been at home for Christmas that year but I knew from other correspondence that his travels took him away for months on end. Not easy for his wife or the children.

Claudia was interrupted at that point because the sentence trailed away and the letter was cast aside. I laid it back in the box file and glanced out of the nearest window. Luke would have gazed at those oaks, their trunks ancient and gnarled in the late afternoon sun. Rooks perched in the top branches; flocks gathering for their sociable evening assembly, their loud gregarious caws rising in the cooling air. I imagined the boy longing to be free from the drudgery of mathematics and grammar; to be able to run across the lawn to the woods. What had happened to Luke and the other children? Where had their lives taken them?

A tingle ran down my spine when the room darkened but it was only a bank of cloud covering the sun. As the light faded, I thought I glimpsed a figure near the window, hands holding onto the middle bar of the sash, forehead pressing against the glass.

I shook my head and smiled. So much for fancies: I had work to do.

I walked to the end of the bookcases beside the door. I didn't believe in ghosts or spirits from other realms but sometimes my imagination took flight. My mother, not in the least creative, and a woman who acted mostly on irrational instinct, used to tell me how I'd invented other worlds when I was a child; worlds that seemed so real to me that they reduced me to laughter or tears and left her baffled. I couldn't remember and used to suspect her of making it up for dramatic effect to amuse other visitors at the time.

I wondered how long it would take my brother to reply to my email. He often disappeared for weeks and wasn't a slave of the internet or social media; never felt the pull to connect with his family on a regular basis. He'd been more distant since Dad died, perhaps feeling guilty about not returning early enough to spend time with him those last months when I lived in our old home and made sure our father ate, drank and washed at regular intervals. I'd taken Archie for walks when Dad no longer had the strength and, after his owner passed away, the terrier attached himself to me. How could I have even thought of finding another home for Archie? He'd soon won me round.

He was a comfort; an affectionate, demanding little pal who kept me company through the sadness. The Jack Russell had imagination and flights of fancy too. For weeks afterwards, he often woke and sat up, staring at my father's empty chair. Did he see him? Or was he just remembering him? Only Archie knew the answer to that.

The dog was lying asleep under the window, soaking up the last warmth of sunlight. I moved along the bookshelf on my left, which held volumes of poetry and natural history. Collected poems of William Wordsworth, Lord Byron and Coleridge. Had Polly read these to the children? I pulled down the Wordsworth and opened a page:

For oft, when on my couch I lie
In vacant or in pensive mood,
They flash upon that inward eye
Which is the bliss of solitude;
And then my heart with pleasure fills,
And dances with the daffodils.

The final verse of *I Wandered Lonely as a Cloud.* The inward eye was an expressive way of putting it. My inward eye had seen the shadow of Luke Manning at the window.

I replaced the poetry volume and returned to the desk and leafed through the pages of the children's journal, their game, as they called it. Solomon was too young to write much but he had been given the job of watching the kitchen. I read several short sentences in his handwriting about what was planned for dinner and what type of cake Cook had baked. A chocolate cake had been underlined several times, so perhaps he liked that one best. As well as Mrs Delaney, there was also a housemaid mentioned. She was the one who liked drinking sherry from the decanter when no one was watching, when she was supposed to be cleaning out the fireplace in the drawing room. Solomon wrote:

> *"I was behind a curtain. Saw Lizzie drink sherry. She drank two glasses."*

I wondered about the housemaid. Was this the servant the villagers told stories about? The one who'd come to a suspicious end while living in the house? I made a note of her name and tried searching the internet. Nothing, but that wasn't surprising when I didn't know her surname. No unusual death mentioned in 1895 at Colgrannagh, in fact nothing whatsoever about Colgrannagh.

Hannah, the next youngest, had the task of following Claudia's mother Dora Burroughs and also the governess Miss Walsh, who was replaced by Miss Brady in March 1895. Hannah's handwriting was large and flamboyant with swirled loops:

> *"Mrs Burroughs spent the afternoon asleep in her armchair in her bedroom. She was reading 'Sonnets from the Portuguese'. Miss Walsh says they are famous romantic poems written by Elizabeth Browning. I didn't know that Mrs Burroughs liked romantic books. I expect silly Miss Walsh does. I crept up close, for she was snoring loudly, and took three of her peppermints from the table beside her bed. It wasn't the same as stealing because she often offers them to me but I won't tell Mrs Manning."*

I smiled. Hannah came across as brave but innocent. Other reports of hers revealed the older lady scolding the maid in a kindly manner and slipping Hannah a treat, usually sweets or biscuits, if she woke up and caught the young spy in the act.

Annie's reports, in contrast, were detailed and painstakingly neat, with no ink smudges or spelling mistakes like those blotting the accounts of Solomon and Hannah. I imagined her looking up the dictionary before writing the words, anxious to be correct and in dread of being thought ignorant. Nowadays Annie might be a lawyer or an accountant. In those days, who knew what happened to her? Married off to a businessman perhaps and obliged to cook for his clients. Annie, in her reports, followed any visitors to the house, as well as keeping an eye on Claudia. Many pages were filled with her immaculate notes.

I turned the pages. The girl mentioned Claudia's patients who came to the house for herbal treatments as well as the times she was allowed to accompany Mrs Manning on trips to local cottages. In one account, she outlined how her guardian had washed a deep cut on a man's leg, applying herbal ointment and a bandage. In another a boy with a high fever lay sweating in an unaired room. Annie had been sent back to wait in the carriage outside and reflected later that he might have been suffering from a contagious disease. I spotted one entry dated June 1895:

> *"Today I watched Mrs Manning meet Mr Kingson in the physic garden. He looked so handsome with a fine wool coat and a burgundy necktie. They walked along the paths and Mrs Manning stopped to point out different plants to him. Perhaps they were discussing their uses for healing. I wish he would smile at me the way he smiles at her. Hannah will laugh when she sees this. She doesn't care for Mr Kingson. She thinks he's…"*

The next three words were crossed out and scored through with obvious emotion until the ink obliterated all trace of them and leaked onto the next page.

Annie had a crush on Kingson. The poor girl had to watch the man's flirtation with Claudia and yearned for him to notice her. A teenage girl's nightmare.

Reports in the notebook from Luke were few. He was older and probably had less opportunity to carry out covert and rather childish activities. His paragraphs were less tidy than Annie's and much shorter:

> *"I watched Robert Kingson in the village today. He was with Dr Fitzpatrick outside the public house. They are cohorts, those two, and not to be trusted."*

Why didn't he trust them?

I flicked over more pages. Only a few were left before the end of the book. No more reports from Luke but Hannah had written out details of Claudia going for a drive with Kingson in the carriage and Solomon had spotted Cook baking scones and shortbread for Annie's birthday tea. Annie's lengthy lines brought The Game notes to an abrupt conclusion that made me wonder if they had written more in other books and hidden them away:

> *"Luke and Hannah say I must write this down although I find it most difficult. Luke says it is important. Today I witnessed an upsetting scene in the physic garden. I followed Mrs Manning and Mr Kingson across the lawn and hid behind the oak tree near the gate. Mr Kingson and Mrs Manning were close by and I could hear what they were saying.*
>
> *She said something about his previous question and that she had an answer for him. His face was all pink and glowing, as*

if he were excited, and I felt my poor heart lurch. Mr Kingson replied that he was anxious to hear what she would say and I held my breath. She smiled and took his hand. She said she had decided to consider his proposal of marriage!

Oh, my Lord, what a shock! I thought I was going to be sick on the lawn or that I would faint and I had to get away before they saw me. I ran back to the house and told Hannah. She said to tell Luke as soon as possible because he will be angry. Hannah is correct. He is angry but I don't know why. I expect it is because he dislikes Mr Kingson so.

Luke now says we must make a plan. We must try to stop the engagement and save Mrs Manning from Mr Kingson. I don't understand why but I have written this down."

I reread the girl's words. Claudia had received a proposal from Kingson. A friend of the local doctor's, it seemed, and not trusted by Luke.

I opened my notebook and consulted the lines I'd written about Claudia, where I'd noted the date of her birth, her death, her burial in the graveyard beside her father. I hadn't found any mention of a second marriage. The death notice in the newspaper decades later stated she was the widow of Gilbert Manning.

Shadows were deepening outside, the daylight slipping away and the rooks growing silent in their nests in the oaks. Who was Kingson? What had become of him? I thought of the skeleton taken away in the undertaker's hearse. Could it be him?

Perhaps Polly Brady's diary would divulge more. I opened the little book and turned instinctively to the last page. Excitement coursed through me for there, in her rounded and rather girlish hand, was the final paragraph:

"I can never write of what has happened because I dread the consequences. A difficult decision lies ahead of me and

I pray, with God's help, that my conscience will help me choose the correct path."

Chapter Twenty-Seven

The present – September 2022

I was sitting on the bench beside the old fig tree in the herb garden reading more of Polly's diary when the breeze gathered strength. Although usually a sheltered spot that caught the last rays of the sun, I saw the treetops above the wall shivering in the wind.

Daniel had warned me that the weather forecast predicted a gale storming in from the southwest; the first I'd experienced in the Wicklow mountains because the late summer had been unusually balmy for Ireland.

The diary lay open on my lap and I continued to read about her trip to Lough Ouler with Luke and the two girls:

> *"An enjoyable day out. The girls were excited and paid little heed to their lessons yesterday. Poor Solomon was distressed at being left behind and not even chess with his grandmother consoled him. He loves chess and is quite a little genius at the game."*

Polly described the journey to Laragh in the borrowed carriage and up the Old Military Road. I had to search for Lough Ouler on the internet because I'd never come across it.

Still only accessible by foot and probably much the same as in June 1895 when Polly wrote:

> *"The lake was similar to a romantic sapphire pendant and most definitely heart-shaped when viewed from the ridge above. We reached it within two hours on our climb from Glenmacnass Waterfall. The girls were tired and Luke seemed worried that we were not enjoying ourselves but the dark blue jewel lying below us took our breath away."*

Polly seemed both fascinated by Luke but also irritated by him. Perhaps the beginning of an attraction that she was trying to resist, reluctant to succumb. Her sentences brought the scene alive: the trek up the mountainside, Annie and Hannah complaining of fatigue and Polly anxious not to get too close to Luke.

Then came the bombshell when the girls had moved further away to rest. The young man produced a photograph of a priest in Brazil with a tall fair-haired man standing beside him. She recognized him immediately. I reread her words:

> *"Oh, what a shock! This man, standing so companionably beside the priest with a hand resting on his shoulder and smiling in his usual charming manner, was Robert Kingson."*

Kingson. There was the name again. What was he doing in Brazil and in the same area as Gilbert Manning? Perhaps Luke was right to be suspicious. Did Kingson know what happened to the plant hunter? Was he involved in some way?

The wind caught the pages of the diary and they flapped like a live creature. It was then that I noticed Archie had gone. The terrier had been lying asleep by my feet. Damn! I glanced around the garden but there was no sign of him sniffing along the newly planted lavender hedge.

Tobie had also disappeared from where he'd been half an hour earlier over by the door leading to the lawn. I checked the time on my mobile. Six o'clock already. Perhaps Archie, bored with my absorbing research, decided to follow him.

I remembered that Kenny and Millicent were organizing a retirement dinner for the president of a golf club that evening and *Madame* had asked Kenny to pass on the message that neither I nor my dog were welcome to attend. That ruled out going back to the house until later. Daniel wouldn't be in his cottage because he was going to the golf dinner.

The first thing I had to do was find Archie. And fast. He might be in the throng of local dignitaries, seeking attention and food. The thought sent me running towards the gate and along the path to the house, Polly's diary clutched in my hand. I should have clipped on his lead and tied him to the bench. How had I been so careless? I silently cursed the little wretch for sneaking off without making a sound.

Kenny was standing at the top of the front steps, a clipboard with a long list of typed names in his hand. As I approached, a sleek silver Mercedes drew up and a woman wearing a tight satin dress and high heels stepped out, accompanied by two men in black suits.

I raised a hand to attract Kenny's attention and he frowned.

"Not now, Fiona, please. I did say…"

"Yes, you did but… I'm sorry about this interruption but have you seen my dog?"

The woman demanded her fur wrap from the back seat of the car as the wind snatched at her sleek blonde hair.

"No," Kenny hissed, "he's not inside. I would have noticed. Now, please, I have to attend to these people or Millicent will have my head."

I left him to his task, red blotches of anxiety erupting on his pale skin, poor man. But I'd had to check because if Archie were helping to host the president's dinner, Millicent might take more than my head.

Tobie. The dog must have followed Tobie back to his mobile home. I'd never been inside it but had seen the pale green structure from the kitchen window, down by the trees near the river. Millicent had refused to give him a bedroom in the house. She'd pointed out that there wasn't another spare one and how fortunate I was to have the dilapidated one on the top floor. Daniel, of course, had to pay for a mobile home for Tobie while he was carrying out garden renovations.

I skirted around the house, ducking under the tall windows of the dining room to stay out of Millicent's view and hurrying towards the old empty stables.

Piles of concrete blocks filled the yard, dumped there by the builders; plastic-covered pallets of timber boards for flooring and several new bathroom suites awaiting their final destination. I threaded my way through them and opened the door into the back field. A mown path through long grass wound under apple and pear trees laden with ripening fruit and there, beside the wood, was the mobile home.

I turned to cast my eyes up at the house. A figure stood at the kitchen window watching me. Hair rose on the back of my neck, but I soon realized it was only Millicent.

I raised a hand in greeting but got no response. No doubt she was checking to make sure I wasn't going to venture anywhere near the golf president's farewell bash.

When I was halfway along the path, I spotted a little brown and white shape frolicking outside the open door of the mobile home. Archie, the little scamp, oblivious to the worry he'd put me through. The landscaper was sitting on the door step, a beer can in one hand and the other tossing a tennis ball for the terrier.

"Hello," I called, not wanting to take him by surprise. "I see you've got my naughty Jack Russell."

Tobie looked up and grinned. "Yes, he's been here for a while. I thought you'd come and find him when your work was done."

"I'm sorry, I never noticed he'd disappeared." I arrived, panting and flushed with embarrassment, and bent to reprimand my heedless dog. "Now you, my little friend, are in serious trouble. I hope you haven't been up to mischief."

Archie tilted his head as if considering my words before bounding away to fetch the ball.

Tobie held up the beer. "Would you like one? You seem flustered."

I laughed. "I feel flustered. I met Kenny on the front steps welcoming the local cream of society but he was keen to get rid of me. I suppose he thought I would lower the tone."

"I also was warned to keep away, if that's any consolation to you." He stood. "I'll get you a lager. Come in. Allow me to show you around my palatial dwelling."

Inside, he led me to the fridge in a tiled kitchen area. Pine cupboards with glass doors were fixed over counter tops and two small striped sofas faced each other across a beige carpet. There was even a mantelpiece over a gas fire.

"Not bad," I said. "Much more luxurious than my bedroom near the schoolroom."

He shrugged, holding out the drink. "Yeah, I'm not complaining. I'd prefer not to live in close proximity to *Madame* and I'd hate to share a kitchen with her."

"I think she saw me. She was standing at the kitchen window when I left the yard."

He pointed to one of the sofas. "Take a seat. The drawback of living here is she can see me from the main bedroom higher up. I'm sure she's been watching me through binoculars from time to time. The sun glints on them."

"Why would she do that?"

He leaned against the cooker. "She likes to interfere in everyone's business, I suppose. She now knows you've come to see me."

I considered this. "Better than intruding when she's got a catering event on. I bet she was relieved to see me keeping out of her way."

"What about dinner? Have you had anything to eat yet? I'm guessing you haven't. When I left the herb garden, your nose was stuck in that little book."

I held up the leather volume. "Polly's diary. It's fascinating. It draws me right into the year 1895. I must show you her embroidery of the herb garden… called the physic garden back then. I borrowed it from the restaurant in the village and it's really very pretty. The sundial is still there and there were circular beds radiating out from it."

Archie ran in and jumped onto my knee to lick my face.

"I'd like to see that," Tobie replied. "What about dinner? I've made carbonara and there's plenty if you'd like it. Bacon lardons, eggs, parmesan, creme fraiche and pasta."

I hesitated. The golf dinner would probably go on until late. I'd meant to go down to the pub in the village and get a bite to eat there but the enticing smell of food made me realize just how hungry I was. "Thank you. That sounds great… as long as you've got enough."

"I've got plenty, don't worry." He turned to the cooker. "You might like to tell me about Polly's diary while I heat this up." He lifted the lid of the saucepan and stirred the contents with a wooden spoon.

The wind was howling in the pines outside and the mobile home shuddered on its concrete blocks.

"What's that strange noise?" I asked.

"Conifers make a completely different sound to deciduous

trees." Tobie explained that narrow pine needles vibrated faster in the wind and created a murmuring. The stronger the wind and the more conifers grouped together, the more various the sounds produced.

The whispering river was alive tonight as the gale gathered force. No longer whispering but wailing, a low but eerie howl that rose and fell with the gusts of wind.

"I suppose country folk centuries ago would have thought the trees sounded like banshees," I suggested.

"Banshees?"

"They are often mentioned in Irish folktales. Ghostly women who wail and scream before a family member dies."

Tobie turned the pasta in the pot. "Creepy. But that noise out there is only the pines."

I smiled. "I realize that." Tobie was always so logical; didn't allow his imagination to spirit him away. It was reassuring.

I sat on the sofa nearest to the kitchen area and snapped open the can of lager, taking a gulp. On a bookshelf opposite, I saw a framed photograph of a woman with short hair, a small boy on her knee. Both were good-looking with high cheekbones. The boy resembled her, the same shaped nose and full lips.

Tobie said, "My mother… and Victor, my son."

"Ah, that's a nice photo. By the way, you might be interested in my latest mystery. Polly Brady mentions a man called Robert Kingson in her diary who proposed to Daniel's great-aunt. She never married him, as far as I am aware. There's no record of any marriage so I'm wondering who he was."

"Did you check in the graveyard?"

"There's no Kingson buried there. Stephen gave me a list of all the names. The Burroughs family, Claudia Manning, Solomon… but not the girls… they must have moved away but that would be normal, wouldn't it? They probably married and went to another county or to Britain."

"And Polly… what happened to her?" Tobie asked.

"I don't know what happened to her after she left Colgrannagh."

"The skeleton in the garden…"

Something fluttered in the pit of my stomach. "You think it might be her?"

"I've no idea but you must consider all the possibilities." Tobie turned off the hob and pointed to a cupboard above my head. "Can you hand me two plates from there, please?"

I helped him to lay the table between the sofas. "Kingson might have just been a regular visitor to the house and perhaps his relationship with Claudia deteriorated and they called off the engagement. If he came from England, and it looks likely that he did, he would have gone home and left no trace in Colgrannagh."

Tobie spooned out pasta in a rich creamy sauce and produced lettuce, cucumber and tomato salad from the fridge. He tossed in a dressing and put the bowl on the table, taking a seat opposite me.

"*Bon appétit.*" He added, "Polly could have married later on and moved away, like the girls. Perhaps that's why you never heard of her again."

I remembered the final lines of her diary. The difficult choice she'd mentioned.

Rain, riding on the gale, lashed the windows. Tobie got to his feet and pulled down the blinds. "What a night! It's like the middle of winter. Where did Polly come from?"

"That man I met near the tower house… Stephen… he told me she was from County Mayo and was brought up by her aunt, a seamstress in a small village. I doubt whether the aunt cared much about her. Stephen said she was glad when the girl grew up and was off her hands. Sounds callous, doesn't it? But if she were paid to take in another woman's child and never warmed to her…"

"She was paid?"

"Yes, by the landlord's son… the father of Polly. It's complicated but common enough in those days. Polly would have had a respectable upbringing if no one realized she was illegitimate, though from her diary entries it seems her aunt never allowed her to forget her birth."

Tobie forked pasta into his mouth. A gust was rising again, the trees moaning. I shivered, suddenly cold. Poor Polly, unwanted in her home. What had become of her and the mysterious Kingson? Where had the two girls, Annie and Hannah, gone? There were too many missing pieces in the jigsaw puzzle but there had to be a link to the truth somewhere. It would just take time. I couldn't contemplate a dead end. I wouldn't contemplate failure.

"We should go to Mayo," Tobie announced.

"What did you say?"

He grinned. "Mayo. We should go there and hunt for information about Polly's aunt. You might find out interesting facts and I'm due a weekend off. I'd like to see more of Ireland while I have the chance… before I go back to France."

I kept my eyes on my plate. Would it be a good idea to go with him, an attractive married man with a difficult wife? No, it wouldn't.

"Why shouldn't we?" he asked.

"I've got a lot of other research to get through first," I replied, avoiding his eyes.

He frowned and made no reply.

"Daniel is more interested in Claudia and her medical background than the governess," I said.

"But if the governess knew what happened here… if she's connected to the skeleton, surely Daniel would be interested in that?"

"Daniel is important to me," I replied. "Without Daniel's support, Millicent would be able to get rid of me, and I need this job."

He nodded slowly. "Yeah, I see what you mean. Without Daniel, I wouldn't be here either. Millicent would kick me out tomorrow and replace me with someone more…"

"Obedient," I interjected and laughed.

He smiled. "Exactly." He held up his beer can. "Well, here's to Daniel."

I joined in the toast, relieved and yet disappointed that I'd managed to steer the conversation away from Mayo. I would have loved to go, of course I would, but it would be a risk with Tobie. It would be asking for trouble.

"I suppose the forensic team will need DNA," I said. "Someone's DNA to compare with the skeleton in order to identify it. But we have no records of Robert Kingson, no notion where the man went after he left County Wicklow, so how can we find any relations? And if it really was Polly left to lie in that shed, Stephen wouldn't be any good for providing DNA for her either because she was adopted and not a blood relation."

"It's a conundrum." Tobie appeared pleased with the word. "Definitely a…"

My phone interrupted him, vibrating on the table beside me. I glanced at the screen. "Oh hell, it's Millicent. What does she want?"

He let out an exaggerated sigh. "You better answer it. She knows you're here with me."

I tapped the screen and switched on the loudspeaker.

"Fiona?"

"Yes, Millicent." I raised my eyebrows at Tobie.

"Fiona, come quickly and bring the landscaper with you. It's Daniel."

"What's happened? Is he all right?"

"No, he's not. He's had a fall… down the stairs. Lying at the bottom and it looks bad, Fiona. He's not able to get up, so please come quickly."

Chapter Twenty-Eight

The past – July, 1895

Hannah held up the silk skirt of her gown and twirled in front of the looking glass. "What do you think, Miss Brady? Is it not exquisite? You stitched it so beautifully for me."

Annie smiled from her perch on the bed. "You look divine. So divine! If only I had such a head of dark hair…"

Hannah's laughter filled the room. "Lizzie helped me with it. She told me she used to be a lady's maid for a French marchioness in Paris. I don't believe her. Such stories Lizzie tells! I told her she'd never been further than Dublin. Will the guests notice me? Will I catch the attention of the gentlemen at Mrs Manning's luncheon?"

Polly stood at the window, resting a hand on the shutter, and watched the carriages arrive; the broughams and landaus of local gentry drawing up on the gravel sweep and unloading their finely dressed passengers, the grooms wearing top coats, white breeches and tall hats for the special occasion.

Eamon had predicted earlier that bad weather was on its way; a storm gathering force out at sea. He said the crows were clustering together and seagulls flying inland. Perhaps he would be wrong. A bright day so far, the horses' coats shining in the sunshine, their harnesses jingling and the leather gleaming.

Dr Fitzpatrick's brougham had just arrived, with its gloomy driver, and the physician alighted, dressed in a frock coat that almost didn't close over his rotund figure and sporting a surprising scarlet cravat. He raised his hat as two ladies wearing matching gowns greeted him. The twin sisters from a nearby estate were loyal and admiring patients of the doctor. They sometimes dropped in for afternoon tea at Colgrannagh and sang his praises.

Such self-importance, Polly thought, the way the doctor smiled and bowed. He'd taken the news of Kingson's proposal badly, according to Mrs Burroughs who had sidled up to Polly on the landing the previous week and whispered that the physician was put out that his friend wished to marry a herbalist. Dora gripped Polly's arm and laughed with sardonic merriment. "He might suspect it to be dark magic! Poor Dr Fitzpatrick," she said. "That a man of science like Kingson should risk such a union… what would this mean for his future career?" Dora's voice brimmed with mischief in the gloom at the top of the stairs.

"Miss Brady! Are you listening to me?" Hannah's question rose to a squeal.

Polly swung round. "I'm delighted you like the gown and I enjoyed creating it. The primrose shade suits you so well with your hair." She glanced at Annie, pale and composed on the bed. "And you too, my dear. Your emerald silk is most becoming. Did Lizzie help with your hair too? I like your silver hair slide with the pearls."

Annie blushed. "Thank you. Mrs Manning gave me this filigree slide for my birthday. Lizzie is surprisingly talented with hair. I like your gown, Miss Brady. You are a gifted seamstress."

"Yes," Hannah said, "it's so… so plain but it's elegant."

"Has Mr Kingson arrived yet?" Annie rose and walked to the window.

She'd been downcast since Kingson's proposal, even though

her guardian hadn't yet accepted him; disappointed that he'd chosen another but what could she expect at her age?

Polly gave her a sympathetic smile. "I saw him walk up the steps and into the house."

Hannah patted her curls and fussed about the lace on the neckline of her dress, peering into the mirror and pouting her lips.

"Oh, there's Luke." Annie let out a soft breath, the window glass clouding as she leaned closer. "The tailor finished that new coat for him last week. Doesn't it look well on him?"

Polly agreed. He certainly stood out from the crowd of young men who surrounded him, his fiery golden hair alight and a serious expression on his face. Perhaps Annie would transfer her youthful fancies to him now that Kingson had escaped her.

"He's looking around for you, Miss Brady," Annie added.

"Don't be ridiculous. As if he…"

Hannah ceased twisting a ringlet to say, "He's very taken with our governess, isn't he, Annie?"

"Yes, indeed." Annie smiled at Polly.

"You could be Mrs Luke Manning, I dare say." Hannah giggled and stepped over to the window, clutching at Polly's arm. "I wouldn't mind except you would have to stop being our governess and that would be sad."

Annie added, "We've grown fond of you."

Polly thanked and kissed them. Claudia's warning in the herb garden still rankled: Luke was not a suitable match for her. It was unlike her mistress to be so snobbish. She'd seemed fond of Luke and often told Polly that he was one of her father's best protéges, so why the sudden unexpected caution? It was out of character, unless Luke had done something to worry Claudia in the past.

A suspicion surfaced. Suppose Kingson had influenced her? He might have sensed Luke's hostility towards him and attempted to blacken the young man's name.

She turned to the girls. "I'm determined to remain your governess for a long time to come, until you no longer need me. Your French still requires much improvement."

They all laughed and Polly lifted her pocket watch to peer at the time. "My goodness, it's getting late! Mrs Manning will wonder where we're hiding. She wishes to show you off to her guests. Come along."

They descended the staircase, admiring the vast floral arrangement in the hallway created by Dora from the summer garden. Dark pink roses towered above frothy sprays of white astilbe. She had an artistic touch with plants.

As they crossed the hall, Luke walked in the front door. He hesitated when he saw Polly and stepped to her side with a quick greeting. The two girls exchanged glances and hurried into the drawing room.

"Miss Brady, how lovely you are…" Luke began.

"Thank you, but please don't flatter me."

His eyebrows joined in a frown. "You sound out of sorts. Have I displeased you again?"

"Of course not."

He bowed with mock humility. "I hope you will forgive me if I have. Would you care to accompany me?" He offered his arm. "Oh please, Polly, it's only a bit of fun. Do try to play along."

Unable to resist a smile, she linked her arm with his. "I never know when you are being serious. That's my dilemma."

"Well, then, you must never take me seriously. That is the obvious answer to your dilemma. There's Dr Fitzpatrick swilling down wine cup over there in the corner surrounded by his admiring lady patients. What a vain toad he is!"

"Hush, they'll hear you." Polly pulled her hand from his coat sleeve as they entered the drawing room, where the chatter of voices rose as Lizzie and another housemaid taken on for the occasion circulated with silver trays of crystal glasses.

"And there, by the far window, is Kingson, looking very pleased with himself," Luke added.

"I do hope you'll be polite to him today, for Mrs Manning's sake… please, Luke."

He leaned close to her ear and whispered, "Today, perhaps today I will be… but tomorrow you are going to help me discover more. It's not too late to put a stop to this engagement."

Polly opened her mouth but closed it again. No use arguing with Luke in front of all these people. She might only aggravate him into taking his suspicions a step further.

Solomon tugged at Polly's dress. "Miss Brady, will you come and see my toy soldiers? Mr Kingson gave me a present."

An attempt to purchase his loyalty perhaps, Polly thought as she bent to examine the red-coated figures and gave her approval.

"Miss Brady, what a happy occasion!" The strident tone of Dr Fitzpatrick made her spin round. His eyes held their usual calculating expression, as if weighing up her reaction.

"It is indeed." She could see Luke out of the corner of her eye, moving towards Annie and Hannah. She hoped he would keep his word and not say anything to ruffle feathers.

The physician raised a bushy eyebrow. "You think them well matched?"

"You refer to my mistress, I presume?" Polly forced a smile. "Perhaps it is a little early to take their union for granted but, if they are happy, isn't that all that matters?"

He grimaced. "Pah, happiness! Happiness is over-rated, in my opinion. It's easy to be happy at the outset when love is in the air and everything seems rosy, but compatibility is much more important. Are they suited to each other?"

Why was he asking her, a mere governess, these questions? Why would her opinion be relevant when he had clearly made up his own mind? "I feel they are suited. They share a love of medicine…"

He laughed, shaking his head. "Medicine! Neither has an understanding of medicine, my dear girl. Kingson is a hawker of drugs and Mrs Manning… well, how shall I put this without sounding disparaging… Mrs Manning is a knowledgeable botanist. I will give her that."

Luke appeared at Polly's elbow. "We have been requested to move into the dining room." He flashed a grin at Dr Fitzpatrick, who returned a cold nod before stepping away.

The doctor's civility towards her obviously didn't extend to Luke. He would know all about the young man's past.

"Horrid man," Polly said as they crossed the hallway. "I do wish he would keep his feelings to himself. If he dislikes Mrs Manning, why does he accept her invitation?"

"Did he say he dislikes her? He doesn't dislike her. Oh yes, he disapproves of her… and only because she is a woman meddling in a man's world… or what he holds to be a man's world." Luke grinned again and leaned closer to Polly, his breath warm on her ear. "Guess what Mrs Burroughs told me."

"What?"

"She told me that Dr Fitzpatrick once asked permission to marry her daughter… years ago, when she was only a young woman."

"My goodness, no! Is that really true?" Polly asked.

"Old Dora promised me it is… and she's very good at keeping an eye on us all. You've noticed how she sees and hears everything, while she's pretending to be asleep in her chair. Dr Burroughs… He actually considered the match a good idea but Mrs Manning wasn't having any of it. She didn't like Dr Fitzpatrick from the start because she thought him overbearing."

"I believe she's correct."

Luke pointed towards a small table in the corner behind the door. "Here's where we sit. You, me… the children. We've been given a table of our own where we won't make the more important guests feel uncomfortable."

Polly ignored his last comment. "Dr Fitzpatrick married years ago, didn't he?"

Luke pulled out a chair for Polly. "Yes. Poor mild Edith, who wouldn't dare to say boo to a goose. Edith is a goose, if you ask me, for marrying a bully like him. She's over there with Mrs Burroughs, see… always has that timid expression on her face."

Polly saw the thin woman with wisps of hair already falling out of its pins. "I expect the doctor took a dislike to Mrs Manning for daring to turn down his proposal. I'd love to have seen his face when she spurned him."

"So would I! Do you think it was Kingson's idea to put us here together, away from the main party? Perhaps he's ashamed of us all. His beloved's lowly adopted urchins. He would have enjoyed going further, I'll be bound, and banned us from the luncheon. We wouldn't be permitted to attend if it weren't for Mrs Manning."

Polly frowned. She couldn't encourage him but she suspected he was speaking the truth. "Luke, please…"

"Mrs Manning would have allowed us to mingle with the guests."

"Oh, what does it signify? I prefer it here at this little table in the corner. I'm only a governess, please remember, and I wouldn't know what to say to local society."

"You would, of course you would. You're an intelligent woman… more intelligent than the empty-headed simpletons here today."

Hannah flopped down beside them. "I'm famished. All this talking… silly questions from old people about how much we've grown, how pretty we are… when are we going to be allowed to eat?"

"Soon enough." Luke nodded at Lizzie, making her way through the throng towards them with a silver tray laden with bowls of steaming soup. "Here comes the first course. Where is Annie?"

"She'll be here soon," Hannah replied. "She had to take Solomon to wash his hands because he insisted on putting them into an urn of flowers to rescue a worm."

Luke laughed. "Solomon will be a zoologist when he grows up. He'll travel the world to study animals and other creatures, mark my words."

When Annie had appeared with the boy and all the guests were seated, Kingson rose to his feet. He tapped his wine glass with a knife and, clearing his throat, he asked for silence.

"Here we go," Luke said to Polly. "He loves to talk… the sound of his own voice keeps him riveted for hours. If only I could say the same for the rest of us." He laughed loudly and Polly shot him a stern look.

"Dear friends," Kingson began, "My dear Claudia and I are so pleased that you could join us to celebrate this happy occasion. I've only lived in the village for just over a year but Claudia has always been so kind to me, including me in activities with her family. I truly feel a part of the community now and that I've known you all for much longer… so much longer, yes indeed."

A murmur of approval rose from the guests.

"I'm sure you'll agree that Claudia, my Claudia, is radiant today…"

"His Claudia," Luke almost snarled, his mouth twisting.

Across the linen tablecloth, Solomon grew restless and sank a spoon into his soup. He slurped a mouthful.

Annie nudged him with her elbow. "Solomon, hush!"

"I have been asked by Mrs Manning to welcome you all…" Kingson continued, while one of the twin ladies seated near Dr Fitzpatrick tittered and clasped her hands in excitement.

Luke grimaced as he spread butter on a piece of bread. "Oh Lord, give me patience."

Polly frowned again. He was worse than a child. "Luke..."

He shrugged and pushed the bread into his mouth.

Kingson opened his hands. "And it is my earnest wish that you will all be able to join us on our wedding day."

A silence descended while this information was digested.

A laugh burst from Dr Fitzpatrick. "Well done, Kingson, well done, man. That's a fast move. A fast move indeed. Are you afraid she might turn you down?"

A blush seeped across Claudia's cheeks and she reached out to place a hand on Kingson's sleeve, as if to restrain him. "Robert, please. It's too early to..."

Luke's scowl darkened.

The speech continued for another five minutes as Kingson thanked everyone again for coming and hoped they would enjoy their luncheon. He requested the guests to stand while he proposed a toast to their hostess.

Lizzie arrived with a platter of poached salmon decorated with slices of cucumber and sprigs of fennel and silver bowls of tiny buttered potatoes. The clatter of silverware and clink of glasses punctuated the hum of conversation as the food was consumed.

After pudding was served, Claudia got to her feet and made her way around the guests. She bent to kiss the twins and held out her hand to Dr Fitzpatrick, who clasped it firmly. They were too far away for Polly to listen to his words but she saw her mistress start and step away. What had he said?

"She is coming this way," she told the children. "Are you ready to smile and thank her for permitting you to attend the luncheon?"

Hannah raised her eyes from a bowl of sherry trifle. "I hope Mr Kingson gives me a present. It's not fair if he only gives one to Solomon."

"I'm certain he will." Polly saw Luke reach into the pocket of his coat as Kingson joined her mistress.

"Ah, here you are, my dears, all sitting together," Claudia said, laying a hand on Annie's shoulder. "Such pretty dresses and Miss Brady is most becoming in hers. The embroidery on the bodice…"

Kingson agreed. "Indeed, she is. And Annie, she…"

"What about me?" Hannah interrupted. "Mr Kingson, do you like my gown? Mrs Manning has seen it already but you haven't."

"Exquisite, quite exquisite. I've never…" he replied, his words fading away when his gaze moved to Luke, who had placed a photograph on the table beside his pudding plate and was leaning over it, as if studying it for the first time.

Alarm brought a flush to Polly's cheeks. The photograph of Kingson with the priest in South America! Should she reach across and attempt to snatch it away?

It was too late, for Kingson was already tilting his head to peer at it. "What's that you've got there, Luke?"

The young man stared at him. "Do you recognize these men?"

Kingson's lips turned white.

"Robert, what is it? What's wrong?" Claudia's hand reached for his arm.

Polly frowned when Luke smirked.

Kingson picked up the photograph and held it away from him, as if he were short-sighted, before tossing it back onto the table and smiling at Claudia. "Nothing, my dear. Nothing is wrong. Come along, let us continue to greet your guests."

Chapter Twenty-Nine

Driving rain hurtled against the window panes as the guests departed, gusts of wind snatching at ladies' hats and the umbrellas in gentlemen's hands. Claudia stood inside the main door, bestowing farewell kisses on her visitors and advising them to make a dash for their carriages. Laughter and shrieks swirled into the hall while Luke and Polly whispered at the foot of the stairs.

Luke said, "Kingson's out on the steps talking to Dr Fitzpatrick. When he comes back in, he'll try to confront me, he definitely will. Now, no, don't argue, listen to me. There's a cupboard behind you, under the stairs… see that small door in the panelling? Hide inside and listen to what he says."

"Oh, for heaven's sake, Luke! You're making too much of this. What would Mrs Manning say if she finds me lurking in the cupboard and spying on her friend?"

"She won't see you… make haste, he's coming." Luke's hand pushed at Polly's back as he fiddled with the latch on the oak panel. "No one will find you… just hide in there and I'll let you out when Kingson has gone."

Darkness yawned in front of her, a jumble of sweeping brushes, feather dusters and an overwhelming smell of oil and turpentine. Polly's breath caught in her throat and she stepped back. There could be spiders' webs amongst the cleaning paraphernalia.

Luke hissed in her ear, his palm forcing her forwards. "Hurry, he'll be here in a minute. He knows we walked towards the staircase because I saw him watching us before he went out on the steps."

The babble of voices and laughter dropped as the door closed behind her. She saw nothing but the musty blackness. She reached out her hands, feeling for the walls of the cupboard, irritated by her own weakness and for listening to Luke in the first place. There was probably a perfectly logical explanation as to why Kingson was in Brazil.

She could lose her position over this nonsense and be sent packing back to Mayo. How would her aunt react if that happened? Polly would never acquire another placement without a good reference. Her aunt would take pleasure in sending her off as a servant, having always said a housemaid's life was all she was fit for. She imagined Aunt Maureen leaning towards her, her words twisted with bitterness. "I told you so. Your mother was a housemaid and a disreputable one at that. You were never good enough to keep company with my daughter and the fancy education funded by your foolish father was wasted on the likes of you."

The position as a governess had been her chance to escape, to rise above her lowly birth and get away from Aunt Maureen.

Polly grew accustomed to the gloom and she could make out the shapes of the brooms. She inhaled slowly and moved towards the panelled door, placing her ear to the wood.

Someone was speaking outside. If only she could hear who was there. If it were just Luke, she would ask to be let out of the cupboard and would escape up the stairs to the sanctuary of her bedroom, away from this madness that threatened to embroil her in serious trouble. She wished she'd never met Luke Manning with his far-fetched imagination.

Dora's high-pitched titter rang out. Luke gave a short reply and the old lady laughed again and cried, "I don't like him any more than you do, my lad, but Claudia won't listen to me… says she's tired of being on her own. She's lonely, if you ask me, since Gilbert died."

Polly couldn't decipher Luke's reply, which sounded more like a grunt than actual words; he must have been desperate to get rid of Dora. Her footsteps pattered towards the foot of the staircase.

Perhaps Kingson wouldn't attempt to confront Luke. He'd looked uncomfortable when he glimpsed the photograph, hadn't he? He might prefer to say nothing and not draw attention to it. His face had quickly regained its usual pleasant expression as he moved away with Claudia on his arm.

But no, heavier footsteps approached as Polly strained her ears. A strong confident stride and Kingson's clear tones called, "Luke… Luke, I want a word with you."

The young man didn't reply.

"Don't turn your back on me like that." Kingson's voice was close, his tone lower and more menacing. "What the hell are you playing at?"

"Playing at?"

"Don't act the innocent with me, my lad. What the devil do you think you're doing?"

"I could ask you the same question."

Polly's heart leaped in her chest, fluttering against her ribcage like a trapped bird. Luke was courageous. Courageous but foolhardy.

"Where did you get that photograph? Tell me!" Kingson demanded.

"Do you admit you've been in Brazil?"

"You don't know what you're talking about. Have you been drinking?"

"I asked you a question," Luke said.

"Now see here, boy, I don't have to answer to someone like you." His words were low, a contemptuous growl.

Dust tickled Polly's nostrils and she swallowed several times, praying that she wasn't going to sneeze. She lifted a sweeping brush further away from her face. What if Kingson found her hiding? What if he hauled her out and asked what she was doing? Please God he wouldn't. What would she say? She suppressed a cough.

"What was that?" Kingson asked.

"What? I heard nothing."

"That hiccupping sound… you must have…"

"I heard nothing," Luke repeated, "but Mrs Burroughs has just gone up the stairs. Perhaps she's still on the landing."

A silence while Kingson either took this in or glanced upwards.

"Why were you in Brazil?" Luke's challenge sounded confident. "The priest in the photograph knows you. He sent it to a friend of mine."

More silence. Was Kingson still there?

"You were there the same time as Gilbert Manning disappeared."

Kingson hissed, "How dare you! I know all about your father. He was a drunkard and a wife beater."

"My stepfather. He always encouraged us to call him…"

"I don't care what the scoundrel encouraged you to do. I know what he was like and I don't have to listen to a blackguard like you. You're going to upset Claudia with your foolish questions and ridiculous suspicions."

Polly shifted her feet in the darkness, pressing her ear to the door.

"Better she finds out in time before…"

A scuffling noise and a sharp cry from Luke, as if Kingson had seized hold of him. A wave of nausea struck Polly and perspiration broke out on her face. What if she vomited or fainted? She would surely be discovered then. She twisted her fingers together and forced herself to remain calm.

"Now look here… I was in Brazil, yes, but I'd been sent there by the company for which I work. New opportunities are beneficial for medicine…"

Luke must have pushed Kingson off because there was a thump against the panel door and Polly stepped back, her foot striking a bucket that rattled like an explosion in the surrounding darkness.

The door remained shut. Outside, the two voices were whispering and she struggled to make out the words.

"South America… tree bark… opportunity… scientific research." That was Kingson.

"Gilbert Manning… English nursery… his discovery." Luke's words came and went.

Blood pulsed in her ears as she held her breath. She wouldn't be much of a witness if she couldn't hear.

The hall must have been empty of guests, because Luke spoke more loudly. "Did you try to steal his discovery? Did you? Did you push him into that ravine?"

An exclamation from Kingson and more scuffling feet on the flagstones. The darkness in the cupboard was suffocating, overwhelming; she couldn't hold out much longer. She might be running out of air. Where was Claudia? She must have gone back into the drawing room because she would have intervened if she'd seen the altercation between the two men.

Kingson shouted, "You're insane, man! What do you take me for?"

"I know what you are. You're a fraud. You don't really want to marry Mrs Manning. You only want to get your hands on…"

Footsteps moved away and Kingson replied threateningly, "I'll see you're dismissed from your position for this."

"As if you could do that!"

"You're only tolerated here because of Claudia… because of her soft-hearted kindness towards you and the girls. You know that as well as I do."

"Leave the girls out of this."

"You're nothing but a troublemaker. I'll make sure that no one ever employs you again."

Luke remained silent.

Kingson added, "You'll regret this when you find yourself back in the gutter where you belong, mark my words." His boots clattered across the hall, growing fainter.

Polly leaned her forehead against the panel. She was a fool to get involved. Luke was stupid to confront a man like Kingson who had influence, too much influence, but the man had admitted to being in Brazil.

The door creaked open. She blinked as daylight dazzled her.

"Did you hear?" Luke reached out to take her hand, helping her out. "He was there… he was there. He admitted it."

Polly bent over and gulped in air. Another five minutes in that dark suffocating space and she would have panicked.

"You heard him," Luke said.

"Yes… yes, I did but…"

"He said he was in Brazil. You must have heard that."

"I did, yes. He was there… but Luke, what if it was harmless, as he claimed?" Polly straightened up. "What if he'd been sent there by his company to discover plants that might help scientists find new cures for illnesses? Could he be telling the truth and have nothing to do with…"

"Why keep it a secret then, eh? Why not tell Claudia and everyone else that he was there? I don't believe it was harmless. We have to contact that priest." Luke reached to pull a cobweb from Polly's hair.

"You're risking your position," she said. "Do you want to lose that? I heard his threat."

Luke snorted. "Are you so cowardly, Polly Brady? It's not like you. If Robert Kingson had something to do with a death, would you only think about yourself?"

"No, but..." Her limbs trembled. "Oh, I don't... I don't know... I can't..." She pressed a damp palm to the panelling. She would have to get away from Luke and consider what had happened. Try to make sense of the doubts reeling in her mind. "I just... I think this is too dangerous."

He tried to prevent her walking away, clutching at her arm and beseeching her to listen, but she pushed him off. She reached the bottom of the stairs and gripped the rail, raising her eyes when a shadow moved on the landing above.

Someone was staring down at her. A dark figure with fine white hair under a widow's cap.

Dora. How long had she been standing there, watching and listening?

Polly's face flushed as she swung away. She couldn't go up to face her. The old lady could have overheard everything; listened to the argument between Luke and Kingson and seen her emerging from the cupboard like the spy she was. If Dora repeated what she'd witnessed to her daughter, what then?

Luke might not be the only one to lose his position.

Chapter Thirty

The present – September 2022

"I can't go with him to the hospital," Millicent shouted above the wind as we watched the paramedics load the trolley bed bearing Daniel into the ambulance. The gale howled around the side of the house and she raised a hand to her hair to stop it from being blown across her face. "You know I've got this important dinner for the golf club… how can I possibly leave now?"

"Well, someone has to go with him," I said. "You can't expect a man of ninety to cope on his own, especially after an accident like that. What was he doing upstairs? I thought he didn't like going up there."

Millicent turned towards the doorway where Kenny stood. "I've no idea… to fetch a photo album, I think. He mentioned it to one of the old guys at the dinner, the man who found him lying on the floor… Stephen, I think his name was."

No doubt Stephen was asking for more information about Polly Brady. If only I'd been there, I could have run up and found it to save Daniel taking the risk with his lame leg. "I suggest his nephew Kenny goes with him."

"No, he can't. He can't go because I need him here to talk to people and to keep an eye on the catering staff. Daniel will be fine, don't fuss about him. They're used to dealing with people on their own these days in A and E."

Tobie, leaning against the side of the ambulance, snorted and Millicent shot him a dark look.

"All right," I replied. "I'll go. I'll stay with him until he's been seen to. We don't know why he fell. What if it was a stroke?"

"The doctors will find out. Don't forget Daniel used to be a surgeon and feels at home in hospitals." Millicent, her face pinched and cold, was moving up the steps to issue orders to her fiancé. She reached the hall door and added as an afterthought, "Thank you, Fiona, I appreciate this. Give me a call when he's had an X-ray or whatever."

"I'll come with you," Tobie said when she'd gone inside. "Millicent is an ungrateful…"

"She owes so much to him and this is how she treats him. Thanks, thanks for offering to come too. Between us, we can keep him company. Quite often a fall can be serious for older people."

"Yes, I realize that. My grandmother passed away after one." Tobie must have noticed my anxiety because he added, "But don't worry, Daniel is used to hospitals, like Millicent said, and he's strong for his age."

"I hope so. I'll tell him and the paramedics that we'll follow in my car."

Almost an hour later, we were sitting in the Accident and Emergency department in a Dublin hospital, Daniel lying flat on his trolley and still looking pale. Light blue curtains with tiny flowers surrounded us.

Tobie removed his sweatshirt and complained about the suffocating heat. Monitors bleeped and staff wheeled machines to test blood pressure and oxygen saturations from one cubicle to another.

I had managed to get some information from a nurse who'd

checked Daniel on arrival. The paramedics didn't think he'd had a stroke but the doctors would tell me more. Was I a relative? No, I explained, I wasn't but he had no relatives to help him. Not strictly true but the nurse nodded and wrote that down on the clipboard notes attached to the end of the trolley, along with my telephone number.

"How are you feeling now?" I asked Daniel when she'd gone.

He attempted a laugh. "Foolish. Like a foolish old man."

"Thank goodness you're all right. When Millicent called me, I thought…"

"It takes more than a fall down stairs to kill me off, don't worry. Thank you for coming with me. And Tobie too. So kind of you both." He drew in his breath and winced.

"Is it very painful?" Tobie asked.

Daniel remained silent for a few moments before saying, "A bit. My left leg hurts. I'm certain I've broken my hip… at least my hip if not my pelvis. I can't move my leg and my foot seems at a strange angle."

My eyes shot to the outline of his legs under the covering. Antiseptic lingered in the heavy air, mingling with another smell. Cabbage? Perhaps someone was eating dinner behind the adjoining curtain.

Across the passageway, a doctor in a white coat was examining a small sobbing boy with a deep gash on his forehead. I turned my gaze away from the blood and tears running down his cheeks.

"Can I get you anything?" Tobie asked Daniel, pulling his cotton blanket straight.

"No thanks. The nurse said not to eat anything in case they have to operate tonight."

"What about you, Fiona? Want anything to eat or drink?"

"Tea would be good, thanks." When Tobie walked away, I leaned closer to Daniel. "You gave me a fright. Why did you go upstairs?"

He looked frail, lines of pain and exhaustion on his forehead. "To find a photograph album for Stephen… he was there at the golf dinner. He used to be the president of the club a few years ago."

"I've never seen a photograph album belonging to your family."

"Millicent came across it yesterday," Daniel said. "She found it in a cupboard in one of the bedrooms they're doing up. It belonged to Solomon, a present from his mother when he was only a young lad."

"That sounds interesting. Are there any pictures of Claudia and the girls?"

"There are a few. And of Gilbert too. I never realized what piercing eyes the man had. There's a larger framed photo of him somewhere that used to hang on the landing. He had long hair to his shoulders and a bushy beard. Quite an unusual-looking man for his day but I suppose years hunting for plants in South America…" He turned his head to the side and groaned.

A nurse pulled back the curtains and smiled at us. "Professor Manning, you'll be going for an X-ray soon. Everything all right?"

Daniel flashed her a ghost of a grin. "That's a relief. They'll soon find out what's wrong with me and send me home."

She laughed and wagged a finger. "Not so hasty, young man. I think you might have to stay with us for a few more days."

I imagined Daniel when he was a heart surgeon; the banter with the other medical staff and women eating out of his hand. How could Millicent be so callous? The golf event mattered more to her than her benefactor. After all he'd done for her! I wouldn't let this go. When I next saw her, I would give her a piece of my mind. And as for Kenny, he was spineless the way he allowed her to bully him.

Tobie reappeared with two plastic cups of tea. "Best I could manage… machine in the corridor, sorry." He passed one to me.

"How is the patient?"

"He's doing fine," I said.

Daniel gave me a lopsided smile, probably in a lot more pain than he was admitting.

"Would you like me to read you some passages from Polly's diary?" I asked, taking a sip of tea.

"Polly? Oh yes, the governess. Have you got it with you?"

"Yes, I brought it to Tobie's mobile home when I was searching for Archie. I hope that dog is behaving himself."

Tobie smiled. "He'll be asleep on the sofa now after all the running around."

I opened my handbag and took out Polly's diary. No reply so far from my brother about any contact in Rio but Anthony might not have even opened my email yet. My mother had called me the day before, saying she'd spoken to him the previous week. She assured me he was alive and well but still no mention of a steady partner, she'd complained. What my brother did was his business and I made no comment.

I ran my eyes down the first page of the journal; the faded neat handwriting from nearly one hundred and thirty years before. March 1895, written while sitting in the waiting room at a railway station, two carpet bags at her feet containing all the belongings she possessed.

"Polly says she finished her education in Paris," I said. "She spent a year in a French school for young ladies learning the language, dancing, music and art."

Daniel attempted another smile. "An accomplished girl for her era. What else does she say?"

"Will I read it out loud to pass the time?" I cleared my throat and began:

> *"I admit to being apprehensive about taking up my new position and I fervently wish that the family, and*

> *the children especially, will take to me. I've never had to discipline children before and hope they will be well behaved, not spoilt and condescending like the ones my aunt tells me about."*

"Governesses had a tough time, when you think about it," Daniel said. "Treated like servants by many of their employers and living so far from home."

"Yes, I can understand her concern. She writes about how she would love to be able to turn back the clock and relive the excitement of warm evenings as she and a companion strolled along the Seine, touring the great art galleries and trotting after a guide in Notre Dame. She says here:

> *I stood breathless in admiration beneath the great rose windows of thirteenth-century glass."*

I turned several pages. "Oh, Daniel, she mentions her first meeting with Claudia here. You might be interested in this description of your great-aunt." I read:

> *"Sleek shining hair and kind eyes. Mrs Manning laid her hand on my arm and squeezed it with what seemed like genuine affection. Her kindness almost overwhelmed me."*

I wondered what had happened to her father after she left for Wicklow. Did he ever see her again? Polly was fortunate as a baby because at least she hadn't ended up in an orphanage, an all too common fate for so many unwanted illegitimate children in the nineteenth century. At least she'd been granted a good education; another rarity for women in that era and I guessed that was her father's wish.

I read on, resting the small dark-green cover on my knees:

"I commend Mrs Manning's decision to continue her father's good work with the two girls, Annie and Hannah. Her mother, Mrs Burroughs, let slip this evening that Hannah's mother had most likely been a wild young woman, with thick dark hair and alluring looks that landed her in trouble. She abandoned poor Hannah as a baby. The girl and I have an experience in common, both cast off by our mothers."

I might have to find out where Hannah and Annie went later in life because they would have known what happened to Polly. "Daniel, were you ever told what became of the two girls?"

His voice sounded weaker. "No. Sorry… never heard of them before you came."

I picked up Polly's diary again. So easy for women to vanish back then, unless they were prolific letter writers or were married to someone well known. I held the little leather book out in front of me. I could hear my excitement as I read aloud:

"15th July, 1895 - Luke has disappeared. I'm worried because it's not like him to vanish without telling me. He missed our meeting at the church. I'm determined to question my mistress at the earliest opportunity because, after his argument with Robert Kingson, I'm deeply concerned."

That name again. Robert Kingson.

An altercation with Luke who'd disappeared. Could that be significant? I glanced at Tobie, thinking of the skeleton buried in the garden shed.

"What?" Tobie looked up from his phone. "What's wrong?"

"Polly says here that Luke has disappeared after a row with

Robert Kingson. That's all she says. This is nearly at the end… nothing else in the diary except those final few lines about her having to make a difficult choice."

Daniel was drifting off to sleep and didn't reply.

"You definitely need to find out more about Kingson," Tobie said.

"I agree. He's been mentioned too many times to ignore. But how?"

"Now, Professor Manning, we're ready for you," the nurse announced as she pushed aside the curtains. "Has he fallen asleep? He must be exhausted after his ordeal but we'll soon get him fixed up."

An orderly appeared and pushed Daniel's trolley away, followed by the nurse.

"What will we do? Wait here?" I asked Tobie.

"I suppose we should. Hopefully the X-ray won't take long. Poor man, I bet he's in a lot of pain. If his hip is broken, will they do surgery on it tonight?"

I closed the diary, placing it back in my bag. "That might depend on how many other people with broken bones are waiting ahead of him. I'm going to stay here and see what they say."

"I'll stay with you." He took his phone from his pocket to check the time. "We could be here for hours, I guess. The main thing is for Daniel to make it through or else…"

"He has to. If he doesn't… if he doesn't…" I didn't want to articulate my thoughts.

Tobie grimaced. My phone bleeped. Anthony.

"It's my brother," I said, opening the email. It was longer than I expected:

> *"Hi Fi,*
>
> *Ma says you've landed some lucrative job up in the wilds of Wicklow. Glad you decided to kick the teaching habit and that*

leech of a husband.

You're in luck, dear sister, because I've a friend in Brazil who worked for the Botanic Gardens there while doing his post grad degree and his thesis was on medicinal plants. How's that for serendipity?

By the way, I'm living in Prague now working for the university, but there's an order of Jesuits running a college in Rio. My friend says they were keen botanists in the 19th century and used to grow herbs in their garden. They discovered that the local people had an innate knowledge of the healing power of plants.

My friend has put me in touch with a priest called Francisco Rossi who just happens to be in charge of the archives of their library. So, I gave him a call and hopefully he'll get back to me soon.

My friend found a grave for Gilbert Manning in the Sao Joao Batista Cemetery in Rio. It's a huge old place, over eighty thousand burials. Do you want me to ask him to take a photo? It might be useful for your client's book."

I typed a few lines in response.

Yes, please, Anthony, a photo would be good and thanks for your help.

I owed him a drink or two when he was next home, whenever that would be.

"So what does he say?" Tobie asked.

"Gilbert has been found. He's buried in Rio. That means he's not our skeleton."

"Cross him off the list," Tobie replied with a grin.

Chapter Thirty-One

The past – July 1895

Polly ran a hand over the nearest gravestone, its soft lichen warmed by the sun. Where was Luke? It wasn't like him not to appear when he'd arranged to meet her and he was usually so punctual.

She looked across the churchyard towards the spires of yew standing on either side of the entrance gate like brooding sentries. What had delayed or stopped him coming?

A crow cawed from the tower of the church behind her and the hair on the back of her neck prickled. She was alone, alone with only the dead for company and yet she didn't feel alone. A foreboding, a stab of doubt made her spin around and peer into the gloom of the trees along the wall. Was Luke playing a practical joke, hiding behind the circle of yew growing near the church? Perhaps he would jump out, calling her name and laughing at her startled expression.

His note, handed to her by Eamon during her early stroll around the physic garden, had stressed urgency:

> *"Meet me on Tuesday at half past ten in the graveyard.*
> *Important details to discuss. I require your help."*

Luke's handwriting appeared so hurried that it was almost illegible. Eamon's wiry figure had vanished into the lane; her opportunity to question him was gone.

Polly stepped through the long dry grass towards the entrance to the church. She remembered her mistress's serious expression when she'd come to the schoolroom the day before. She wished to offer advice, she'd said, advice about taking Luke's words too seriously. Claudia pointed out that she was very fond of him, knew his idiosyncrasies, but Polly would do well to avoid being influenced by his more irrational fancies. Her employer's words were low and kind but a sudden flash of irritation had prevented Polly from replying. How could Claudia say that?

She admired her mistress, tried her best to please her, but she'd noticed a change in her since she'd grown closer to Kingson, a change for the worse. The man was able to work his charms on her, no doubt about it. He seemed capable of twisting her beliefs.

Where was Luke? Polly took out her pocket watch. Almost half past eleven, an hour late. He wouldn't come now, must have been delayed and she couldn't linger there all morning. The two girls had gone in the trap with Claudia to a shoe fitting in Wicklow town and Solomon was helping his grandmother with a jigsaw, so Polly had a few hours to do as she pleased.

Perhaps Luke was inside the church. That idea hadn't occurred to her and she clicked her tongue in exasperation. How foolish she was! Yes, that's what he must have meant; that they should meet inside the building where, in the chilly shade, no one could see them or eavesdrop on their whispered words.

Hurrying to the arched entrance and turning the iron ring handle, she pushed open the heavy door. A protesting complaint whined from the hinges and cold air hit her; the clinging smell of damp in her nostrils. She glanced along the rows of wooden pews, her footsteps muffled by a carpet running up the aisle of paved stone. Light filtered through a stained-glass window above,

Christ and his apostles seated at a table and Judas the betrayer by his side.

Behind her, the door groaned again. Polly swung around as a figure moved from the shadows near the font.

"Luke!"

Not Luke though. A taller man staring straight at her, dressed in a wool coat and riding breeches. Too late to hide behind a pillar, Polly's heart missed a beat.

Robert Kingson.

"Miss Brady, how pleasant to find you here." His mouth stretched into a smile that didn't quite reach his eyes.

A warmth bloomed on her cheeks. "Oh, Mr Kingson… I beg your pardon. I thought…"

He tilted his head to one side. "You thought I was your good friend, I suppose. You arranged to meet him here, didn't you? An assignation… a secret tryst. Well, my dear, I must say I find that most romantic." His tone was light, mocking.

Heat spread to her forehead. "Oh… no, nothing like that, I do assure you, sir. It was just a… we were just going to take a walk… the girls being away and the weather so fine but…" She was babbling like a child and stopped to take a breath.

His lips twitched. "Ah, a walk, and it's a fine day for a walk, to be sure."

She remained silent, looking at the cold paving under her boots.

"Miss Brady, forgive me, I'm only having a little fun. Is Luke not here then?" His tone sounded warmer and she glanced up.

"He is not."

He was standing in her way, blocking the aisle and her escape, resting a hand on one of the pews. "I am sure he will be here soon." He waved at the altar. "I thought I would take a look inside the church… for wedding plans, you understand."

"Yes, I understand. Have you seen Luke?"

"No, but I expect he's on his way to you and may already be waiting in the graveyard." He stood aside to allow her to pass but touched her arm with a forefinger as she moved away. "By the way, Miss Brady… Polly, if I'm to be a more… if I'm moving into Colgrannagh in the future, I would like us to be friends… you know that, don't you?" He gripped her, his fingers pressing into the sleeve of her gown.

She flushed again. "Of course, Mr Kingson." Let him think her an innocent. Perhaps that would be safer.

"Call me Robert."

"Oh, yes… Robert, I also would value your friendship." Her words sounded hollow as they echoed in the dim light but what else could she say? She would have to be polite to him and, after all, what had he done to upset her? Nothing, nothing at all. It was Luke who'd placed doubts and suspicions about him in her mind.

He squeezed her arm one final time before releasing it. "That's good… pleasing to hear. I hope you find your young man and I wish you an enjoyable stroll."

"Thank you." She moved towards the door with relief.

Blinking in the sunlight outside, she gazed up at the bell tower around which a cloud of jackdaws circled, uttering their short *tchawks*. Had she mistaken the date on the note? Luke may have suggested meeting her the following day and not that morning. She took the piece of paper from the pocket in her walking dress and skimmed through the words again. No, something must have happened and she would have to find out. If she asked Eamon to saddle Misty, she could ride over to the house of Luke's employer. Perhaps he'd been delayed at work.

She threw a quick look over her shoulder to ensure that Kingson hadn't appeared from the gloom of the interior and walked towards the lane leading along the river.

An old man with a fishing rod cast a curious glance in her direction when she passed by and raised his cap in greeting. She nodded her head and hurried on.

Thoughts tumbled over one another. She would ask Eamon about the note; find out when Luke handed it over. Kingson's half-mocking smile in the church taunted her. Had he told her the truth or did he know information that he chose not to reveal?

A group of children stood on the bridge, the tallest one with dark curly hair and a rather insolent expression. Polly had seen him in the village on a few occasions and Luke told her he was the ringleader of a gang of boys. He suspected them of lighting the lanterns in the tower house at night.

They watched her in silence as she walked past, their tousled hair uncombed and bare feet peeking out below threadbare trousers. They came from the thatched cabins at the other end of the village; their fathers were miners in the Glendasan pits and their mothers were probably tired and hungry with more babies on the way. Luke, Annie and Hannah would be like these children if it weren't for Claudia and her father whose magnanimity had saved them from a life of poverty.

She smiled at the boy but he scowled back.

Polly discovered Eamon in one of the stables, grooming a carthorse, brushing off the mud from the fields and whistling as he worked. The huge animal shifted its weight onto three feet, resting a hind one, and munched contentedly on hay pulled from the rack above.

"Eamon, excuse me…"

The man turned and his face creased into a smile. He stopped brushing and muttered, "Miss Brady… and what can I do for you?"

"Oh, I beg your pardon… I don't wish to disturb you but have you seen Luke?"

The horse turned his head and regarded her with dark liquid eyes, as if recognizing the name. He blew down his long nose and nudged at his groom.

Eamon stroked the side of the animal's head and replied, "I have not, miss. Not since he handed me the note to give to you."

"Yes, but… when did he give you that?"

"Yesterday evening it was, aye, it was yesterday just before milking time. He arrived in the cow byre… said it was urgent and not to forget about it in the morning." He frowned at her. "Is there anything amiss?"

Polly hesitated, wondering how to begin.

Eamon lifted the brush and began to groom the horse again. "I know I've no right to ask but if you think I can assist you…"

"Luke didn't appear," she said. "I went to the churchyard but there was no sign of him."

"Ah, Luke's a wild one, indeed he is, he's like a two-year-old colt. He'll come later… or tomorrow maybe. I'd go back to the house and forget about him, miss, if I were you."

The muscles in her throat constricted and she turned her head away so the man wouldn't see the tears brimming. So silly, she thought, why was she distressed? The encounter with Kingson had unsettled her and she recalled his cool calculating stare. Luke was a fool to make an enemy of the man and she would tell him so; she would try to convince him that he was only stirring up trouble for himself.

She said, "I have the morning off. Luke and I were going to meet for a walk so I'm worried because he hasn't appeared. It's not like him. Perhaps I should ride over to his employer and check if he is there."

The brush dangled in mid-air. "Ride over? I didn't know that you could ride a horse."

"I can indeed. My… my father taught me to ride on the beach in Mayo. I'm well capable of managing a horse." She forced what she hoped was a reassuring smile because he was regarding her with surprise. "May I borrow the pony?"

"Borrow the pony? And what will the mistress say if anything befalls you? If you take a tumble or worse, I'll be the one to blame."

"Please, Eamon, I can ride competently, I assure you. Misty is there at the end of the passageway. I can see her white head. She is small and quiet… the girls say she is trustworthy. If they can ride her, so can I."

Uttering words under his breath that sounded like a remonstration against strong-minded women, Eamon tossed the dandy brush into a wooden box near the door and beckoned. "Come this way and I'll fetch a bridle and a lady's saddle. If Mrs Manning says…"

Polly replied, "Don't you worry, I'll take the blame. I'll tell her I persuaded you. Thank you, Eamon, thank you so much for, to tell the truth, I'm worried about Luke."

The man shook his head. "Worried about that lad? You're wasting your time… wasting your time. Luke is well able to take care of himself."

Misty seemed none too pleased to be snatched away from her hay and led out into the yard. Eamon tacked her up and checked the girth before giving Polly a leg up onto the saddle. "Are you comfortable? Now give the mare her head and don't be pulling on the reins for she doesn't like that. She's a grand quiet lass and knows what to do but, like all ladies, she can't abide being pushed around." He chuckled and handed her a whip. "And don't you go using that, you hear me? It's only for emergencies in case you meet a mad dog or need to give the mare a tickle to pass a donkey, for she can't abide the creatures with their long ears and braying." He laughed again and gave the pony a gentle slap on her broad behind. "Off you go, Misty my girl, and make sure you bring Miss Brady safely back to us or I'll be thrown out on the road."

The pony walked down the avenue at a sedate pace, attempting to turn her head on several occasions, unwilling to part from her equine companions in the stable yard and letting out a few shrill whinnies of protest. Polly urged her on with soothing words. After ten minutes of adjusting to Misty's rather choppy stride, a surge of joy coursed through Polly. A long time since she'd been on horseback and she hadn't realized how much she'd missed it.

Once through the tall granite pillars and onto the road to the village, the pony broke into a trot and passed several side cars and a farm cart loaded with turnips without even flicking her ears back. Polly began to relax and breathed in the sweet warm air, wafts of honeysuckle drifting from the hedgerows.

She leaned forward to stoke the mare's sturdy neck. "We'll find him, won't we, girl? We'll discover that my concerns are for nothing."

She rode on past two shops with folk chatting in huddles in the doorways, past the rows of thatched cabins beyond the public house and the tall house belonging to Dr Fitzpatrick. A woman stood on the granite steps in front with a small baby in her arms, her face blotched from crying. Polly turned her head away. Pity for the mother welled inside her but she'd no wish to encounter the doctor and be subjected to inquisitive questions about her journey, because he had an uncanny way of guessing her thoughts.

The gateway to the big house at the end of the village loomed and she turned Misty into the tree-lined avenue, dark and gloomy out of the sunshine. She pulled on the reins and the pony slowed to a walk, her hooves crunching on the gravel.

Was she being foolish? No, she couldn't allow misgivings to sway her. There were the pillars of the front portico and the heavy door with brass fittings. She'd hoped to find a servant outside, one she could ask about Luke, but the sweep before the great building was deserted. Her gaze lingered on the window above the portico as she recalled the girl who'd lain in that room, pronounced dying by the doctor until Mrs Manning had stepped in with her herbal cures and common sense.

A wave of nausea rose from the pit of Polly's stomach. She would have to summon her courage, climb down from Misty's back and approach the front door to pull the bell wire and send its urgent message jangling to the kitchen area. Polly secured the reins behind the stirrups and left the pony at the bottom of the steps. Hopefully Misty would stay put and not wander off or decide to head homewards.

As she reached for the bell, she wondered what she would say. They might think her brazen and would have no idea who she was. She would introduce herself, mention her mistress and… and what? Should she tell a lie and imply that Mrs Manning had sent her to ask after Luke? If that got back to her employer, who'd advised her to keep Luke at a more cautious distance, how would she explain?

The door swung open and a small woman appeared, with a sharp nose and enquiring look. "Yes?"

"Oh… I… well, I am…" Polly stammered, silently cursing her ineptitude.

"Yes?"

"I've been sent… I've come to ask about Luke Manning, ma'am."

No reply came this time, just another appraising stare from those chilly eyes. The housekeeper, for this must be she, wore a severe dark blouse and skirt with a collection of long keys attached to a leather belt. She was obviously accustomed to seeing off unwanted visitors and barring entry, protecting her wealthy employers. Perhaps Polly would be sent round the back to use the servants' entrance.

"I'm wondering if he's here this morning, ma'am."

"Luke Manning, you say?"

"Indeed, yes… for I'm Polly Brady, Mrs Manning's governess, you understand, and I've been sent to…" The lie slipped out and it was too late to retract her trembling words.

The housekeeper's lips formed a firm line, as if weighing up Polly's introduction and finding it lacking. "Mrs Manning… Mrs Claudia Manning?"

'Yes, ma'am."

The older woman cleared her throat, glancing over her shoulder into the hall behind, checking no one was there, before saying, "Miss Brady, I regret that you will have to inform Mrs Manning that the young man she seeks is no longer employed by the master."

"No longer employed?" Polly asked. "What can you mean?"

The woman began to ease the door shut. "You may take that message to your mistress, Miss Brady, and although it's not for the likes of me to say, this is what comes of giving too much charity to those who don't deserve it."

The door closed in her face and Polly remained standing on the steps. How dare she! How dare that rude woman say that about Luke! And as for her insinuation about Mrs Manning…

She returned to the pony and wound her fingers in her wiry mane, unable to suppress her grief. As she wiped away her tears with the back of her glove, a suspicion dawned. Was this Kingson's doing? Had he told Luke's employer that he couldn't be trusted?

Polly snatched the reins from under the stirrups and looked for a mounting block. She had to get back up on the pony and leave; get away from this place. She glanced around, cursing her long skirt and the awkward ladies' side-saddle. If she were a man, she would be able to vault onto Misty's back without having to ask for assistance.

A short distance away, a garden boy appeared from behind some laurels, pushing a barrow full of chopped wood.

"Excuse me," she called, waving a hand. "Excuse me, would you assist me to mount, if you please?"

The boy obliged and she turned Misty towards the oak trees

that formed an arch at the top of the avenue, urging the mare forwards.

Luke was gone. She had no idea where. As she rode down the gloomy avenue of trees, conviction rose inside her. Kingson was involved in this. That was why he'd regarded her in that mocking manner in the church. He knew what had become of Luke and she would waste no time. She would go to Mrs Manning, express her concerns and she would make her listen this time. Her mistress would have to listen.

Chapter Thirty-Two

Polly found Claudia on a sofa in her upstairs sitting room and waited inside the door while her mistress finished writing a paragraph in her medical journal, putting down her pen and inserting a bookmark, before placing it on the wine table.

"Ah, my dear, sometimes I need to remember what I've achieved… helps me to keep striving." Claudia smiled. "Hannah told me that you wished to speak with me. You're not feeling poorly again?"

"I am quite well, thank you."

"Do come over here and sit beside me." She patted the pale blue upholstery.

Polly sat with her knees together, her palms resting on her muslin dress, thoughts racing in her mind. She would have to be prudent with her choice of words; careful not to blame Kingson because Claudia might take offence.

Her mistress continued, "Hannah said you are concerned about Luke. Indeed, Hannah herself seemed upset. What did you say to the girls?"

Polly tried to swallow a lump in her throat and remained silent.

"You look worried. Tell me what's wrong."

"Oh, ma'am. It's Luke… he's… well, he wasn't at his place of work when I rode over…"

"You rode to his employer's house? On your own?"

"Yes, ma'am, I…"

"Why Polly, I didn't even know that you could ride. It was foolhardy to go alone when anything could have happened."

The muscles in Polly's throat tightened. What could she say? She would have to sound calm and sensible, rein in her indignant feelings, because she didn't want Claudia to think her hysterical. "I'm a good rider. I learned at home in Mayo. My father taught me."

"I'm relieved to hear that as I'm worried about you having an accident. So, tell me, why did you go to where Luke works?"

Polly explained about the note she'd received and how he hadn't appeared at the appointed time. Claudia listened in silence, observing Polly.

"And then I was afraid something had happened to Luke, so I asked Eamon for Misty and rode over to the house and the housekeeper was so haughty and cold… Oh, Mrs Manning, she told me that… told me that Luke no longer worked there. What could have happened? It doesn't make sense."

Claudia moved to take Polly's hand, squeezing it for a few seconds before releasing it. "Don't be upset, please. I know the reason for Luke's departure and it's unfortunate, most unfortunate. I found it hard to believe that he would do such a thing."

"What… what has he done?"

Claudia glanced towards the fire where a flame leaped up around a log with a sharp hiss, a scent of pine and damp wood floating out into the room. "I'm sorry to say a serious discrepancy was discovered in the accounts ledger. A page torn from one as if to hide an entry… and more entries missing."

Polly sat upright. "You surely don't… I don't believe that!

Never! It's not possible. Luke would never do such a thing. He never would."

"My dear, I understand you are friends with Luke and I know... he lived here under our roof for years," Claudia replied. "I am most disappointed. I assure you, I couldn't comprehend it at first but Robert..."

"Mr Kingson told you this?"

Claudia's gaze fell to the Persian rug at their feet. "Mr Kingson told me that bookkeeping discrepancies had been noticed in several ledgers. When questioned, Luke had no explanation to offer so he was told to pack his belongings and leave."

Polly jumped to her feet and hurried over to the window, her hands shaking. It was Kingson who'd done this. Kingson who must have tampered with the ledgers so that the blame would fall on Luke. But how? How had he managed to interfere with them? No wonder he had seemed so smug in the church earlier; that mocking smile when he asked her to call him Robert. And now Claudia had turned against Luke because of the man's lies.

She gripped the middle bar of the sash window, resting her forehead against the cool glass.

"Polly, please come back and sit beside me. I know this is hard for you to comprehend but you must listen to me. I have no wish to upset you but we must try to face the truth."

"It's not the truth. These are lies. I won't believe them." Polly remained by the window, gazing out at the expanse of lawn that swept away to one of the chestnut trees near the avenue. A red squirrel ran across the grass and up the trunk, disappearing into the leaves. Eamon appeared with the lawnmower and bent to start up the engine.

She could hear her mistress's voice behind her, her calm low tone.

Claudia got to her feet and walked towards Polly. "You must try to understand. If Luke hadn't run off, it would have been so much better, but the fact that he's disappeared makes it look… makes him seem more culpable. I'm the last person who would blame him but he should have come to me to explain. I haven't seen him. You must understand how that appears."

Her mistress was right, of course. If he'd been blamed unjustly, he would have come to Colgrannagh to plead his case, to lay his case before his guardian in the hope that she would speak up on his behalf. Where was he? What had happened to him?

"Mr Kingson…" Polly stammered, "I met him earlier. He must know why Luke didn't turn up."

Claudia's frown deepened. "Polly, please… you don't know what you're saying."

"He was in the church and he knew… he knew that Luke hadn't come to meet me because… I think that…"

"This is nonsense, utter nonsense. I must ask you not to continue speaking, if you truly feel that Mr Kingson had anything to do with Luke's dismissal. It's preposterous to suggest such a thing."

"Excuse me, Mrs Manning, but… the photograph Luke was given of Mr Kingson in Brazil… you must have seen how angry it made him."

Claudia turned pale. "I can't permit you to speculate like this… This is Luke's doing. Now come back to the sofa, please, and allow me to explain." She caught hold of Polly's arm, none too gently, and pulled her across the rug. "Sit down, sit there and listen to me!"

Polly knew she'd said too much but it was too late to withdraw the words.

"Mr Kingson has nothing against Luke, let me assure you." Claudia placed a hand to her throat. "He has only the best of intentions towards Luke… but I'm sorry to say Luke's recent accusations and actions have eroded our trust. For some reason…

no, pray don't interrupt me for I will speak my mind… his attitude towards Mr Kingson is incomprehensible, who has only ever shown him kindness and somehow Luke… or this priest from the reformatory, has poisoned his mind. I don't understand it… I really don't understand how he can behave like this after all we've done for him."

Polly stared into the fire and made no reply.

"Have you nothing to say?" Claudia asked. "I'm surprised at you, to be honest. Robert had no involvement in my husband's death. Why? Why would he? I have in my possession the bark that Gilbert sent home before he died so why would Robert have any reason to conspire against him?"

Polly watched a flame licking up the side of the logs in the grate. A fire in July? The room was warm, too warm. Was that the blackened piece of an envelope in the grate? Perspiration broke out on her brow.

Had something happened in South America, something Kingson didn't want known, and perhaps her mistress was burning correspondence from him?

"He has offered to help me find a laboratory to run tests on the bark… says it might be valuable. Oh Polly, I might be able to afford to study medicine now that the Royal College of Surgeons in Dublin has opened its doors to women. You must understand how important that is to me… how important the money would be to me. All my life I've longed to be a doctor… to stand on equal footing with my male counterparts."

Polly replied, "I understand, I do understand but…"

"I can only surmise that Luke's animosity towards Robert is because of jealousy. Perhaps he resents him in some way… feels replaced in my affections… for we are a household of women and I did rely on Luke to help me. I don't know, I really don't and I can't understand why he would behave in such a manner." Claudia took a breath, before adding, "It's hurtful, you must see how hurtful it is."

"Luke showed me the photograph and the man looks like Mr Kingson."

Claudia waved her hand towards the fireplace as if to dismiss the accusation. "I can assure you that Robert would never have harmed Gilbert. He would never have had Luke dismissed unfairly from his position."

No point arguing further, Polly decided. Her mistress was determined to support her admirer. Kingson's charm and his promise to help her achieve her lifelong ambition of studying medicine had swayed her opinion.

Polly got to her feet, smoothing down the skirt of her dress. "I'm sorry, ma'am. I apologize for taking up your time. I must return to the schoolroom."

"One moment, if you please. I'm not finished speaking." Claudia reached for Polly's hand to prevent her moving away. "Sit down." Her tone was colder. "Now, are you listening to me? I would like you to take a couple of weeks away from Colgrannagh…"

Polly flushed. "Are you dismissing me?"

"No, certainly not." Her mistress forced a smile. "You have been here for several months without much time off and you seem, if you'll forgive me for saying so, to have fallen under the spell of Luke. I can understand why. You are only in your early twenties, as also is he. You have interests in common perhaps. Colgrannagh is a quiet place with few amusements for young women. I suppose it's to be expected but I would like you to go home to Mayo for two weeks and take the time to reflect."

"No, I can't."

"You don't have a choice, I'm afraid. Robert suggested this to me several days ago and I was reluctant to follow his advice but I see now that it's a good idea. You have grown too close to Luke and time away from him and this house will give you an opportunity to consider your future."

So, she was to be punished for taking Luke's side, for believing in him! Tears stung and she raised a shaking hand to brush them away.

Claudia's tone softened. "I'm sorry you're upset but I must insist. I can't allow you to hold feelings of suspicion against Mr Kingson. Perhaps when you return, you'll find Luke has reappeared and made peace with his employer. I'm certain that the constabulary won't be involved because, with Luke's background, it might not be... but I've been assured... Robert says he has put in a good word for him."

Polly stifled a sob and pulled a handkerchief from the pocket of her dress, dabbing at her eyes.

"There now, my dear, don't be distressed. Your aunt will be pleased to see you after all this time. She'll enjoy hearing about your work and then, after a fortnight has passed, we shall welcome you back here and never speak of this sorry incident again."

Polly buried her face in the soft linen and struggled to hide her feelings. She'd feared this would happen, that she'd be dismissed. But this was not outright dismissal. No, it was only a warning. Polly was to forget Luke and his claims and return to the cold oppressive cottage in Mayo to consider her future. If she continued to support him, there would be more serious consequences, of that there was no doubt.

Mrs Manning hadn't articulated the threat aloud but it was there, hanging between them. Kingson, with his alluring smile and handsome looks, had won her mistress's loyalty while Luke had been cast aside.

Polly pushed the damp handkerchief back into her pocket and stood once more. "Thank you, Mrs Manning, I will do as you say. I will write to my aunt this evening."

Claudia's smile broadened. "I knew you would see sense. We are often guilty of foolish alliances when young. Our heads are turned by dashing men. I tried to warn you not to become too fond of Luke. One day you will understand."

"Yes, ma'am."

"And one more thing… please don't think me cruel. A short time back in Mayo will give your father a chance to speak to you. There is an important detail he needs to tell you."

Polly hurried towards the door. What could that be? Had her mistress already written to him expressing her doubts about Luke? Claudia obviously suspected she was in love with him. Was she right? She'd never been in love. Was that what love felt like? Perhaps love increased her horror of harm being done to Luke and her rising panic at the thought of never seeing him again.

"Miss Brady! Tell me what ails you." Dora stood by the staircase on the landing, peering at her.

"Oh, oh… I've just had distressing news."

"Not your aunt, I hope?"

"No, she is well, I thank you. It's not that. Forgive me, Mrs Burroughs, but I must hurry back to the children… a French lesson."

Dora called out as Polly ascended the staircase, "It's Luke, isn't it? I've heard what happened. He has upset you." She sighed dramatically. "Poor child, I feel for you, I really do. Young love can be so painful, so terribly painful."

Chapter Thirty-Three

The present – September 2022

"I wonder how Daniel is getting on." Tobie leaned against the window seat in the pub. "I'm glad they decided to go ahead with the surgery tonight. A fractured pelvis and hip at his age is going to be a challenge to recover from."

I watched a young woman sitting at the bar, legs crossed as she gesticulated and laughed with her companion, a man of the same age. They could be Polly and Luke over a century before except she wouldn't be sitting so casually in a public house. Women's lives were much more limited in the Victorian era and yet there'd been some who defied the restrictions placed upon them by society.

"You're in another world," Tobie said, giving my leg a gentle push with the toe of his shoe. "Would you like another lager?" He got to his feet. "This is a nice pub. I like the old-style décor and the view of Dublin."

I followed his gaze out of the window. Darkness had fallen; below us lay the twinkling lights of the city and, over to the right, the ink-black water of the Irish Sea. It was quiet in the bar, with only a few people sitting at the round pine tables; their conversations rising and falling in the glow of candles.

I remembered Daniel lying unconscious in a bright hospital

theatre. The medics had carried out tests before his operation and pronounced his bloods and heart in good order so that was a relief. He still had to make it through the surgery.

Tobie exchanged a few words with a dark-haired girl behind the bar. She gave him a wide smile, obviously attracted by his slight French accent and his healthy complexion. A sudden stab of jealousy pricked me and, annoyed with myself, I turned to my handbag to retrieve Polly's diary.

The handwriting was less tidy on the final pages of the journal and her tone no longer that of the cautious governess. She'd been summoned to Claudia Manning's sitting room and told to sever her acquaintance with Luke who was still missing.

> *"At present I am in my bedroom and must gather my belongings, for Eamon has been instructed to take me to the railway station tomorrow morning, along with all the clothes and books I shall require for a fortnight in my dreary home. I'm still shocked at how Mrs Manning is so unconcerned about Luke's disappearance but she has changed; most definitely she has changed since the strengthening of her friendship with Kingson."*

Polly sounded far from happy at the prospect of returning to Mayo for an enforced holiday. I ran my finger down the lines of looped writing, searching for any mention of Luke. I looked up to see Tobie still chatting to the girl, two glasses of lager between them on the counter top.

I turned away and read on:

> *"Mrs Manning told me that she sent a telegram to alert my aunt about my arrival. I dread seeing her for it will certainly not be a kindly welcome home. My only consolation is that I may meet Papa because I have missed*

him over the last few months. I wonder what he wishes to speak to me about."

Polly appeared to hold her father in high esteem and I was glad that, in spite of being illegitimate, her father seemed kind to her and hadn't disowned her, which was unusual for the era. Hardly the way a man who was prepared to abandon his lover would behave. If Polly's mother ran off and died in poverty, perhaps it wasn't her father's fault.

Polly mentioned her employer's ambition to study medicine and how Kingson had promised to help her achieve this lifelong dream. Was that how he'd manipulated her feelings towards Luke? As Claudia's affection for the young man diminished, Polly's love seemed to be increasing. The governess almost admitted that in her diary. She was clearly worried that something had happened to him and she didn't trust Kingson.

I noticed Tobie walking towards our window table and I dropped my eyes to the diary. Didn't want him to think I'd been watching him or listening to him chatting with the girl.

"I hardly dare write this and, indeed, this will be the last entry in my journal about the subject, but I am worried about what has befallen Luke. It is unlike him to stay away from us for so long and I'm certain that Kingson knew more than he divulged when I encountered him in the church. He was laughing at me, mocking me beneath his gentlemanly veneer. I can understand how Mrs Manning has been taken in and I forgive her, for I was as foolish in the past months, but the scales have now fallen from my eyes. I'm certain that Kingson uses women to get what he wants."

Strong words from a young woman, but was it possible they'd

been written with a certain amount of jealousy? Was she bitter because she'd been passed over and he'd transferred his affections to her mistress?

I felt her anxiety concerning Luke came across as genuine and probably provoked her outpouring. If Polly were in love with Luke, she might not be a reliable narrator. Kingson might not be the villain she suspected him to be.

I turned the page but all that was left was the paragraph about making the difficult choice. Nothing about her return to Mayo; no entry about Luke reappearing. What had stopped her writing more? Or perhaps she'd never gone back to Colgrannagh and gave up writing a journal. Frustrating, but I would return to the large box of letters belonging to Claudia and check if any of her correspondents mentioned the young man at a later date.

"A lager for you, my friend." Tobie sat down and pushed a glass across the table.

"Thanks."

There'd been no sign of a Robert Kingson mentioned in the 1901 census so I wondered if a search through the archives of newspapers around 1895 might produce more information. Luke had vanished, Polly had been sent home to the west of Ireland and Kingson didn't feature in the census after the turn of the century. Mystifying.

The age and gender of the skeleton in the underground storeroom was still unknown, the pathologists taking their time. Daniel had been told that they had a backlog of work after the lockdowns of the Covid-19 pandemic.

I took a sip of beer. "Was it Luke buried in the garden… if he was never found?"

Tobie shrugged. "Who knows? You might never identify who it was. So long ago and no DNA, unless it was a family member."

"That would rule out Kingson, Luke and Polly because their descendants aren't recorded... at least not in any of the papers

I've seen so far." I closed the diary with a frown.

The research was frustratingly slow and I tried to suppress the feeling that I should have ignored Tobie's gruesome discovery, concentrating instead on Claudia's medical education and career. But if tree bark sent back from Brazil by her plant hunter husband had helped pay for her university fees, surely that was relevant? Besides, Polly's diary and her beautiful embroidery of the old herb garden had brought her alive. I'd held in my hands a work of art that she'd created. I was drawn to her predicament and longed to discover more about her.

"That needlework of Polly's, what do you make of it?" I asked.

"What do you mean? It's very professional."

"Yes, but does it possess a hidden meaning? Victorians sent special messages with flowers, especially messages to do with romance. Why choose those plants around the outside?"

Tobie shook his head. "I don't know. They're common-enough plants, ones that are found in ordinary gardens so it might have been a random choice. Maybe she chose them because she liked them best."

"I'll take a more detailed look at it later," I said. "I don't suppose we'll ever know why Polly chose those seven flowers. You could be right and it's only a decorative piece of work." I realized I was running out of ideas. I was tired, clutching at straws.

"Fiona, what are you going to do tonight?"

"What do you mean?"

"What if we find a B & B… stay the night somewhere near Daniel?" he said.

"I can't… the dog, I can't leave the dog locked up all night on his own."

He nodded. "Yeah, I forgot about Archie."

A silence yawned between us. Tobie shifted his weight on the bench in the window and ran a finger along the top of the table, frowning.

"What's wrong?" I asked.

"I didn't tell you the truth," he said, without looking up. "Not the whole truth."

I asked quickly, "About what?"

"About my wife."

What was he going to say? For a few seconds, I didn't want to listen and opened my mouth but closed it again.

"She left me," he said.

"Oh."

"Six months ago."

"I'm sorry to hear that." A surge of pity for him swept through me. "Another man?"

"Yeah, at first. Later she told me it had meant nothing, a stupid mistake, but she still wanted time away from me."

"I'm sorry," I said again.

"When I told you she preferred living in Paris, I should have admitted that she moved back there. We agreed to a trial separation… and it's dragged on longer than we expected."

I attempted to keep my voice steady. "That's tough. Does your son live with her?"

"We share him but he's with her now, since I got this job, although he goes to my parents for weekends sometimes."

"Thanks for telling me." It wouldn't make any difference to me because I wasn't going to get involved with Tobie. Absolutely not.

"What I suggested about Mayo… going to Mayo to track down Polly's relations… does that appeal to you?"

I glanced out of the window. A couple were walking off into the dark, arms wrapped around each other, their heads close together. "I've been too busy to look into it."

His mouth twitched. "If she were sent back to Mayo by

Claudia, wouldn't it be a good idea to go there, in her footsteps so to speak, and find out where she went? I could take a few days off... even a long weekend, if you like?"

Why had Tobie mentioned his wife and their separation before returning to the topic of Mayo? Clearing the way?

I said nothing.

He raised his eyebrows, leaning towards me. "Fiona..."

"I can't get involved with you, Tobie. I'm sorry, I just can't." The words tumbled out before I could stop them.

"That's not what I meant."

"It is what you meant."

He smiled. "All right, so why not? Is it a crime? Why can't we just let things drift and see what happens?"

At the bar, the cheerful girl behind the counter was talking to an older man and also to the young couple on her left. Happy, carefree people. I wished I was like them, their lives so much simpler than mine.

"A weekend away in County Mayo," Tobie repeated. "We'll enjoy the scenery, you can ask about Polly... I'll buy you dinner."

I smiled. "You make it sound so easy."

"It is easy."

"Then why didn't you mention your separation until now?"

"I didn't want to put you off. I understand that you're nervous... afraid of getting involved again. Maybe you're afraid of being hurt again. It won't be like that, Fiona. I promise you."

"Oh, please..." I shook my head. "Let's not go there."

"Don't you want to find out what happened to the governess?"

"I do, of course I do, but I don't want to..."

"You don't want me to go with you." He frowned into his glass of lager.

"That's not true. I would enjoy your company and you seem interested in my research... in Daniel's research."

He reached out a hand. I thought he was going to take mine

but he picked up a beer mat in the middle of the table and twirled it between his fingers.

I wondered if it would be a bad idea to reach out and touch his. But I didn't. I placed both my hands on my lap.

He grinned, as if reading my mind, and said, "I'm going to book two rooms in a guest house in… what did you say the place was called?"

"Mulranny."

"Yes, Mulranny. Two rooms there for the weekend after next and we'll do our best to find Polly's family and learn what happened to her. Is that a deal?"

Impossible not to laugh. "You're very persuasive."

"We'll forget all about Dominic and Isabelle… won't mention them. It will be a working weekend for you and a chance for me to visit more of Ireland before I go home."

"When are you going back to France?"

"That depends on Daniel's progress… on what else they want me to do at Colgrannagh. I miss my son. I hope to go back for a weekend soon."

My phone pinged with an email coming in. I grimaced before looking at it, hoping it wasn't another from Dominic's solicitor. The only emails I seemed to get those days.

"Aren't you going to check who it is?" Tobie asked, lifting his glass of lager and taking a gulp.

I noticed my brother's name on the screen. Relief coursed through me.

"Hi Fi,

Good to hear from you again. Francisco got back to me and he has looked through some of the papers for you. There's a lot of them, so I sent on your thanks! I'll ask him to take a photo of Gilbert Manning's gravestone."

I raised my eyes but Tobie was scrolling on his phone so I read on:

"Francisco is excited about your tree bark and yes, you're right, the tribes used it for fever and infections, especially yellow fever. Gilbert Manning was staying with the missionaries on the edge of the Amazon rainforest and it sounds like he posted some of it home to his wife. There were quite a lot of cures for various ailments at the time, all plant based.

I asked Francisco for information about how Manning died but no luck there. He's promised to check the archives and old local newspapers and, if anything shows up, he'll get in touch with me. He's found no sign of a Robert Kingson. Was that the guy's real name?

So, what do you think, Fi? Sounds like you might be onto something here. Some sort of early pharmaceutical discovery and rival jealousy? I suppose if the bark had the potential to be transformed into a drug that would act as a powerful painkiller and replace the earlier forms of aspirin, it would be likely to become a valuable commodity. Pharma breakthroughs can make a fortune these days, such as cures for cancer, dementia and other serious illnesses. It was no doubt the same back then."

I sent him a quick message:

"Thank you, Anthony, how could I have doubted you?"

I laughed aloud and Tobie looked up.

"My brother Anthony is proving helpful," I said.

Was that the guy's real name? A good question and I had no answer for it. Who exactly was Kingson? A man connected to a pharmaceutical company, according to Polly's diary. All the more reason for him to want to acquire what might be a medical breakthrough. I remembered how valuable new discoveries of ornamental plants were in the nineteenth century. The Dutch mania for tulips in the seventeenth century was another example, where a single tulip was said to be worth much more than an average man's wages until the market for them collapsed. Surely a medicinal plant with good commercial prospects would be fought over? All sorts of devious shenanigans went on among plant hunters.

If only I knew the name of the tree, I could have checked the internet. Daniel had never come across an exciting discovery attached to Colgrannagh or his great-aunt. Perhaps it had all come to nothing.

"Useful information?" Tobie asked.

"The priest has found details about Claudia's husband and the bark he sent back to Ireland. He says Gilbert was staying with the Jesuits near the Amazon rainforest, so he would have had to package the sample and send it on a lengthy journey by ship in those days. Unfortunately there's no sign of any name for this tree. I'm going to have to look up early pharma companies… and cures for fever."

"Kingson's employers must have got wind of the discovery and thought it valuable enough to send him to Brazil in the hope of tracking down Gilbert."

I nodded. "Yes, Polly wrote earlier that Kingson's job was to travel Ireland, selling patented preparations to local doctors. He was well paid and presumably had influence in the right area if he'd agreed to help pay for Claudia's university fees to study medicine, though that might have been a ruse in order to get his hands on the tree bark. Suppose he was leading her on and that was his intention all along? It could have been why the couple never married."

And Luke Manning? What was his role in this, if any? If he'd tried to expose Kingson…

"Your brother has done well," Tobie replied. "He's confirmed your suspicions. If Kingson really wanted that bark, if he was determined to get it, he might have been ruthless enough to get rid of anyone in his way."

"Yes, yes," I cried and a bearded man at the next table turned to stare at me. "If he was challenged by Luke who threatened to expose him… who probably suspected him of pushing Gilbert into that ravine. Then Kingson might have decided to make Luke disappear."

We gazed at each other; our previous embarrassment forgotten.

The excitement in his eyes must have mirrored mine. "And that means… that means, my dear Fiona, Luke might have lain in the shed below the ground for well over a century."

Chapter Thirty-Four

The past – July 1895

Polly pulled open a drawer and took out a blouse. She might need a few of them in Mayo where she would be expected to wash her own clothes, with no Lizzie to do it for her, and probably have to clean Aunt Maureen's as well.

Outside, the full moon dangled over the spires of trees beside the river and threw a silvery path across the lawn. Polly placed the clothes on her bed and walked to the window, glancing at her pocket watch. After eleven o'clock and she should be in bed, resting before the long train journey to Westport in the morning. Mrs Manning had mentioned at luncheon that Eamon would drive her to Wicklow railway station after breakfast.

Polly hadn't received a reply to her brief letter to Aunt Maureen but that was to be expected. Attempts at communication were often rebuffed.

A knock sounded on the door, two short raps. Was that Mrs Burroughs dropping in for a cup of hot chocolate? A bit late for her but she slept badly and often prowled around the corridors at night seeking entertainment.

The old lady would be a trial that night, with her endless questions and knowing smiles. Polly had avoided meeting her on her own since the tearful encounter on the stairs.

A tap on the door came again, impatient and demanding.

"I'm coming," she called out. "Who is it?"

Hannah stood before her, hair tied with a yellow ribbon and wearing only a cotton nightdress. She pushed past Polly into the room and hurried to the window.

"See there," she said. "Have you noticed?"

Polly sighed and shut the door. "You should be in bed. What are you doing up at this hour?"

Hannah ignored the question and pointed across the moonlit lawn. "See there… above the treetops."

Polly joined her at the glass pane and her chest tightened. Lights. Lights in the tower house.

Hannah added in a whisper, "There's someone there. Lizzie told me on the way to her bed… came into my room and woke me up to tell me."

"I'll have a word with Lizzie tomorrow. She had no right to wake you."

"Oh no, Miss Brady, I asked her to… next time she saw the lights. Lizzie thinks they're a bad omen, a sign of a death. Would they be a sign of death? She saw them before Mr Manning…"

"Yes, yes, I was told about that. It's nonsense. Just gossip and superstition."

"Oh no, it's exciting! You don't believe her? But he died… he died the following week."

Polly pointed to her watch. "See the time, young lady? It's after eleven. You should be in bed and not amusing yourself with ridiculous tales. I'm sure those lanterns belong to a gang of local boys."

"Boys?"

"Yes, Luke told me they like to use the tower house for their night-time games. Up to no good, I'll be bound. I saw them standing on the bridge only recently. We shall ignore the lights and go to bed. Now, come along, if Mrs Manning finds you…"

Hannah murmured, "If I tell you... if I tell you, will you promise not to mention it to..."

"I can't promise," Polly replied. "What if Mrs Manning asks me?"

A sulky expression crept over the girl's face. "You used to be kinder, miss. It's because... it's because you've been sent away. I'm sorry you're going. We all are... me and Annie and Solomon."

"Annie, Solomon and I."

Hannah hissed through her teeth before calling out, "Look! There's a light near the top of the tower. Are you not dying to find out who's there?" When Polly made no reply, the girl added, "We used to go into it sometimes but not at night. We used to meet Luke and have a picnic. Miss Walsh never found out. We'd run away when we were supposed to be doing our schoolwork."

"That was naughty of you. Now, go back to your bedroom."

Hannah clutched at Polly's skirt. "Please come with me... to the tower."

"I will not, indeed. What a suggestion! Do you wish to have me dismissed from my position? I'm in enough trouble as it is."

She shouldn't have admitted that but Hannah merely nodded without surprise. The girls knew everything that went on in the house. And Dora too. They took pleasure in ferreting out the secrets of others. No doubt Lizzie and Mrs Delaney had been discussing Polly's trip home to Mayo over bread-baking in the kitchen.

"It might be Luke in the tower," Hannah suggested with a sly grin. "What if it's Luke?"

Polly made no comment. Was it him? It was possible Luke was hiding there, spying on Kingson and Claudia, afraid that his employer would have contacted the constabulary after the bookkeeping discrepancies. Should she do as Hannah suggested, go out into the moonlit night and discover who was there? She placed her hands on the window sash while she considered.

Would she be brave enough to do that? If there were boys there or, worse still, robbers or republicans, what might become of her?

"Miss Brady?"

"No, Hannah. We are both going to bed. We'll leave whoever is hiding in the tower alone. I'll accompany you to your room now and make sure you go back to bed."

Hannah laughed. "You're frightened, aren't you? You're afraid to go out into the woods, and you're afraid you might meet dangerous men there. You're just like Annie who is pretending to be asleep. She hates the tower house but I'm not frightened."

Polly decided it would be best to let her think that because Hannah wouldn't encourage her to go if she were afraid. "Yes, you're correct, my dear. I'm not going to risk prowling around an old haunted ruin in the dark with all those evil stories whispered about it. Why, there might be armed men there. Imagine what they would do to us! I'm certainly not brave enough." She took hold of the girl's hand and led her to the door. "Now, hush, go quietly along the corridor. We don't want to raise the household."

Hannah kissed her goodnight at the door of her chamber and closed it softly behind her, the sleeping form of Annie under a blanket in the other bed.

Polly stood on the landing for a few minutes, the house draped in shadows, the casement clock ticking in the hall below. At half past eleven it would chime the half hour. A muttering rose and died away in Solomon's bedroom but he often called out in his sleep.

Claudia's cat stole up the stairs and sat to regard her with round yellow eyes. She bent to stroke his smooth black fur.

Hannah's words lingered in her mind. Luke used to meet them in the tower house when Miss Walsh was their governess. Suppose he was there, hiding from his employer and Kingson. Where else might he go when he'd been asked to leave? She'd come across him in the wood the last time, claiming to be feeding the fox and he'd warned her about robbers using the ruin but perhaps he'd made up that story. An untruth to keep her away from one of his secret haunts.

The clock ticked on, minutes passing while she considered. Would it do any harm to creep up to the tower and check if Luke were there? No one else need ever find out. If she slipped out of the house… it was a warm night so she had no need of a coat.

She put her ear to the door of the girls' bedroom. Silence. Hannah must have climbed into bed and fallen asleep.

Polly stepped towards the staircase, anxious every time a floorboard creaked. The cat ran down in front of her, hoping to be allowed out into the garden. She reached the hall and crossed the flagstones, casting a glance over her shoulder to ensure no one was watching her from the landing.

She turned the huge key in the lock and pulled back the bolt, a clatter echoing in the hallway. She held her breath but no shout rang out, no hurried footsteps followed her.

A warm night but there was dew on the grass. Better to avoid the moonlit path across the lawn. She turned left towards the walled physic garden. She would slip into the wood further down, passing through the gate from the garden; along the side of the underground potting shed. If she kept to the shaded parts, it would be less likely anybody would see her.

Polly walked faster, not daring to look back at the shuttered windows of the house. The wrought-iron gate into the trees squeaked on its hinges. She hesitated for a few seconds, waiting for the snap of twigs as someone approached. No, nothing, only the breeze in the branches above her head. The whispering of the pine needles and the answering gurgle of the river as it flowed under the footbridge.

The full moon was a blessing, illuminating her way, bright against the dark sky, like a white face pitted with scars but kind and benevolent, smiling down on her. All she had to do was creep up to one of the windows on the other side of the tower house and peer in. If the lanterns inside were glowing, no one would see her outside in the dark.

She hurried along the path, safe among the trees where no one would see her from the house. The tall mossy rock rose above the pool where she and the children had swum during the heatwave. Like a massive creature in the half-light, squatting above the water. No need to cross the footbridge, just follow the track under the pines.

The ruin came into view, standing in the clearing, a beacon in the moonlight, the side nearest to Polly draped in shadow. She slipped behind a tree trunk and peeped out. She would have to be careful moving across the long grass towards the window but, if she kept to the trees, she might be able to slip behind the building unseen.

A pale shape moved overhead and she flinched, but it was only a barn owl, hunting on silent wings for mice and voles. She watched it glide over the tops of the trees.

A voice rose on the warm air. A man's shout of anger, making her breath catch in her throat. Light flared behind one of the arrow slit windows higher up and for one moment she imagined an archer with his bow trained on her figure amongst the trees, calling out a warning to keep back. The words died away and silence fell again. She waited another five minutes, her limbs stiff with fear.

What was she doing in the woods on such a foolish mission? There was still time to get away, to creep back along the path to the sanctuary of the house.

Was that Luke talking? It didn't sound like him but she wasn't certain. If so, he wasn't alone.

The glow from the lantern danced up the tower, on the spiral stairs that Eamon had climbed before. There weren't many windows on the lower floor but there was an arched doorway near the trees. All she had to do was cross the ten yards of long grass and peep in.

Casting a glance above her head to ensure no one was standing on the open parapet, she hunched her shoulders and hurried to the door. The granite was hard and cold under her hand as she twisted her body to see inside.

A huge fireplace yawned before her, uneven stone slabs on the floor and glowing embers in the grate. Logs had burned there earlier that night. A tin mug sat on the hearth; a blackened kettle hanging on an iron crane above the remains of the fire and an old plaid blanket lying in a heap on the floor.

Polly noticed a cavity in the wall beside the steps leading upwards. If she were to run across to that niche, she would be hidden if anyone came down the spiral staircase. She slid along the wall and into the dark space.

Not a moment too soon. Footsteps echoed above; the scrape of boots on stone. She pressed her body against the granite blocks, holding her breath and praying she was hidden by the darkness. The moon lit up the middle of the great room, beaming through a hole in the roof. A queasiness churned in the pit of her stomach.

The boots on stone grew louder and an oath rang out. A coarse hand, its fingernails grimy with dirt, clutched at the pillar beside her and she shrank back. His rasping breath was followed by a hacking cough, as a glob of spittle landed on the paving at the foot of the steps.

"A curse on them all!" the voice cried out. "I'll curse them all." Another fit of coughing.

Polly pressed back against the wall. Not Luke. How foolish she'd been to think he would be there, to imagine it might be him in the lonely tower. No, it was more likely to be a thief or someone on the run from the constabulary, lying low in a place where people were too terrified to venture at night.

She had no choice. She would have to wait and hope that he wouldn't see her; remain where she was until he'd gone or settled down to sleep under that filthy blanket. Only then would it be safe for her to try to escape. Please God he wouldn't see her because he looked like a man who would show no mercy.

The figure stepped into the shaft of moonlight and reached for a long stick that was leaning against the wall. He gave the dying fire several pokes and a flame shot up. Polly saw the man's back, his ragged coat, hunched shoulders and greasy white hair falling over his face as he rearranged the charred logs with the end of his staff. It was possible he was a tramp, with nowhere else to sleep, or a poacher who roamed the woods at night to snare rabbits for his dinner.

The man moaned, a shallow rattling breath, and peered into the fire for several minutes. He gave it another jab, before tossing the stick away and rubbing his palms together in front of the flames.

The draw in the chimney was poor, smoke belching downwards into the room, no doubt blocked with nests of jackdaws. A sooty cloud floated towards the steps, causing an acrid taste at the back of Polly's mouth. She bent over, stifling a cough. Her eyes watered and she clamped her hand over her mouth, swallowing hard. A loud hiccup shot into the blackness around her and the man turned his head.

It took him two strides to reach her, stooping to snatch up the blanket on his way.

"What have we here, eh?" He caught her by the arm and hauled her out of the niche. "A girl, a girl spying on me." He gave her a shake.

He pushed his face close to her. A stench of stale sweat hit her before he threw the blanket over her head, blotting out all light. He pinned her arms behind her back as she screamed and struggled. She kicked out at his shins but he gave her head a smack as she wriggled under the stinking greasy wool.

"Silence," his harsh tone breathed in her ear, "or you'll regret it. Silence, I said!" He twisted her hands so hard that she sank to her knees in pain.

He fumbled with something, cursing under his breath, while her chest tightened with fear and lack of air. Was he going to suffocate her? Tears pricked but she would not cry. She raised a foot to kick back at him again but he drew a rope around her waist and pulled it tight, so tight that she toppled forward. She whimpered as he bound the blanket in place. Another twist of the rope and he secured her ankles.

"Let's see you escape from that, my little beauty," he said with a laugh that ended in a fit of coughing. "I'll leave you to your fate." He gave her a push that sent her sprawling on the flagstones.

Polly lay still. Was he still there watching her? She forced herself to breathe, battling with waves of panic. There would be air coming through the blanket. She would not suffocate. For a moment she feared she might faint, her head light with dizziness.

Footsteps sounded on the stone, growing more distant until the man reached the grass outside the doorway. He was gone. Thank the Lord. He was going to leave her there in the dark, with the foul blanket over her head but he hadn't tried to attack her apart from that one blow to her head. The man was a lunatic, his eyes red-rimmed and swimming with hatred. What little she'd seen of his face seemed unnaturally pale, covered in sweat, and his lips a dark hue. Perhaps he was ill, suffering from a fever. What if it was contagious and she caught it and died there alone under the thick wool blanket?

She screamed. "Help, please help!" Her cries might bring the villain hurrying back, but a wave of terror at being abandoned overwhelmed her.

Outside the breeze hissed in the pines, like people conversing with each other. Panic gripped her throat, squeezing like taut fingers. She struggled to free herself, her head thumping on the ground.

Minutes passed, long painful minutes while she struggled to draw air into her lungs. Gathering her strength to sit upright, she lifted her head and called out again, "Help me, help me..."

Footsteps. Lighter this time. Were they only in her imagination? She lowered her head to the floor and groaned.

"Miss... miss!"

A girl's voice. One she recognized with a surge of joy.

"Where are you, miss?"

"Hannah, oh, Hannah, help me please..."

Fingers fumbled with the rope binding her.

"Annie, a knife, we need a knife. There's a plate over there, see the knife? Fetch it... hurry."

Polly was crying with relief, tears coursing down her cheeks. She would never scold Hannah again. Never again. The girl must have waited in her bedroom before sneaking to open the door and watch her leave the house. She must have woken Annie and they followed Polly through the woods.

"Oh... thank you... thank you," Polly sobbed. "How can I ever thank you?"

"Hush, miss," Annie said. "No need to fret. Hannah is cutting the rope now. Don't cry, please don't cry. You're safe now."

A moment later she was free. The girls pulled off the blanket and tossed it aside. Polly enfolded them in her arms, expressing her gratitude.

"We saw you go," Hannah said. "I was sure you wouldn't be able to resist going to the tower when you thought Luke might be here. We watched you leave from the window at the top of the stairs."

"What happened to you?" Annie asked.

Polly forced out the words. "A man… a terrifying man. I think he was ill because… but he discovered me spying on him and threw the blanket over my head."

"You were fortunate," Annie said. "He might have done worse."

Hannah reached out to stroke Polly's face. "We saved you, Miss Brady, didn't we?"

Polly managed a weak smile. "You did… indeed you did. I can't contemplate what would have become of me if you hadn't followed me. I thought I was going to die here."

Hannah held a finger to her lips. A harsh cough barked outside.

"He's coming back," Polly whispered. "I recognize that sound. Oh, dear Lord, he's returning. Quick, girls, out the back… we must get away."

Chapter Thirty-Five

The past – July 1895

Polly's aunt punched the dough, thumping it onto the pine table. "You let me down, indeed you did, and you have yet to offer an apology." She flipped over the sticky mass and tossed flour over it before shaping it into a round. "A right young madam you've become in Wicklow. I knew you should never have gone. It put grand ideas into your head… airs and graces you've no right to have."

Polly didn't reply as there seemed little point attempting to argue when her aunt was in a bad temper. The dough would soon be left to rise on the back of the range and Aunt Maureen would sink into her armchair and demand laudanum for her headache which would, of course, be blamed on Polly. Nothing had changed during her absence from home.

"Poor Mrs Manning… an embarrassment to your family, that's what you are. If Mrs Manning weren't such a lady you'd be out on your ear, you mark my words!" She threw the dough into a pan and tossed a cotton cloth over it, brushing flour from her hands. "Are you listening to me?"

To remain silent would be considered a further affront, but what could Polly say that wouldn't antagonize the woman further? She looked up at the wooden ceiling, where shadows danced when the door of the range was jerked open and more sods of turf flung onto the flames.

"Well?" Aunt Maureen demanded, placing the pan on the warm surface behind the plate and, hands on hips, she turned to glare at Polly. "What have you to say for yourself? Look at me when I speak to you."

Better to leave the kitchen; escape from the accusations before Polly uttered words she might regret. Since she'd departed from Colgrannagh, a long week before, her aunt had uttered a daily admonishment berating her ingratitude.

The apology, when it fell from Polly's lips, was barely audible and she wondered if she'd spoken the words aloud. "I'm sorry, Aunt."

"What did you say? Speak up, girl!"

Polly cleared her throat. "I said I'm sorry. I never meant to bring disgrace upon you. That is the truth."

"Indeed! You would have done well to have considered that before you went meddling in affairs that don't concern you. The mortification of it! A young woman like you, poor and with no decent prospects… kindly permitted to educate another woman's children and you take it upon yourself to behave in an ungrateful manner."

If her aunt had been in Mrs Manning's position, she'd have ordered her to pack her belongings and depart; have taken pleasure in it. Polly gazed down at the flagstones under her boots and shifted her weight from one foot to another.

Aunt Maureen gave another snort of displeasure and swung away. "Get out of my sight, girl, and don't come back until teatime."

Her cheeks burning, Polly ran to the door and out into the cool air where she leaned against the wall of the cottage. Her thoughts whirled as the wind blew her hair across her face, the cold calming her after the heat in the kitchen. So many things she could have said to defend herself but why make the effort? She would never win against her aunt and so it had been for as long as she could remember.

Memories flooded back: standing as a small girl with her head bowed while accusations were hurled at her; tiny fingers clutching her pinafore and her mouth squeezed shut to stifle the sobs. She'd rarely given her aunt the pleasure of witnessing tears.

Her aunt's daughter had managed to leave home, finding employment in a mill in Lucan in County Dublin away from the ferocious lashings of her mother's tongue. She was always the pet, but she too could flame irritation if Aunt Maureen were in one of her moods.

Polly shivered and set off to follow the stony path down to the beach, where the wild sea, a monster with white-crested waves, pounded against the rocks. A day when the incoming tide devoured the sand with foaming jaws. Stepping over rocks onto the beach, Polly admired the power of the Atlantic Ocean. A walk would do her good, releasing pent-up frustration after the altercation with her aunt. She only had to endure one more week before she could return to her position in Wicklow and continue her search for Luke.

No letter had arrived from him and no reassuring missive from her employer. Polly's fears were increasing by the day. How strange that he'd contacted no one, and she wondered if he was lying low somewhere, hiding from Kingson and Claudia. He had friends among the locals and there was kind Brother Eugene in the Glencree Reformatory School. Had Luke gone to him for shelter and food? His dismissal without a reference would make it difficult to secure another post, especially if people chose to gossip about the bookkeeping discrepancies and believed him to be untrustworthy.

Polly marched faster, her heart pounding to the rhythm of her footsteps on the sand as she breathed in the sharp salty air.

Overhead a herring gull circled, its harsh cry piercing the roar of wind and waves. Her hair fell loose from its pins and streamed behind. She let it be, no longer caring, for there was no one on this long, deserted strand to take offence at her unkempt appearance. If Aunt Maureen saw her, she would accuse her of being slovenly.

Polly recalled the words she'd overheard whilst hiding in the cupboard under the staircase; Kingson's threats and the fact that he hadn't denied being in Brazil. She put a hand to her glowing cheek. If he were involved with Gilbert Manning's disappearance, he might show no mercy towards Luke. If he were desperate not to be exposed, he might do anything.

She was being fanciful, allowing her anxious thoughts to gallop away like the native ponies in the fields beside the beach. If only she could have seen Luke before she left for Mayo. If only she had some way of knowing that he was safe.

Polly swept hair from her face and walked on, the sting and taste of salt on her lips, whether from the ocean or the tears that now coursed down her face, she cared not. What if she never saw Luke again?

Annie and Hannah had promised not to tell about the night in the tower. Well used to keeping secrets, the girls understood how Polly could lose her position permanently if Mrs Manning discovered she'd been out looking for Luke after dark.

A figure in the distance brought her to a standstill. A tall man dressed in a dark coat and riding breeches with long boots, standing where the shingle met the sand. She felt a rush of joy. Could it be him? Yes, it was because there was Hero the spotted dog frolicking in circles with his tail between his legs, while his owner threw back his head and laughed at his antics.

Polly gathered her skirts in her hands, hoisting up her blue cotton gown and running towards the man who turned to stare at the young woman waving and calling into the wind, "Papa, Papa!"

For one heart-stopping moment she feared she was mistaken when he didn't react but stood watching her, as if frozen to the grains of sand and shell beneath his feet.

"Papa!" Polly shouted again but the breeze snatched her words and threw them back in her face. A herring gull perching on a nearby rock uttered a mocking screech.

At last the man moved towards her with long strides as the Dalmatian chased a black and white bird along the surf, until the oystercatcher took to the air, indignant squeaks coming from its orange bill.

"Polly! Is it you? Can it really be you?" Her father called across the distance between them. "Good Lord, it is, it truly is."

She ran the final yards and he caught her in his arms, lifting her up and swinging her around.

"It's you!" he cried again as he brought her feet to rest on the beach and held her close.

She threw her arms around his neck and leaned her face against the familiar wool coat that smelled of horses and tobacco, swallowing hard to force down the lump in her throat.

He smoothed her hair back and took her face in his hands, raising her head and gazing into her eyes. How blue his were! She'd forgotten how blue. "You are crying, my love! Why are you crying? I thought you would be happy to see me."

Polly sniffed and smiled. "Oh, I am, I am… indeed, so happy to see you, Papa."

Aunt Maureen hated her calling him that but he always encouraged her. He looked tired, deeper lines pulling at the corners of his eyes and a sprinkling of grey among his dark curls.

He slipped his arm around her shoulders. "Let us walk back towards the lane over there because I have left my poor mare tethered to a tree and she may become restless if left for long. Tell me all about Wicklow and how you are getting on. Are they being kind to you?"

She hesitated. "Oh yes." To change the subject, she added, "Did you know I was coming home? I've been here for a week."

He frowned. "A week…"

Polly said, "I wondered if… if Aunt Maureen mentioned anything."

"Not her. She wouldn't let me into the house but I received a letter from Claudia Manning." He pointed to a stand of misshapen trees, crippled by the wind. "Over there behind the rocks, that's where I left the horse."

"I'm in disgrace. My aunt does nothing but scold me."

Her father smiled and leaned to pick up a stick of seaweed which he tossed for the dog, who jumped away, scattering sand over their boots and racing off with a yelp of excitement.

"I suppose that's to be expected." He raised a hand to shield the wind. "That damn woman delights in scolding."

His bay mare stood where he'd left her, tied by a rope and halter placed over the bridle to the trunk of a birch. She raised her head at their approach and nickered a welcome.

Polly rubbed the horse's forehead, her fingers caressing the soft hair while the mare nuzzled her cheek.

Her father watched, his face remaining expressionless and she couldn't guess his thoughts. "What happened in Wicklow?" he asked. "Sit down here beside me and tell me. Don't be afraid." He patted a large boulder sheltered from the wind by a clump of trees. "Tell me, my girl."

It was a relief after her silence at home and, once she began to speak, the words fell out, tumbling over one another. Her father remained silent throughout but reached into his coat pocket and offered her a large linen handkerchief.

"I heard there was a young man…" he said, when she stopped to draw breath.

Polly replied, "He's a… a friend I met in Wicklow." Her mistress must have told him about Luke.

He took the dried seaweed from the eager dog and hurled it towards the beach. "I also heard he's been dismissed from his position."

"Yes… and now he has disappeared. I'm worried for him but he never would have stolen money. He never would."

"I suppose you feel you know this young man well?"

"I do, Papa. He's a little wild, but I'm certain he's honest… I'm sure of it." Polly twisted the damp handkerchief between her fingers. "He wouldn't steal money."

"And yet you say he has disappeared. Hardly the actions of an honest man."

"Perhaps he had good reason… or perhaps he had no choice."

"No choice?" her father asked. "Please explain. What do you mean?"

"I… well, there's a man who wishes to marry my mistress, a man called Robert Kingson and he doesn't like Luke. Luke confronted him, you see, about… it's a long story but it involves the death of Mrs Manning's husband in Brazil. Luke thinks Mr Kingson was involved somehow."

"I've never heard of this Kingson."

She nodded. "Mrs Manning was fond of Luke until Mr Kingson came. It isn't like him not to keep in touch with us. He used to ride over every second day to see Mrs Manning and the girls and…"

"And you? Did he come to see you?"

She gazed at a tuft of marram grass on the sandy path at their feet. A plant that helped to give sand dunes their structure, her father once explained because he'd always been interested in botany. "I suppose he might have. We became… good friends."

He reached out to grasp her hand in his firm one. "You like him, don't you?"

She made no reply, a silence hanging in the air between them.

"Tell me, my dear. You can confide in me."

She would have to admit it. "Yes, I do. I like him because we think the same way… most of the time. We have interests and feelings in common. But then Mrs Manning warned me not to get too close to him… but I don't understand why she turned against him for she was always so fond of Luke." She added, "It has to be Mr Kingson's doing."

"You have changed, Polly. I believe that you've grown up since you left home. What if Mrs Manning is correct and Luke is not a good friend for you?"

"Why? Why would you say that? You've never met him!"

"Don't pull away like that. Please don't take offence for I was only suggesting… I'm concerned your employer fears for you."

She relaxed again, leaning her head against his shoulder. "I don't understand why she would be afraid."

He picked up a twig and twirled it in his hands, before saying, "She might know more about him than you, have you considered that?"

"Like what?"

"About this fellow's character. She knows him since he was a teenage boy. He came from a difficult background."

Polly turned to him but he was staring at the piece of stick between his fingers. A thought struck. "How do you… how do you know about his background?"

Her father made no reply but his mouth tightened.

She reached out a hand and laid it on his sleeve. "How do you know?" Her fingers gripped his arm. "Tell me, Papa, please."

She thought for a moment that he was going to jump to his feet and stride towards his horse, saying it was time he went home in the way he often had in the past if she asked questions he didn't wish to answer. "Tell me," she pleaded.

He tossed away the stick and swung round to take her face in his hands. "Polly, my sweet Polly, how I wish I could tell you. I could have told you years ago and it might have been for the best but…" He dropped his hands and turned away.

She was aware of an ache in her chest, like a band tightening, making it difficult to breathe. She gripped his arm again. "Told me what? What, Papa?"

"I have been foolish… I was a young and foolish man."

"You've mentioned that before."

A half-smile flickered. "Yes, and I repeat it now. Perhaps I will always be foolish. Perhaps Aunt Maureen is correct and I will always be foolish. God knows, she doesn't think much of me. She wouldn't like to see me here, talking to you like this."

"No aunt… no relation of mine." She spat out the words. "She's bitter and hard-hearted. That's what she's like. She resents me… she resented having to take me in as her own and, if it hadn't been for your money, she would never have agreed."

"Don't say that, please don't say that, my dear. You make me regret my actions even more but I know you're right. She's not a kind… never was a kind woman. My father didn't choose a good woman. He should never have made that arrangement with her and I was too immature and weak to object. If only Mama had lived. She would have understood and helped you… she would have stood by me. You should have remained with me… with us but you realize he was a cold proud man who wanted nothing to do with his son's…"

Polly cried out, "Yes, yes. Aunt Maureen told me so many times. She said if it hadn't been for her, I would have been sent off to the workhouse in Westport. What would have happened to me there? You know what those places are like and if I'd survived the fever and dysentery… She said girls like me, girls who were a disgrace to their families, used to be packed off to Australia. I heard it so many times that I believe she wished me there."

He winced at her words and replied, "If I hadn't been so young… I was eighteen, Polly, eighteen years of age and only a boy, a stupid impulsive boy who fancied himself in love." He looked up and forced a smile. "But what good does it do to dwell on the past and the mistakes I made? What matters is now. I have to get you away from Maureen Brady and her cruel ways. My God, the whole countryside sees how she maligns you. I thought Colgrannagh would be the solution."

"It was... it can still be."

"My father's dead now and no longer able to dictate what happens. He made me marry an heiress from England, you know that. He found a wife for me, the daughter of a friend of his in the army with enough of a fortune to keep our great barracks of a house running. I would have you with me, living there, Polly, if it weren't for her. You know that, don't you? She cares too much about..."

Polly stroked Hero's head when he laid it in her lap. "I understand. She cares about what people think."

He sighed. "It's not a good marriage. I should never have agreed but my father insisted. He wanted me to produce an heir... the usual story."

"I'm sorry to hear that." Had he always loved her mother, her real mother? The wild servant girl who'd run away and left her baby behind.

She was about to ask but he spoke first. "Polly, my dear, will you return to Wicklow? Do you wish to return there because if you don't..."

"I want to go back, of course I do. I enjoy working with the children and Mrs Manning is usually kind... and I want to find Luke. I have to discover what has happened to him."

"This Luke has certainly made an impression on you. I want you to be careful, Polly. Please, be careful, don't let him steal your heart."

She shook her head but didn't reply.

"Promise me that. Promise me that you won't let him steal your heart."

"I can't, I can't. Why do you say the same as Mrs Manning? Why do you both think that Luke can't be trusted?"

He took her hand in his, raised it to his lips and kissed it. "Not your… it's not your fault… and it's not Luke's either, truth be told. I can't help but feel I've made another foolish mistake in sending you there. I never knew…"

"Knew what, Papa?"

"Claudia Manning and I have known each other since childhood. Her father was an uncle of a schoolfriend and I spent time with him at Colgrannagh years ago. I thought she would be a good person to take care of you… for your first position. I thought she would watch over you and keep you safe… when I couldn't."

"Oh, but she has been good to me. She has."

"I'm sure she has but now… now you doubt her judgement about this Kingson fellow." He was still grasping her hand. "She wrote, yes… and last time, a few days ago, she asked me to tell you the truth. She thought it only fair."

"The truth?" What could he mean?

"Claudia thought I should be the one to tell you… said it wasn't her place."

Polly put a hand to her throat.

"I must tell you, my child. For years... all this time I've said nothing and now I see that I have caused more hurt, more heartache for you… if only you've not fallen in love with this young man. Can you at least assure me of that?"

She faltered at the expression on his face, the concern in his eyes. "I… I can't. I can't assure you."

"Then this will be hard for you to hear and I'm truly sorry, believe me."

"You must tell me," she said. "What could be so bad that you can't tell me?"

Her father got to his feet, pushing a hand through his thick hair and holding out the other to help her up, but still made no reply.

"You *must* tell me."

He touched her cheek, a quick stoke with his forefinger. "How grown up you are! I would hardly recognize the timid little girl on the beach… the child I used to play with all those years ago. You have strong feelings now, I see that. I am almost afraid of you!"

She tried to smile. "What nonsense!"

"I must tell you. I am sincerely sorry but I've only recently found out…"

"Tell me, please."

"Very well. A priest came to see me, a priest who taught Luke at the reformatory school who knows his background."

"Brother Eugene?"

"Ah, I see you've been told about him. So, this Brother Eugene paid me a visit and said he had news for me. What he said… I couldn't believe it at first. All these years I've remained silent because I feared he was dead. Polly, my dear, the reason Claudia Manning didn't encourage a deeper friendship between you and Luke is because… because he is my son."

Son. The word struck her like a blow and she gasped.

"My son," he repeated more loudly, his voice sounding hoarse. "Luke is my son. His mother… your mother… ran away and left you behind but she took him." He cleared his throat. "She took your brother with her. I'm sorry… I'm so sorry."

Polly shrank back. "Luke is my brother…"

"Yes." Her father's words sounded distant, as if he were speaking from a long way off, barely audible above the roaring in her ears. "Luke is your twin brother."

Chapter Thirty-Six

"I've no need to ask where you've been. You've been cavorting with that useless father of yours," Aunt Maureen shouted from the door of the cottage, hands on her hips, a scowl twisting her face.

Polly kept her eyes on the copse of wind-worn pines where she'd said goodbye to him.

"Answer me, girl."

She'd put up with her antagonism for years, too timid to answer back and afraid of attracting more anger. It was time to change that. She turned to face her aunt. "He's not useless. I'll thank you to use kinder words to describe your benefactor."

The older woman snorted, uttering a mirthless laugh. "My benefactor, if you please! That is certainly a good jest, indeed it is. He's far from being my benefactor. His father, now, he was a different man… understood how to command respect and keep people in their place."

"You should remember that my father paid for the education of your daughter."

"Now, miss, I don't like your impertinent tone. Paid for my daughter's education… why, that was payment for services rendered. It was for bringing up his illegitimate brat and concealing her true identity from the world but you… ungrateful hussy that you are, risk bringing shame on us when you're seen in his company. What will people think?"

Polly lifted one shoulder in a half-hearted shrug. "What they always think. It's not as if they don't know. They know only too well and I suspect that you told them because you can't resist boasting about your so-called magnanimous…"

The seamstress reached out, grabbing Polly's arm and digging fingernails into her flesh beneath the thin cotton sleeve. "How dare you! How dare you answer me back like that! Your time in Wicklow hasn't done much for your manners. Go to your room!"

It would be better to leave, to hurry away before her aunt's temper reached boiling point and she lashed out with whatever object was near to hand; a rolling pin once and the soup ladle on another occasion. The local doctor had tutted when he'd seen the bruises on Polly's limbs after one such beating but he'd said nothing. No one dared to stand up to the village seamstress. She had too much information about everybody's business.

Polly pushed past the woman and hurried up the narrow staircase to her tiny room overlooking the yard at the back of the cottage. She slumped onto the bed, startled by her reflection in the dressing table mirror. How defiant she was with her flaming cheeks and hair tossed by the breeze! If Aunt Maureen threw her out the next day, ordering her to pack her belongings and never darken the doorway again, what difference would it make? Polly was an educated woman with experience as a governess and she would ask her father to help her. He might persuade Claudia Manning to give her a reference. She would go to Dublin and teach other children if she were no longer welcome at Colgrannagh.

Her father would help her, he definitely would. He wouldn't mind if she asked him for money; a loan to pay for lodgings in the city and she would work hard to repay every penny.

She lay down, overcome by the walk in the sea wind, her

father's revelation about Luke and the quarrel with Aunt Maureen. She must have drifted off to sleep because, when she next glanced at the window, night was descending. Polly got to her feet and peered out into the darkening yard. She could just make out the shorthorn cow standing in the byre, pulling hay from the rack.

The cow withdrew her head and Polly glimpsed a figure hiding behind the animal. She dropped to her knees on the bare boards, pressing her face to the glass. No, she was mistaken. Nobody there. Had her aunt asked someone else to look at the cow? But wouldn't he have brought a lantern? No, it was just a figment of her imagination, conjured up by her overwrought state of mind.

She was rising to her feet when the shape reappeared, this time a head peeping over the door and turning from side to side, as if making certain nobody was watching.

Polly laid her palms flat on the window ledge. The man in the tower house. Had he followed her to Mayo?

Shadows were creeping along the back wall of the cottage and a crescent moon dangled above the crooked hawthorns behind the cow byre. Polly sat back on her haunches. Or could the man be a thief, come to steal their belongings and beat the two women senseless after nightfall?

Polly watched the figure open the door of the byre and slip away into the gloom near the donkey shed, stooping under the branch of a hawthorn at the corner of the building.

A thought struck her. Was he a messenger sent by Luke? She had a choice: lie on her bed and read a book or go out and follow the man; discover what he was up to. It didn't take her long to decide, but she had to move silently so as not to attract the attention of her aunt.

She pulled on her wool shawl and, holding her breath as her bedroom door creaked open, she tiptoed down the stairs. The kitchen was empty, the lamp extinguished and wooden chairs tilted against the table where her aunt had been sweeping. There was the brush leaning against the sink, a bad omen. If her aunt had made no effort to put it away, the obsessively tidy woman was in a very bad temper.

Polly lingered at the foot of the stairs, straining her ears for any sound. She would have to be quick.

Lifting the latch, she stole out and pulled the door closed behind her.

Where had the man gone? She'd last glimpsed him under the hawthorn as he turned away from the cottage. He might still be there, waiting in the shadows until the two women were asleep. He wouldn't be expecting her but she'd have to be careful. Best to creep round the back of the cow byre and approach the yard with the field behind her. That way, if the man turned violent, she had a way of escape across the grass and down to the trees that sheltered the road. He might not know the lie of the land as well as she did, if he wasn't from the area. She decided to take a gamble on that.

She turned to the left and edged along the back wall of the cottage, ducking under her aunt's window where a candle glowed behind the curtains. The slap and suck of waves came from the beach. High tide and no sand left; the water licking the stones near the pathway. If she had to run, there would be no point heading that way.

She stretched out her hands in the dim light, running her fingers along the rough whitewashed wall of the turf shed. The byre came next with its comforting smell of sweet hay. How many times had she taken refuge in there when her aunt was in a fury? Safely concealed in the cool dark space while the cow nosed her hair.

She reached the corner beside the hawthorn, its branches clutching at the thatched roof of the donkey shed. Polly leaned against the stone wall, holding her breath. No sound except for the sigh of the sea. Minutes passed and wind stirred in the twigs above her head. The cow stamped a hoof in the byre, munching her hay.

Polly stood listening, wondering what to do and if she should slip back the way she'd come to the safety of her bedroom. Was she risking unnecessary danger out there in the dark? She remained where she was. The man was nearby, she was certain.

A shadow fell on the stones at her feet, a shape thrown by the light of the moon, and Polly froze. He was there, only a few yards away. She waited again and, hearing nothing, took a step forward, edging around the corner of the donkey shed.

"Who are you?" she demanded in a low fierce whisper.

A slim figure moved towards her. "Polly?"

That voice! It must be… it had to be. "Luke?"

"Yes, I thought… I was afraid you were the woman," he said. "It was difficult to see in the darkness and I never heard you creep up on me."

She glanced up at Aunt Maureen's window and replied, "I saw you in the cow byre and I decided to… but what are you doing here?"

He took her into his arms, pulling her close in an embrace, his mouth in her hair. "Oh, Polly, I am glad to see you… so glad to see you." He held her face between his hands, as if trying to read her expression. "Are you… are you pleased to see me?"

"Of course, of course I am. I was so worried about you. I thought something had happened… that something terrible had befallen you."

He smiled in the half-light, a familiar grin stretching across his freckled face.

"But, Luke, tell me why you are here," she said. "What made you come to Mayo and how did you find me?"

"I have a lot to tell you, but first… where can we go where we'll be away from prying eyes?"

Polly pointed towards the candlelit window. "We can't stay here. That's my aunt's bedroom and she has ears like a bat. She'll hear us."

"So where, then?"

"The shore… I think the shore. The tide is in but we can sit on the shingle at the top of the beach. I'll lead the way… you follow me."

With a glance back at the cottage and the gleam from the candle dancing up Aunt Maureen's curtains, Polly crept towards the wall behind the shed and climbed over the stones, her hands on their covering of velvet green moss. She heard the scrape of Luke's boots as he scrambled after her. Luke, her brother. Her twin brother. Thank the Lord he was safe.

He'd no idea she was his sister. His embrace at their meeting told her that much. How would she tell him? The revelation might come as an unpleasant shock.

No time to examine her own feelings, she had to keep moving because, when the moon slid from behind the clouds, the countryside would be illuminated in a silver glow.

A wooden gate stood at the entrance to the lane leading down to the sea; a stout rope knotted to the post. Polly gripped the top bar and climbed up, hoisting her skirt over and dropping into the long grass on the other side.

Luke landed beside her with a chuckle. "Aren't we a pair of miscreants?"

"Hush, say nothing yet. This way, down this lane. Another few minutes and we'll be at the beach."

She led him to the sanctuary of a large boulder and they sat behind it, facing the ocean. The water glimmered in the darkness.

"You live in a fine spot, there's no doubt about that." He leaned closer and stroked her cheek with a finger. "Thank you, thank you for caring about me. I heard how you rode to my employer's house and how you spoke to Mrs Manning and tried to defend me. Let me assure you, I was dismissed for nothing, for absolutely nothing. It was just a fabricated story… but that's what happens to men like me… with my background."

Polly withdrew from his caress but caught his hand and held it in her own. "Was it Kingson?"

"It was him. I'm sure of it. The snake came to my master and told him that he'd heard me boasting about taking money from him… that I'd deliberately altered the account ledgers to cover my crime."

Polly let out a breath and said, "Oh, it was him! I guessed it was him."

"Kingson is a credible liar and he has the backing of the doctor… and now Mrs Manning too."

"So unfair! What will you do?"

"Kingson told me the constabulary was coming, so I had to get away," Luke replied. "I had no time to alert you… I believed what Kingson said would convince them I was guilty, so I ran. He assured me that I had bad blood and no magistrate would trust me. And he's right about the law, he's correct about that. They wouldn't believe me."

She squeezed his hand. "Where did you run?"

"To Brother Eugene in Glencree. He agreed to look after me. He hid me in an empty shed in the reformatory and brought me food. It was kind of him… there would have been trouble for him if we were caught. I owe him so much."

Polly watched the dark shifting water. "Your disappearance only made you appear more guilty."

He frowned. "Don't I know that?"

"I couldn't understand why you didn't come to Mrs Manning for assistance but I realize now. Kingson would have sent for the constabulary if he saw you there at Colgrannagh. He has my mistress under his control now. When I tried to defend you, she turned on me and sent me home," Polly said, shivering and pulling her shawl around her shoulders.

Luke gazed up at the moon for a few moments. "Hannah and Annie told me there is to be an engagement soon. The girls are good at keeping an eye on what goes on at Colgrannagh and informing me. We have a secret way of sending messages to each other… one of the trees in the wood, near the bridge, has a hole in the trunk and we slip them into it."

"You shouldn't encourage them," Polly replied. "You'll get them into trouble. They sneaked out into the dark after me and…"

"Ah, you sound like the governess now!"

"Let me finish, if you please. I saw a light in the tower house and thought it was you. I went to investigate. Oh Luke, there was a man… a man like a thief or a tramp there and he tied a blanket over my head and…"

"My God! Who was he?"

"I've no idea… I didn't see his face. He had longish white hair and looked dirty from living outdoors."

"A thief, no doubt. They must use the ruin for sleeping, if they're on the run from the constabulary." Luke shook his head and added, "A foolish thing to do… to go there on your own in the dark. But listen to me, there's to be a dinner before the engagement is announced, so I intend to put in an appearance."

"No, Luke, no… you can't risk it."

"I'll expose him!" he cried. "I'll stand up and tell everyone what he did and how he's only marrying my guardian for the tree bark and the money."

"You can't. They won't listen to you. Not even Mrs Manning will listen to you anymore. No, Luke, please, you'll be arrested and thrown in jail. You can't risk it."

"Brother Eugene is helping me. He has heard from his friend in Brazil and Kingson was definitely there with Gilbert Manning. He knew about the bark, about its potential value as a cure for fever… Brother Eugene's friend said it might be the discovery of the century. No wonder Kingson is interested in it."

"Does he… does he think Mr Manning was killed because of it?"

Luke nodded. "He's certain of it. Kingson is ruthless. Brother Eugene says he'll try to discover more about his past before he came to Ireland."

Doubt lingered in Polly's mind. Luke would be foolhardy to try to stop the engagement without real evidence, without a witness who could help expose Kingson.

He continued, words spilling out. "He let it slip once when talking to me that he came from London. Brother Eugene has contacts there. They'll track him down and when they do…"

"Then wait, please wait." She grabbed his arm. "Wait for definite proof before you try to expose Kingson."

"I have no time, don't you understand? I have no time because the dinner is in two weeks. I have to do this… have to stop her marrying him."

"No, Luke. You must wait. Do you want to go to jail?"

He turned to her, putting an arm round her shoulders and drawing her to him. "I want you to come with me. That's why I'm here. I want you to help me."

"I will, let me do this. Let me be the one who exposes him at the dinner."

"Would you? Would you be brave enough?"

"Let me do it," she said again. "I may be dismissed but they can't put me in jail. It's too risky for you."

He smiled. "I'm so grateful to you, Polly, for caring about me… caring enough to offer to take my place."

The water shimmered in front of her. "I will probably lose my position if Mrs Manning doesn't believe what Brother Eugene has to say."

He leaned closer, peering into her face. "If you're concerned…

about getting into trouble, about losing your position…"

"I will help you but… I need to talk to my father, Luke."

He wasn't listening, struggling with guilt. "I shouldn't allow you to do this but we have to stop Kingson marrying Mrs Manning. He will take everything from us… from her… from the girls… you too, Polly. He will get rid of you… of anybody who challenges him. He won't rest until he has his hands on the bark."

"I must speak to my father first," Polly replied. Papa might be able to help. He'd known Mrs Manning since he was a boy.

Luke added, "Kingson pretends he wants to help her with her career… with her application to the Royal College of Surgeons. He claims he has influence there."

"Luke, my father… Papa might help us. Let me talk to him."

He frowned at her. "Your father? Why would he be interested?"

"He might know how to help. He knows Mrs Manning and he might be able to influence her." She could say the words; tell Luke that he was his father too but they stuck in her throat. No, it wasn't her place to tell him. Papa would have to do that.

"I don't trust your father," Luke said. "I don't trust the man, and he abandoned you so I don't like him."

"He never abandoned me. He never did."

"He sent you to live with that woman you're obliged to call your aunt… the one who beat you and treated you like a social outcast. Others told me what she did, Polly. I asked questions when I arrived in this county. The locals have no love for her."

Her voice trembled when she replied, "Papa had no choice. His father made him give me up. Papa always kept in touch with me… paid for my education. It was his father who washed his hands of us."

"Us? You mean you and your aunt?"

She'd nearly given it away. Pity for Luke swept over her. His earnest expression only made her feel worse and she hated lying to him. He would have to learn the truth about his father but she couldn't tell him. "Me. Papa's father… my grandfather wanted nothing to do with me."

"Well, that's typical, isn't it?" He snorted. "That's what he tells you. Blames his own father."

"Will you come with me to meet Papa?"

"If I come with you, he'll report me to the constabulary."

"He's not like that," she said. "I promise you… Papa isn't like that. He wants to meet you."

"A likely story."

"He does. I know he… I told him about you… that we're friends and he wishes to meet you."

Luke looked so forlorn, so boyish as he sat on the pebbles beside her, that she leaned forward to stroke his hair. "I'll speak to Papa and he'll meet you tomorrow, perhaps. He knows Claudia Manning and he wouldn't want her to come to harm. He helped me to find the position in Colgrannagh."

"Did he, now? And how does he know her? I suppose you're going to tell me he had heard about me too… and the girls and where they came from? I bet he has a lot of sympathy for children abandoned like we were," he said with scorn.

"All these questions!" She forced a laugh. "It's late. I must get back because Aunt Maureen is a light sleeper and if she discovers me missing… if she locks me in my bedroom, I won't be able to meet you again tomorrow night."

His eyes brightened. "Will I come back here to this beach?"

"No more talk, Luke. I have to go." She planted a quick kiss on his cheek and got to her feet. "I'll meet you here tomorrow night… here after dark. No, don't interrupt. I'll leave out some bread for you tonight on the windowsill opposite the byre. Bread and a glass of milk. A slice of bacon too if you like because you must be starving."

He mumbled his thanks, reaching for her but she spun away and hurried into the darkness of the lane.

Chapter Thirty-Seven

The present – September 2022

I turned to smile at Tobie on the old Victorian causeway, resting my hands on the railing. "This was built in 1889 as a link from Mulranny village across Trawoughter Bay and the salt marsh over to the main beach."

"Spectacular, isn't it, Archie?" he replied, looking down at the Jack Russell panting beside him.

I could see the village along the shoreline with the nineteenth-century hotel on the hill, and I imagined ladies in long dresses with bustles and lacy parasols over their heads descending the steep steps of the hillside. I yearned, as I often did, to be transported back for even a single hour to observe and eavesdrop.

"It's beautiful," Tobie murmured.

I smiled. "Isn't it wonderful? The vast sweep of sandy beach and hardly anyone here apart from those teenagers over there by the pier. Apparently the wild flowers are spectacular in May… a carpet of sea pinks covers the marsh. You should come back and you could also drive down to the Burren in Clare and see the wild flowers there."

"I could. Perhaps you would be kind enough to volunteer as my guide."

"I went to the Burren once on a school trip with the geography teacher… assistant with forty-five kids, all wild with excitement at escaping from the city for a long weekend."

"You'd be the perfect guide," he said.

"Oh, I might be expensive."

We both laughed.

My phone pinged. A text message from Daniel, which I read.

"How's he doing?" Tobie peered over my shoulder.

"He says he's doing well. The physiotherapist is making him walk further each day. At the end of next week, he'll be going to stay in a rehab clinic and spend another few weeks there until they're happy he can go home." I pointed across the causeway. "We might as well walk out to the beach. What do you think? It's supposed to be worth seeing."

He waved a hand. "Lead on."

When we stepped down onto the sand, I said, "I'll let Archie off the lead." The Jack Russell ran around me in frenzied circles before barking at a seagull and running off. "Do you think Polly walked across this causeway? I imagined her living in a more isolated area… the beach close to the door of her aunt's cottage. I remember reading in her diary that the house wasn't far from the ocean."

"She might have come here for a day out, if she was allowed such a thing, though it sounds like her aunt was a tyrant." Tobie bent to pick up a shell and held it aloft, twirling it in the sunlight. "See this. Very pretty. Probably dropped by a gull or washed up by the Atlantic Ocean. You keep it… here, take it, and keep it to remind you of…" He gripped my hand for a few moments and pressed the shell into my palm.

"Thank you." We conversed in unfinished sentences more and more, leaving unspoken words floating between us; words that could have beckoned us down a different path. The wrong path? I didn't know but I was cautious and too much of a coward to take the risk.

I'd finished Polly's diary two days before, completing my notes and deciding to follow in the governess's footsteps to Mayo. Even in modern times, the county was still a long way from Wicklow: four hours in a car across Ireland. Millicent and Kenny had gone to Cork for the weekend and weren't at Colgrannagh to prevent Tobie from coming with me.

Tobie had booked two rooms in a guest house on the outskirts of the village. With a soaring sense of happiness which I chose to ignore, I filled up my car with fuel and we headed off.

Pushing the tiny shell into the pocket of my jeans, I said, "Polly might have gone further down the coast. If only she'd continued with her diary. What made her stop writing?"

"Concern about someone reading it… the aunt might have been an inquisitive type, or maybe she didn't want her employer to find it… or that guy Kingson who sounds like he might get his hands on anything."

"We only have Polly's side of the story," I replied. "We don't know what Kingson was really like. She might have imagined he was responsible for Luke's disappearance."

"I'm becoming more convinced that Luke is the one I found in the underground shed. The carbon dating of the bones might give us an idea of the man's age… or can they do that sort of thing?"

"I don't know how specific it is… and I suppose an old skeleton from more than a century ago isn't a priority," I replied. "They must have more pressing investigations."

We fell silent and walked on until we reached Mulranny beach, where the sand stretched away from us, a golden arc with glistening water.

I found a sheltered spot behind a large rock and, pulling the rucksack off my back, I opened a bottle of water and passed another to him. Archie flopped down beside me and rested his head on his paws.

"Thanks," Tobie said, twisting the lid and raising the bottle to his lips. "I think you have a nice job. You can play the detective without the gory bits. It's like solving a crime mystery, digging up evidence from the past."

"That skeleton was my first." I smiled. "I mostly get clients who want me to draw up their family trees… not very exciting, although my first project in Wexford three years ago… a man murdered in a wood over a century before, that was interesting."

Tobie lay back against the boulder, closing his eyes. "Sounds good. More fun than planting gardens for people like Millicent."

"I suppose some family research is like a cold case… a mystery concerning people from the past who disappear. If families knew where they went, they wouldn't need me."

"You don't regret giving up your full-time career as a history teacher?"

I peeled off my sweater, resting my head against it on the rock. "I hope I won't. It's too early to tell. I would be back in the classroom by now if I were still in that school. Maybe I'll run out of money and have to go begging to the principal for my job."

He didn't smile but gave me a sudden piercing stare before fixing his gaze on the sparkling sea again.

Another silence fell between us, more words unsaid. I heard the lapping of waves on the shore, the tide creeping towards us.

"If Polly's father lived in a big house near here," Tobie said, "then it might be easier to find than her aunt's cottage, which might have crumbled away by now."

"You'd think so. It would help if we knew his name but she never mentions it in her diary and he doesn't feature in letters from Claudia's acquaintances and family." I sat up and scratched at the sand with a small piece of driftwood, writing my initials and rubbing them out with a sweep of my palm.

I watched a figure approach, but it was hard to see her face against the sun. A woman with a golden retriever and dressed for a much colder day in a long mac and jeans. I wondered if she was foreign and unused to our climate.

She cast a glance in our direction and walked on, whistling to the dog to follow.

Tobie jumped to his feet. "Excuse me," he called after her. "Excuse me, please."

She looked over her shoulder at him.

"Are you a local?" Tobie enquired, as I also stood up and brushed sand from my clothes.

The woman frowned and looked like she wasn't used to being hailed by tourists in this quiet spot.

"Do you live near here?" Tobie tried again, giving her a cheerful grin. "Only, we're doing family research, you see… at least, Fiona here is and we're looking for a seamstress from the late nineteenth century called Mrs Brady."

The retriever trotted over to Tobie and sniffed his legs, as if checking him out on behalf of his owner, before crouching down and uttering a playful woof at Archie. The terrier yelped with excitement and took off across the beach with the bigger dog in pursuit.

"I'm sorry," I said and shouted at my dog, who ignored me.

The woman shrugged. "Don't worry. He does that. My fault for not putting him on the lead when I came up to you." She had a Scottish accent. She repeated toTobie, "Brady, you said."

"Yes," he replied. "Lived somewhere near here, perhaps this village or one nearby."

"I'm from Edinburgh so I'm not that *au fait* with the people who live in the area. Only moved here two months ago."

Archie and the golden retriever were in the shallow water on the edge of the sand, leaping and splashing. I tried calling again but they were having too much fun to pay attention.

"Is there a mansion near here?" I asked. "Have you seen one? We think a young woman called Polly Brady was born somewhere like that."

The woman checked her watch. "I'm meeting my husband for lunch soon. A big house? There's one on the road to our place. A long avenue and tall chimneys behind a clump of trees… never been there but it's an old Georgian building. I don't think anyone lives there now so that might not be any help to you."

Tobie pulled out his phone and opened a map. "Somewhere here?" He pushed it towards her.

She peered at the screen. "Need my glasses to see. Is there a sizeable house mentioned about four miles away? The name is… what is the name? Begins with Glen. There was also a village once, I think."

Tobie enlarged the map with his fingertips and I pointed. "There, See! Glenbegnal House."

The woman smiled. "Yes, that's it. Glenbegnal House. There's only a water pump left where the village used to be. I take the dog along that stretch of road sometimes because there isn't much traffic. A lot of the cottages were abandoned when people moved to the city for work."

"They probably emigrated to England or America in those days," I replied.

"Thank you," Tobie gave her a smile. "We'll drive over and check it out. I hope you catch your dog."

She laughed and waved a dismissive hand. "I'll walk on and he'll soon follow. Goodbye and I hope you find your Polly."

"I envy her," Tobie said, watching her walk away.

"Why?"

"She's going to have lunch."

"Oh, for goodness sake. We have a picnic in the car, don't forget."

"She's probably got a treat like seafood chowder or mussels in wine waiting for her and all I've got is a chicken and salad roll."

"You Frenchmen and your food."

"Ha! Does it have to be all work this weekend?"

"What do you mean?"

"What I mean is… do you need to work all the time? We could go for this drive, find Glenbegnal House and then what? I'd like to see more of the Mayo coastline. It's a waste to come here and not see more of the area. How about we drive to Achill Island and I buy you dinner somewhere later this evening?"

I bent to click the lead on an exhausted Archie who'd given up chasing his large companion and returned to us, flopping down with his tongue lolling. "Okay."

"Okay? Is that all you can say?" Tobie twisted his mouth and made a face like a disappointed child.

I laughed. "Dinner sounds good, thank you."

He sighed and lifted his shoulders. "Yeah, you're not a romantic, are you, Fiona?"

"Are you used to women falling in romantic heaps at your feet?"

"Women rarely fall at my feet. You shouldn't let one bad experience put you off, you know. We're not all like Dominic."

I looked down at the terrier at my heel. "I know."

He caught my hand in his and gave it a squeeze, holding onto it while my cheeks flamed like those of a teenage girl. "Hey, you're blushing. Why the embarrassment?"

I extracted my fingers from his grip and swung away, pulling on Archie's lead. "I'm not embarrassed."

Tobie followed me in silence as I walked towards the causeway. He was married, I reminded myself, and although he and his wife were separated, it mightn't always be so. Some couples made up their differences and got back together. Even Dominic, after his fling with the journalist, had tried to get me back when she dumped him. I could allow a flirtation with Tobie to develop into a more serious relationship, but then he would go back to France, back to Isabelle and his son. She'd be tired of Paris and want to return to Provence and the security of her marriage. No, no, I would be crazy to consider a liaison, however casual, with the charming Frenchman.

He led the way up onto the bridge, stopping to offer a hand which I refused. He shrugged and moved away as I watched the sunlight on the back of his head, his broad shoulders and strong arms from physical work. Tobie was an outdoor man, so different to Dominic who sat hunched over his computer screen for hours on end and used to snap at me in irritation if he suspected I was checking up on his gambling addiction.

We climbed the steps up to the main street, stopping to catch our breath on the steep hill. I looked back through the trees to the beach below.

"A memorable place," Tobie said again. "I won't forget today." He offered to drive my car to give me a rest and held out his hand for the key.

I sat in the passenger seat, my elbow leaning on the open window, admiring the countryside, the narrow roads lined with stone walls, the brilliance of the ocean, wind tossing my hair. Was that a skylark above? I couldn't tell because it was too far away but my father would have known.

He was keen on ornithology and I'd packed all his books in cardboard boxes, awaiting my new home. I couldn't give them away; didn't have the heart to because they were part of my childhood, part of my memories of him. He'd taken Anthony and me to bird sanctuaries to watch starling murmurations and geese flying in from Greenland. I would have to get serious about finding a home; an apartment or small house in Dublin, or perhaps Wicklow. That might not be so expensive. But I would have to get Dominic out of my life first. Otherwise he would arrive on my doorstep demanding a bed.

After about ten minutes, large pillars loomed ahead on the right-hand side of the road. "Is that it?" I asked.

Tobie stopped the car and checked the map on his phone.

"Might be. We've driven far enough."

I leaned across him. Rusty ornate gates stood in front of us. One slumped on the ground, its hinge broken, and long grass ran along the middle of the avenue.

"Looks unused, don't you think?" I said. "But it's the only entrance we've passed that could lead to a large house. Perhaps the family has fallen on hard times."

"Or they could have all died and the place is empty," Tobie replied.

"Let's drive in and see."

He swung the car between the pillars and we bumped over potholes where rain had washed away the gravel. A copse of battered pines stood nearby, huddled together against squalls from the sea.

We passed the trees and the lane took a sudden turn to the left.

"Oh look!" I pointed in front of us.

A vast house lay ahead, with windows shuttered and steps running up to double doors under a portico. Jackdaws circled overhead and several slates in one corner of the roof had crashed to the ground, leaving gaping holes like missing teeth. I glanced at Tobie and his eyebrows joined together in a frown.

"No one lives here," he said. "It's almost a ruin. The timber is rotten in some of those windows. Nobody has lived here for years."

Chapter Thirty-Eight

The pair of doors appeared solid, with an ancient brass knocker faded to a green patina from lack of polish. The entrance was flanked on either side by ornate vertical windows with their glass still intact. Heads of dandelions peeked from crevices in the stone steps, golden in the sunshine, and a cloud of bees droned overhead.

"Honey bees, look at the swarm!" Tobie pointed up. "They must have a hive inside the door… or perhaps inside the wall of the house. See that small hole in the stonework on the left. I bet the queen bee went in there and the rest of the hive followed."

"I believe that's supposed to be good luck for a house, isn't it? Bees living in a home."

He frowned at the missing slates and the grass poking long fingers from gutters eaten away by rust. "Not so lucky for this old place. Looks like it has been empty for a long time. There could be anything living in the house… and not just bees… other wildlife and maybe the occasional ghost or two." He jerked his head towards the building. "Shall we go around to the back?"

The glass in some of the bottom windows was cracked, a few panes missing with sheets of plastic taped into position to keep out the rain.

I called out, "Let's see what the inside of the house is like. Empty, probably, because I'm sure the family departed many decades ago." I climbed up on a stone trough to peer in.

Inside was a ballroom, with a faded rug on the dusty floorboards and cobwebs in corners of the ceiling. A chandelier still hung in the middle, its crystal glass dull and lifeless in the shadowy light.

"It's still furnished, Tobie. Isn't that odd? I expected it to be empty."

Books white with mildew lined the shelves and an armchair with only three legs was propped in the other corner beside an upright piano, its lid raised as if ghostly fingers hung over the yellowed ivory keys waiting to play.

I shivered and turned away.

"What's wrong?" Tobie asked.

"It's so weird. Like someone just walked out and left everything in place. It's a bit spooky… makes me feel… well, it makes me feel that someone might still be here."

Tobie raised his eyebrows and grinned. "There's no one here. I reckon the place was deserted long ago when the last owner passed away. That happens… it happens in France too. Let's go on around the corner. Perhaps there's a yard at the back."

He kept close to the wall, stepping over clumps of nettles thrusting their way up through what remained of the gravel. A row of old sheds ran along a field at the side of the house, many slates whipped off by the sea gales and lying in forlorn heaps on the ground. They might have been stables once upon a time.

"Perhaps we should try to climb into the house," Tobie suggested.

The interior yard was cobblestoned but covered with a mat of grass and tiny flowers of scarlet pimpernel. The house reared up behind us, three storeys of cut stone battered into submission by the wind.

"Imagine how much it would cost to restore this place to its former glory." Tobie sat down on an iron water trough in the middle of the yard and ran his hand along its smooth rim. "I wonder when the family moved out."

"If they didn't die, then they probably left when the south of Ireland became independent in 1922," I said. "A lot of big houses were abandoned at that time and families moved back to Britain. The fear of the unknown, I suppose… that probably drove many of them out… that and the lack of staff after the First World War. So many lives were lost in that war. A lack of money too after the war. These huge places became a liability and no one wanted them. If the houses weren't rescued by orders of priests or nuns, they were often doomed."

"That's interesting… and sad," Tobie replied. "I suppose it was a time of great turmoil and change. Life would never have been the same for the owners of these grand mansions."

I sat beside him on the trough and we watched swallows swooping in and out of the empty stables and the lofts above with their row of tiny windows. Perhaps staff had lived in those upstairs rooms long ago. I imagined their faces peering out through the dusty glass.

A sudden noise, the bang of a door slamming, made me jump and I swung around.

Drawing in a breath, I nudged Tobie. "Look… look behind you."

A woman was moving towards us. She had straggly grey hair and was wearing a long coat and wellingtons. Her face was lined with deep grooves of displeasure as she regarded us, thin lips pressed together. Her bony hands gripped the stock of a shotgun, the barrel of which was pointing straight at our faces.

Tobie and I exchanged glances and slowly raised our hands in the air.

Her finger twitched on the trigger as she barked, "Who are

you? What do you want, eh? And what the hell are you doing on my property?"

It seemed safest to answer the first question.

"My name is Fiona Foley and I'm a family history researcher."

She kept the gun pointed at my head. "Oh Lord no! Not another one."

Not quite the reaction I'd been expecting. Perhaps she made a habit of shooting researchers and hiding their bodies in the sheds. I slid closer to Tobie along the water trough. Wasn't there a law preventing landowners from threatening visitors at gunpoint?

She jerked the weapon at Tobie. "Who's he?"

"A landscaper," I said when my companion appeared to be struck dumb. "We were told about this house by a woman we met on the beach in Mulranny." I pointed at the gun. "Is that thing loaded?"

She sniffed loudly and nodded. "So, you came in without so much as a by your leave, eh? Is that how you treat other people's property?"

"Oh… oh no, definitely not," I stammered, "It's just… the house seemed deserted and…"

"Well, it's not deserted. Turn around slowly and walk back to your car before I blow your brains out."

"Before you do that, may we know your name?" Tobie asked, keeping his tone polite.

She glared at him. "You don't sound Irish."

He risked a quick smile. "I'm not. I'm half French."

"You don't sound French."

"Do you mind lowering the gun, please?" Tobie said. "You're making us feel uneasy."

A tabby cat with white paws strolled out of the shade near the door, three striped kittens in tow. The woman gazed down at them and dropped the butt of the shotgun to the ground.

"Thank you," I said.

She bent and extended a hand to stroke the cat's head. "Can't trust anyone these days. A poor old woman like me living on her own with fellas walking in to sell me all sorts of rubbish… insurance, tarmacadam, farm gates… it never ends and all the time they really want to knock me on the head and steal my belongings."

"You appear well capable of defending yourself," I ventured with a smile.

She chuckled and the lines on her face softened. "I am, I am surely. Shot a fella in the leg once… had to have sixteen stitches."

We said nothing but the hair on the back of my neck rose. What had the man done to deserve that?

She tilted back her chin, her pale eyes alight with amusement. "Ha! If you could only see your gullible faces! I'm joking… I never shot him but I gave him a hell of a fright. You should have seen him run back to his van like a scalded cat!"

I glanced at Tobie. "I bet he did. Don't worry about us, we'll go now. I'm sorry we disturbed you."

For a second, I thought she was about to raise the shotgun again but she just shifted her feet on the cobblestones, while the cat rubbed against her wellingtons and purred.

"Cat's hungry," the woman said. "With all those little ones to feed, small wonder."

"We'll go back to the car and you can forget we ever came." Tobie prodded me in the ribs with his elbow.

She held up a hand. "Not so fast, my lad… what did you want here? What brought you poking your nose into my back yard, eh?"

"Nothing… we were just curious to find out about the family here."

"Family researcher, eh?" Her eyes rested on my face. "What family?"

"I'm working for a client in Wicklow," I replied. Honesty

seemed the wisest choice at this stage. "My client is a retired heart surgeon and his great-aunt once employed a governess who came from this area."

"I don't hold much faith in those surgeons." She sniffed again, rubbing the back of her hand across her nose. "Cut you open and charge you thousands. It's a racket… money is all they're after. I don't trust those fellas. Nothing wrong with my heart… I'm as strong as an ox."

"I'm sure you are but I think my client is reputable… but anyway, yes, the governess was called Polly Brady and was born near here. I believe her mother might have been a servant in this house."

"Brady? That's a common enough name in these parts." The woman frowned down at the cat.

"Do you know the name of the family who lived here in the late Victorian era?" I asked.

She jerked up her head, with a flash of pride. "I certainly do. It's my name, isn't it? I'm Eleanor Staunton." She added, "But it's no use you standing there all day asking questions and wasting my time… you'd better come in."

Chapter Thirty-Nine

When Tobie and I said nothing, the woman's fingers tightened on the barrel of the shotgun. "You'll come in and have a cup of tea now that you've put me to all this trouble."

"Oh, well, I think… I think… that's kind of you, thank you," I stammered. "You mentioned another family researcher…"

Tobie caught my eye and shook his head, an almost imperceptible movement. "We should go now. We need to get back to the guest house."

"Yes, that Canadian lad," Eleanor replied, ignoring him and moving towards the back door. "Endless talk… heavens, you should have heard him. I reckon he was obsessed with his family's roots. Sent me letters, so many of them… I never read half of them."

What did the eccentric woman spend her hours doing? It was tempting to accept her invitation, though. Fifteen minutes in her kitchen with a cup of tea and a chat and we might discover useful information.

"Was he a relation of yours, the Canadian?" I asked, following her into a damp scullery with peeling paint and a profusion of ancient raincoats hanging on hooks.

"A descendant from my great-uncle's line of the family... the one that married the heiress in Nova Scotia and never returned home again, sensible man." Her pale face split into a grin.

"I see... it would be good to talk a bit more about the Staunton family, if you don't mind, and I'm particularly interested in the late Victorian period."

We followed her into a dark corridor, flagstones strewn with old boots and stiff leather bridles lining the whitewashed walls. I imagined our hostess as a fearless horsewoman decades before, galloping across the countryside, roaring abuse at anyone who dared to get in her way and leaping fences on a creature as crazy as she was. I turned to smile at Tobie who shook his head.

She pushed open a kitchen door, its hinges creaking in protest, and waved at two chairs and a long table.

I sat down and surveyed the room. Cardboard boxes of newspapers sat on the counter top; a lurid green dresser dangled chipped mugs coated in dust and an old cream Aga stood in the middle of the far wall. A small basket with a pink cushion had been placed at the bottom of the cooker and into this the cat and her three kittens scrambled; the mother curling up and blinking at us as if we were regular visitors.

"Tea or coffee?" Eleanor barked.

"Oh, tea please... tea would be lovely," I said.

"If it's okay, coffee for me," Tobie added.

"I've no cake, mind. I might have some biscuits if you look under those papers on the table. Is there a red tin with horses on it? No? Ah well, I must have put it away after the biscuits were finished." She lifted one of the Aga's lids and hauled a large kettle from the shadows at the back of the hot plate. "Local supermarket delivers food but not until next week." She eased herself into an armchair by the cooker. "Never been fond of housekeeping... too many other exciting things to do with my life."

I smiled. "I can sympathize with that feeling."

"When the kettle boils, you can make the tea and coffee," she told me. "You do know how to make tea, don't you? Not with those modern tea bags, mind, but with real leaves."

I assured her that I did. Tobie pushed away more papers to clear space on the table in front of his chair, and moved a box of letters with flamboyant handwriting on the envelopes and foreign stamps. This was the Canadian descendant's correspondence, no doubt.

Eleanor saw my eyes on the box. "Yes, those are from that fella. Look at them all… and one page isn't sufficient. He has to send me at least six in each envelope. Still, he's a nice young man… polite, asks my permission before he arrives."

That was obviously a rebuke directed at us.

"Do you have much information about your ancestors?" Tobie asked.

She frowned. "Not as much as that young man… Wilber, he calls himself. He knows every date and every name… took him five years to write the book. At least five years."

I sat up. "He wrote a book?"

She coughed, swallowing and patting her chest. "Excuse me, dear, I've had a bad cold. Left me with a bit of a wheeze."

I thought a reluctance to go to the doctor might not have helped and suggested, "If you need antibiotics…"

"I don't need antibiotics, girl. I don't go near those medical charlatans. What were we talking about? Oh yes, the book that Wilber wrote. The longest most detailed saga you ever saw. I only had the patience to read the pages about my own family… the ones I can remember, that is."

I leaned forward. "Is it just a family tree or are there anecdotes and stories too?"

She pointed at the Aga. "Kettle's boiling. No need to let it boil dry."

"Sorry." I got to my feet and searched for the tea leaves.

"Orange tin over there by the sink. Yes, yes, under the dishcloth. Lord, girl, can't you see it?" She made as if to struggle out of her armchair but I snatched up the tin and opened it. "Four spoons and one for the pot. No coffee here, just remembered. Bad for my digestion. The young man will have to put up with tea."

"Yes, Mrs Staunton." I grinned at Tobie.

"It's Miss." She cleared her throat and twitched her lips. "Not the marrying type, I'm afraid. Too many horses, dogs and cats to look after, so I'd no time for a whining man as well."

"I understand," Tobie said, keeping his expression serious. "Men can be a handful at the best of times."

A laugh shot from her. "You're right. You're right, Frenchman. Got a wife and kids?"

He hesitated.

"Tea's ready," I called out to distract her.

"No, it's not. It has to brew first. Don't know much about making tea, do you, miss?" She turned back to Tobie. "Tell me about your wife and kids. I presume you're not married to this woman here."

A faint heat rose on my cheeks. Why did she presume that?

Tobie sighed and stretched out his legs under the table. "I have a wife and a son. My boy is seven years old… in Paris at the moment."

Had I hoped he would admit that his wife had left him? I stirred the contents of the teapot. He wasn't going to tell her that and it was none of the old lady's business.

"Ooh, Paris, that's very grand," she replied with a chuckle, followed by another hacking cough.

Tobie muttered his thanks as I handed him a striped mug of steaming tea.

Eleanor studied his face for a few moments before turning to me. "And how about you, young lady? I don't suppose you are married."

"I am… I was. I'm separated."

She nodded, holding out both hands for her mug. "Yes, that's why I didn't bother. If you don't keep pandering to men, they clear off with a younger woman. I'd no time for all that nonsense. Give me animals any day… much more faithful and devoted. I'd advise you to get a dog, my dear. A dog will never let you down."

I thought of Archie asleep in my car after his exercise on the beach. "A dog is definitely a true friend. Miss Staunton, may I ask you about your family?" I reached for my handbag and pulled out my notebook and biro.

"Call me Eleanor, for goodness sake." She pulled her heavy coat tighter around her thin frame. "Ask away. I won't promise to answer though."

Tobie laughed softly and sipped his tea.

"How far back can you remember? About your family members, I mean."

She snorted. "My memory of the past is as good as it ever was, I tell you. It's the short-term one that's failing. My grandfather, I remember him although I was only five when he died in 1940, just after the evacuation of Dunkirk. Grandpa was eighty-five years old, a great age in those days, but his second wife, my grandma, died young."

I scribbled down notes. "Your grandfather's name was?"

"Cameron Staunton. A kind man, loved dogs… used to have Dalmatians, I remember. There are photographs of them in an album somewhere. He married twice but I never found out that until Wilber the Canadian told me. His first wife was a rich socialite… couldn't stand Mayo. They divorced in about 1900."

"Your grandfather lived here in this house?"

"Yes, of course. He married first when he was thirty or thereabouts. And then he married my grandmother and their son, my father, was born when he was in his mid-fifties. He lost his wife soon after but that's life, isn't it? It was tough in those days… tougher than now. TB carried her off, poor soul."

I chewed on the end of my biro and frowned. Could he have been Polly's father? The age seemed correct. I glanced at Tobie but he'd taken out his phone and was scrolling through text messages.

The cat let out a contented mew in her basket and continued licking the nearest kitten.

"Cameron Staunton. A wild young man in his youth, my dad said. Cameron's father worried that he'd never settle down. Got into all sorts of mischief." She cupped her creased hands around her mug and nodded. "Yes, all sorts of trouble. He was handsome, you see, and he probably knew it."

Was she aware of the liaison with the servant girl? I would have to ask that question tactfully although she didn't seem the type to be offended.

"I'm eighty-seven." She beamed at us. "There, that surprised you, didn't it? Eighty-seven years old and I can still fire a gun and hit the target."

"Impressive." Tobie laughed, a hearty chortle. "I couldn't hit the target even now."

She inclined her head, pretending modesty, but seemed pleased.

"Did Wilber find out anything about your grandfather?" I asked.

"Oh… too much, far too much. He had letters, you see, and he showed me the letters. That's how I found out about the details of the scandal. I didn't hear before because the family hushed it all up. They did that back then. The disgrace and the locals talking… all that nonsense and claptrap."

"You mean about the illegitimate daughter?"

She stared at me. "How could you have heard about her?

It was supposed to be a family disgrace, a secret no one would speak about. I bet all the locals knew anyway. Such a load of codswallop."

"I met her great-nephew Stephen in Wicklow… not a blood relation but he's another man interested in your family history."

She slurped her tea. "Bit weak for me… the tea. Sorry, my dear, you were saying…"

"Her great-nephew… Polly Brady's great-nephew. A bit complicated because he's only related to the woman who adopted her… took her in."

"I see. No relation of mine then, if he's a Brady. Yes indeed, they paid some local woman to bring the girl up. I've no time for that sort of hypocrisy myself. I suspect my great-grandfather was a snobbish old tyrant and Grandpa Cameron had to toe the line." She shrugged and coughed again, before pulling out a handkerchief and pressing it to her mouth.

"Are you sure you don't need a doctor?" Tobie asked.

"I haven't got that plague… that Covid virus, if that's what you think," she replied. "I'm fine, don't fuss."

"Do you have anyone to care for you? Anyone to drop in to make sure you're okay?"

"Young man, please don't worry. I might be found dead on the floor and eaten by rats one of these days, but nobody will care."

"I didn't mean that."

"Yes, you did. That's what you were thinking. That's what everyone thinks. The district nurse calls out regularly to dress the ulcer on my leg and she wants me to go into a home. God forbid, I'd rather die." She pointed at the faded fawn corduroys pushed into her wellingtons. "And there's a nice young girl who keeps a Connemara pony in the field over there." She waved a hand at the window above the sink. "She pops in to talk to me now and then, so she'll probably be the one to find me stretched out on the tiles, dead as a dodo."

"I hope not." I looked at the wooden-framed clock ticking on the wall above the dresser. We'd already been there for over half an hour. I wrote down the ages of Cameron and Eleanor Staunton.

"Polly was your aunt," I pointed out.

"Yes indeed, by blood but our paths never crossed. People like Polly, born on the wrong side of the blanket, as they say… people like her lived in the shadows." Eleanor fixed her gaze on me. "There was another child too… but you probably heard that. A boy."

"What do you mean?"

"Polly the illegitimate daughter had a brother. The housemaid ran away with him… the other baby, the twin."

"The twin? Polly had a twin?"

She nodded. "Yes, that's what I said. The maid had twin babies… left the girl and took the boy. Wilber traced her to Dublin… said she died in poverty and was buried in Glasnevin cemetery. There might be more about it in the letters I didn't get around to reading."

My thoughts raced as I leaned over my notebook. A twin. A boy. What had happened to him? Polly never mentioned him in her diary so perhaps she never knew. How sad if she didn't, if she never met him.

"I'm surprised by that," I said. "There's no mention of a twin brother in anything I've seen so far."

Eleanor took a sip of tea and made a face. "That man in Colgrannagh adopted him. A philanthropist, apparently. Took in orphans and educated them. Luke, the boy was called Luke."

I blinked at her and she laughed, asking, "What's wrong? Recognize the name?"

Luke Manning was Polly's twin! I shot a look at Tobie. "I hope Polly found out because… well, from what she wrote, she seemed to be in love with him."

"Cameron probably told her at some stage." Eleanor shrugged, losing interest. "Any more questions?" Her face was paler, as if the coughing fit had taken away her feistiness.

"I don't want to tire you… to delay you but…"

"Ask away, my dear. I have all the time in the world."

A wave of pity swept over me. She would be lonely, living in this old draughty house on her own with nobody to mind her or keep her company during the long dark nights. Despite her earlier show of bravado when wielding the shotgun, she appeared vulnerable and frail. I would mention her to Stephen. She was almost a relative of his and perhaps he would be enthusiastic to meet her and help her.

"I'd like to learn more about Cameron's daughter, if you don't mind talking about her. She ended up in Wicklow working as a governess for the great-aunt of the man who's paying me… for whom I'm doing this research."

"What was her employer's name?"

"Claudia Manning, daughter of Dr Burroughs… the man you mentioned," I replied.

Eleanor sat upright.

"Do you remember Claudia Manning?" I asked.

She sucked in her cheeks, making a whistling sound. "Claudia Manning… I certainly do. That's the woman who poisoned a man… she poisoned the man who wanted to marry her."

"No! She couldn't have," I said.

The gleam in her eyes was more cunning. "She did. They never found the body, of course, because it must have been hidden away. She understood all about herbs, I believe, and how to poison people."

My first thought after the initial dart of shock ebbed away was of Daniel. What would he say if I revealed his great-aunt was a killer? This couldn't be true. Eleanor Staunton's long-term memory might not be as accurate as she claimed.

What was the expression on Tobie's face? Sympathy, it seemed like sympathy but tinged with excitement.

"How… how do you know this?" My face reddened. It was suddenly stifling in the hot kitchen. How could she sit there in her coat? But elderly people felt the cold and Eleanor was thin, worryingly fleshless.

"She murdered that man. She used plants from her herb garden. Common garden plants but poisonous. She had the skills to do it, I tell you."

"How do you know this?" I asked again. Was she was joking, treating us like gullible strangers?

She leaned her head against the back of her armchair. "The Canadian suspected her… found a clue in a letter. He wrote it down somewhere." Waving a hand at the nearest box of letters, she added, "It's in there, I think. A long story from my great-uncle, Wilber's great-grandfather, about Claudia who thought that the man had killed her husband out in South America. She was lucky not to be found out because she would have been hanged in those days."

Chapter Forty

The past – August 1895

Candlesticks gleamed on the dining room table; silver-plated serving dishes polished until they shone. Austere portraits of Mannings hung on the walls surrounding Polly, gazing down at the preparations for the dinner with obvious indifference.

She moved to the head of the table where Robert Kingson would sit. Her fingers gripped the envelope in her pocket, her eyes searching the place setting. Where could she leave it? It had to be somewhere discreet where he wouldn't discover it until dinner had started, when all the guests were seated and would bear witness to his mortification. That was Luke's plan and her task was to ensure it happened.

"Miss Brady, I didn't expect to see you here." Kingson's voice rang out from the doorway and she stiffened, her opportunity lost. She moved towards him and he inclined his head in a slight bow. "You've returned from County Mayo."

"Yes, sir." Polly struggled to remain calm. "Mrs Manning asked me to come back to be with the children and said they were missing me."

"How gratifying. What a shame we haven't room at the table for you this evening but never mind, it sounds like you will be well employed in the schoolroom."

"I shall enjoy being with the girls and Solomon."

"And Luke, have you seen him, by any chance?"

"I have not." Polly flushed, releasing her grip on the letter in her dress.

"You don't know where he is? Indeed, Miss Brady, I'm surprised because you two seemed such close friends." He raised an eyebrow and tilted his head to one side, a mocking smile on his lips.

Did he suspect her? No, surely not. She hoped he'd been convinced by her guileless expression. Her untruth had slipped out easily, too easily, and she turned her face away to hide her disquiet. The man was making a liar of her.

Polly peeped into the hall but they were quite alone. "I suspect," she said, "that you've driven him away."

"Really?" he replied, leaning closer to her, still with the same teasing note. "Ah, but you jest… no, perhaps not… I see by your severe expression that you're in earnest. What would make you say such a thing?"

"Luke would never steal money from his employer. I know he wouldn't."

Kingson lifted his hands in the air, a theatrical gesture. "Indeed, my dear girl, I only wish I had your confidence in the lad. I fear your trust is misguided."

"Time will tell, sir."

He gave her a sharp glance but she hurried away, aware of his eyes boring into her back as she walked across the hall. Kingson, for all his habitual confidence, did not appear to be well. His face looked pale. On several occasions, he'd rested a hand on his stomach.

She should have sympathized and asked if he was feeling poorly, but his comments about Luke irritated her. She would have to be careful not to antagonize the man. It was not her place to reveal his secret dealings in Brazil and his attack on Gilbert

Manning. Brother Eugene's letter would do that, if only she could find another opportunity to leave it under his table mat.

Luke, waiting with impatience in the bathing hut for her news, would be frustrated with her lack of progress.

Dora appeared on the landing above and raised a wrinkled hand in greeting. "Ah, Polly, there you are. I'm told Cook has excelled herself with the feast for tonight. I shall be up half the night with indigestion."

"I pray not," Polly replied with a quick smile.

"And poor unfortunate Lizzie," Dora continued. "Sick as a dog and taken to her bed. Mrs Delaney is frantic and had to hire two extra maids for the evening."

"I wonder what Lizzie ate?"

"Or drank." Dora chuckled. "Warm tonight, too warm for me. Robert doesn't look well, does he? I hope he's not feeling poorly on his big night."

"I hope not, indeed. I saw him touching his stomach."

"Nerves, perhaps," the old lady said with a cackle of laughter. "I'm sorry you won't be with us. Instead I shall have to listen to the foolish prattle of Dr Fitzpatrick and his admiring ladies. I would prefer to spend time with you and Lizzie's hot chocolate."

The mention of the housemaid sparked an idea. Polly decided to slip into the kitchen corridor and wait by the servants' door into the dining room to hide the letter when Kingson went upstairs to change.

Rounding the corner near the scullery, she bumped into a flustered Mrs Delaney.

"Oh Miss Brady, such an evening! Everything is going wrong. I'm all a dither, what with Lizzie falling ill and now the other one."

Polly sympathized, adding, "What other one?"

"A young local girl taken on for the evening, miss, and now she can't come… she sent word with a boy. A slight fever."

Another maid down. Polly replied, "I have an idea."

"Thank you, miss."

"Let me be your assistant in the place of the sick housemaid."

The cook regarded Polly with astonishment. "You?"

"It would be a help to the family, surely?"

"Yes indeed, miss, and very kind of you to offer but… but what would Mrs Manning say? And Mrs Burroughs? A governess asked to wait at table. I'm not sure…"

"I'll talk to Mrs Manning. Let me try to persuade her because I would like to help you." Polly left the flabbergasted cook and hurried in search of her mistress. Luke would be pleased with this idea. He'd expected her to linger outside one of the windows to keep an eye on Kingson during dinner but now she might have a more entertaining excuse. If she were to act as a maid for the evening, she would be able to stand in the dining room and keep an eye on what happened.

Spying her employer rearranging one of her mother's flower vases in the drawing room, Polly approached her. "Mrs Delaney has just informed me that one of the extra maids hired to help tonight has come down with an illness."

Claudia looked up. "Good heavens, that's a blow, Polly. Our cook has too much on her plate tonight."

"Ma'am, if you please, may I suggest an idea?"

"By all means."

Polly hesitated before rushing out the words. "I will take the place of the second maid. I would like to help." She imagined Luke's grin of approval.

"Oh, I'm not sure…"

"It would only be for one night and many of your guests… with the exception of Dr Fitzpatrick… they won't know me and, to be honest, would they object? I really don't mind doing this if you approve of it."

Claudia turned to the roses in the arrangement, adjusting a

long-stemmed cream blossom and frowning. "Very well then. If you're happy… and it would be a great help. I shall make sure you are paid extra for the inconvenience."

"Thank you. I'll go and tell Mrs Delaney immediately. She'll be so relieved."

The red-faced cook seemed delighted, exclaiming and clapping her hands together.

"You'll have to tell me what to do," Polly said. "I've been a servant to my aunt most of my life but I've never waited at table for a grand dinner party."

"It will be simple, miss. All you have to do is carry the plates of food and place them in front of the guests. I'll hand them to you on trays in the kitchen and you can distribute them. I'll tell you exactly where to place them, never fear."

She disappeared into the servants' area to unearth another maid's dress and apron while Polly waited near the dining room. Kingson had moved from the other doorway but she could hear his voice in the hall. She couldn't risk trying to hide the letter until she was alone.

Mrs Delaney returned with a starched uniform and handed it over. How fortunate Polly and Lizzie were both of a similar build, although the skirt might be a bit loose around the waist but that wouldn't be noticeable when the white apron was tied.

Polly changed in her bedroom, pinning up her hair and putting on the maid's cap. Her red hair gleamed in the candlelight and her eyes shone with a mixture of excitement and apprehension. She was already looking forward to telling her brother later.

Her brother. Luke hadn't said much after Papa had told him the truth. She'd seen the two men from the door of her aunt's cottage; the tall man pacing in circles on the sand and the younger one sitting on a rock, his head in his hands.

Luke chose not to mention that conversation, only uttering a few words when they boarded the train in Westport on their way back to Colgrannagh. Shocked or disappointed perhaps but it was hard to tell. He'd taken her arm amongst the throng on the smoky platform and said, "Come, sister, the adventure begins." That was all but, knowing Luke, his mind was already preoccupied with his latest obsession: exposing Kingson. A fortnight had passed and Polly, who'd felt alone all her life, was overjoyed at having a brother.

She followed the cook to the kitchen and received her orders. "Don't spill the gravy when serving it. Small spoonfuls, mind, and on no account allow the guests to handle the hot gravy boat themselves or it will be splashed over the fine linen tablecloth." Mrs Delaney concluded her advice, giving Polly a broad smile, and patted her on the shoulder before hastening back to the huge range and the leg of lamb roasting in the oven.

Polly returned to the dining room and found it empty. She took Brother Eugene's letter from the pocket of her apron and slipped it under the table mat in front of Kingson's seat. With luck, he might not notice it until he looked down at his dinner plate.

The guests were beginning to arrive, Claudia and her mother at the front door smiling greetings. Half an hour passed, the grandfather clock in the hall chimed and their eighteen companions took their places in the dining room.

The maid arrived from the kitchen with a steaming tray bearing the first course and handed it to Polly. "Off you go, miss. Consommé à la Royale to begin. That's a clear soup to the likes of you and me."

Robert Kingson raised his eyebrows when she approached. "Miss Brady, I hardly recognized you. Is this your new position?" He smiled, waiting for her reaction.

"Just helping out for the evening, sir, because the other maid fell ill."

He thanked her for the soup and looked away. Would he

notice the corner of paper under the mat? No, not yet. Polly moved on, placing the consommé in front of Dr Fitzpatrick's wife.

Lobster followed the soup, accompanied by a Hollandaise sauce. Mrs Delaney was an excellent cook, in spite of her lack of patience and occasional furious outbursts.

This time the physician raised his eyes to Polly's face. "I believe that I know you."

"Miss Brady, sir, the governess."

"Good gracious. And you are used to waiting at table? How extraordinary!"

She gave him a quick smile and moved away. It wouldn't do to have the doctor draw attention to her, especially if Kingson spotted the letter and began to wonder who might have hidden it. It would be better if he didn't find it until her duties were completed and she could slip away.

The roast lamb arrived in due course, neatly carved and served with green peas and new potatoes from the garden, grown and picked by Eamon.

The maid circulated with the wine and filled crystal glasses.

Kingson got to his feet. "A toast, ladies and gentlemen, if you please. To Claudia, our lovely hostess."

Dora rose slowly to her feet opposite, clutching at the table to maintain her balance as she reached for her wine. She held the glass aloft and called out, "Claudia."

Polly waited. Was he going to mention the betrothal now? Had anybody else noticed his hands shake and his voice falter? Apparently not, apart from Dr Fitzpatrick who regarded him, his brow furrowing with concern. Not for the first time, Polly wondered if the physician had come to an agreement with Kingson about the bark from South America and its possible potential. They were always so close, so conspiratorial.

Kingson reached for his glass again and knocked it over. Polly remained near the sideboard as he attempted to dab at the scarlet liquid spreading like blood across the damask cloth. The maid hurried over to assist.

He must have drunk several more glasses than usual before dinner. The alcohol had obviously gone to his head. Polly retreated to the doorway leading to the kitchen stairs while the other maid lifted the damp end of the table cloth and exposed the letter soaked in wine.

"What's that?" Kingson demanded.

She pointed at the handwriting. "It's for you, sir," she said.

Polly slipped behind the door, keeping one eye on him, holding her breath as he tore open the envelope.

Kingson glanced at the handwriting and his face turned white. He reached for the table with one hand, leaning forward and stuffing the sodden paper into his jacket pocket. He looked up and searched the room.

Polly stepped back and hastened down the steps to the kitchen in the basement.

Mrs Delaney started with surprise when she entered. She was sitting at the scrubbed pine table, her boots thrown off and her swollen feet up on a stool as she puffed on a cigarette, her work nearly over for the evening. "Lord, miss, you gave me a fright. I was afraid you were that Mr Kingson. He's the very devil for checking up on us."

"I'm sorry. Don't let me disturb you. No, don't get up. I've come for the serving of meat and vegetables that you prepared for me."

The cook sighed and waved a plump finger towards the top of the range. "That man thinks he owns the place already, and that's the truth, God help the poor mistress." She watched as Polly took a platter from beside the hot plate. "Yes, that's it. You're feeling peckish tonight." She laughed and winked.

Polly murmured her thanks and winked back.

"Tell him we miss him," the cook added before Polly pulled the door closed.

She drew on a shawl to hide her uniform and slipped outside. The night was still, the air almost as warm as the kitchen when she moved into the shadows outside the back door. A fox called in the distance, a hoarse, almost supernatural cry.

Polly made her way across the bleached grass to the physic garden, passing the dark outline of the potting shed and walking towards the river. Her boots made no sound. Luke would be waiting in the trees by the river, impatient for food and information. Hopefully he wouldn't be an outcast for much longer. Kingson would be gone, Luke's name cleared and he would be back amongst the family where he belonged.

A sound behind brought her to a standstill. What was that?

Her heart jumped as she held her breath, her fingers gripping the material of her dress. That sound. Was it a crunch of footsteps on gravel? No, nothing, only her imagination getting the better of her.

She took a step towards the gloom of the wood.

Was that a muffled cough?

She swung around and peered into the dark. The moon had vanished behind a cloud and it was difficult to see. Was there a figure waiting near the shed? She strained her eyes but saw nothing except its dark entrance.

"Hello," she called. "Is there somebody there?"

No sound, no reassuring answer.

She lingered for several seconds, steadying her heartbeat and willing herself to remain calm.

Further off, the fox barked again, its rasping cry sounding eerie in the silence around her. Polly cast a quick look over her shoulder and, seeing only the great bulk of the house with candlelit windows glowing, she hurried on. She would have to make haste or Luke's dinner would be cold.

Polly stumbled over the hem of her dress and hoisted it higher off the ground, lengthening her stride and peering into the trees. She couldn't see Luke. Was he there, watching and waiting? He might make a call like a fox and, for a moment, she wondered if that unnerving sound had come from his lips. A signal to her, perhaps.

A pair of rabbits appeared from the undergrowth and hopped away, their fluffy tails bobbing. The call of a barn owl, a loud screech, came from behind the huge chestnut tree and Polly smiled. That would be Luke. She'd often heard him hooting owl imitations to amuse Solomon.

She whispered, "Hello, I'm here."

A hand grabbed her neck and she screamed. The dinner plate fell from her grasp and shattered on the path.

She struggled and lashed out with her fists.

"So, this is what you're up to, girl!" A man snarled in her ear and the grip on her throat tightened as she gasped for breath.

Kingson!

She tried to kick back at his legs but he stepped to one side. He must have noticed her leave the house and followed her out.

"Let me go!" she cried, straining to push him off, but he was too strong. "Let me go or I'll scream again."

He laughed, releasing his hold on her neck and twisting her arms behind her back. "Go on then, scream all you wish. They won't hear you in the house above their merriment and chatter. No one will hear you except your lover in the wood and it's him I want... not you." He thrust her from him.

She lost her balance and fell to the ground. "No... no..." She lay panting on the gravel, a stabbing pain in her side where her ribs had struck the brick edging. Hard to breathe. "Luke, get back... go back. He's here."

The moon slid out from behind the clouds as Kingson threw her a scornful glance. "I think he'll come, my dear... I think your brave young man will come to your rescue, if he thinks you're in danger. Shall we see what happens?"

She groaned. So hard to take a breath. "What… what do you mean? You can't seriously… seriously intend to do me harm?"

He shrugged, smiling.

Polly cried out, "Luke, don't come… stay away.'

"I've got her, Luke," Kingson shouted. "I've got your little lady friend and you'd better hasten here now, or God knows what may happen to her."

"You wouldn't…"

He pushed his flushed face close to hers. She could smell the wine on his breath. "I wouldn't… do you really think not? What wouldn't I do? I don't like meddling women interfering in my business. I know it was you… you who left that letter tonight for me to find. Dressed as a maid and pretending to help Claudia… very clever, but you didn't fool me." He stood upright, grimacing and clutching at his stomach.

"We know what you've done," Polly replied. "I'm not afraid of you."

"You don't know what you're talking about. The word of a foreign priest against mine? Do you think the constabulary will believe him?"

Polly rolled away on the lawn and struggled to her feet. Her breath came in painful gasps. Had she cracked a rib when she fell? "Brother Eugene… he knows… what happened in Brazil. He has friends there. He knows what you did."

With one hand still pressed into his stomach, Kingson lurched at Polly, sinking his fingers into her shoulder. She screamed and kicked at him, striking him on the knee.

"You… you little…" He was panting, his face sweating and bloodless in the moonlight.

Where was Luke? The ache in her shoulder was worse than the rib. Her stomach churned and she twisted to escape from his vicelike grip.

A figure streaked across the lawn behind Kingson. Polly turned her head away. She couldn't let him know that Luke was there.

"You interfering little madam!" Kingson was shaking her, like a terrier with a rat, his face contorted and spittle gathering at the side of his mouth. "I'll show you…"

Luke struck him from behind, knocking the taller man off balance and sending him sprawling on the ground. He lay groaning on the dry grass, both arms around his midriff.

"Oh, Luke, you were only just in time… he… I thought he would kill me. Just in time."

"Get up, Kingson, get up like a man and stop that moaning!" Luke seized him by the collar of his coat. He clenched a fist and punched him in the face. "Stand up for I have words I've been saving especially for you. Come on, man, on your feet now."

Blood trickled from Kingson's nose as he stared and shuddered. He lifted a trembling arm. "Behind you, behind you…"

Luke shouted, "I won't fall for that trick. Get up, I say!"

"Luke, he's…"

Kingson fell onto his side and vomited, his body hunched in pain.

"This doesn't make sense," Polly breathed. "You didn't hit him that hard."

The other man's eyes were wide open, round with terror as he pointed over Luke's shoulder. He sat upright and retched again. "My God, my God…" He bent over and writhed on the lawn.

"He's ill," Polly said, glancing towards the trees. "There's nobody there. He must be ill."

Kingson's limbs shook again and his body doubled over in a spasm. He moaned and pushed his face into the grass before lying still.

"Should I fetch Dr Fitzpatrick?" Polly cried. "I don't like this… he's… he's…"

Her brother kneeled on the lawn and placed his fingers on the other man's neck. He pushed them hard against the artery below the angle of Kingson's jaw.

"Is he…"

Luke looked up at her, forcing the words through pale frozen lips. "No pulse. I think he's dead."

"But how… are you certain?"

"There's no pulse, I tell you. He must be dead." He held his fingers against Kingson's neck again, his eyes fixed on the other man as if willing the prostrate form back to life. "Polly, what will we do?"

"Dr Fitzpatrick… I'll run and fetch him."

Luke stood and laid his hand on her arm. "No. If you do, you know what the doctor will say? You understand who will get the blame for this? He'll blame me. He'll say that I killed Kingson."

"No, he won't… how can he say that? I was here. I saw what happened."

"Perhaps I did kill him… I hit him. I punched him. Maybe he had a seizure of some sort. No, don't go. You think they'll believe you, a mere governess? They'll think me guilty because of my past. Dr Fitzpatrick will pin this on me. I can't, Polly, I can't take the risk."

Her thoughts spun as she raised her hands to her face. A knot tightened in her stomach and she thought for one moment that she was going to be sick. Was it the food? Lizzie was ill and perhaps some of the guests were suffering the same fate. The lobster? But the cook said it had been delivered fresh from the quays in Wicklow town that morning.

Luke held out his hand. "Give me your shawl. I'll throw it over his face. His expression, it gives me the horrors, that it does."

She did as she was bid. "It was as if he saw something or

someone horrible over your shoulder. Something that terrified him before he died."

Luke shook his head. "He couldn't have. You saw nothing. He was delirious… he was raving." He laid the wool shawl over Kingson's head. "There, now we don't have to look at him." He turned to Polly. "What happened here tonight? I don't understand…"

They would have to act quickly. They couldn't leave Kingson lying on the lawn where somebody might stumble across him and Luke would be blamed for his death. Could they move his body? "Luke, the underground potting shed…"

A burst of laughter came from the house. The door into the garden was thrown open and several men emerged. The moonlight illuminated the figures as they moved onto the lawn, cigars glowing in their fingers.

"Dr Fitzpatrick." Polly hissed in Luke's ear. "I recognize that laugh. Go… go now, into the wood and leave me to explain what happened."

Luke pushed her back and grasped her face in cold hands, his words forced from between clenched teeth. "No, you listen to me… that's a good idea… the potting shed. Walk towards them and leave Kingson to me. Distract them… say anything but don't let them come down this path. Go! Go quickly!"

She hesitated but he gave her a shove that sent her reeling backwards.

"Hurry… they're coming. Go now!"

Polly gathered her skirts in her hands, casting a desperate glance over her shoulder at her brother. She drew in a breath and froze when she saw the shape behind him, the figure at the edge of the wood. The man from the tower, with straggly hair and a crooked leer on his features, began to limp towards them.

Chapter Forty-One

The present – September 2022

A chaffinch sang from the branches of the Scots pine above us in the garden of the guest house, an outpouring of fluid notes. Eleanor's cardboard box of letters sat between Tobie and me on the grass, papers fluttering in the breeze.

Tobie rolled onto his back and yawned. "Do we need to read all these today? It will take hours and hours. There are things I'd much rather do. What happened to our planned drive to Achill Island and the dinner I said I'd treat you to, eh?"

"I'd love to… you know I would, but I can't. At least not yet. We have to get through these papers and deliver them back to Eleanor tonight. I promised her and, if I fail to keep that promise, you can only imagine what will happen. She might actually be tempted to fire the shotgun next time."

"You can tell her it was my fault when you go back to see her alone." He raised his head and smiled at me.

We both laughed. I supposed I'd always felt at ease with him, right from our first meeting, as if I'd met him before in another life, ridiculous as that seemed. Old friends drawn to each other. On the same wavelength. There were plenty of clichés to describe my feelings.

I lifted my eyes to the bird as it began its song again and

fancifully imagined it was singing only for us, a unique melody to serenade our weekend in Mayo.

Why hadn't I met Tobie years before? I would never have wasted all that time pandering to Dominic and his selfish whims but I was naïve back then, supposing that was how most husbands behaved.

I picked up another letter and nodded at the book on Tobie's lap. "Get going. The sooner we finish this, the sooner you get to Achill and your dinner."

"Yes, miss."

I shook a finger at him before returning to the letters I was reading from the great-uncle to Polly's father in Mayo. They were mostly explaining about Canadian agricultural practices and providing ideas for Cameron to emulate. We lapsed into silence, the chaffinch finishing its song and flying off to entertain someone else.

"Hey," Tobie said, sitting up. "There's a note here about those two girls, Annie and Hannah."

"Oh, that's interesting because I often wonder what happened to them. What does it say?"

"It mentions one of them came to Nova Scotia to stay with Cameron Staunton's uncle. That was Hannah. Was she the younger sister?"

"Yes, she was, and I'm not surprised she emigrated because I found no mention of her in Wicklow. When was that?" I asked.

He skimmed the page, flicking away a fly that landed on his nose. "In November 1915. Within eighteen months, she married a great-nephew of the uncle, who was the owner of a hardware store in Halifax."

I juggled in my mind a picture of spirited Hannah of the children's game journal, with her outspoken manner, and an image of her settling down as a spouse in her thirties. Was she the same lively woman as she grew older, and did she ever return to Colgrannagh on a visit? Unlikely, because voyages by steam ship took so long and were, presumably, expensive in those days.

"That sounds good. I often wondered what happened to the girls," I replied. "Any mention of Annie?"

"Yeah, here's a footnote at the bottom of this section. She worked as a nurse in France during the First World War. Later on, in her forties, she also moved to Halifax and found a job in a hospital. It's possible that she wished to be near Hannah."

I smiled at the thought. "She'd love babysitting the big brood of babies when their restless mother was off on an adventure."

"Are you guessing Hannah had a lot of children? It doesn't state that… appears from this record that she had only three sons."

I waved a hand. "Tobie, please don't take me so literally! Just my imagination taking flight and it seems like something she would do. What or who was the connection between the girls and the Staunton relation in Canada? Was it Polly?"

"Perhaps it was," he said. "She might have kept in touch with them and organized Hannah's trip there, or her dad did."

The Ireland in which the adopted sisters grew up changed radically as the years went by. It was a different country in 1915, with the political drama overheating into the rebellion of the following Easter, against the backdrop of a world war and so many young men sent off to fight.

"I like the idea that Polly remained close to the children in the end," I said. "Nice to feel she helped them to find a future."

I resumed reading the letters beside me.

"The owner of the guest house has a pretty garden," Tobie muttered after another five minutes. "She's got a good sense of which plants go well together, though I wouldn't put those bergenias in the middle of the border. Elephant's Ears is the common name and suits the large rubbery leaves… drought resistant and excellent for dry…"

"Tobie, please… concentrate on the book!"

Had I always considered him good-looking? I'd been struck from the start by how fit he was; his muscles hardened from physical exercise and I always liked the sudden smile that lit up his face. I remembered him as a bit sulky when we first met but that was before I discovered his sense of fun.

He glanced through a few pages of Wilber's family research, then pointed. "Hey, this paragraph is underlined in red. It mentions the twins, Luke and Polly and their mother. A housemaid when she gave birth to them and only twenty-one."

"What age was Cameron? Does it say?"

"Yeah, eighteen. She was offered a cottage on the estate but took off one night with the baby boy. I wonder why she did that."

"Ran away with the boy?" I asked.

"Sounds like that. Why not live in the cottage and keep her two children?"

"Restless… didn't want to settle down. Very difficult for Polly to be the abandoned child but she didn't know for years and, to be honest, it sounds like her father looked after her well… educated her and organized a position for her. He was interested in her. Not an irresponsible man… later on, that is."

The guest house manager arrived, a petite woman with boundless energy, carrying a tray with a jug of homemade lemonade and a plate of tuna and salad sandwiches.

"Thank you, that's very kind," I said, standing to take it from her.

"How are you getting on with your research?" She had neat blonde hair, cut into a layered bob.

"It's slow and unrewarding so far," I replied.

"I hope it improves." She added, "A woman phoned for you. She couldn't get through on your mobile so she tried all the hotels and guest houses in the area. Millicent North."

I looked up, alarmed. Had something happened to Daniel?

"Don't worry. She said it's not a life or death situation but she wants you to call her back later today."

I thanked her and she headed back up the path.

"Isn't that typical of Millicent?" I said. "Imagine phoning every guest house in the village! She can't leave me alone… has to be controlling me wherever I am. I'd have thought she would be happy relaxing in the five-star hotel in Cork with Kenny but no… She's probably sitting in the jacuzzi dreaming about how to get rid of me now poor Daniel is out of the way."

"Let's not spoil the day by talking about her. What Eleanor said… about the poisoning. Claudia Manning with her knowledge of herbs. Could that really be true?" Tobie yawned, turning his head on the lawn to gaze at me. "Suppose Claudia was suspected but it was actually Luke… or Polly. That suspicion hanging over them would make them leave the country."

"If the body in the underground shed was Robert Kingson… We know he accused Luke of stealing from his employer but did Luke kill him?"

"If they'd come to blows… you mentioned Polly's suspicions about Kingson in her diary and her anger at how he'd treated Luke. We know that Luke thought Kingson was involved in the disappearance of Claudia's husband. Suppose something happened… a row or a fight… and Kingson died."

I reached for my notebook and scribbled down a few words. "Was Kingson's death covered up? I can't find any mention of him in the death records here or in England. It's like he vanished into thin air."

"Perhaps he was made to vanish. Someone placed him in that section of the shed and bricked it up… a person who had a good reason for his body not to be found. If I hadn't come along with the digger, he would still be there… lying in that dark secret place."

I took a sip of lemonade. In the peaceful garden, Tobie's

words seemed plausible. Someone in the Manning family must have known about Kingson's death and covered it up. If Claudia poisoned the man, it was unlikely she lifted his body on her own so that meant Luke was probably involved.

"Let's say the skeleton is Kingson, then." I attempted to organize my thoughts. "Kingson might have been a deceiver, a liar and a fraud but he came from a pharmaceutical background. It sounds like he was trying to get Claudia to marry him but was only after the tree bark… wanted the money he presumed it was worth if processed into a drug. That's why he might have tracked Claudia down after he came across her husband in Brazil."

"You think he killed her husband?"

"Well, Luke certainly suspected that he did… but how can we possibly find out, all these decades later… more than a century later? We would find that very hard to prove. I'm hoping my brother will come up with more information from the priest's connections out there."

Tobie sat up and leaned his shoulders against the trunk of the Scots pine. "Here's the possible scenario… Kingson disposes of Gilbert Manning, or arranges for someone to do so, then arrives in Ireland with his job of supplying country doctors with pharmaceuticals or whatever potions the Victorians used."

"All sorts of patented potions, some quite lethal back then with opium or arsenic in them."

"Yeah, Kingson is employed by one of those new pharmaceutical companies and persuades them to send him to Ireland where he attempts to endear himself to Claudia Manning so that he can get his hands on the bark which Gilbert sent home. Luke, through his connections with priests at Glencree Reformatory School… and we all know what a network the priests have throughout the world…"

"Yes, yes, Luke found out what Kingson was up to, with the help of his guardian angel, Brother Eugene. Luke informs Polly and gets into a fight with Kingson and kills him, maybe even accidentally."

Tobie added, "And Luke has to flee the country as he would have been hanged if caught."

"Or perhaps Eleanor is correct and it really was Claudia who poisoned him? She wanted revenge for the death of her husband so she created some concoction and fed it to him. He died and she asked Luke to help her hide the body." I frowned. "What will Daniel make of this?"

"Daniel will want proof. He worked in the medical world and he won't like conjecture. He will need hard evidence before he writes a book about his great-aunt."

"I'm sure you're right. Millicent will have a fit when she hears this and she'll focus only on her reputation. She'll imagine people won't want to stay in a place where there was a deliberate murder."

Tobie chuckled. "I bet they would. They'd be fascinated and want to hear all about it."

"Try convincing Millicent."

"No thanks. I'll leave that to you… or Daniel. Daniel should be the one to tell her. He controls the purse strings."

Maybe not for long, I thought. If Millicent and Kenny could make a profit from their wedding and conference venue, they wouldn't need him. If Colgrannagh could function without his money, poor Daniel would be discarded, cast aside. How depressing that would be.

I looked at another letter addressed to James Staunton in Canada in Cameron's thin sloping handwriting. The several I'd already read were short and about the farm in Mayo. Polly's father had been fascinated by land and its management. He'd enjoyed experimenting with different methods of agriculture and, in this letter, was considering breeding pedigree sheep. No wonder the socialite heiress from Yorkshire had found life dull because Cameron struck me as a man who preferred the company of his farm employees to London society.

"My dear James,

I offer you my sincere apologies for my tardiness in replying to your letter at Christmas. My work here in Mayo is all consuming and I'm now convinced that sheep farming is better suited to the west of Ireland than my futile attempts to clear the land of stones in order to grow tillage…"

The letter was dated 1896, a year after Polly's diary. He outlined several breeds of sheep, some of which I'd heard of, and then, unexpectedly, Cameron's thoughts changed tack:

"You might be interested to learn that my childhood friend's cousin, Claudia Manning, has been accepted as a student in The Royal College of Surgeons. I'm full of admiration for she has long dreamed of becoming a doctor and I'm certain that she will make an excellent physician. I remember how, even as a girl, she used to enjoy mixing potions from the flower garden. She had an impressive and thorough knowledge of botany at a young age.

Her father, Dr Burroughs, encouraged her, as also did her mother. You will remember my writing of old Mrs Burroughs before. She's quite the character and children always adore her because she treats them with civility and feeds them peppermints. I remember with great affection how she used to tell us stories about folklore and ghosts and ghouls. She often made my hair stand on end as a young lad."

I scanned the next few paragraphs. "Tobie," I called out, "You'll have to listen to this. Polly's father writes that Dora Burroughs was an expert on plants and wild animals. I'll read you this bit of his letter which is particularly interesting."

"She was another who understood much about the flora and fauna in County Wicklow. She could name every mushroom and toadstool in the wood along the Whispering River and often picked them when in season for the kitchen. I was always nervous we would be poisoned. Mrs Burroughs once told us an alarming tale about the Death Cap, 'Amanita phalloides', a mycorrhizal fungus that lives off the roots of oak and beech trees. Known as a lethal poison by the Ancient Greeks and Romans, she said that Agrippina supposedly used the fungus to dispose of her husband, the Roman Emperor Claudius. A wonderful way to kill your enemy, Mrs Burroughs declared with enthusiasm, because the Death Cap not only looks similar to our common edible mushroom when young but it is palatable with a pleasant nutlike taste. It can also be dried and it only takes half a mature cap to cause death. Victims die slowly, over several days. Beware of old ladies, I say!"

Tobie shrugged, his face twisting in a scornful grimace. "Huh, in France we know which fungi to use for culinary purposes. We would not be so stupid."

"No, that's not what I mean. Don't you understand? Dora Burroughs, according to Polly's papa, had the knowledge to poison people."

He made no immediate comment but I could see comprehension dawning in his eyes.

"You see what I mean?"

"Ah yes, that Dora might have been the poisoner and not Claudia," he said.

"Exactly. That's exactly what I'm wondering. I've heard of the Death Cap and it's fairly common in Ireland. If it were growing under trees along the river close to the house, then it would have been simple to pop out and pick one and slip it into Kingson's food, especially if it was easy to disguise. I always imagined poisonous fungi would taste vile."

"As far as I know, rabbits and hares can eat *Amanita phalloides* without harm," Tobie replied. "Weird when you think about it. Why does it just kill humans? Perhaps the other wild creatures that live in the woodland evolved to cope with its toxins."

I wrote Dora's name into my notebook and drew a circle around it. I would have to go back to Polly's diary and see if there was any reference to animosity between her and Kingson. Being Claudia's mother, she might not have relished the thought of him as a son-in-law. Perhaps she was eccentric or crazy enough to believe that feeding him toadstools was a good way to get him out of their lives.

"Oh God," I said. "We're never going to work this out. There are too many possibilities."

My phone rang and I glanced at the screen. Millicent. I'd already forgotten that she wanted me to ring her back. I hesitated. Let her think my phone was out of battery, or out of range, or whatever. My sense of responsibility got the better of me. "Hello Millicent. How are you?"

Her voice, cold and curt, replied, "Where are you, Fiona? I've been trying to get you all day."

Tobie grimaced again and went back to reading Wilber's book.

"I'm in County Mayo."

"And the landscaper, is he with you? Kenny and I had to return earlier than expected and I see no sign of him here or of any recent work. It's all exactly as it was when we left on Friday."

Tobie, who could hear what she was saying, waved an urgent hand and shook his head.

I wasn't a good liar. "He's here with me. We're doing more research for Daniel… the governess's family."

"Fiona, can you give Tobie a message from me?"

Tobie shook his head more vigorously.

"Um… he's not here at the moment, I'm afraid," I said. "He's… he's gone to the shop for ice-creams."

"Ice-creams? Oh my God, you're both having a jolly time, aren't you? Meanwhile, Daniel is demanding to know when he's coming home from rehab and I've got a wedding booked for Tuesday and the lawn is an absolute disgrace. The grass has shot up. You'll have to come back immediately."

Typical of the woman. We were expected to drop everything to do her bidding. "No, sorry."

"What? What did you say?"

"I said no."

There was a silence.

Tobie smiled and gave me a thumbs-up signal. I was learning to defend myself.

"Fiona, I don't think you realize how serious this is. The whole future of Colgrannagh rests on my wedding events. It's vital that the place looks well. I mean, for God's sake, we've been paying that landscaper for months and this is how he treats me."

"Now, Millicent, calm down, it's not a crisis. Tobie can mow the lawn when he gets back tomorrow. Plenty of time."

"But there are other jobs I want him to do."

"Tomorrow. We will be back tomorrow. We have an important meeting tonight that is vital for my research and Daniel's book."

Dinner in Achill. Tobie grinned, the lines beside his eyes crinkling.

"Daniel's book won't happen now." Millicent sounded more frantic. "How can it? He's not able for it. He's going to have to go into a care home because I can't possibly manage him. If he falls again, it could be the end of him. Kenny and I both think…"

My grip on the phone tightened and I said through clenched teeth, "Millicent, Daniel must be allowed to decide his own future."

She uttered an impatient clicking sound and said, "I was

looking for you, Fiona, because I want to tell you that I've had to clear the schoolroom of all that paper. I've got a painter coming tomorrow morning at eight. We're going to convert it into a luxury bathroom."

"What? No! What did you do with the papers?"

"I tipped them into plastic bags. They'll have to be burnt. Daniel isn't coming back and the care home won't have room for them. Kenny and I have found him a lovely place… near Dublin. It has quite a large garden and…"

I could listen to no more. I jabbed the phone screen with a forefinger to end the call and threw my mobile on the grass.

Tobie jumped to his feet and reached out, pulling me into his arms. "Don't pay any attention to her. Don't let her upset you."

I could have stepped back and pushed him away, but I didn't. I rested my forehead on his shoulder and allowed my tears to stream down my cheeks. Tears for Daniel, for what seemed like the end of my project and goodness knows what else.

Chapter Forty-Two

The present – September 2022

I knew I was too late as soon as I flung open the schoolroom door. All the letters in boxes, my handwritten notes and even Polly's diary had gone. Millicent stood by the bare table, snapping instructions at a young man with a paint roller who was clinging to a stepladder. The bookshelves were empty.

"Careful, you're splashing it on the sill." She swung round when the door banged against the wall.

"What the… what have you done?" I shouted. "Why didn't you wait for me? You didn't have the courtesy to wait until we got back."

Was that a smirk on her glossy lips? She raised a hand to her face, as if enjoying my fury and frustration, but made no comment.

I squeezed my fingers into fists. "What will Daniel say when he hears you've destroyed his research?"

Millicent caught the eye of the painter on his perch and nodded at the door. He slid down the ladder and disappeared into the corridor. I slammed the door shut with the toe of my shoe.

"Fiona…" Millicent fiddled with her fringe, affecting calm. "I gave you plenty of time… you and Tobie, to return from your little love nest in the west. You kept that quiet, didn't you? You never let on there was a budding romance… or is it even a romance because his English is terrible? I can't imagine a decent conversation with the guy."

I stepped closer. "Anything between Tobie and me is personal and none of your damn business." Alarm flashed in her eyes and I added, "I've had enough of you, Millicent. I'm going to tell Daniel that you've thrown out his papers… thrown them out of his own house. This is his house, even if you and Kenny feel you own it."

"Not his for long."

"He owns it."

"His accident… he needs constant care." She shrugged and turned to look out of the window, across the lawn towards the trees by the river, the Whispering River. She said, "The time has come and he needs looking after. Daniel is happy… he told Kenny he's happy to go."

"You're lying," I yelled, losing control. "I bet you never asked his permission. You've planned this all along, haven't you?"

"You shouldn't involve yourself in the affairs of others. This family… our family is not your business, Fiona," she said, casting a scathing look in my direction. "It will be your downfall… one of these days."

"Really? That's exactly what you do… you interfere in people's business. My work… research, involves searching into families… important information from the past that can't be recovered if it's destroyed. How can I do my job if you've burned the letters and diaries?" My cheeks flamed with rage. I was close to tears but wouldn't let her witness them. "You had no right… no bloody right to do it."

Millicent strolled away from the window towards the door, reaching for the brass knob. I spun around and pushed her aside, leaning my back against it. "Oh, no you don't! You're not going to walk away… you'll listen to me. No wonder Tobie finds you impossible to work for!"

"Did he say that?"

"No, he didn't but I imagine that's what he thinks." I didn't want her to blame him. "You interfere so much with his work that it takes him twice as long to get through it and then you complain about…"

"I am the boss… in case he's forgotten. Move away from the door."

"No, you'll listen to me this time. Poor Daniel… I'll warn him about your nasty little plot to push him out of his home as soon as he's vulnerable. Let's see who has to leave then."

Like many bullies, Millicent was a coward. She stepped back as I thrust my finger in her face and shook it.

"Fiona…" Her reply was lower, less arrogant.

"I'm going to tell Daniel… and I'm going to make sure he knows you deliberately burned his papers. How dare you!"

"Fiona… I didn't."

"What? What did you say?"

She dropped her gaze to the floorboards at our feet. "I didn't burn the damn papers."

"What did you do with them?"

She flicked her eyes to my face and away. "They're in the underground shed in the garden. I packed them into plastic bags and I thought you could continue your research in that damp hole instead of up here. I need this room."

Relief seeped through me. "You deliberately misled me."

She said nothing, but a pink blotch bloomed on each cheek. I'd alarmed her, no doubt about it. I'd given her a fright. Nobody else dared to stand up to the woman and her incessant demands. Kenny ran around like a headless chicken as he carried out her orders. Tobie opted out by refusing to speak to her while Daniel was too kind and generous for his own good. All three of them, in their own way, enabled her obnoxious attitude.

Millicent stretched a hand towards the knob and I moved away, my anger abating.

She gave me a cautious smile. "You'll find the plastic bags in the shed and I would be grateful if you wouldn't mention what I told you to Daniel. Nothing has been arranged as yet."

"I should hope not," I replied. "He has a right to be consulted… especially as he'll end up paying for a care home. You can't force him into it. He's not senile yet."

Her smile died when she opened her mouth, but she clamped it shut again and swept out, leaving me alone in the forlorn room.

I watched the shadows thrown by sunshine slanting in the open window. The caw of rooks in the oak trees across the lawn helped slow my racing thoughts.

Minutes passed. I pulled out my phone and rang Tobie.

"Yeah."

"Meet you in the potting shed. That's where she's dumped the papers."

"Okay."

He got there first and was already standing in the dim light with Archie when I descended the steps. He pointed at the bags left by Millicent in the middle of the floor, a pile of black shiny plastic.

"Not too many," I said. "I hope she's left all the paperwork here. I don't trust her."

Tobie reached for the nearest refuse sack and peered into it. "Do you want to check through them or will we carry them up to the garden first? This one looks like it's just old clothes."

No papers, only a jumbled mass of suits, socks and collarless white shirts from decades before. Solomon Manning's clothes, perhaps. Tobie held up a faded jacket, the faint smell of mothballs clinging to it.

"Where did she find these?"

"Maybe she cleared out drawers or wardrobes in the bedrooms on the top floor. For the recycling bin, I suppose?"

"Yes. No point keeping them. What's in the next one?"

We leaned together, elbows brushing, as he untied the knot in the top of the bag and opened it.

"Letters… I recognize some of those," I muttered. "They're the ones that came from Claudia's relatives and friends in England…"

"They never mentioned the death, the man buried here?"

"No. They might never have known about it." I glanced at the bricks in the far corner, where dust-laden cobwebs dangled from timber beams and drooped in swags. "He must have been carried down these steps… then somebody bricked up the wall. Makes me shiver to think about it."

"Claudia or Dora needed help to build the wall. One of the gardeners?" His gaze held mine. "A long time ago. He's gone now… will soon get a proper burial. No wonder local people imagined figures on the lawn. I bet somebody knew… somebody knew what happened here."

Who had struggled under the weight of Kingson's body across the grass in the dark? Who left him in this secret burial place, this silent bricked-up tomb? Luke, Polly, Claudia, Dora? Some of the servants too, like Lizzie, the wine-swilling maid? Servants like her watched what happened in families. Had she been fond of Gilbert Manning and suspicious of Kingson? Love could create murderers of passionate people.

"It's possible Luke bricked up the wall," I suggested.

"It's all guesswork though, unfortunately." Tobie replied, picking up the bag of clothes. "I'll take this up and leave it outside, ready to take to the recycling depot. You try another bag. That one there looks heavy and there might be books or Claudia's journals in it."

"Are you coming back?"

"You're not afraid, are you?"

"Don't be ridiculous. No, I just…" I couldn't explain. Maybe it was the realization that it was likely to be Kingson who'd lain behind the wall all through the decades, his body hidden away for more than a century. I hadn't cared before, when it was just an unknown skeleton but now, now that I suspected who it was, it was unnerving.

"You're worried his ghost will suddenly appear to haunt you?" Tobie asked in a mischievous tone.

"No, of course not. Ghosts don't exist."

The Jack Russell was sitting at my feet, one ear cocked.

Tobie turned away with a grin, slinging the black sack over his shoulder.

The terrier barked, scampering towards the open hearth in the middle of the back wall.

"Now what?" I exhaled through my teeth. Dogs had good hearing and a sixth sense.

Tobie chuckled from the bottom step and called out, "He hears him… he hears the ghost of Robert Kingson. Wait, what was that noise? Ha, there it is. That scraping… surely you can hear it?"

"Shut up, Tobie."

"Definitely a scratching noise. I'm not joking, I promise."

"Oh, be quiet!" I said. "Stop fooling about."

"No, I'm serious. That sound… there? You must have heard it that time. It's like there's an object stuck in the chimney."

Archie stood in the fireplace, gazing upwards and whining. Tobie dropped the bag onto the ground and walked towards the back wall.

The terrier jumped up, placing his front paws on an old iron firebox and barked again, both ears standing erect as he tilted his head from side to side.

"He knows there's something there," I said.

A flapping came from the chimney and a few twigs fell onto the stone, sending my dog into a frenzy of yapping.

I hurried over to Tobie and we stared into the black space above our heads.

He suggested, "Is it stuck? An animal? It's so dark up there… can't see anything."

A loud croak as another bundle of sticks tumbled down.

Tobie grabbed my arm and pulled me away. "Careful. Is there a dark shape up there?"

"What could it be?" I asked, fumbling for my mobile phone.

"It's a bird… has to be. One that's fallen out of a nest in the top of the chimney. Or one of the parent birds." As soon as the words left his lips, an object plummeted to the ground accompanied by a shower of debris; twigs mixed with soot. Among the filthy mess, a creature got to its feet and blinked at us with pale blue eyes.

Tobie leaned forward, reaching out his hand. "Aah, poor thing… it's a bird, a young jackdaw." He swept the dust away and gathered up the jackdaw with gentle hands. "Poor little guy."

I ran my forefinger along its soft head and the feathers down its back. It peered up at me, curious and fearless. "Take it outside. I wonder how we can get it back into the nest? I'll have a look up the chimney… shine my phone flashlight up there."

Tobie hugged the sooty shape to his T-shirt with cupped hands. "We'll need a ladder. I left one in the herb garden where I was pruning the top of the fig tree."

His boots rang out on the flagstones, accompanied by the clickety-clack of Archie's little claws as he trotted after him, still whining with excitement. I stuck my head into the funnel of the chimney and flicked the beam of light around.

A small rectangle of blue loomed overhead, the sky above a shaft blackened by centuries of smoky fires. But what was that on a ledge just out of reach where another larger brick sat askew?

Was it an old biscuit tin that the flapping bird dislodged?

I clambered onto the top of the grate and placed my hands flat against the inside of the chimney to maintain my balance. The taste of soot made me cough. Balancing in the gloom, I stretched upwards and managed to touch the brick but couldn't reach the metal tin. I swung the light towards it. Yes, a square shape that might have been a biscuit container but covered in grime, the same sticky tar that lined the flue of the chimney, with a coating of dried twigs and leaves.

"Found anything?" Tobie reappeared on the steps. "I've left the ladder up above… if we need it."

"Come over here. There's a tin on a ledge. Do you think it might have money in it?"

"Money?"

"Some people hid their money and valuables up chimneys years ago in the days when they didn't trust banks."

"Pass the tin down to me."

"I can't. I can't reach it. You try. You're taller."

I climbed down and he leaned his hand on my shoulder as he stood on the fire box. He handed me the tin, its lid stuck tight with rust.

"I can't open it." I placed it on the wooden potting bench and searched around for a tool with which to force off the top.

Tobie bent to pick up the head of a spade. "Let's see what happens when I hit it with this." He turned the box onto its side and raised the implement above his head, bringing it crashing down.

"Don't damage it."

"Hey, do you want to get it open or not?" He struck it again and this time the lid flew off and clattered across the flagstones. He held out his hand for my phone and I passed it to him. We leaned together to peer into the tin as Tobie positioned the beam of light on a rectangular object.

"A book…" I said. "It's like another diary." I picked it up and ran my fingertips over it. "A clothbound book. It's similar in size and shape to the one in the schoolroom… the one I found with reports written by Luke and the children when they followed family members and wrote down their observations for their game. See the beginning… the names of the children. All except Luke, his name is missing." I squinted in the darkness, attempting to decipher the various handwritings while Tobie held the flashlight.

Names were printed in capital letters on the front page: Annie, Hannah and Solomon Manning and the date 1895.

"Tobie, look! The date is right. Could the answer be here, the children's account of what happened?"

I never finished my sentence because Tobie snatched the book from my hands and headed for the steps. "We can see it better up here."

"Where's the jackdaw?" I asked as I followed.

"It's fine, don't worry, perfectly content in a wooden box I found in the herb garden with Archie keeping an eye on it."

"I hope he doesn't frighten the poor bird. Could the tin have been there all along, hidden in the chimney? All this time."

He offered his hand and pulled me towards the daylight.

"Why not? Like you said, people hid boxes of money and other valuables in chimneys."

I sat on the grass and opened the green cover, the yellowed pages musty and foxed with age. Excitement pricked inside me.

The first entry was an account by Annie about a dinner party attended by the family, their friends and Robert Kingson. She and the other children had watched from the landing. She described the fine dresses worn by the ladies and smart uniforms of the coachmen who drove the carriages. Solomon disappeared at bedtime and was found hiding in one of the broughams.

I turned the pages. Solomon had created a childish drawing

of the more modern carriages and noted the various parts.

Perhaps the notebook held nothing more than youthful accounts of parties, visitors to the house and normal goings on. Lizzie had been in trouble with the cook for finishing off the remains of a bottle of cooking sherry and for smoking Mrs Delaney's cigarettes in the kitchen when she was supposed to be washing dishes. Hannah wrote that account with obvious glee, reporting word for word what the maid had told her the following morning. Lizzie had laughed so much that tears ran down her cheeks.

"Anything interesting?" Tobie asked.

"Amusing, but nothing relevant so far. Perhaps I was wrong to presume..." I turned another leaf of Hannah's slanted writing and ran my finger down the page. There were more details about fine dresses and shining carriage horses, although Miss Brady had managed to persuade Solomon to go to bed on that occasion. Then I found the simple statement:

> *"Mr Kingson was taken ill after dinner and went home early."*

"Hey, here's something. Kingson was ill."

"Read it," Tobie commanded. He was sitting beside me, stroking Archie.

I cleared my throat and began:

> *"Mr Kingson was taken away by Dr Fitzpatrick last night. Mrs Burroughs told us this morning before breakfast."*

I added, "She didn't witness anything because the girls were sent to bed before the dinner ended. That's a pity. I wonder where Dr Fitzpatrick took Kingson."

"If he took him anywhere."

"You mean Dora was making it up? An excuse given to the children."

He nodded. "You hardly expect her to tell them that she poisoned him."

"Well, no."

"Read on."

"Annie mentions further down that Dora stayed in her bedroom all day and that the late night was too much for her."

"That could mean anything," Tobie said.

"Well, listen to this… what Mrs Delaney the cook… what she told Annie."

"Read it, Fiona, don't keep me in suspense."

> *"Cook told me after breakfast that Mr Kingson had food poisoning and that Lizzie is very ill and has been taken to the cottage hospital."*

I reread the girl's sentence in silence. Kingson might have died that night. And Dora had stayed in bed all day. Worn out from the ordeal? She might also have had food poisoning if the maid was ill.

I turned the page and saw, with a flash of frustration, that Hannah took over with a description of a new garden boy, who was an assistant for Eamon. The boy was tall with dark good looks and had, unsurprisingly, attracted the attention of the two girls.

"It's all so normal, isn't it?" I said. "Disappointingly normal."

"Yeah, but wouldn't Claudia and Dora make an effort… to make things seem normal?"

"You've got a point there. Annie says here that Claudia took them in the carriage to Wicklow where they bought a present for Dora, whose birthday was the following week." I read aloud:

"I asked how Mr Kingson was, and she said she wasn't sure but expected to hear from him soon."

"Typical of Annie to enquire after him," I added. "She was infatuated with him. A teenage crush."

"The answer is there somewhere, between the lines. It has to be."

Only five more pages of handwriting were left and the rest of the book was empty. There was more girlish excitement about the garden boy and Solomon's joy when he taught him to catch minnows from the river in a jar. The last entry was scrawled by Hannah, perhaps in a hurry.

"Oh, see here, Tobie. The maid is dead."

He peered over my shoulder. "Read it."

"A horrible week. Lizzie has died. I can't believe we will never see her cheerful face again. Mrs Manning told us she will be buried in Dublin."

"She died of food poisoning?" I asked. "Is that likely? And see here, Polly is leaving Colgrannagh. She's giving up her job. Listen to this." I continued reading:

"Yesterday Miss Brady was angry with us. She discovered Solomon composing an account about her leaving us and how he'd seen her packing her trunk. She took our book and read parts of it. Annie told her that it was only our game and just for amusement but Miss Brady was cross. She said it wasn't polite to spy on the family and that Mrs Manning would be displeased. She said bad things happened to people who eavesdropped and spied on others. She took the book away and was going to burn it in her

> *bedroom fire. I think she wanted to read it and see what we wrote about her."*

Tobie interrupted, "Hannah was probably right. Polly would be interested to see what they wrote about Kingson, if she knew anything about his disappearance or his illness."

"There are only a few more paragraphs. Hannah says she crept into Polly's room when she was at dinner and stole the book back. This is what she says:"

> *"Miss Brady is leaving early tomorrow morning. Before dinner she came to kiss us goodnight and she said she will write to us. She had tears in her eyes. Annie and Solomon cried too. I didn't because I never cry but I will miss her. She was much kinder than horrid Miss Walsh. She gave us a present, our last present. It's the pretty embroidery of the physic garden which she finished this week. She told us to keep it safe and that it has a secret. Perhaps she will tell us the secret one day. She said she felt guilty, terribly guilty but that must be because she is leaving us.*
>
> *It is now the following day and Miss Brady has gone. We waved from the doorstep when Eamon drove her away and Annie and Solomon cried again. Mrs Manning didn't come to see her off but maybe she was busy with a patient. Annie refuses to play the game anymore because she says she's no longer a child. I think she was frightened when Miss Brady got cross and said bad things happen to people who spy. Annie wants me to burn this book but I won't. I'm going to hide it where no one will find it and when no one is watching I'll take it back."*

I closed the journal. "If Hannah left it in the chimney, she didn't take it back. She must have forgotten about it. Grew up, like Annie… no longer interested in childish games. What do you make of Polly feeling guilty? That's what she wrote in her diary too… her last entry. The terrible choice she had to make and her feelings of guilt."

"Guilty for leaving the children? Guilty for another thing? I don't know, Fiona. This could be just another dead end, I'm afraid."

I sat up. "Possibly, but Polly left them the embroidery. Is it the one I have in my bedroom? The one from the café? It has a secret. What did Polly mean?"

"I've no idea. Has it got anything to do with the plants? Victorians gave special meanings to plants. They used them for messages of love and other emotions."

I frowned. "She was fond of embroidery… says in her diary that Mrs Manning sometimes asked her to create gifts for her friends. Polly was good at sewing. I wonder why she gave the children the framed embroidery of the herb garden. Solomon obviously kept it and it was sold with the contents of the house after his death. That's how the café owner got it."

"It's nearly lunch time," Tobie said, pointing at his watch. "I'll drop into the rehab clinic to see Daniel afterwards. Do you want to come with me? You could update him on all this."

"Okay. I'll bring Polly's embroidery with me so we can look at it."

My phone pinged, an email arriving. I tapped the screen. "It's from my brother. He might have more information for me about Brazil. Let's see… quite short, typical Anthony, and yes he mentions the priest Francisco."

Tobie got to his feet. "I'm hungry."

"Frenchmen are definitely ruled by their stomachs," I said, reading on. "Tobie, listen, the priest found out this… Anthony says Gilbert Manning recovered from an assault beside a ravine. He died of yellow fever, a common disease in those days. Francisco claims Gilbert died in January 1896."

"At least you know what killed him… definitely not him in the bricked-up shed. Come on, Fiona, I need food."

I stared up at him.

"What?" he asked. "What is it?"

"1896… the year after Polly left and the girls mentioned Kingson became ill. The death notice in the newspaper that I found soon after I came here…" My fingers groped for my little notebook in the pocket of my jeans. I turned the pages and pointed. "Here it is… Gilbert's death notice stated he died in 1894."

Tobie glanced at my writing and shrugged. "So? The priest might be wrong about the date. People often get dates wrong… make a mistake."

"The priest isn't wrong," I said. "The notice of the death is wrong… perhaps deliberately falsified. Anthony has attached the photo of Gilbert's headstone in the cemetery in Rio. Gilbert died in 1896. He could have come back to Colgrannagh before that to confront Robert Kingson."

Chapter Forty-Three

The present – September 2022

"Why do you think Gilbert came back?" Daniel glanced from Tobie to me. "He must have wanted to stop Robert Kingson, if that's even his real name… stop him from getting his hands on the tree bark."

"Gilbert had access to bark in Brazil… he knew where to source it but perhaps Kingson didn't," Tobie replied.

"Surely it was more than that? I bet it was more personal." I drew the floral curtains around Daniel's bed in the corner of the ward so we would have some privacy. We were speaking in whispers, like conspirators. The man in the next bed lay asleep, soft regular snores rising above our conversation.

Daniel shifted his weight on the bed and winced. "This damn leg… but, from a medical point of view, if Gilbert had bouts of yellow fever, he might have wanted to experiment with the bark and see if it would help him. Claudia knew more about processing medicinal plants than him. He might have needed her assistance."

I stood up to adjust Daniel's pillows and straightened the blanket. "Or else it was just plain old-fashioned revenge… or jealousy. If Kingson attempted to push him over the edge of the ravine in Brazil, Gilbert might have decided to take the law into his own hands. If he thought Kingson was in love with his wife…" I bent down to pick up Polly's embroidery, her signature stitched in the bottom right hand corner and the date: August 1895. I positioned it on my knee, holding it upright so that Daniel and Tobie could examine it. "Take a look at this. Is there some sort of clue hidden here?"

"Just a typical piece of Victorian needlework," Daniel replied with a smile. "Do you think the girl Hannah was telling the truth about her governess saying it held a secret? I admit it's very pretty and an interesting historical plan of the physic garden back then."

"I believe her." I looked down at the tiny silk stitching. "Tell me if you notice anything. Polly was good at detail… the roses and sundial, then the swirls of other plants coming out from the middle."

"From a distance, it's almost like a painting. She featured seven plants around the outside. Why seven?" Tobie pointed at them. "Each with its common and Latin name underneath."

A nurse with a cheerful expression and brown hair tied in a bun popped her head through a gap in the curtains. "Everything all right, Daniel? Painkillers are on the way. I know you've been asking for them."

He raised a hand. "Thank you, kind lady." Turning to me, he said, "I still need the damn tablets… this hip is taking a long time to heal."

"Have patience. You've been here less than a week." The nurse flashed him a smile before disappearing behind the folds of material.

He let out a long breath. "It's frustrating. I'm not used to being so restricted. Anyway, enough of my moaning… what did you say, Tobie, about the plants?"

"Perhaps they're significant," I agreed.

Tobie leaned closer to the framed embroidery. "Ivy, leaves of common ground ivy, *Hedera helix*, is displayed down the left side. That's still used as a tincture for coughs. Then there's *Lobelia inflata*, used for centuries as a herbal treatment. Maybe you should be checking these online, Fiona, in case the names have other meanings and I'm getting it wrong."

Daniel raised his bushy eyebrows and grinned. "What a wild goose chase! Still, it's the most exciting thing that's happened all week."

I tapped at my phone screen and looked up at Tobie. "Yes, you're right. *Lobelia inflata*, called Indian Tobacco, can be grown from seed here in Ireland and was used for various ailments including asthma."

"Good, thanks. At the top there's borage… easy to recognize with its little blue flowers. I see a lot of that in cottage gardens."

"Borage oil," I read out, "for skin disorders including eczema. Here's a modern medical website… amazing how these plants are still in use."

"I know the next one," Daniel said. "Elderflower. That shrub is a pest in the garden because it self-seeds everywhere but it makes a nice cordial made with sugar and lemon."

I keyed the name into the search engine. "An extract from elder flowers is used for sinusitis, colds, flu… usually consumed as a tea."

"There's nothing else significant about any of these plants so far," Tobie replied. "Down the right side she's placed a well-known and much-loved herb… rosemary. You don't need to look that one up, Fiona. Best used with roast lamb."

"Typical of you to say that." I laughed and tapped him on the arm. "The following one is…"

"I like my food." He winked at Daniel. "Bright yellow button flowers. That's tansy. You see it growing wild nowadays, especially among ruins for some reason. I saw clumps of it near the tower house."

I read out, "Traditionally used for women's ailments, pains in the back and heart palpitations."

"And the last one is a gentian. Another pretty flower."

"It's coming up on the medical website too. Used for digestive disorders," I replied.

"Are we any the wiser?" Daniel asked with his burst of laughter. "An assortment of blue, yellow and green plants. What could Polly have meant?"

I got out my notebook and wrote down the herbs. "Is the clue in the names? Like a code in the names?" I frowned and chewed the end of my biro. "Ivy, lobelia, borage, elder, rosemary, tansy and gentian."

"Anagrams?" suggested Tobie with a yawn. "Move the letters around."

The heat in the rehab ward was both overwhelming and exhausting. I also yawned as I scribbled letters on the page. "No, nothing jumps out at me. Perhaps the order of the plants is important."

Tobie peered at my notebook again. "Maybe. I used to do a lot of crosswords when I was a student. Quite good at them, believe it or not, and my mother thought I was a genius. Is it an acrostic? Move the names around."

I tried a few different positions with each word. An acrostic. That was an interesting idea. I, L, B, E… I cried out, "I've got it. Tobie, your mother was right, you are a genius. It is an acrostic. The first letter of each name is the clue… but we should have started with gentian. G for gentian. See?" I pointed at the embroidery. "G, I, L, B, E, R and T. The first letter of each plant spells out his name."

"Good Lord, you're right!" Daniel said. "Gilbert. Surely this must be more than just a coincidence. It fits with your brother's email about Brazil… that he didn't die until 1896."

I looked down at Polly's intricate and painstaking handiwork from so long ago, and yearned to know what had happened on that night in early August. I was certain she was a witness, must have seen Gilbert or been involved in some way. "It's a complicated clue though, isn't it? The girls and Solomon might never have worked that out… probably didn't, especially as they had no idea Kingson was dead. I'm sure they were told he left the country… went back to England."

"If Gilbert were responsible for poisoning Robert Kingson, Claudia probably covered up his crime," Daniel added.

"Polly was probably sworn to secrecy and that's why she felt the terrible guilt she mentioned at the end of her diary… didn't dare write down what happened. She was a witness to a murder and couldn't say anything," I said. "Gilbert and Claudia must have demanded her silence… and Luke's too, if he was there. Kingson's body was hidden in the underground shed and Gilbert went back to South America where he died the following year."

"The maid Lizzie also died. I wonder what happened to her? And what about the tree bark?" Tobie leaned back in his chair. "If it led to a famous discovery, you would have known, Daniel… you would have heard about it."

The older man shook his head. "I heard nothing and I never found anything about the Brazilian bark on the internet, so was it a failure in the end? I'm sure Claudia had it examined and tested. She wouldn't have thrown away an opportunity to make money… an important medical discovery. She qualified as a doctor, don't forget, a clever woman and determined for her era. No, it mustn't have worked out for her. A pity but perhaps…" His words trailed away.

"Perhaps she didn't deserve it." I closed my notebook. "Looks like Kingson died for nothing. Where did Polly go… and Luke, her twin? Where did they end up?"

Tobie shrugged. "So easy to disappear in those days with no computer records. Perhaps there's more information in Eleanor Staunton's boxes of letters from the Canadian great-uncle." He raised his eyebrows.

"I'd like to go back to her house," I said. "I'd like the opportunity to go through more of Eleanor's papers. I can't leave without finding out."

Daniel reached for my hand, patting it. "Thank you, my dear. I'm most grateful for all your hard work… and your help too, Tobie. You've given me a lot to think about. I shall have plenty to do in my new care home."

I swung round. "No! You're joking, aren't you?"

"I'm not joking." He let out a sigh. "I'm getting old, old and infirm. Millicent has found me a modern place near the sea."

"But you can't… you can't let her take Colgrannagh away from you."

Tobie frowned a warning at me.

"It's for the best, Fiona. I'm wise enough to know that," Daniel said, easing back against his pillows. "I'll be well cared for. My meals on time, lots of people to talk to… I'm used to institutions, don't forget. I spent my working life in hospitals."

"But…"

"I can't turn back the clock. I would dearly love to but I can't turn back the clock."

"But what about your book… Claudia's story, what will you do about that?"

He smiled. "I'm hoping you'll advise me. I feel I can't write about the murder at Colgrannagh. It would be too much for Millicent and Kenny. I don't want to upset them. Let them take the house, it's what I'd planned all along. Let them have the house and make the best they can of it."

I fell silent, defeated.

He squeezed my hand. "You've been a wonderful help to me. I'll write Claudia's story, don't worry. You might give me a hand if I get stuck."

I looked in his eyes, those sensible grey eyes that had seen so much over the years, and I knew he was right. In my heart, I knew he was right. Sooner or later he would have had to give up Colgrannagh and Millicent would have got her way. It stung though. It didn't feel fair.

Daniel turned to Tobie. "And you, my friend. What will you do?"

"I'm not going to continue working for *Madame*, if that's what you mean. I won't do it, Daniel, not without you there. I'll go back to France. I haven't seen my son for months. It's time I went home." He stood up and stretched his arms above his head, yawning. "I think we should leave you in peace. Time you had a rest. I'll drop in to see you tomorrow." He beckoned at me. "Are you coming, Fiona?"

I got to my feet and kissed Daniel on his forehead before drawing back the curtains. Tobie followed me out of the ward and into the corridor. We stood beside a fire extinguisher hanging on the wall. I fixed my gaze on the nurses' station on our right. *Time he went home*, those were Tobie's words.

"You're disappointed, aren't you?" he said. "About Daniel, I mean. About him leaving Colgrannagh."

"Yes, I suppose so but I see… I understand what he said. It just seems unfair, that's all. I'd like to think of him staying in his own home."

"He'll be fine. Daniel will enjoy the company of others in the home and he'll be better looked after. I can't see Millicent as a caring assistant, can you?"

"Certainly not, no, and I can see why you don't want to work for her."

He grinned. "I don't speak her language, remember."

"So, you're going back to Provence… or to Paris."

"Provence, yes. What will you do?"

I waved a hand. "Oh, I'll do more research and help Daniel get his book started. After that I'll probably end up homeless on the streets in Dublin when Dominic takes me to court and cleans me out for the final time."

He recognized my mocking tone and continued to smile. "Doesn't sound like fun. Or…"

"Don't worry, I have a few friends who might take pity on me." Perhaps I would end up on Jessica's sofa; an awkward third in her new apartment with her partner.

"Or…" Tobie prompted again.

"Or what?" I reached out a hand to fiddle with a chain on the fire extinguisher. A doctor in a white coat walked past, stethoscope round his neck and clipboard in his hands. He gave us an assessing stare.

"Or you might like to come and visit me… when you're homeless, that is," Tobie said.

Was he being serious? "Ah thanks. That's kind of you."

"I mean it, Fiona. Perhaps I'll even find you some work. A French family tree that needs researching… or skeletons rattling in the cupboard… a project like that."

I laughed.

"Daniel is moving on," he said. "I think it's time you did too."

"Good point," I replied. "I'll think about it."

He slipped his arm round my shoulders, giving me a quick squeeze. "You're as romantic as always. I see I might need to be a bit more persuasive. Let's discuss this… but first a beer. The heat in Daniel's room was overpowering and I need a beer."

Chapter Forty-Four

The past – January 1896

A cold Sunday morning in London, with frost sparkling on the glass when Polly glanced out of the drapery window at the steady flow of carriages rumbling along Leopold Road. Inside, she looked at the rolls of fabric perched on tables: luxurious new silks in shades of blue and green from Paris; cottons and linens from the mills further north in England and, on the shelves behind, the trimmings for her millinery creations; satin ribbon and lace, feathers and beads.

Designing hats was what she loved best, hidden in the workroom at the back of the shop where she pieced together unique confections that made her customers' eyes open wide with delight. She knew she was a good milliner. The more mundane alterations to ball gowns, day dresses and walking outfits could be left to her assistant, a bright-eyed young woman well able to charm the ladies of Wimbledon with her good-natured chatter.

Polly's gaze rested on a letter lying on the counter, ignored all morning but not forgotten. The cream envelope displaying Claudia Manning's handwriting sat waiting like an unwelcome visitor impatient for attention. Polly also recognized her father's scrawl. He had forwarded it on from Mayo to her address in Woodside Parade. She frowned as she walked over to reach for the correspondence, anxiety mingling with relief that Claudia had no idea where she lived. Papa had remained true to his word and had not divulged her whereabouts.

Pushing the letter into her reticule, she pulled on an emerald green wool coat, an indulgence she failed to resist on her last trip to Paris before Christmas with Luke. He was such a help with the purchase of fabrics and adept at bargaining the merchants down, merely shaking his head while she translated. Useful also at keeping her account books in order.

Polly walked out the door onto the street, twisting the key in the lock. Papa, who'd spent years in London in an attempt to escape from his tyrannical father, recommended Wimbledon to them when they left Colgrannagh and Polly had no regrets. Its population was increasing rapidly, just as he'd said. A perfect place to start a little business where Luke and she could be together, their past lives unknown to the affluent occupants of the area.

The shop their father had found for them was also perfect. The floor below was occupied by the owner of the property, a kindly widow who'd married well, born in Dublin and a cousin of Papa's farm steward.

Polly passed the greengrocer's and waved at the boy inside the door. She would wait until she reached Lake Road before finding somewhere to sit and open Claudia's letter.

After another few minutes, she noticed an unoccupied wrought-iron seat under a plane tree, close to the railings of the big manor house. The lake had been designed by the famous Lancelot Brown in 1765 from what had once been wetland. It was true the estate was diminishing, pasture being sold off to rich industrialists and gentlemen from the city, but such regeneration was reassuring. The wives and daughters of those wealthy newcomers required hats and dresses.

Polly sat down and spread out her skirt. The moment had arrived to open the letter, a moment she'd been dreading, truth be told. What news did it carry from Colgrannagh? Fear caught in her throat and her fingers trembled. She and her brother might never be free of the place and the terrible memory it concealed.

She unfolded the sheet of paper, her heart lifting a little on finding only one page, and began to read:

> *"My dear Polly,*
>
> *I trust that this will find you in good health. I have no idea where you are and your father has been most secretive. No matter, for he told me you and your brother are content and that is good news indeed.*
>
> *I am writing with sad tidings received from a close friend of my husband in Brazil. Gilbert passed away earlier this month after succumbing to another bout of that horrible fever. I wished to inform you myself and believe that you may think this yet another ruse but I assure you it is the truth. I regret his deception in the past but Gilbert believed it was necessary.*
>
> *You may feel now that we should reveal what happened at Colgrannagh last summer but I hope I can rely upon you and Luke to remain silent. There is too much at stake. You must understand how none of us can possibly gain from such a disclosure. Indeed, it would only bring the law down on us all and I'm sure both you and Luke will be aware of how the constabulary would consider your involvement. Neither of you have what we shall call an unblemished past."*

Was this a threat? Claudia, determined they were to say nothing, demanding their loyalty? To remain silent forever. Her eyes slipped down the remaining lines of hurried handwriting. No mention of Kingson's death or of how she, Luke, Gilbert and Claudia had carried him down the steps to the potting shed. Or the hours of darkness it took Luke to brick up the wall. It would be foolish to write of that in a letter in case the correspondence fell into the wrong hands. They were accomplices in the crime and Claudia was taking pains to remind them of the fact.

> *'I'm certain you will comprehend why it is necessary to say nothing about this. Your father tells me you have set up a little business and how wonderful to hear that it is thriving! He wouldn't tell me the nature of your enterprise but it would be a pity to lose it, don't you think?*
>
> *I, too, have set plans in motion. I have at last applied to study medicine in the Royal College of Surgeons in Dublin and have great hopes of being accepted this time. You know that it has long been my ambition.*
>
> *Let us agree to say no more about that night in August. It is for the best and I hope to receive your confirmation in due course.*
>
> *I wish you and Luke good fortune in life, my dear, I really do.*
> *Your affectionate friend,*
> *Claudia Manning."*

A pain stirred in Polly's stomach, a cramp forcing her to lean forward and draw in her breath. She twisted her hands together. The shadows on the lawn moved under the moonlight, the silent body on the ground beneath them. A sweating white-faced figure stumbled from the trees, wearing a heavy coat, with long straggly hair and his fingernails ingrained with dirt.

She'd never discovered how long Gilbert had lived in the tower house awaiting his opportunity but it must have only been a month or two. Alarmed to come across her, he had thrown the blanket over her head to prevent her identifying him in the future. Claudia promised she had no idea he was there, claiming his illness had made him obsessive and determined to seek revenge on Kingson. She'd claimed to know nothing about his plan to attack Kingson and believed her husband to be dead.

Polly wasn't so sure. Who had brought him food and water? Those evenings Claudia claimed to be out administering to her patients, tending at sick beds, had she spent those hours with him? Or was Lizzie, whose lips were sealed forever, looking after him?

Gilbert had remained in hiding, his health deteriorating as he grew more delusional, until the summer drought was gone and the rain arrived. Until the fungi under the trees in the wood sprang to life.

The Death Cap, it was called. Luke told Polly later that he knew what the mushroom looked like. Half a cap was all that was required and it took several days to kill, destroying internal organs. An innocuous taste meant it could be slipped into food without detection. The perfect poison.

Gilbert admitted he'd given the chopped pieces of Death Cap to Lizzie and instructed her to fry them with onions and add to Kingson's plate of stew two days before. Poor gullible Lizzie, not blessed with intelligence, she would have done anything for her master without question. Gilbert assured her that Kingson requested the fresh mushroom and Lizzie wouldn't have realized it was poisonous. That was why she'd eaten some of it herself and suffered the consequences.

Luke, with his suspicious mind, believed Gilbert had suggested that Lizzie should try some of the deadly mushroom because it was an easy way to remove a witness.

And Dora? Did she know of her son-in-law's crime? Perhaps not. She'd gone to her bedroom when the guests were leaving. Had she stood at her window and watched the little group huddled together? No, for she would have given some sign of suspicion, incapable of keeping such a secret. Dora was innocent. She wouldn't have sent Polly to the tower house on that first occasion if she'd known Gilbert had returned.

Robert Kingson had left him beside a ravine and, but for a

local tribesman, Gilbert would have bled to death. He'd been nursed back to health by the priests living on the edge of the Amazon forest but the yellow fever returned and twisted his thoughts.

Polly shivered as a breeze stirred the dry leaves of the plane tree around her feet, sending them scurrying towards the railings. She'd been sitting too long. She placed the letter back in her reticule.

Would she reply? She didn't want to, preferring to ignore its veiled warning, but it might be best to agree to Claudia's request and perhaps then it would be over. She would have to ask Luke for his opinion but she already knew what he would say.

Nobody had discovered the clue she'd left in her embroidery of the garden and it seemed unlikely anyone ever would. It was a foolish and rather desperate gesture to salve her conscience at the time.

Polly took out her pocket watch and peered at its tiny ornate hands. Three quarters of an hour had crept past. Luke would be walking towards the shop, on his way to count the takings for the week, with his sweet young fiancée on his arm. Polly would make tea and they would laugh and talk and enjoy the rich chocolate cake that her brother always purchased at the bakery on Leopold Road.

His fiancée would again assure her that her eldest brother was longing to meet her, a cheerful steadfast man who worked in the same bank as Luke. Polly smiled at the thought. Did she look like she needed a steadfast husband? Her work demanded all her energy and attention.

She would write back to Claudia and it would be over. The wind was blowing the dead leaves into frenzied circles as she got to her feet and set off, swinging her arms and facing into the winter sun.

To the reader

Thank you for reading *The Whispering River*. I hope you enjoyed it and, if you did, perhaps you would be kind enough to leave a review. This makes a big difference to authors these days and it can be as short as you like. Your help is much appreciated.

If you're interested in receiving my newsletter by email with information about my other novels, special offers, background research, gardening tips, folklore and historical photographs, please visit www.suzannewinterly.com and complete the form. All are welcome!

You can also find me on the following social media platforms:

Facebook

www.facebook.com/suzannewinterly

Instagram

www.instagram.com/suzannewinterly

Pinterest

www.pinterest.ie/suzannewinterly

Author's Note

People often ask me where I get ideas for stories. It's a good question and one that I can't always answer. I think it might have been the garden owned by the Botanic Gardens at Kilmacurragh in County Wicklow, with its huge rhododendron and tree collections dating from the Victorian era, that sowed the seeds for the plot of this novel in my imagination.

The quest for new plants in the Victorian era

Kilmacurragh is now open to the public but was owned by Thomas Acton during the 19th century. Acton collaborated with the curators of the Botanic Gardens in Glasnevin, Dublin at the time and some of the new species brought back from around the world succeeded in the milder climate of Acton's Wicklow garden after failing to grow in the harsher conditions at Glasnevin. It must have been an exciting time for lovers of gardening.

A plant hunting life

The life of a plant hunter in countries like Brazil, Chile, Peru and even North America could be dangerous. While the botanists were usually well paid by the plant nursery owners, they needed a spirit of adventure to endure the many hardships they encountered. Plant hunters had to survive shipwrecks and pirates, numerous accidents and tropical diseases like dysentery and yellow fever, so some never came home. William Lobb, originally from Cornwall, is buried in the USA.

An inspiring female botanical artist

One 19th century woman who impressed me was Marianne North. Over 800 of her botanical paintings are on display in a gallery in Kew Gardens, London. In an era when many women had a very limited lifestyle, North travelled the world to paint plants in their natural habitat. She brought home beautiful colour drawings in an age when there was only black and white photography. You can imagine what a reception her artwork received. I haven't been to the gallery in Kew yet but it's on my list.

The Chelsea Physic Garden

This famous four acres is London's oldest botanic garden. Hidden behind walls and on the edge of Thames River, it was originally known as the Apothecaries' Garden. It was founded in 1673 for growing plants as medicine. The garden has the largest fruiting olive tree in the UK and around 5,000 other plants. In 1983 the Chelsea Physic Garden was opened to the public and became a registered charity.

Acknowledgements

A big thank you goes to everyone who helped me with *The Whispering River*, especially Hilary Johnson for her eagle-eyed editorial advice. My thanks go to Stuart Bache for his lovely cover design. Many others helped along the way: from proof reading the manuscript to making sure Tobie's French was accurate, and I would like to thank Rosemary, Tara, Maggie, Anne, Danièle and, of course, my husband William.

And to you, the reader, my sincere thanks.

Suzanne Winterly – 2023

About the author

Suzanne Winterly was born in County Tipperary, Ireland. She has an English degree from Trinity College, Dublin and has written three mystery novels and articles for specialist newspapers and magazines. She loves visiting old houses and gardens.

She has two sons and lives in the country with her husband and a variety of four-legged friends.

Website

www.suzannewinterly.com

Facebook

www.facebook.com/suzannewinterly

Instagram

www.instagram.com/suzannewinterly

Pinterest

www.pinterest.ie/suzannewinterly

Printed in Great Britain
by Amazon